S0-AWG-627

Praise for Elizabeth Fackler

"Crisply told, this action-filled tale conjures the thrills of the Old West.... A genuinely gripping story."
—*Publishers Weekly* on *Backtrail*

"Seth Strummer books are a study of a man who lives by violence, what made him that way, and what might save him from himself."
—*El Paso Times*

"Elizabeth Fackler has a gift for dialogue. She brings her reader close to her subjects and makes him touch their hearts and minds."
—Earl Murray

Praise for Elizabeth Fackler's
Billy the Kid: The Legend of El Chivato

"Compelling tragedy laced with irony and fueled by friendship, loyality, and love. Most memorable though is Billy himself.... Billy and the time he lived in come off the page and capture the imagination."
—*Kirkus Reviews*

"A magnificent achievement in historical fiction."
—*Roundup Magazine*

"Other novels have been written about Billy the Kid, and it is likely that more will be, but it is unlikely that any will surpass Elizabeth Fackler's in epic scope, emotional depth, and in rich characterization. She makes the legend live."
—Elmer Kelton

BADLANDS

Elizabeth Fackler

FORGE®

A TOM DOHERTY ASSOCIATES BOOK
NEW YORK

This is a work of fiction. All the characters and events portrayed in
this book are either products of the author's imagination or are used
fictitiously.

BADLANDS

Copyright © 1996 by Elizabeth Fackler

A Forge Book
Published by Tom Doherty Associates, Inc.
175 Fifth Avenue
New York, NY 10010

Forge® is a registered trademark of Tom Doherty Associates, Inc.

ISBN: 0-812-57761-2
Library of Congress Card Catalog Number: 96-18275

First edition: October 1996
First mass market edition: June 1998

Printed in the United States of America

0 9 8 7 6 5 4 3 2 1

To Michael

AUTUMN 1883

1

Crossing the yard toward the open door of Esperanza's casita, Seth could see her sleek black hair nearly touching the floor as she sat on a stool before her vanity. When he stopped on the threshold, she sensed him there and looked up.

"Seth," she said, her dark eyes laughing a naughty invitation. "Come in."

She seemed happy enough, which was more than he could say for himself as he sat on the edge of her bed and leaned back on his elbows, meeting her eyes.

At forty-four, she was ten years older than he and living on his charity. It was generous and stemmed from friendship, but carried no guarantees. She smiled warily. "Would you like a drink?"

"You keep whiskey in your room, Esperanza?"

"You left it here last time."

"I'm surprised Blue didn't drink it up."

Her smile vanished. "Does it bother you I sleep with him?"

Seth shook his head. "It bothers me that you're scaring Rico, though."

"Scaring her? I wouldn't."

"She's crying 'cause I'm going to town tonight. You got any idea why she might do that?"

Esperanza looked away from his cool gray eyes, across the yard to the light shining from Rico's bedroom, then turned back to Seth. "I don't control the cards," she said softly.

"You control what comes out of your mouth," he retorted, "and I'm tired of your gloomy predictions."

Slowly she crossed the room to kneel on the floor in front of him. "Don't be angry with me, Seth," she pleaded.

He just watched her.

"I won't read Rico's cards anymore, if that's what you want."

"That's what I want."

"Okay." She smiled. "Okay?"

"I don't know," he said. "I should burn the damn things."

"You wouldn't!" she whispered. "I brought them from México and they are very ancient."

"What good are they?"

"They predict the future."

"Bullshit."

Seeing a playfulness in his eyes that told her he was no longer angry, she laughed and leaned against his knee. "Ay, Seth. Why don't you come see me anymore, eh?"

"I'm here now."

She sighed, then asked mischievously, "How are you getting along with Rico?"

"We were doing fine before you told her I was gonna get killed in a saloon."

"It was in the cards, Seth."

"When it happens, you can all cry your eyes out. Until then, I don't want to hear about it. Is that plain enough?"

"But it's a warning. It's not a fact yet. You can prevent it."

"By staying home the rest of my life. That's what you and Rico want, ain't it?"

Demurely she dropped her lashes and said softly, "It would be wise."

"It would be hell," he said, angry again. "Get up."

She rose quickly and backed away from him.

Watching her closely, he asked, "You afraid of me?"

She shook her head. "I trust you with my life."

"Since that's the case, you think maybe my advice might be worth taking?"

"Not on this. You are wrong."

He stood up, so much taller that he towered above her. "What am I gonna do with you, Esperanza?"

"Shoot me?"

He nodded at her humor. "I might," he said, then turned and walked out.

The yard was dark, lit only by two fingers of light that didn't quite reach. In the casita behind him was a woman he'd taken on because her man threw her out, not through any fault of hers but because Seth had brought a younger woman to their home and she'd stolen Esperanza's man. In the house in front of him was a woman who held the place of his wife, a legality denied her because he had abandoned a wife back in Texas. Asleep in the house were their infant daughter and his seven-year-old son, the child of yet another woman. As he crossed the yard, Seth felt a fleeting inclination to kick himself free, as if the people dependent on him were shackles dragging at his stride.

He walked into the kitchen and saw Melinda sitting at the table over a cup of cocoa. He could see she'd been crying, and he silently sighed at yet another confrontation that sucked at his patience. But he didn't want to go back to Rico, who would resume their argument, so he sat down across from Melinda.

She sniffed. "Want some cocoa?"

He shook his head. She was a pretty woman, with dark

sun-streaked hair and a delicate face just beginning to show signs of aging. At twenty-six she was half a decade older than Joaquín, Seth's partner, with whom she'd been living for two years now. As he watched her try to hide her tears, he wished he hadn't sat down. At least Rico was crying over something he could deal with. Melinda was crying over Joaquín, and Seth didn't want to edge so much as a knife blade into that situation.

"I'm sorry," she said, wiping her eyes with her fingertips. She sniffed again, then gave him a smile. "I feel like an idiot, Seth."

"Maybe you are."

She laughed. "I wish Joaquín was more like you."

He almost got up right then, suspecting what was coming. Instead he decided he might as well direct the conversation toward a constructive conclusion, so he asked with a fortitude he didn't feel, "How like me?"

She stared past him into the darkness outside. "I guess I worked in saloons too long."

He waited.

She gave him a teasing smile though her eyes were brimming with tears. "Remember when we were together?"

"Me and you?"

She nodded.

He frowned, unsuccessfully trying to recall her body among the hundreds of saloon girls he'd enjoyed over the years.

"I'm not tryin' to take anything away from Rico," she said. "I just keep rememberin' how you were."

"What do you remember?" he asked.

"You took what you wanted," she said.

"Yeah, that pretty well describes it."

"That's what I need," she whispered. "But Joaquín . . ."

"Cares about your feelings?" he bit off. "Doesn't want to hurt you? Treats you like a lady?"

"It's not my fault, Seth," she retorted, tossing her head defiantly.

"It ain't his."

"Maybe it is. Maybe he just needs to learn some new tricks."

Seth kept quiet.

"I was waitin' for you here," she said. "I was hopin' you'd talk to him, teach him something, maybe."

"No," he said.

"It would be easy," she said. "Just take him into town and share a woman with him. Show him how it's done."

"How what's done?"

"You know," she said, holding his gaze.

"Take a belt to you, is that what you want?"

"Just a little spark, that's all, Seth."

"Maybe you oughta think about moving on."

She stared at him. "Are you throwin' me out?"

"That ain't my decision. It's Joaquín's."

"You're ruler of this roost. What you say goes."

He sighed, wishing he'd heard those words from Esperanza. "I ain't got nothing to do with Joaquín's bed. If you got problems, he's the one to solve 'em." He stood up, looking through the parlor at the closed bedroom door, then turned and walked back outside.

The stable was dark, no light coming from beneath Joaquín's door at the end of the aisle. Seth lit a lantern then backed his sorrel out of the stall and led it over to the rack of saddles, shouting down the distance, "Hey, Joaquín, want to ride into town?"

He was reaching under his horse's belly for the cinch when Joaquín came out. Neither of them said anything until they were away from the yard, trotting along the trail that wound toward the road into Tejoe. When Seth looked over, the kid gave him a bittersweet smile and said, "Melinda was crying."

"So was Rico," Seth said.

"Why?" Joaquín asked with concern.

"Esperanza predicted I'm gonna die in a saloon, so Rico

wants me to stay home the rest of my life.'' When Joaquín didn't reply, Seth asked, "What about Melinda?"

The kid took a long time to answer. Finally he said, "She has been hurt by many men."

Seth looked across at his friend, who had once wanted to be a priest and still dressed all in black. "I was one of 'em, did you know that?"

Joaquín nodded, meeting his eyes. After a while the kid said, "Melinda will be all right."

Seth didn't believe it, but he meant to stay clear of the explosion he saw coming.

The Blue Rivers Saloon was crowded when they walked in the back door and climbed the stairs to a private room. Seth stopped on the threshold, assessing the woman on Blue's lap.

She was a succulent jewel of a female, her well-curved body encased in a gown of maroon brocade embroidered with a golden vine running rampant around her skirts. Leaping to her feet as the door opened, she stared at the men who had just come in, her laughter sounding forced.

Blue laughed, too, a much more pleasant sound. "Hey, Seth, Joaquín. I want you to meet my new manager, Lila Keats."

"Seth Strummar, no doubt," Lila said, coming forward and extending her hand.

Her green eyes nudged him with a memory he couldn't put a handle on except to think that Blue had just made a bad mistake. As with Joaquín and Melinda, however, Seth kept his opinion to himself and shook the soft hand that felt cool as a grave.

Lila turned toward his *compadre,* her smile deepening her dimples. "And Joaquín Ascarate. I would have known the two of you without an introduction."

Joaquín shook with her as quickly as Seth had, then met his eyes with a cautious amusement.

Blue said, "Sit down. You want a drink?"

"Yeah," Seth said, though he walked over to the window and looked out. The entire block was saloons, their hitching rails crowded with horses illuminated in the yellow rectangles of light falling from the windows. Seeing his own shadow on the street, Seth stepped back and closed the shutters. When he turned around, Lila was watching him. Again, her green eyes nagged him with a memory he couldn't quite catch. "Why don't you sit down," he suggested.

"Thanks," she said, settling herself carefully in her tight skirt. With a taunting smirk she asked, "Aren't you going to inquire as to my qualifications to manage a saloon?"

"Should I?"

"Aren't you Blue's partner?"

"Silent partner. He makes all the decisions."

She laughed. "That's a relief. I thought I had two bosses to please."

Blue handed everyone a drink then raised his in a toast. "To Lila's success," he said.

"As long as it's helpful to yours," Seth muttered before downing his shot.

Lila laughed deep in her throat. "Since I get a percentage, it behooves me to do well."

Seth left his glass on the table and walked over to the window again, lifted a slat of the shutters and peered out.

Joaquín asked, "How long have you been in Tejoe, Miss Keats?"

"It's 'Mrs.' but you can call me Lila." She laughed again, and Seth thought she was so free with her laughter it had to be camouflage. "I just got here yesterday," she said.

"You were lucky," Joaquín said, "to find employment so quickly."

Blue chuckled. "I was sitting here at nine o'clock this morning feeling sorry for myself 'cause I'm always penned up inside this saloon, then the answer to my prayers came sashaying through the door and asked for a job."

"Nine o'clock," Joaquín mused. "So you must have come to the Blue Rivers first."

"That's right," Lila said, tension hardening her voice.

"Why?" Joaquín asked.

"Maybe it was the name," she answered. "It made me think of a fresh start, which is what I want."

Seth turned around and met her eyes. "Where're you from?"

"Wherever the wind blows."

"Where did it blow last?"

"Austin," she said in a tone entirely too intimate for his comfort. "I've seen Jeremiah."

Seth felt a cold slice of anger, the remnant of a rage he'd thought to expel by hanging the man who'd lynched Jeremiah. He'd discovered, however, that the rage lingered despite his vengeance, even though his kid brother had been dead for thirteen years.

"He's a fine boy," Lila said. "You should be proud."

"Who're you talking about?" Seth asked in a low voice.

"Your son." She laughed with self-deprecation. "You may wonder how a woman such as I would cross paths with a senator's grandson, but I saw him in the park along the river. I was walking with a gentleman friend who pointed out the child and his mother. And their bodyguard. They're accompanied by an armed protector everywhere they go. Did you know that?"

Seth shook his head, assimilating the news that his wife had named their son after his brother.

Lila smiled with barely hidden glee into his stony silence, then said softly, "I thought you'd like to know that they appear to be happy and healthy."

"Thanks," he said, not meaning it.

Turning to Joaquín she asked lightly, "You know her, don't you, Joaquín?"

He finished his drink and set the glass on the table, looking at Seth. "I'll be downstairs."

Seth smiled at his partner's wiliness in not answering her question. "See you later."

The noise of the spinning roulette wheel, men laughing and a few high-pitched squeals from the working girls flooded the room until the heavy door closed.

Seth poured himself another drink, then studied the woman over the rim of his glass as he sipped at the whiskey. Finally he said, "As a silent partner, I only make one demand on Blue's business: I get to try out all the new girls." He watched her face tighten with control. "That agreeable to you?"

"Yes," she whispered.

"Right now?"

She nodded.

He turned back to Blue. "There you are," Seth said. "She's a whore without virtue. Don't forget it." He set his glass down and smiled into her angry green eyes. "Don't take it personal. I got what I want at home."

Seth walked into the noise of the saloon, pulled the door shut and stood on the balcony a moment studying the scene below. Joaquín looked up, meeting his eyes across the congestion of tobacco smoke floating in the air. When Seth walked down to join his partner at the bar, the keep set another glass in front of them, and Seth poured himself a drink from Joaquín's bottle.

"What do you think?" Joaquín asked.

"She's trouble," Seth said, sipping the whiskey. He turned around with his back to the bar just as a man came through the front door. Their eyes locked, the newcomer's hot with hostility. Softly to Joaquín, Seth said, "Here's more."

Joaquín looked at the man who had just come in. His face was hidden behind a dark beard, and his clothes were covered with so much dust he looked as if he'd ridden a hundred miles in a hurry. He didn't head for the bar, though. He edged along the wall, watching Seth. Joaquín asked, "Who is he?"

"Don't know him," Seth said.

"He knows you."

"Looks like it," he said. Remembering all the times

he'd faced a man's challenge in the past, Seth smiled in anticipation.

As the stranger continued to edge around the perimeter of the room, keeping a dozen crowded tables between them, the girls flitted across Seth's vision like brightly colored butterflies among the barely perceived field of dusty men. The stranger stopped at the end of an empty aisle and shouted across the din of noise, "You seen me."

The room fell silent in the catch of a breath. "Don't know you," Seth said in a normal voice that carried in the quiet.

"I know you, though." The man grinned through his thick beard. "You're my bonanza. Or will be soon as you're dead."

Men knocked chairs over scrambling away from the tables lining the aisle. "Maybe you'll be dead," Seth answered.

The man shook his head. "I'm still in business and been getting a lotta practice. You been living soft, retired as you are."

The upstairs door opened and Blue came out, his shuffling gait loud on the wood floor of the balcony. At the top of the stairs, he glanced at Seth and Joaquín, then demanded of the stranger, "What's going on?"

"None of yours," he answered without taking his eyes off Seth. "I'm collecting a bounty on a killer. Only one way t'do that and I aim t'do it."

"He ain't alone," Blue said.

"What's the matter, Strummar?" the stranger gibed. "You lose your nerve to face a man one on one?"

"Stay out of it, Blue," Seth said. "You too, Joaquín," he said in a softer voice, not taking his eyes off the stranger.

Joaquín stepped a scant distance away, feeling the chill of his partner's intention. Never having faced such a challenge, his mind spun through possible alternatives and consequences in a tumble of confusion which he knew could be lethal in such a situation, and he admired Seth's unified calm.

The stranger was no longer smiling. A magnetic intensity hovered in the air between him and Seth, seeming almost to hum with the escalating tension until the stranger reached for his gun. Seth's .44 appeared in his hand—Joaquín didn't see him draw it—and he fired once. The stranger grunted and staggered backward, dropping his gun as a stain of blood soaked through the front of his shirt. He stared at his gun on the floor, looking sick, then lost his balance and fell from the weight of a bullet in his heart. The room was silent, acrid with smoke from the barrel of Seth's gun. The stranger hadn't fired. Joaquín gave Seth a smile of congratulation, but he was scanning all the other faces watching him.

Seeing a cunning admiration behind a cruel indifference, Seth knew few of the men in the room would grieve for him any more than they did for the stranger. He raised his eyes to Blue at the top of the stairs. Lila stood beside him watching with an amused smile, and Seth felt an uncomfortable suspicion that the dead man was no stranger to her. He looked at the barkeep. "Sheriff's out of town, ain't he, Gus?"

Gus nodded.

"He knows where to find me," Seth said, holstering his gun. Then he smiled at Joaquín. "Let's go home."

Rico was awake when they returned from town. Lying in her dark bedroom listening to the hoofbeats of their horses in the soft dust of the yard, the creak of the corral gate, then the heavier moan of the stable door, she felt tears of relief that Esperanza's prediction had been wrong. After a few minutes she heard Seth approach the house, the silver jangle of his spurs accompanying his footsteps.

She listened to him enter through the kitchen, heard the crossbar laid in the latch, then his steps crossing the parlor and going into Lobo's room. He stayed there a long time, and she smiled, thinking of him looking down on his sleeping son. When she heard him go into Elena's room, however, her relief was swamped with a cold fear that he was saying goodbye to his children. Finally he opened her door and stood on the threshold. "Evenin'," he said.

She always marveled that he knew she was awake despite the dark. "Hello," she said, then listened as he crossed the room until she could see him standing silhouetted against the starlight outside the window. Sensing something wrong, she struggled to amend it. "I'm sorry, Seth," she apologized. "I shouldn't have carried on so."

He was quiet, surveying the yard for anything amiss. "I told you what to expect," he finally said without turning around. "Nothing's changed."

"I know. The longer we're together, the more I want you with me."

"Can't argue with that," he said, still staring out the window.

She often watched him study the yard before he came to bed, taking comfort from his strength between her and the darkness outside. Tonight, however, he did something she hadn't seen before: he pulled his gun and opened the cylinder, removed a spent shell, flicked it out the window and replaced it with one from his belt, then reholstered his gun. With accumulating dread she asked, "What happened in town tonight?"

Still not looking at her he said, "I killed a man."

Fear froze her heart. "So Esperanza was right."

"He died. I didn't."

"Who was it?" she whispered.

"A bounty hunter. I didn't catch his name."

"Then it was self-defense."

"He drew first," Seth agreed.

"So they won't hold it against you."

He shrugged. "Sheriff's out of town. We'll see what he has to say when he gets back."

"There were witnesses, weren't there?"

"Yeah," he said. Then, after a moment, "I shouldn't be here, Rico."

"Where?" she whimpered, afraid of his answer.

He turned around and faced her, though she still couldn't read his eyes in the dark. "What do you think the kids are gonna say to Lobo in school next week?"

"I'm sure he doesn't care," she answered. "Do you think they mean more to him than your love?"

"Sometimes I think they should." He closed the shutters, leaving the room in the ink of darkness.

She listened to him cross to the bedside, the rustle of the box of matches, then the hiss of the match as he struck it. In the flare of light, she nearly cried at the pain in his eyes.

"I ain't going to court," he said, lighting the candle and dropping the match to flicker out in the saucer. "I ain't surrendering my gun to any officer of the law for any reason. I'll die before I let 'em cage me, and the odds are good you and Lobo are gonna watch it happen."

"I don't believe that," she whispered.

"Which?"

"If we watch you die, it will be of old age in your bed."

"That ain't what you were saying this afternoon, is it?"

"I was wrong. I lost my courage for a while. We can see it through together, Seth. Without you, Lobo and Elena and I will be lost, to say nothing of Joaquín and Esperanza."

"That's a heavy load to carry, you know that?"

"Yes," she said.

He nodded, then unbuckled his gunbelt and hung it on his side of the headboard. She felt the weight as if the bed had tilted, though it hadn't. As she watched him sit down and tug off his boots, she restrained herself from touching his back.

He leaned his elbows on his knees and held his head. "Thing that bothers me most is the indifference I saw in all those men. I was no more to them than that bounty hunter. They didn't care which one of us died."

"They don't know you, Seth."

"I've been living here for two years. I go into Blue's saloon nearly every damn night."

"And do what?" she asked carefully.

He snorted in recognition of her point. "Drink with Blue and Joaquín behind a closed door more often'n not."

"Exactly," she said softly. "All they know is your reputation and what you look like passing through. And whatever their children learn from Lobo, which can't be much since you've told him not to discuss his homelife at school. If they could see you being a father like them, trying to raise your family with decency, they would accept you as one of them. Maybe not the same, but close enough." When he didn't answer, she said, "Tomorrow's Sunday. Maybe it would be a good time to join the community."

"You mean go to church?" he scoffed.

"What an excellent idea," she said with a laugh.

He looked at her and laughed, too. "It wasn't mine," he said.

"It would make you real to them instead of just someone living on the outskirts of town attracting certain unpleasant consequences."

"Attracting scum, is what you mean." He stood up and crossed to the washbowl, then poured water in the basin. As he pulled his shirt out and unbuttoned it, he faced her and asked, "You think they'll forgive me for shedding blood in their town?"

"If you'd prove to them you've changed, that you're not the man you were."

"You think if I show up in church, I'll sprout a halo for them to see?"

She smiled. "None of them have halos either, Seth."

He took his shirt off, crumpled it into a ball and threw it into the laundry basket in the corner, lifted handfuls of water to wash his face, then ran a wet cloth over his torso. The cloth, too, he threw into the basket. "I ain't been to church since I was a kid," he said.

"I've heard Mrs. Engle at the mercantile say good things about Reverend Holcroft," she said softly.

Seth emptied his pockets on the bureau, the coins clanking loudly, stepped out of his trousers and sat down naked
to peel his socks off, then threw them all in the basket,
blew out the candle and slid under the covers beside her.

Still he didn't touch her, and she waited in agony. He
had killed men before but all that had been in his past and
he rarely spoke of it. When he did it was to make a joke,
as if his proclivity for homicide were nothing more than
an amusing riddle. Now for the first time she realized it
made him feel everyone he valued was threatened rather
than protected by his presence, and she suddenly understood why he had always moved on after a killing, drifted
to another place where he could build a new world he
sustained on hope until it was shattered again with a bullet.
She wanted to tell him this killing wasn't his fault, but she
knew he would scoff at the notion; wanted to hold him
close and love away his thoughts of leaving, but was afraid
her touch now would be perceived as another demand he
couldn't satisfy that would drive him away for good.

Across the dark space between them his voice was hollow. "Rico?"

"Yes," she whispered, turning on her side to face him.

"I heard news of my wife tonight."

"From who?" she asked, feeling another stab of dread.

"A woman working for Blue. Said she saw Johanna in
Austin, and the kid, too. A boy named Jeremiah."

She held her breath, waiting.

"It's odd to think there's a new Jeremiah Strummar in
the world." Abruptly he pulled her close and buried his
face in the crook of her neck. "Jesus, Rico," he murmured, his breath warm on her skin, "I wish you were my
wife. If there was only one thing in my past I could
change, that would be it."

"It's enough to hear you say that," she answered.

He lay back with a sigh. "You think it'll be enough for
the good people in church?"

"They only know what we tell them."

He chuckled. "Then we're married and I'll kill the man

who says otherwise.'' He snorted with self-mockery. ''I've made that joke and seen men dive for cover. Maybe I'll let the churchgoers think I'm unarmed. What do you think of that? Seth Strummar without a gun.''

''You won't really go without one?'' she asked with new worry.

He laughed again. ''You think the do-gooders might kill me?''

''No,'' she said, ''but anyone can go inside a church, Seth.''

''I'll be proof of that,'' he said, ending their conversation with a kiss.

2

Homer Holcroft was forty-eight years old and had come to the Southwest for his health. When a series of debilitating lung infections forced his resignation as pastor of a modestly affluent parish in St. Louis, he came west seeking a comfortable hermitage in which to die. The hot, dry sun, however, cleared his lungs, and his hermitage turned out to be a thriving town without a Protestant church.

Holcroft decided to establish a place of worship in competition with the Roman Catholic diocese. To attract as many parishioners as possible, he chose to remain independent of the denominations which funded missions on the frontier, and he named his endeavor the Unified Christian Church of Tejoe. Using his own money he built a modest white edifice boasting a bell tower and enough pews to seat a hundred worshippers. Alongside the church he built a small adobe rectory, and he employed an old Mexican woman to care for him and the sanctuary. Tulia was Catholic and attended daily mass at Our Lady of Sorrows, but since there were no respectable Protestant women in need of employment, the reverend made do.

His parish consisted of the families of men employed in the local silver mines and the merchants who catered to their needs, as well as scattered ranchers who rarely made it into town for Sunday services. Except for the mine owners and the president of the Bank of Tejoe, none of the reverend's parishioners evidenced wealth. If their tithes were truly one-tenth of their incomes, he would be forced to conclude that his parish existed barely above subsistence.

Also pivotal in starting the first public school in Tejoe—though the school board was as poorly financed as his charity endeavors—Reverend Holcroft had reviewed the tax rolls many times searching for a citizen with hidden assets who might be induced to share what he had. There was only one whose record gave any hint of wealth. Unfortunately, it was unlikely he would join the church.

It was said he had a sizable balance in the Bank of Tejoe, was the financial backer of the most popular saloon in town, and lived on unmortgaged land without an income. He was reputed to be responsible for the support of six people besides himself, and gossip had it they mail-ordered their clothing from St. Louis and Chicago. His family came to town to buy groceries—always accompanied by a Mexican gunman who watched them with eagle eyes—and his seven-year-old son attended the public school. The teacher said that little Lobo was bright, and also, upon questioning, that he never talked of his home-life. If the subject of his father came into a conversation, the child fell silent. Miss Perkins had whispered that to the reverend, as if wary of saying the father's name.

Seth Strummar was the name, though few people said it out loud. Usually they referred to him as the outlaw. Reverend Holcroft had never heard of him before coming to the Southwest. After discovering the outlaw was living in his parish, the reverend did some research and learned that in the late sixties Seth Strummar and Ben Allister created havoc in Texas, robbing banks and terrifying citizens across the state. They escaped the law's retribution through eight years of pillage that finally ended when Allister was killed by his own wife. Strummar hanged the woman in vengeance, then disappeared. He was reported seen here and there, usually in connection with a killing, but the stories of his ultimate fate were varied and wild. It seemed only the people in Tejoe knew he was living five miles outside their town.

His presence was seen as a curse waiting fulfillment. Whenever his name came into a conversation, before the talkers were through they expressed their fear that a bounty hunter would find Strummar and then they'd have a killing in their town. If Strummar died the problem would be over, they would say, lowering their voices, but if his luck held and the hunter died, another would show up before too long.

The fateful event had finally transpired. Late on Saturday night Tulia knocked on Holcroft's bedroom door, jabbering in an hysterical Spanish that yanked him from sleep in alarm. Tying his robe as he hurried to open the door, he led the frightened woman into the kitchen and sat her down at the table, trying to calm her enough to speak in English so he could understand. She had been praying with friends at the wake of their father, she finally managed to say, when they were interrupted by the news and she'd hurried home to tell him.

"Tell me what?" he asked kindly, heating milk at the stove.

"He has brought death, as we knew always he would," she announced solemnly, her beady eyes sharp and black, her frizzy hair skewed out of its bun so it stuck up like a grizzled halo around her head. "It has come, the curse he carries."

"Who? What curse?" Holcroft asked, straining for patience. The woman was superstitious and excitable, and this wasn't the first time he had placated her fears.

"The outlaw," she whispered. "He has killed a man, just now, in the Blue Rivers Saloon."

Holcroft turned away and took the tin of cocoa from the cupboard, measured two spoonfuls into the simmering milk and stirred the mixture methodically while he tried to imagine the event Tulia was describing. He had never seen a gunfight and found it difficult to picture men coldly squaring off in deadly opposition. His mind full of questions he knew she couldn't answer, he splashed a shot of whiskey into the cups before filling them with hot chocolate.

"Now," he said, setting the cups on the table and taking the chair across from her, "tell me again what you heard."

"Just that, no more," she answered, greedily slurping the cocoa without letting it cool. "He is the devil walking among us," she said, her eyes glinting through the steam rising from the cup.

Holcroft smiled sadly. "He is only a man, Tulia."

"A man with the devil inside," she hissed. "He will kill this town, as he killed the bounty hunter tonight."

This new fact nestled into Holcroft's mind with a reassurance he couldn't credit to logic. "It's unfortunate, Tulia, but not as much as you seem to think. A bounty hunter, after all, is seeking someone's death, is he not?"

"Not his own!" she retorted fiercely.

"No," he answered with a smile. "And it's not an action we can condone, but we can't blame Mr. Strummar for defending himself."

"He is defending the wrongs he has done! I blame him for bringing his wrongs to our town so all of us must pay."

Holcroft sipped his cocoa, thinking of his sermon in the morning.

"He has doomed Tejoe," Tulia pronounced, setting her empty cup on the table.

Holcroft smiled gently. "No one is doomed living in the love of God."

"The love of God is for the heaven of eternity," she answered. "The outlaw has brought hell to us now, alive in our town."

Holcroft shook his head. "The act of one man cannot doom a pious community."

"Judas doomed the whole world," she argued. "He was only one man."

Holcroft smiled with indulgence. "Judas doomed only Jesus of Nazareth. Through His sacrifice, Jesus became Christ and His crucifixion redeemed the world."

"Who will redeem Tejoe?"

"The same Christ," he answered. "And all of His servants who unite against the coming of violence."

She shook her head. "The outlaw is stronger than all of us together."

"How can he be?" he asked with paternalistic patience.

"Because he has the evil eye of Satan inside him! You will see, Padre Holcroft. You are new to this country and don't know it as I do. The desert is the Devil's homeland; he rules here."

"Go to sleep," Holcroft said with compassion. "In the light of day you'll see that things aren't as bad as they seem in the dark of midnight."

"I will go to my room," she said, "but I will not sleep. I will pray for God's mercy."

He watched her trundle from the room, then Reverend Holcroft sat up late rewriting his sermon. He chose for his text Matthew 5:30: "And if thy right hand offend thee, cut it off and cast it from thee, for it is profitable that one of thy members should perish and not that thy whole body should be cast into hell." He felt dissatisfied with the message he was giving his congregation, but he hoped that in uniting against the outlaw they could achieve a strength of community he had found lacking among his widely scattered parish.

The autumn morning was bright and warm as he greeted the arriving worshippers. In his white robe, he stood on the steps of his white church, feeling humbled as he saw the effect of the killing in the faces passing before him. People were frightened that violence had disrupted the peace of their somnolent town, and they came craving leadership, many more than on any other Sunday since services had begun. Holcroft smiled and touched the people in greeting as he prayed that he not disappoint them and fail what he understood to be the true beauty of the church: the satisfying union of the congregation.

He left the doors open to catch the breeze, ascended to the pulpit, and faced the people with pride yet trepidation as he nodded at the pianist to begin the opening strains of the invocation. The people rose and began to sing: "Praise God from Whom all blessings flow."

Holcroft watched a buggy stop outside the door accompanied by a Mexican gunman dressed in black and riding a black horse. The weapon on his hip caught sunlight as he dismounted. He tied his reins to the back of the buggy, then went to the head of the team and held them.

"Praise Him, all creatures here below," the congregation sang as the outlaw's boots stepped into the dust. He wore a dark suit and no gun, his dark hat pulled low above his eyes as he turned to help his wife.

"Praise Him above the Heavenly Host," sang the congregation as Mrs. Strummar reached inside the buggy for a blanket-clad infant.

"Praise Father, Son, and Holy Ghost," the people sang as little Lobo jumped down with a grin.

The rustle of the congregation being seated covered the approach of the arriving family. Holcroft stood stunned, trying to force his mind to rearrange his sermon in light of this new development. The people saw him staring through the open door, and they turned to see what had caught his attention.

The outlaw stopped silhouetted in the door, his face still hidden by the brim of his dark hat. His right hand held the small hand of his son, whom most people had seen in school or around town. His left hand was on the waist of his wife, a pretty woman most people hadn't seen. Her blond hair was braided and wound at the nape of her neck beneath a pert bonnet that matched her dress, which was sky blue with a fashionably narrow skirt snug on her slender hips, and she held a baby wrapped in a yellow blanket against her breasts. The outlaw's eyes were pale, roving across the silent faces of the congregation. Letting go of his wife, he reached up and took off his hat, then nudged his son to do the same. Lobo complied, watching his father as the outlaw asked softly, "Is there room for us?"

Holcroft found his tongue. "There is room for everyone in the House of God," he said, searching the crowded pews for someplace to seat them.

Abneth Nickles leaned across his wife and whispered quickly to his oldest sons, then stood up. He was the outlaw's neighbor but had never garnered the courage to ride over and meet the man. "We'd be pleased if you'd share our pew, Mr. Strummar," he said as his three boys filed out to sit on the floor against the wall.

"Obliged," the outlaw said, guiding his wife forward with his hand on the small of her back. The two women, each holding a baby, sat beside each other, then the boy, then the outlaw on the aisle.

Reverend Holcroft watched the congregation drag its eyes away from the newcomers to face forward expectant of his wisdom. He looked down at his notes and knew they were wrong. His righteousness had been humbled by the very sinner he was prepared to castigate coming forward to worship God. Holcroft was not a simple man. He knew the outlaw had an ulterior motive for choosing this Sunday to attend, but Holcroft also guessed what that motive was, and he approved. Strummar wanted to be accepted as a citizen; citizens paid taxes and tithes and stipends to school boards. So Reverend Holcroft smiled at the outlaw, then opened his Bible.

"My text today comes from the Book of Job," he said solemnly. "Chapter three, verse twenty-six: 'I was not in safety, neither had I rest, neither was I quiet; yet trouble came.'"

He looked up and searched all the faces watching him for understanding. "What do those words tell us?" he asked rhetorically, wishing someone would answer him. "That life is a vale of tears no matter how virtuous we are? That we can do our best to build a decent God-fearing community, and the hand of Satan will always defeat us? Moses said, 'Look to it: evil is before you.' Did he mean it was preferred by God? 'Before you' can mean above you or in your line of vision. I think it is the latter. Evil is all around us, but nowhere in the scriptures does it say that evil will triumph."

He paused to meet the outlaw's eyes. "Yet it was alive last night, wasn't it? None of us can deny that in the noise and bustle of a typical Saturday night in the Blue Rivers Saloon, when the room was crowded with men gambling away their earnings and fallen doves wandering about in the hope of catching the spoils from the drunken men, the very cacophony of hell on earth—a human hell, ladies and gentlemen, one we built without any help from either God or Satan but with our own bare hands from the desires of our hearts—into that human world, the Devil walked. Who was the Devil in that room last night?"

He paused again, sweeping his gaze over all the men. Softly, he asked, "How many of you were there?" He smiled his forgiveness. "I understand from certain parishioners who operate businesses in competition with Mr. Rivers that his establishment takes more than a little of their trade." A murmur of chuckles followed his words. "It's a popular place, the Blue Rivers Saloon. Maybe it's the name." He stopped to smile at the outlaw again. "Sounds like new beginnings, doesn't it? Fresh starts? Making amends for wrongs done in the past and living clean again?" He looked at the women in the congregation. "There were three entities in that saloon last night: two actors and an audience. The audience did nothing. They watched. Whatever they felt about what was coming—and they all knew from the first instant of confrontation what was coming—they kept their opinions to themselves. You know why? They didn't want to attract attention. They didn't want either one of the actors to think they had taken sides. They were neutral. They had no effect. They were like a herd of mares waiting to see which stallion would rule.'' He looked at Mrs. Strummar. ''Forgive me if I'm being too blunt.'' He looked at everyone else again as he softly said, ''But I am talking about control, ladies and gentlemen. Control of evil.''

He paused for effect, then let his voice ring out: '' 'I was not in safety, neither had I rest, neither was I quiet; yet trouble came.' '' He sighed deeply. ''It's the 'yet' that's puzzling, isn't it. You expect that verse to end with God's reward, not with more trouble. Yet trouble came. Trouble always comes seeking destruction and death. The man who sought death last night in the Blue Rivers Saloon found it. The man who delivered it did not bring it, he met it. And this morning, ladies and gentlemen, he has brought his family to worship among us. As we bow our heads in prayer, let us remember Job's warning—I fought trouble, yet trouble came—and decide in the secrecy of our hearts whether Job would welcome into his sanctuary a man adept at meeting trouble.''

He nodded at the pianist, and she began to play the quiet chords of ''Nearer My God to Thee'' as the ushers rose to pass the collection baskets. Locked on the minister, the outlaw's eyes were so pale and cool that Holcroft couldn't read anything in them. He knew he should look away but couldn't bring himself to break the gaze. Finally the outlaw broke it, looking down at the basket his wife held. He reached for his wallet and took out a hundred-dollar bill. It was United States currency, which Holcroft rarely saw in the territory, and his eyes picked out the amount hungrily. Handing the basket to the usher, the outlaw met Holcroft's gaze with a sardonic smile, and the minister laughed, making several people in the congregation look quickly back and forth between them.

''Next Saturday,'' Holcroft said, his voice booming happily, ''the Ladies Auxiliary is holding our autumn picnic. We hope everyone will attend. On Wednesday . . .'' his voice droned on with the announcements of the prayer meeting, the arrival of a new baby and an impending visit from relatives, his mind racing with an excitement he couldn't define except to know he felt pleased to have Seth Strummar among his congregation. Holcroft closed his book and left the pulpit, expecting the opening chords of "Beulah Land," the hymn he and the pianist had chosen. Instead she began a melancholy melody that arrested everyone with its haunting sorrow.

The members of the congregation had risen to their feet and a few were preparing to leave, but all stopped as if turned to statues as they listened to Miss Gates play. She began to sing, her husky contralto filling the room with a spiritual Holcroft hadn't heard since leaving St. Louis.

"Sometimes I feel like a motherless child," Miss Gates sang as Holcroft walked down the aisle to the door, his hands folded within the voluminous sleeves of his white robe, his eyes on the floor, his thoughts far away in another time where sorrow was perpetual. "A long ways from home," she sang, "a long, long ways from home."

Slowly the people filed out. A few of the women were dabbing at their eyes with handkerchiefs, their husbands gruff and impatient. Buck Stubbins, owner of the Red Rooster Silver Mine, leaned close to mutter, "I know what you're tryin' to do, Rev, and I admire your ambition but you're playin' with fire, ya know that, don'cha?"

Holcroft met his eyes with determination. "All of life is playing with the fires of hell, Buck. I'm experienced and know my way."

Buck laughed softly. "I think ya done bit off more'n ya can chew and I expect ya to be spittin' it up 'fore winter's come."

"I hate to disappoint my parishioners but in this case I hope I do," Holcroft said gently.

Buck shook his head. "Try defendin' him after the next killin' and then tell me how optimistic ya feel." He slapped the minister affectionately on the back and walked down to his buggy where his wife and children were waiting.

Holcroft shifted his gaze to the Mexican who had come with Strummar. He was standing by the team, watching the crowd, his hand loose by his gun. Holcroft saw the stock of a rifle on the seat of the buggy, an extra weapon ready for use, and he raised his eyes to meet those of the Mexican's. Holcroft knew the gunman's name to be Joaquín Ascarate, that he had several killings in his past and was living at the Strummar ranch with a fallen dove from Tombstone. Holcroft had also heard that Ascarate had intended to be a priest before meeting the outlaw. Believing the story for the first time, Holcroft smiled into Ascarate's dark eyes, which spoke of a depth of kindness that didn't match his reputation.

Holcroft turned away and walked into the church to see Strummar and his family just standing up. The pianist continued to play softly though everyone else had left. Holcroft walked forward, extended his hand to the outlaw and introduced himself.

"Seth Strummar," the man said, and it sounded odd to hear the name spoken outright. "My wife and daughter," he said, "and my son."

Holcroft smiled at all of them. "I'm very pleased to see you among us this morning. I hope you'll favor us with your presence next Sunday."

"What're you gonna talk about?" Strummar asked with a playful light in his eyes.

"Perhaps the rewards of generosity," Holcroft said with a smile.

The outlaw laughed. "Well, I'll tell you," he said, turning around to give Miss Gates a smile, "I'd come back just for the music. That's a talented lady you got at your keyboard."

Miss Gates blushed. Holcroft saw Mrs. Strummar cast a worried scrutiny at her husband, who said, "You know Rico sings and plays a pretty guitar." He looked down at his wife. "It's a shame to let talent go to waste." She looked flustered at his words.

Holcroft said, "We'd be delighted, Mrs. Strummar, to

have you sing for us. Perhaps you could get together with Miss Gates and choose a song you'd like to perform.''

"I couldn't," she said, throwing her husband a puzzled frown.

"Well, you think about it," Holcroft said. "Is there any chance we'll see you at our picnic on Saturday?"

"No," the outlaw said. "But we'll be back next Sunday." He looked down at his son. "Won't we, Lobo?"

"Reckon," the boy said unhappily.

The outlaw shared a smile of friendship with the reverend, then guided his family down the aisle and out of the church.

3

Melinda and Esperanza sat at the kitchen table finishing off the breakfast coffee. Outside the open door, Joaquín's white dove cooed from the roof. "I hate that damn bird," Melinda said, draining her cup and studying the grounds left in the bottom.

Esperanza watched her warily.

"Can you read coffee grounds?" Melinda asked with a laugh. "Look at that pattern. Don't it resemble a hangman's noose?"

Esperanza stood up without looking at it, carried her own cup to the sink and washed it in the water left from the dishes.

Melinda laughed again, a harsh sound without joy. "You don't like me, do you?"

Esperanza looked over her shoulder as she placed the clean cup on the shelf. "I like you well enough."

"Seth doesn't, though, does he?"

"He's never said nothing to me about it," Esperanza answered. She carried the dishpan to the door and threw the dirty water out. When she banged the pan against the side of the house, the white dove flew away from the noise, then coasted to land on the top of a golden cottonwood. Esperanza considered the dove an emblem of love on the homestead, and Melinda's dislike of the bird was worrisome. When she went back inside, Melinda was pouring whiskey into her cup.

"That's Seth's whiskey," Esperanza said. "You think he'll be glad you drank it?"

"I ain't gonna drink it all! Seems like every time I turn around, somebody don't like something I'm doin'."

"You think that's our fault?" Esperanza asked.

Melinda looked at the large, dark woman who had been a beauty in her youth. Traces remained in the smoothness of her plump face, the flash of her black eyes and her equally black hair wound in a glistening bun on the nape of her neck. As if her words didn't carry a barb, Melinda asked, "Don'cha think it's funny Seth's had every woman on the place?"

Esperanza remained silent, wiping the stove with a wet rag that hissed with the heat.

"You think he didn't take us along," Melinda asked, "'cause he didn't want to walk into church with his harem?"

"Did you want to go?" Esperanza answered, tossing the rag into the sink.

"Nah. Who'd want to go to church?" Melinda muttered, refilling her cup with whiskey.

"You gonna be drunk when they get back?" Esperanza asked.

"Maybe," she said with defiance. "Maybe I'll take all my clothes off and run around nekkid. What d'ya think of that?"

Esperanza smiled. "I think you will get a sunburn."

"Will I get a reaction from ol' Seth is the question," she said, sipping his whiskey.

"Is *that* what you want?"

"Yes," she said earnestly. "If I could do it without hurtin' Rico."

"What about Joaquín?"

Melinda smiled wickedly. "Think he'd fight for me?"

"With another man, perhaps. Not with Seth."

"He'd just hand me over and tell us to have a good time?" She laughed bitterly. "You're right. That's exactly what he'd do. How d'ya get away with it?"

"Away with what?"

"Sleepin' with Seth and not hurtin' Rico."

"Who says I sleep with him?"

"I've seen him go into your casita so late the coyotes are already in bed. You don't light the lamp and he don't come out again for a good hour, so it ain't hard to figure what you're doin'."

"You watch, do you?" Esperanza asked coldly.

Melinda sighed. "I don't mean to. It's jus' that I can't sleep so I'm awake a lot in the middle of the night. Don't be mad at me, Esperanza. Everyone else seems to be and I can't figure it out."

"It's because you're making Joaquín unhappy," she said softly.

"That's 'cause he's makin' me unhappy! Don't anyone care about that? I wanta stay here but Joaquín can't cut it and it's drivin' me crazy."

"What are you saying?" she whispered.

"You know what I'm sayin'," Melinda retorted.

"I don't believe he had a problem before you."

"Maybe it's not me. Maybe it's Seth. You know how Joaquín feels about him. He'd lie down in the mud and let Seth walk on him to keep his boots clean."

"You misunderstand," Esperanza murmured.

"I don't think so," Melinda said. "There's only one stud on this range, and it ain't Joaquín." She poured herself some more of Seth's whiskey.

"I agree," Esperanza said softly. "If it's a stud you want, Joaquín is not your man. But he is the only man here for you, so maybe it is time you weren't here."

"Thanks," Melinda muttered. "Your kindness is over-whelmin'." She drained her cup and refilled it. "I never could figure Seth choosin' weak little Rico. I wonder why he did."

"She is not weak," Esperanza argued.

"You'd think he'd want a woman to match his passion for bein' alive," Melinda said.

"You think you do?"

Melinda nodded, then spoke softly, staring into her cup. "When I first hooked up with Joaquín, I thought we could make it work. Everything was good at first, so good I thought even when Seth came back my love for Joaquín would carry me through. But that was a mistake 'cause it all fell to pieces soon as Seth rode into the yard. It wasn't 'cause of my love, though. It was 'cause of Joaquín's."

Esperanza didn't want to hear any more but she stood rigidly in place, listening to the woman's lament.

"It happened that first night Seth came home." Melinda paused for a sip of whiskey, then went on. "Joaquín was restless and wouldn't come to bed though I coaxed and pleaded. Then Seth came to the door and took him away. Just came and asked and Joaquín was out that door in less'n a minute. He was gone a long time, and even when he came back, he still wouldn't come to bed. He stood at the window and looked out at the dark 'til I fell asleep. When I woke up in the mornin' he was gone. And when I walked into the kitchen and asked Rico if she'd seen him, she said he and Seth and Lobo went ridin' and wouldn't be back 'til late. When they came back, Seth took Joaquín into town." Melinda emptied her cup. "He came home so drunk he was clumsy in bed, and I threw Seth's finesse in his face. Any other man would've slapped me. You know what Joaquín did? He took his blankets to the loft and he's slept there ever since."

"All this time?" Esperanza whispered.

Melinda nodded. "It's something, ain't it? Any other man would've kicked me out of his bed if he didn't want to share it with me. Not Joaquín, though.'' She laughed bitterly as she refilled her cup.

''Don't you think you've had enough?'' Esperanza asked with worry. ''You've drunk nearly half of it already.''

''No,'' Melinda said. ''I'm gonna be good'n snockered when they come home.''

''Why?''

''Maybe so I can see if Joaquín'll defend me when Seth throws me out.''

''Can't you wait 'til tomorrow when Lobo's in school?''

Melinda laughed, twisting in the chair to face her with a grin. ''Don't you want Lobo to see his heroes in their true light? Ain't that what you're always sayin' about the cards, that they tell the truth and it's always better to know the truth?''

''I don't think you know it,'' Esperanza intoned. ''But I know I don't want to see what you cause with your ignorance.'' She walked out of the house, across the bright, hot yard to her casita, feeling a strong foreboding of dread.

In the dim coolness of her room, she took her tarot cards from the cedar box over the mantle and sat at the table shuffling them, clearing her mind as she stared through the open door. Across the yard, the white dove landed gracefully on a saguaro. Esperanza took it for an auspicious omen and dealt the cards for Melinda.

Behind her was disappointment; covering her was a fiery woman with treachery in her heart; before her was Death; his aspect was the cup of abundance. Esperanza stared down at the cards for a long time, unhappy with the recurrence of Death every time she laid a cross for someone at the homestead. She gathered her cards and returned them to the mantle in their cedar box, then she stood at the door and felt the hot wind ruffle her dress, dreading what would happen when the family returned from church.

She heard them coming from beyond the mountain, and for a moment she doubted her inaction. It seemed there should be something she could do to prevent the catastrophe she saw coming. She was too late, however. The pair of matched chestnuts cantered into the yard pulling the buggy. Seth reined up in front of the door and stepped down to hand Rico out. Lobo leapt to the ground and ran ahead of them, and Rico called for him to change his clothes before playing outside. As she carried the baby into the house, Seth drove the buggy back toward the corral where Joaquín was just swinging off his horse.

Seth stepped down, then looked across the yard at Esperanza. He studied her warily a moment before turning to unharness the team. Asking herself what he would have her do, she decided it would be to get Lobo out of the way. Hurriedly she trudged across the yard, through the front door and into Lobo's room. He had shed his church clothes and was pulling on his dungarees. She smiled at his skinny arms and pale chest beneath the line of sunburn around his neck. ''Where's your shirt?'' she asked, picking his suit off the floor and shaking it out.

In her bedroom, Rico laid Elena in the cradle and sat down on the bed, letting herself fall back to stare at the ceiling. It was a marvel to her that they had comported themselves acceptably among the respectable people, that the preacher had actually asked her to sing in his church. It wasn't her talent she doubted. Rico had sung in public to high acclaim in her past. In fact, praise of her voice had been the topic of Seth's first conversation with her. That had happened in a Pinos Altos saloon where she was an entertainer fighting the lure of prostitution's wages. Though she'd managed to hold that line over the years, she and her friends were a far cry from respectable.

Rico was proud to be Seth's woman. Although she was denied the honor of being his wife, she considered herself fortunate to have the man she loved stay with her and their children. Seth was an outlaw, however, and despite her happiness, never in her wildest dreams had Rico hoped to be accepted on the proper side of town.

She giggled with pleasure remembering how everyone in church had stared at her and Seth walking in. All those wives who would have shunned her in Tombstone were admiring her now. She had seen it in their faces, how they pursed their lips as they took in the latest fashion of her frock and bonnet, their envious eyes acknowledging the power of the man at her side. Rico hugged herself, unable to believe it. Only last night Seth had come home with news of what seemed like doom. Only yesterday Esperanza had driven Rico to tears predicting his death. Now it was Sunday and she could still hear the church bell ringing, see the sun sparkling on the white church, the women's faces watching her without rancor.

In Rico's past, respectable women had been altogether another breed from the harlots who'd been her friends. She had known a few other girls like Melinda over her career in saloons: young and single, loose and lost in a world definitely not arranged for them, they latched on to each other like sisters, often sharing rooms where they ridiculed the men they had to please all night. Sometimes they even found love in each other's arms, but their intimacy was always brief. Invariably, a man came between them.

Melinda and Rico had been sharing a room in Tombstone when Seth walked into the saloon where Rico was singing and resumed the romance they'd started in Pinos Altos. When he left her again, she had been so devastated she'd tried to kill herself. It was Melinda who kept her alive, bandaged her wrists and gently chided her for ceding any man that much power, then spent her own money on food and lodging until Rico could fend for herself. After Rico gave up on Seth's return and married Henry Lessen, it was Melinda's friendship that helped her endure the hell her marriage became. It was even Melinda who convinced her to see Seth when he came back, then handed her into the wagon as Seth tied his horse on the back and she said goodbye to Tombstone and hello to being his woman.

Rico had felt pleased when Melinda liked Joaquín. Both she and Esperanza watched with concealed amusement as the experienced woman led the shy man through a mating dance delightful to witness. He was like a wild creature who needed to be coaxed to come near, so different from the men all three of the women were accustomed to, men who habitually barged in and took what they wanted. Joaquín seemed to doubt what Melinda was offering, or that it was really him she was offering it to, even whether he wanted it. When he finally decided he was reading her right, he still hesitated before giving in.

Rico understood. Joaquín was a thoughtful man who sought the deepest value in everything he did. He was also disciplined and didn't easily let loose of his passion. He lived deliberately, weighing every act, assessing every thought, honing himself in his quest for the truth though he was neither stuffy nor self-righteous. Delicate in his playfulness, his subtle humor often turned on the ambiguity of a word, and to Rico his company was like a cooling breeze across the desert. Yet Melinda had grown weary of his delicacy.

It started when Seth came back from Isleta with Blue Rivers. At first Rico thought it was Blue who had caught Melinda's eye. Certainly he was a more obvious choice for her than Joaquín. But as far as Rico could tell, Blue's lack of interest went beyond respect for Joaquín's claim to downright dislike of Melinda. He slept with Esperanza, seemingly content with her maternal commodiousness, until he moved into town. Rico thought everything would settle down after that, but she was wrong.

Joaquín became quieter and slower to smile, Melinda louder and quicker to laugh. Seth began avoiding her company, then Esperanza did too, so that during her pregnancy Rico was often alone with Melinda. In those last months of her confinement, and then after Elena was born, Rico felt grateful to Esperanza for taking on the responsibility of managing the household. She had taken on far more than that, but Rico was blissfully ignorant until Melinda chose to enlighten her.

It happened one afternoon when they were sitting in the shade beneath the cottonwoods behind the house. Rico was nursing her daughter and remembering more often than not the things Seth had said and done the night before. They had only recently resumed sex after a hiatus of several months, and Rico found as much delight in his lovemaking as she had in the beginning. Her memories elicited secret smiles that had no bearing whatsoever on anything Melinda happened to be saying.

Melinda wasn't dense. She knew the source of those smiles and could remember a time when she herself had smiled over her own memories of Seth. Now, however, that time was gone, and though she loved Rico as a sister, she couldn't resist pricking Rico's bliss with doubt. "Do you ever wonder," she asked in a tone of innocence, "what Joaquín and Seth do when they're alone?"

Rico laughed. "I'm sure it would bore us to tears."

"They're awfully close," Melinda said. "Does Seth talk about Allister much?"

Rico shook her head, suppressing a frown as she laid Elena in her cradle and pulled the netting over the top to keep the flies away.

"I suspect it's the same," Melinda said.

"The same as what?" Rico asked, feeling a nudge of discomfort.

"Men together." Melinda shrugged. "You know, like we were once."

"It's not the same," Rico argued.

"Why not?" Melinda asked flippantly.

"We shared affection, that's all. And comfort 'cause we had so little. It's not the same with men."

"How is it different?" Melinda asked, amused.

"You know," Rico murmured. Then lowering her voice even more, "The way men violate each other."

Melinda laughed. "Don'cha think Seth and Allister did that?"

"Why don't you ask Esperanza if you're so curious?" Rico answered sharply. "She knew Allister."

"She knows Seth, too," Melinda replied.

Rico stared at her.

"Shoot. I didn't mean to say that, Rico." Melinda

grinned with feigned embarrassment. "Spilt the beans, didn't I. Jesus, I'm sorry."

Rico tried to pretend she'd known all along and didn't care. She shrugged, actually managed to laugh, then said, "Seth has so much hunger I'm happy for a little help once in a while."

Melinda snickered. "If you need any more help, let me know."

"Don't you think Joaquín would object?" Rico asked, appalled.

"He'd never find out," Melinda answered.

But Rico hadn't believed it. She felt certain Joaquín would sense the change not only in Melinda but also in Seth. It was Rico's greatest fear that something would destroy their friendship; without Joaquín's stabilizing influence, she suspected Seth would leave.

The happiness she'd brought home from church tarnished by her memory of Melinda's comments that day, Rico stood up and saw that the baby was asleep, then walked through the parlor and on into the kitchen seeking someone to unhook her dress. Melinda was at the table with a nearly empty bottle of Seth's whiskey. Knowing the bottle had been unopened, Rico warily sat down at the table and asked, "Is something wrong, Melinda?"

"Nope," she answered, shaking her head emphatically.

"Did you drink all that by yourself?"

"Yup. Felt bad bein' left behind. First I thought it was 'cause I ain't good enough to go to church, but I figured out now why I had to be left behind."

"Why?" Rico asked, confused.

" 'Cause ol' Seth," Melinda said in an earnest tone, as if all she wanted was affirmation of her great discovery, "couldn't walk into church with a harem, now could he?"

Slowly, Rico stood up. "You've had far too much to drink, Melinda. I think you should go sleep it off."

She shook her head. "I ain't done yet."

"Please go," Rico pleaded, "before the men come in."

"Why? You can't tell me Seth's never seen a drunk

woman 'cause he's seen both of us drunker'n skunks. 'Member that time we shared him? Or did he halve us?'' She laughed. ''I can see why you need help pleasin' him. You was always drawin' the line short of what he wanted.''

Rico turned to walk out but stopped when she saw Esperanza and Lobo blocking the parlor door. Esperanza put her hand in the middle of the boy's back, impelling him forward. ''Go outside and find your daddy, Lobo,'' she said. ''Keep him and Joaquín out of the house for a while.''

''Why?'' Lobo asked.

''I'll explain later,'' Esperanza said, meeting Rico's eyes.

''All right,'' Lobo said, looking curiously at Melinda as he passed.

Esperanza pulled a chair out from under the table and lowered herself into it. ''Sit down, Rico,'' she said.

Melinda tried to laugh but her voice broke with tears. ''What is this, the ladies ganging up to throw the harlot out of town?''

Esperanza waited until Rico had sat down. A quick glance told her Rico wouldn't be much help. She looked back at Melinda. ''Earlier you asked me to read your cards. I read them a little while ago when I was alone.''

''What'd they say?'' she asked with studied indifference as she poured herself more whiskey.

''I saw your death,'' Esperanza answered.

Melinda stared at her, then laughed. ''You're layin' it on a bit thick, don'cha think? Why don'cha jus' come right out and say you want me to leave?''

''I already advised you to.''

''How 'bout it, Rico?'' Melinda jeered. ''Do you want me to leave?''

''I don't understand,'' Rico whimpered, her eyes on Esperanza. ''Will we all die?''

''What the hell're you talking about?'' Seth asked as he strode into the room. He glared down at Esperanza, then at Melinda and the well-gone bottle of whiskey. He picked up the bottle and threw it out the door where it shattered in the dirt. "Think you had enough," he said.

In an effort to hide her tears, Rico stood up and moved toward the stove. Seth caught her arm and pulled her back, looking down at her with a frown of regret. Then he turned hard eyes on Esperanza. "What'd I tell you about those cards?"

"I have not disobeyed you," she answered without flinching.

They all looked at Joaquín coming through the door with Lobo.

"Sorry," Lobo said to Esperanza. "They wouldn't do it."

She nodded, thinking she should have known that when Lobo told his father the women wanted him out of the house, being Seth, he'd come find out why. She stood up and scooped the boy from the floor. "It's all right, Lobo. Now you and I will stay outside."

"No!" he protested. "I don't want to."

Softly, Seth said, "Go with Esperanza."

Joaquín had seen the broken whiskey bottle, and Melinda's drunkenness was as obvious as Rico's tears, though she gave him a hopeful smile. When Seth dropped his gaze and led Rico from the room, Joaquín felt ashamed. He listened to their bedroom door close, then looked at Melinda. "Get up," he said.

She laughed. "Not sure I can."

He crossed the room and yanked her chair out, caught her as she started to tumble, and lifted her to her feet. The whiskey on her breath reminded him of his mother and all the nights she'd tucked him into bed with the smell of liquor on her kisses. Joaquín had hoped to save Melinda from the sordid death his mother had earned working in brothels, and his heart ached at his failure as he led her from the house. When she stumbled as they walked across the yard, he wished he could simply put her to bed and let her sleep it off, but he knew the situation demanded a more drastic remedy. In his room, he set her in a chair and began gathering her belongings.

"So I'm to be turned out," she said, her voice slurred.

He kept quiet, trying to neatly fold her voluminous dresses to fit inside her valise.

She laughed at him. "You know what Seth would do with those? He'd throw 'em in the fire."

"I am not Seth," he said quietly.

She sighed. "What're you gonna do, Joaquín? Drop me off in a saloon, say that's where I found ya, sweetheart." She laughed bitterly. "Now that's something Seth would do."

Joaquín walked out without answering. As she sat on the chair looking at her closed valise and listening to him back a horse out of a stall, then the creak of leather as he saddled up, the finality of her leaving struck her with regret. If it hadn't been for Seth she could have loved Joaquín, but Seth was between them like a stallion flaunting his power to rule. Even now she was being kicked out because she'd become a problem to Seth. Joaquín would tolerate anything from her. He'd proven that by giving up his bed and sleeping in the loft without complaint. But she'd become a problem to the lord and master; she'd made his woman cry by telling her the truth. Though the suspicion that she'd said more than was actually true nudged at Melinda's mind, she dismissed it. Even if Seth hadn't touched her, she wanted him to. It wasn't fair that everyone else shared his bed and only she was shut out.

Joaquín returned and lifted her gently by her arm, then took her valise in his other hand and led her from his room, not bothering to shut the door. He put her on his black horse and swung up behind, his arm around her waist as he reined the horse out of the stable. When he dug in his spurs, the horse leapt to a gallop and jumped the fence. Even though Joaquín held her safely in front of him, Melinda clung to him with fright, then as they cantered along the trail, she clung to him with regret, knowing he had been a tender source of solace she had betrayed.

4

Rico watched Seth close their bedroom door then turn around and face her as he took off his jacket. He wore a shoulder holster with a Colt's .41 beneath his left arm.

"What was going on in there?" he asked, tossing his jacket across the footrail of the bed.

She picked up the jacket and hung it inside their chiffonnier, then quietly closed the door and looked out the window, seeing the white dove on the saguaro. "Don't you think it's surprising Joaquín's dove has stayed around?"

"Yeah," he said. "You didn't answer my question."

She shrugged. "Melinda got drunk."

"Why?"

"She was hurt that Joaquín wouldn't take her to church," Rico said, keeping her eyes on the dove.

"Joaquín stayed outside and watched the door. It wouldn't have looked real respectable for me to walk in with two women."

"That's what she said," Rico murmured. "That you didn't want to go with your harem."

He was quiet a minute then said, ''If she told you I touched her, she lied.''

Hearing him toss the gun and holster onto the bed, she turned around to watch him unbuttoning his vest.

''Is that what she said?'' he asked.

Rico shook her head and sat down, pulled the pistol out and opened the cylinder with its five live shells and one empty chamber. She snapped the gun closed again as Seth threw his shirt into the laundry basket. He opened a drawer for another, shook it out and put it on, watching her as he buttoned it.

She thought about Esperanza doing the laundry, taking special care in ironing his shirts and stacking them in the drawer so he always had a fresh supply. Seth was particular about his clothes and changed shirts two or three times a day, and Rico was thankful she didn't have to keep up with the laundry as well as care for the baby and watch Lobo too. She met Seth's eyes and tried to smile.

He came closer but didn't touch her. Instead he lifted his .44 off the headboard and buckled it on walking across to look out the window as they both listened to a horse gallop away.

''Was that Joaquín?'' she asked.

''Yeah, with Melinda. Looks like she's gone.''

''How far?'' Rico asked mournfully.

''You gonna miss her?''

''Yes,'' she said, not looking at him.

''You're not gonna tell me what's going on, are you?''

''There's nothing going on, Seth,'' she answered, meeting his eyes again.

''The hell there ain't.''

She shrugged. ''Melinda was drunk. I'm not going to believe anything she said.''

''What'd she say?''

Rico knew accusations of infidelity would not stand her well with Seth. Whenever he expressed regret that he couldn't marry her, she always answered it was enough that they were together. Most of the time it was because it seemed he truly considered her his wife. At other times, though, reality came clear in how easily he could leave her. A wife would still be a wife whether wanted or not, but if Rico caused too much trouble she became an expendable problem. Since the only remedy had been stolen by his legal wife in Austin who refused to divorce him, Rico couldn't fault Seth. She smiled bravely and said, "I'll handle it."

He gave her a smile of admiration. "You want me to unhook your dress, or can you handle that too?"

"Please," she said, standing up and turning her back. She felt his fingers open the row of hooks and eyes, his breath on her neck, then his kiss on her cheek as he slid his hands around her waist inside her dress. She leaned into his strength, the enveloping protection of his arms, feeling the buckle on his gunbelt in the small of her back like a threat of doom. Death was everywhere; she could feel its humid presence swamping her home with an overpowering sensation of dread. From outside the window, Joaquín's dove cooed its rhythmic murmur of reassurance.

Melinda cried against Joaquín's shirt as they rode through the suddenly overcast afternoon. She tried to tell herself it was because of the way the light fell on the earth, golden sunbeams slanting from between the clouds at such a deep angle that they appeared to be a stairway to the sky, but she knew it was because she had lost this man who held her gently while getting rid of her.

When they reached the outskirts of town he reined up behind a house with yellow shutters on a back street. He swung down and tied his horse to a palo verde tree, then lifted her to the ground beside him. Carrying her valise and holding her elbow, he led her into the house and up the back stairs to a corner room. He pulled a key from his pocket, unlocked the door, then pushed it open, guided her inside, and set her valise on the floor.

"I have taken this room for you," he said. "You may stay as long as you wish; I will pay the rent." He handed her the key, his eyes dark with the same melancholy she felt. "It has a nice view of the desert," he said, then turned to go.

"Joaquín?" she whispered.

He turned back on the threshold and watched her in silence.

"Is that all?" she asked.

"What else would you like?" he answered gently.

"When did you rent this room?"

"Last week."

"Was it Seth's idea?"

He shook his head. "Seth hasn't mentioned you for a long time. That was how I knew you had become a problem to him."

"What about you, Joaquín?" she asked mournfully. "Are you gonna live in his shadow for the rest of your life?"

Joaquín smiled. "I am his shadow, and he is my abyss, but I don't expect you to understand that."

"Abyss?" she mocked. "Isn't that like death?"

"Yes, and all the wisdom it contains."

She laughed. "You're gonna be dead, all right. You oughta get Esperanza to read your fortune. It might make you think twice about being Seth's shadow."

"I have thought of it a thousand times."

"Yet you're still there!" she jeered.

"As you would be if you could. You are like his wife, full of ambition but without the discipline to achieve it."

"I'm like Seth's wife?" She laughed again. "Thanks, Joaquín." But when she turned away, she blinked back tears as she looked out the window at the desert stretching empty all the way to the mountains, then she looked at him over her shoulder with a teasing smile. "See you around?"

"Perhaps," he said.

Listening to his boots on the stairs, then the hoofbeats of his horse trotting away, she felt forlorn. The barest of breezes moved through the room as she sat on the bed and

opened the crocheted bolsa Rico had given her as a birth-
day present the summer before. Inside was a tiny mirror
which Melinda didn't look into, knowing too well what
she would see. Almost as well she knew the contents of
her coin purse, but she opened it anyway and counted all
the money she had in the world: twenty-one dollars and
seventy-two cents.

She heard a door open and close in the hall and then
the tap of feminine footsteps and the rustle of a satin gown.
Through the door Joaquín had left open, Melinda saw a
woman stop and look in with discreet curiosity. The dé-
colletage of her dress marked her for a lady of the evening,
and beneath a cascade of auburn curls, her eyes were a
clear pale green as she looked Melinda over. "New in
town?" the woman asked.

Melinda nodded.

"Need a job?"

"I hadn't thought that far ahead," Melinda said, "but I
guess I do. The man who left me here paid the rent but
didn't give me any money."

The woman chuckled with sympathy then asked, "Ever
work in a saloon?"

Melinda laughed. "That's where I met him."

"Well then," the woman said in a husky voice that
rippled with camaraderie, "come by the Blue Rivers later,
if you're interested in a job."

"The Blue Rivers Saloon?" Melinda asked with a mischievous smile.

The woman nodded. "Ask for Lila Keats. I'm the manager."

The afternoon was fading fast as Joaquín ambled toward
home, the clouds steaked with crimson on the horizon, the
silence around him heavy. He felt melancholy with failure,
yet also relieved Melinda was gone, and satisfied that he
had acted before the situation caused irreparable harm. She
had originally come to the homestead to keep Rico company while the men were gone, so had been Rico's re-

sponsibility until Joaquín took her into his bed. Then suddenly Melinda was his, and when she turned sullen it had been his chore to get rid of her, even though he had long ago relinquished any claim.

He smiled now in the falling shadows of twilight, remembering the times he'd chastised Seth for resisting being stuck with a woman he didn't want but had slept with and so taken on. Now Joaquín knew how easily that could happen. It started with a tantalizing game that ended in bed, then suddenly the man was responsible for what became of the woman.

Joaquín was determined not to play that game again. If the time ever came that he brought another woman to his bed, he would marry her first. Even with that thought, however, he couldn't see himself a married man. His first loyalty belonged to Seth. If Seth decided to leave Rico and his children behind, Joaquín would go with him even if he himself had a wife and children. So he couldn't see taking on a family with any kind of clear conscience, and it was important to Joaquín to keep his conscience clear.

He had killed two men in his past, the first to protect Seth's wife and the second to protect Seth. Those deaths did not sit lightly, but what Joaquín felt was sorrow, not guilt, believing a man's defense of his family was no sin. The puzzle was why Joaquín's family was one and the same as Seth's, why their interests were identical and had been from the moment they met.

They were not kin, not even of the same race. They had grown up speaking different languages yet were brothers in a way stronger than blood. They understood each other without words, complemented each other's skills so they stood united against the world, maintaining a potent defense steeled by Seth's instinct for the kill tempered by Joaquín's need for mercy. Together they survived. Alone, Seth would have trapped himself in his own rage, and Joaquín would have martyred himself to his pious ambitions. Their finding each other was proof of God's care. Joaquín believed that, and he'd learned from Rico that Seth did too, but Joaquín and Seth had never discussed it. Though they talked of many things, the power that held them together was a knowledge too tender to threaten with words.

The world was poised on the cusp of night, the sunset still dying on the horizon, when Joaquín saw a buggy approach on the road ahead. As he studied the small black run-about pulled by a single horse, he couldn't sense any hostility from whoever rode in the shadowed interior, but he stopped anyway in the deeper darkness beneath a cottonwood and slipped the keeper strap off his pistol.

The buggy pulled abreast of him and stopped. Leaning halfway out to reveal himself, the preacher asked pleasantly, "Mr. Ascarate, isn't it?"

Joaquín smiled, thinking the Protestant padre had an interesting face, creased with a depth of understanding lightened by an ironic humor. "Buenas tardes, Señor Holcroft. I'm sorry I missed your sermon today. May I ask what scripture you quoted?"

"Job 3:26," Holcroft said, running it through his mind so he would get it right when he recited it.

"Yet trouble came." Joaquín laughed softly. "A good choice."

"You know the Bible?" Holcroft asked with surprise.

"I have studied it," Joaquín answered.

"We should have a discussion over brandy sometime." Holcroft immediately regretted mentioning that he imbibed spirits, then remembered he was talking with a Catholic and a gunman at that, so his smile deepened.

Joaquín had no suspicion the smile was related to the consumption of spirits. He credited it to Holcroft's remembering whom he was speaking with, and he liked the amusement in the padre's eyes. "Do you think we would learn anything?" he teased.

"Perhaps to understand what we know a little better," Holcroft answered.

Joaquín laughed again. "Seth told me he enjoyed meeting you."

"Was kind of him to say so. Maybe next Sunday you can join us."

He shook his head. "My job is outside. I don't need a church to worship God."

"I've always considered the fellowship of a church its most constant blessing."

Joaquín looked at the empty desert lit with the last glimmers of sunset. When he had made his decision to follow Seth, he hadn't realized how much human fellowship he would be sacrificing for the sake of his partner. He looked back at the padre. "Would you like to join us for supper?" Joaquín asked lightly, as if it weren't the first invitation ever extended from the homestead.

"I would be delighted," Holcroft beamed.

Joaquín swung down and tied his horse to the back of the buggy, then climbed in beside the minister. They smiled at each other as Holcroft turned his horse around on the road.

"I should tell you," Joaquín said, looking away again, "that I am returning from taking a woman to town. She had lived with us but became a problem. If you feel an oddness among us, it will be the newness of her being gone."

Holcroft smiled with understanding. "Will she be all right on her own?"

"I don't know," Joaquín said softly. "The path is just ahead, beyond those boulders."

Holcroft turned onto the trail marked by a huge saguaro growing from an outcrop of rocks. "I was visiting with the elder Mrs. Nickles, who's been ill," he said. "Mr. Nickles said this morning in church was the first time he'd met his neighbors." He smiled at Joaquín. "Abneth is a good man, more broad-minded than most. You would do well to win his friendship."

Joaquín said nothing.

After a moment the minister asked softly, "You were in the saloon when the killing happened, weren't you?"

"Yes," he said.

"Do you think it could have been avoided?"

"No."

Even more softly, Holcroft said, "That's an odd answer from a man who once wanted to be a priest." To his surprise, Joaquín laughed.

"Even the most disciplined zealot for life cannot abstain from death," he said.

"No, that's true." Holcroft smiled. "I came west to die. I had a lung disease and the prognosis was terminal. This land revived me. This air, this sky, these mountains towering with such sublime arrogance. There's power in land, any land anywhere, but the desert is shorn of ostentation so its power flows into us unhindered." He stopped himself, then gave his companion an embarrassed smile.

"I like the desert very much," Joaquín said.

"Have you always lived in it?"

He shook his head. "I was born deep in México."

"What brought you to this country?"

"I came seeking work."

"Did you find it?"

"Yes, and something more: the scaffold on which to hang my life."

"That is more," Holcroft agreed. "May I ask what it is?"

"Protecting Seth," Joaquín answered without hesitation.

"From his enemies, you mean?"

"He doesn't need me for that. I protect him from himself."

"Ah." The minister smiled. "How fortunate for both of you."

Joaquín watched him, wondering if he really understood, then asked, "What do you know of us?"

"Just the gossip around town." Holcroft shrugged. "I try to take it with a grain of salt."

"What do they say?"

He was unable to recall anything complimentary so answered honestly, "People fear what they don't know."

"We mean trouble for no one," Joaquín said earnestly.

"I believe you," Holcroft said, impressed with the intensity in the Mexican's dark eyes.

The outlaw's homestead was more humble than Holcroft had imagined: a small adobe home with a tiny casita in the yard, a modest stable with a corral holding fewer than half a dozen horses. Behind the house, cottonwoods loomed in the twilight, and a windmill creaked in a sudden breeze as the outlaw stepped through the dark door of the house—a barely discernable silhouette holding a rifle.

Joaquín jumped from the buggy while it was still moving and jogged toward the man in the shadows. By the time Holcroft pulled his horse to a stop, Strummar had set his rifle aside and was walking toward him.

"Evenin', Reverend," he said. "Glad you could join us for supper."

"Thank you," Holcroft answered, climbing down to accept the proffered hand.

The outlaw turned a playful smile on Joaquín. "For a minute I thought I was about to witness a wedding."

"More like a divorce," Joaquín answered wryly.

The outlaw laughed and slapped him on the back with affection, then grinned at Holcroft. "Come on in, Rev."

"I'll put the horses up," Joaquín said.

Holcroft stopped in his tracks, but the Mexican gave him an encouraging smile, as if knowing Holcroft felt vulnerable following the outlaw into his home, and the minister took reassurance from the gentle humor in the gunman's dark eyes.

The parlor was spartan, the wood floor bare, the only furniture a settee before the hearth. There were three closed doors and one threshold without a door. Holcroft followed his host through it into a brightly lit kitchen where Mrs. Strummar looked up from the stove with surprise.

"The rev's staying for supper," the outlaw said. "We got enough, don't we?"

"Of course." She smiled at their guest. "We're glad to have you, Reverend."

"Thank you," he said, turning to the large Mexican woman sitting at the table with Lobo.

"This is Esperanza Ochoa, the backbone of our family," the outlaw said, giving the woman a wink as he sat down. "This is Reverend Holcroft, Esperanza. Have a seat, Rev, you know my son."

"How do you do," Holcroft answered, nodding at the woman as he took the chair across from her, thinking she was still a beauty though no longer young. He smiled at the boy. "Hello, Lobo. Do you remember me?"

"Sure," he said. "You're the preacher."

The outlaw asked, "Did you pick up that broken glass?"

"Not yet," the boy said, drawing a pattern on the table with his finger.

"You gonna do it soon?"

Holcroft watched the boy look at his father. There was no fear in the appraisal but the challenge was clear.

The outlaw smiled at their guest and said, "If I had some whiskey, I'd offer you a drink."

"Esperanza's got another bottle in her room," Lobo said.

The outlaw laughed. "After you pick up the broken glass, why don't you fetch it for us?"

"I don't feel like it," Lobo answered.

"I will get it," Esperanza said, standing up and walking toward the door.

"Not the glass," the outlaw called.

She stopped and looked back at him, then at Lobo. "No," she said, going out.

Joaquín came in, dodging her in the door. He smiled at everyone, then crossed the room and picked up the dustpan from where it leaned in the corner behind the stove.

"What're you doing?" the outlaw asked.

"I'm going to clean up that broken glass," Joaquín answered.

"Lobo's gonna do it," the outlaw said.

Joaquín looked at Lobo watching his finger draw circles on the table. "When?"

"I don't know," the outlaw said. "When you gonna do it, Lobo?"

"When I get ready," he said, not looking at his father. Joaquín put the dustpan back and took a chair at the table. "Too bad we can't offer the padre a drink."

"Blue left some whiskey by Esperanza's bed," Lobo announced. "She's gone to fetch it."

"You're a little loose with your information," the outlaw said softly.

Lobo looked around the table with a quizzical frown, meeting the eyes of each of the men. Holcroft wanted to reassure the boy that he wouldn't hold the information against the family, but he couldn't think of anything appropriate to say. They all sat in a silence broken only by the spoon as Mrs. Strummar whipped potatoes at the stove.

"Ay," Esperanza said, walking in the door. "All that broken glass, a person could get hurt." She set a half-full bottle of Magnolia Pike on the table, then brought three clean glasses from the cupboard.

The outlaw filled each glass and raised his in a toast. *"Salud,"* he said.

"Salud," Joaquín said.

"Salud," Holcroft echoed. He sipped the whiskey and smiled at the men, feeling comfortable in the kitchen full of the good smells of supper and the bustle of women at the stove, even the pouting of the little boy who was now kicking one of the table legs.

"Quit it," the outlaw said. The boy instantly stopped, then watched his father ask, "How long you been in Tejoe, Rev?"

"A little over three years. As I was telling Joaquín on the way in, I came for my health, not expecting to live." Holcroft smiled. "But here I am."

The outlaw laughed. "I could say the same thing." Watching Lobo walk over to pick up the dustpan and carry it outside, the outlaw quickly looked away when the boy passed, then winked at the minister and said, "The desert has a way of reviving people, don't you think?"

"Yes, indeed." He smiled. "You have a fine son. Miss Perkins tells me he's her best student."

"Thanks," the outlaw said, standing up. "Excuse me."

Holcroft watched him walk into the parlor. Joaquín followed him as the women moved away from the window, and only then did Holcroft hear the hoofbeats of an approaching horse. Lobo came to stand just inside the door, holding the empty dustpan by his knee as he peered around the corner of the house. He looked back inside and whispered, "It's the sheriff."

"Lord have mercy," Mrs. Strummar murmured.

"They're coming in!" Lobo said, hurrying to finish his chore.

Holcroft stood up and smiled at the sheriff walking into the kitchen. Rafe Slater looked surprised to see him.

"Guess you two know each other," the outlaw said, settling himself at the head of the table again. "Have a seat, Rafe. You got another glass, Esperanza?"

She set it next to the whiskey, then retreated again as the outlaw poured the sheriff a drink. Joaquín remained standing by the door, his hands loose at his sides and his face shuttered against emotion. Holcroft glanced quickly at the women, huddled together before the stove. Mrs. Strummar was watching the sheriff with worry, while Esperanza glared at him with outright hostility. Lobo returned to stand in the door, his dustpan full of broken glass.

Sheriff Slater sipped his whiskey then gave the outlaw an awkward smile. "Guess you know why I'm here, Seth."

"What I don't know is what you're gonna do about it," he answered with an easy smile.

"There'll be an inquest tomorrow. It'd be helpful if you'd show up."

"You got a whole slew of witnesses. You don't need me."

"Can I take your statement now then?"

"This is it: the man called me out and I beat him."

Slater sipped his whiskey again. "You know who he was?"

The outlaw shook his head.

"Name was Bart Keats. His wife's working for Blue now. Guess I should say his widow."

"Sonofabitch," the outlaw muttered, meeting Joaquín's eyes.

"You know her?" the sheriff asked.

"I've met her."

"She didn't have anything to do with you killing her husband?"

The outlaw glanced at his wife before looking coldly at the sheriff. "What are you implying?"

"Nothing," Slater said, keeping his voice light. "Just asking questions. That's my job."

"I met her ten minutes before he called me out."

The sheriff sighed. "Well, like you said, there were plenty of witnesses as to how it happened. Why is the question."

"He said he was after the bounty," Joaquín said.

Slater twisted in his chair to study Joaquín a moment, then returned his gaze to the outlaw. "Mrs. Keats says you and her husband were associates back in Texas and there was bad blood between you. She said he came looking for revenge."

"I'd never seen him before last night."

The sheriff looked at his whiskey.

"You gonna believe her or me?"

"I'll take your word over hers," Slater said, "but it doesn't matter a whole lot. You acted in self-defense regardless of his motive. I just wonder why she'd lie."

"When you find out, let me know," the outlaw said.

Slater nodded. "Don't suppose you'd change your mind about the inquest even if I subpoenaed you?"

The outlaw shook his head.

Slater sighed again. "Well, I'll be going, then." He stood up. "Goodnight," he said to everyone.

"I'll walk you out," the outlaw said, leaving with him.

Holcroft looked around and saw Lobo still standing in the door with his dustpan. The boy's pale eyes met his, then Joaquín's. "What's it mean?" Lobo whispered.

"Nothing," Joaquín said. "The sheriff called it self-defense."

"He's not gonna try'n arrest Seth?"

"No," Joaquín said.

Lobo looked at Holcroft. "Seth wouldn't let him. I wouldn't either."

Holcroft didn't know what to say. On the one hand he admired the boy's loyalty, on the other he couldn't condone resisting the law.

"Neither would I," Joaquín said, meeting the minister's eyes.

"Nor I," Esperanza said.

"Don't leave me out," Mrs. Strummar added with a laugh.

Holcroft laughed too. "Let's hope it doesn't come to that," he said sincerely.

They all heard the sheriff's horse loping away, then from beyond the parlor a baby began to cry. After a moment the outlaw came into the kitchen carrying the infant against his shoulder. His wife moved across the room to take her, and Holcroft admired the family tableau, the gentle love in the outlaw's eyes as he smiled down at his daughter, quiet now in her mother's arms. Yet when he looked at Joaquín, the outlaw's gray eyes glinted with a cool anger, then softened again as he smiled at Lobo still holding his dustpan of broken glass. "You get it all?" he asked.

"Yes, sir," the boy answered.

"What're you gonna do with it?"

Lobo walked outside and dumped the broken glass into what sounded like an empty barrel. He returned the dustpan to its corner, then pulled a chair over to stand on while he washed his hands at the sink.

The outlaw lifted the bottle of whiskey. "Another drink, Rev?" he asked in a pleasant tone.

Holcroft shook his head, then watched the outlaw refill his own glass and slug down the shot. Quickly Esperanza whisked the bottle from the table. "Sit down, Seth," she said gently. "Supper's all ready."

As Reverend Holcroft drove his buggy back toward town later that night, he remembered the sound of the broken glass falling into the empty barrel, and it seemed the most cogent symbol of the outlaw's family. Love and loyalty were strongly evident, but beneath the surface of their fellowship cracks of fear threatened to shatter the courage of their smiles. Holcroft mused on the enigma of fear in his community.

Most everyone feared the outlaw and the repercussions of his presence, while his family feared the community as well as strangers who could destroy their home without warning. Yet the outlaw himself seemed fearless. Holcroft remembered his wink as Lobo left to perform the chore, the silent unity of father and son strung on a rope of battle the outlaw kept taut with control. Holcroft knew it required unceasing vigilance to raise a child without violence, a constant attention that kept its distance, allowing the child freedom to make choices yet never failing to judge the results, again from the distance of granting the child the same rights of integrity granted an adult. The ultimate aim was nurturing the growth of a man any town would be proud to count among its citizens. Seth Strummar was not such a man, but that he was so passionately involved in the raising of his son proved he could be, and Holcroft saw Lobo as his strongest ally in bringing the outlaw into the community.

5

Blue Rivers was twenty-five years old but that wasn't the only achievement he owed to Seth Strummar. Blue's silent partner had provided the financial backing to establish the Blue Rivers Saloon, and his reputation and patronage inspired more than a little of Blue's business. Blue was capable of gracefully acknowledging all that without losing any of his innate arrogance.

Despite a slight limp in his right knee, Blue walked through life with a leonine stroll of possession. His cocky self-assurance had initially drawn Seth into their friendship, and his mental agility and amiable disposition kept Seth there even after learning Blue's responses weren't as effective as his promotion of them. Blue knew Seth forgave him for being tardy when speed counted, relying instead on the constancy of his loyalty, because Blue's allegiance wasn't built on ignorance of any aspect of their partnership.

The Blue Rivers Saloon was the only establishment in Tejoe that Seth patronized. He had a private room where he could drink with men of his choice, and sometimes he mingled in the crowd around the gaming tables or drank at the bar knowing he was on home turf where no man could successfully challenge him and live to walk out the door. Blue hired his bouncers and barkeeps with the stipulation that if the time came when they were needed they would defend Seth Strummar, and an arsenal of loaded Winchesters was kept under the bar for that purpose.

Word of such circumstances wasn't kept secret. Everyone knew Seth Strummar could often be found in the Blue Rivers Saloon, and everyone knew if they made a move against him they would die. So it bothered Blue that Bart Keats had walked in on Saturday night and challenged Seth flat out. Blue wasn't surprised Seth had handled the man on his own; they had agreed the riflemen would be backup for disaster, but he couldn't figure why Keats had thrown his life away.

His connection with Lila was bothersome, too. Blue would have fired her except that he liked her too much. He knew it was too much in light of the short time he'd known her, and he suspected it was partly because she wanted him to like her and was doing her best to make it happen, but he no longer believed it was because she was desperate for a job. Joaquín had seen through her instantly, questioning why she'd come to Blue's in search of employment. At the time Blue had thought Joaquín was just down on women because he and Melinda were having problems. Even after Seth humiliated Lila by demanding she sleep with him then saying he wasn't interested, Blue credited Seth's hostility to resentment that a woman was nosing into their male sanctuary. He still thought those two motives were operational, but the death of Lila's husband made him realize his friends were closer to seeing the truth than he was.

There were two possible explanations. The one he wanted to believe was that Keats had followed Lila here and stumbled onto Seth, then made his decision on the spur of the moment to try for the bounty, maybe thinking with a thousand dollars in his pocket he'd look better in Lila's eyes. That had been her explanation and it left her guilty only of trying to escape an onerous husband. The other explanation was that Lila had agreed to meet him here as part of a plot. When introduced to Seth and Joaquín, she said she'd know them anywhere. Five minutes into the conversation she claimed to have seen Seth's wife and son in Austin. She had been interested in whether or not Joaquín knew Johanna. Then an hour later her husband tried to kill Seth for the bounty. If it was a plot, Blue wanted to understand it before he acted. He also figured there was no harm in enjoying Lila in the meantime, especially as she was trying so hard to please him.

He felt hungry to see her again, to admire the curves of her body in her elegant gown, the auburn flash of her hair and the wicked smile she wore as often as not, so he left his office and stood on the balcony looking down at the swirl of activity on the floor below. Among the tables of men playing poker wandered working girls, available for a laugh or a trip upstairs, and among their colorful flock Blue spotted Melinda.

She wore a yellow dress cut low in front, and her sun-streaked hair fell nearly to her knees, turning heads as she walked through the room, smiling and chatting like the professional she was. Knowing that neither Joaquín nor Seth was there because they always came up and visited him first, Blue was left with the undeniable conclusion that Melinda was working.

He called to Nib Carey who was standing at the head of the stairs. Nib was a bear of a man with a thick black beard and small bullet-hole eyes. When Blue nodded at Melinda and told Nib to bring her upstairs, Nib grunted and said, "I been waiting for that." Then he turned and walked heavily down the steps and across the room. Blue watched Melinda look up at him on the balcony as she listened to Nib, and he sighed as he turned back into his office.

Blue had avoided Melinda as a troublemaker from the

start, recognizing she was the kind of woman who tried to trade cards in the middle of a deal. She'd repeatedly thrown herself in Blue's face and Seth's too, and Blue knew it had been just a matter of time before she went too far. He figured what she needed was a man ornery enough to make her toe the line, but Joaquín wasn't one to make anyone do anything, and Blue wondered what had finally happened to exile her from the homestead. It worried him, too, that whatever it was had happened the day after Lila's husband destroyed the carefully nurtured peace of his saloon. The coincidence seemed ominous with foreboding.

When she knocked on the door, he told her to come in then watched as she quietly closed and leaned against it, her mouth wearing a teasing smile while her eyes begged for mercy.

"What're you doing here, Melinda?" he asked.

"Workin'," she said. "Didn't Lila tell you?"

He shook his head.

Bravely she asked, "You're not gonna say I can't, are you?"

"I'm afraid I am. You should've known that."

"Don't, Blue," she pleaded. "What's to become of me?"

"There're other saloons all up and down the street, but my advice is to go back to Tombstone."

"I won't," she whispered. "I can't face it again."

"You'll make more money than in Tejoe."

"Do you think that's all I care about?"

He shrugged. "Seems to me you oughta be putting some aside for the future."

"I just need to get better at pickin' men," she retorted. "Joaquín didn't give me nothing."

"Were you there for wages?" Blue asked coldly.

"A partin' gift would've been nice!"

He shook his head. "You never did understand one whit of that man. He thought you were enough of a lady that giving you money would have been an insult. Besides, I can't imagine him just dropping you off on the street and saying adiós.''

''He rented me a room,'' she admitted.

''For how long?''

''He said I could stay as long as I want,'' she answered defiantly. ''Does that sound like he's tryin' to get rid of me?''

Blue shrugged again.

''Can't we wait and see,'' she argued, ''if Seth takes exception to my workin' here?''

''We're talking about Joaquín,'' he said softly.

''They're the same man,'' she sassed back.

Blue turned around and looked out the window, thinking if he hadn't hired a manager this wouldn't be happening. He'd already lost control with Lila's presence: the saloon had seen its first gunfight the day of her arrival. Now one of his girls was a keg of dynamite waiting for a fuse.

Behind him, Melinda said, ''They won't come to town tonight. At least let me finish the shift so I go home with a little money.''

As he turned around and looked at her, he decided he could give her that much. ''All right,'' he said. ''But if they walk in the door, I want you out of here. Understand?''

''Thanks, Blue.'' She smiled, looking as though she'd give him her heart on a plate.

He knew it was an act, though. He didn't think Melinda had a heart.

Esperanza stood in her darkened doorway admiring the stars in the black sky. Lowering her gaze, she looked with affection at the small jumble of buildings that housed her family, though none of the people on the homestead were kin to her. She was the oldest, however, and had achieved a stature of wisdom among them. Her knowledge of harvesting medicine from the wilderness was valued, as were her meals and labor, her constant stance of giving comfort where she could.

The house across the yard was dark except for a single lamp in the kitchen. As she watched, it was extinguished, then Joaquín came out and started for his room in the stable. Softly she called to him. He came willingly, almost invisible in his black clothes, only the row of bullets in his cartridge belt catching starlight as he walked. She remembered the boy he had been when she first met him, how his eyes had shone with admiration for Seth, his every move aimed at winning Seth's approval.

Joaquín had become a man in the time between that first meeting and when she'd seen him again. He had taken Seth's wife to Austin and the journey had been long and difficult. Immediately afterward, he had started on his search to find Seth, and that journey too had been ripe with lessons. The next time Esperanza saw him, he and Seth were coming home to Rico with little Lobo. When during that visit Joaquín became angry with Seth, Esperanza had watched him challenge his former teacher with the courage of an equal.

For nearly three years now, Joaquín had willingly taken on the stigma of riding with an outlaw, earning his place by proving he could be lethal when necessary. Yet he had started out to be a priest, and his mission in life was to bring Seth to God. He worked toward that achievement by demanding Seth accommodate himself to his new partner's notions of virtue as much as he had accommodated Allister's habitual vice. Seth had told Esperanza all that in bed one night, laughing softly when he said Joaquín was determined to save his soul. She thought it an admirable ambition, and tonight she saw a chance to help the savior.

She watched him stop a scant distance away, a slight young man half a foot taller than she was, his dark eyes sad, his smile compassionate. She whispered, "Wouldn't you like to come in for a minute?"

He had never been inside her casita, and she could feel him following her with concern. She didn't light a lamp but turned to face him in the dark as she said softly, "I feel sad, Joaquín."

"Why?" he asked.

"So many things have been happening. Will you talk with me a while?" She didn't wait for his assent but took his hand and led him to sit beside her on the bed. "I feel lonely," she murmured, leaning against his shoulder. "I am happy with Seth's family, but sometimes it is hard to come to my casita alone."

"I know," he said, sliding his arm around her waist and holding her close. "Sometimes I am glad to hear the horses at night."

She laughed softly, laying her cheek against his chest and listening to his heartbeat. "You are a good man, Joaquín. I have always felt close to you."

"I have loved you as a sister," he replied.

"Is that why you never come visit me at night?" she teased. "Because you see me only as a sister?"

"You are also a mother for Lobo," he said.

She sat up in surprise. "What about Rico?"

Joaquín shook his head. "Lobo is too much like Seth in the way he controls her. She answers Seth with sex but has no power over his son. You are the one he shares himself with. Rico is a competitor for his father's love."

"So you don't visit me," she asked, "because you see me as Lobo's mother?"

"No," he answered with a smile. "I've seen Seth come to your door in the middle of the night, and I've thought of doing that, but my manners made me wait for an invitation." He laughed softly. "I am half your age, Esperanza. Do you think I am experienced enough to please you?"

"Your wisdom humbles me, Joaquín," she said. "We have waited too long to share love."

When he leaned closer and kissed her, his hesitant caresses told her of the damage Melinda had done. Esperanza pulled him into her bed and cradled his slender body within her ample solace, suckling him through the night to a rebirth of self-confidence in his prowess.

*   *   *

In the morning she walked into the kitchen to see Seth at the window watching Joaquín return to his room in the stable. Seth turned around and grinned at her. "How'd it go?"

She sighed with exaggerated fatigue. "I didn't sleep all night."

He laughed and swatted her bottom as she walked to the stove to start the coffee. Rico came in carrying Elena, frowned at the swat, and said, "Don't let Lobo see you doing that."

"Doin' what?" Lobo asked, hobbling into the room carrying one boot.

"Go saddle the horses," Seth said. "I'll ride you to school this morning."

"Is Joaquín sick?" the boy asked with concern.

Seth shook his head. "I just thought I'd ride my son to school. Is that all right?"

Lobo grinned. "The kids have been wantin' to see you."

"Maybe I better dress up," Seth said.

Lobo laughed and ran from the house. Through the window, Seth watched him cross the yard toward the stable, then turned around and looked at Rico. "You got a problem with me touching Esperanza?" he asked with an incredulous tone.

"No," Rico said, concentrating on mixing the biscuits.

"Look at me," he said. When she'd raised her eyes to his, he said, "Esperanza ain't no threat to you."

Rico glanced at her watching warily, then looked back at Seth. "I know that," she said.

"Why don't you act like it then?"

"Why don't you act like it?" she retorted.

"What the hell is that supposed to mean?"

"When you've got your hands all over every woman in reach, what am I supposed to think?"

"What women?"

"Melinda, for one."

"If she said I touched her, she lied. I told you that already."

Rico nodded. "Like Lila Keats is lying?"

"Damn straight! You gonna believe them over me?"

"I don't want to!" she cried. "But I'm having trouble not believing something I hear so often."

"Is that my fault?"

She blinked back tears. "It might be. Why don't you think about it?"

"Okay, I'll think about it," he said. "Right now I'm gonna help Lobo with the horses and see if Joaquín wants to go with us. We'll get breakfast in town."

Both woman watched him take his hat from the peg and leave them behind.

Rico began mixing the biscuits again. After a minute she said with false bravery, "We'd make out."

"No problem," Esperanza agreed, setting the table for three, then remembering Melinda wasn't there. "You know where Joaquín took Melinda?"

"No," Rico said.

"He rented her a room in town. I don't think it was far enough, do you?"

"She'll probably work for Blue," Rico said.

"Uh-uh," Esperanza said. "He once told me she's trouble and he wouldn't want her in his saloon."

Rico laid the biscuit dough on the breadboard. "I'm beginning to suspect," she said with a smile of forgiveness, "that all the important conversations around here happen in your casita."

"It is the power of the cards," Esperanza answered with a twinkle in her dark eyes. "Their truth brings it out in everyone near."

6

The schoolyard was crowded with children, the girls playing jump rope or talking in clusters, the boys running in packs. They all stopped and watched as Lobo rode up with Seth and Joaquín. Sunlight fell through the trees and danced in patterns across the children's faces.

The girls wore short skirts, their hair in braids, their eyes wide with a curiosity that reserved judgment. In overalls or sporting suspenders on their trousers, the boys watched with excitement shining from their eyes.

Drawn outside by the sudden silence, the schoolmarm came to the door and saw Lobo with his father, a man she had never met but knew instantly because the boy was his spitting image. She nodded at the father, then at the Mexican who was usually waiting in the shadows beneath the trees when school let out, a dark figure on a black horse. Now the three of them sat their horses on the very edge of the yard. The outlaw tipped his hat, and all the children turned and looked at her then slowly looked at him again.

Lobo grinned up at Seth. "See you later," the boy said,

kicking his horse toward the corral. He unsaddled and let the pinto loose with the others, a sorry collection of broken down mounts, mostly scruffy burros and ancient mules, then left his gear on the fence and sauntered through the silent schoolyard to the steps. He looked back and waved before walking in alone. When Miss Perkins began ringing the bell, the children filed inside.

Watching the kids look over their shoulders to catch a last glimpse of him, Seth noted how different they were from his son. Lobo dressed the same as he did, a store-bought shirt and vest over serge trousers and boots, while the other boys had homespun smocks and even now, so late in autumn, bare feet. In the corral Lobo's pinto shimmered like gold among the pitiful herd. His saddle was new, while the others on the fence had been patched so many times they were barely above worthless. Seth remembered, too, that Lobo had crossed the yard without greeting anyone. He'd walked in like a pansy bookworm who couldn't get along on the schoolyard.

Turning his horse away, Seth looked across at his friend. "What were *you* like in school?"

"I never went to school," Joaquín answered.

Seth thought about that a minute then asked, "How'd you learn your letters?"

"Johanna taught me."

Seth looked at the mountains hovering like a ridge of trouble on the horizon. "Think we'll ever see her again?"

"Do you wish to?" Joaquín asked with surprise.

"I'd kinda like to see Jeremiah." Seth smiled. "It pleases me she named him that."

"It was a wise choice."

"If she'd divorce me, I'd invite them all out here to visit. But the way it is now, I can't see putting Rico through that."

"It would be difficult," Joaquín agreed. "Besides, what if Johanna chose not to leave? Since she's your wife, what could you do?"

Seth laughed. "I could become a Mormon."

"Would you like that?" his friend asked earnestly.

"God, no. Imagine trying to keep more'n one woman happy."

"I haven't yet succeeded with one," Joaquín said.

Seth laughed again. "You're doing better'n I was at your age. Least your women leave without any bruises."

"I'm good at not doing things," Joaquín said, looking away.

Seth leaned closer and said, "We oughta go down to Tombstone for some carousing, Joaquín."

"Why Tombstone?" he asked unhappily.

Seth shrugged. "It ain't home."

"You're known there. I don't think it's a good idea."

"Let's go to Mexico, then. Some little pueblo south of nowhere. Stay drunk all week, share women, raise a little hell covering each other's backs."

Joaquín studied him a moment before asking, "Why are you restless?"

"Things don't feel the same," Seth said, looking at the distant mountains again. "Or maybe too much the same. Some days the only useful thing I do is feed the damn goat. Rico's unhappy over one thing after another, all of 'em falling in a chain that feels like it needs breaking. Besides, a bounty hunter found me and it won't be long before another one shows up. Maybe it's time to move on."

"Without Rico?" Joaquín asked with studied indifference.

Seth smiled into his partner's dark eyes. "Maybe she'll be happier somewhere else."

Joaquín shook his head. "I don't think moving is the answer."

"What is?"

"It's hard to say since you can't pinpoint the problem." When Seth remained silent, Joaquín asked, "What is it exactly you want?"

Seth twisted in his saddle and looked back as if he thought someone might be tracking him. "Real enemies instead of ghosts." He met Joaquín's eyes, then laughed at himself. "I spent a lot of years on the move. Maybe I just want to feel that kind of freedom again."

"What freedom?" Joaquín scoffed. "Being chased out of town by lawmen? Sleeping with a pistol in your hand and one ear cocked for the approach of death? Assessing each new friend and situation as a potential trap?"

Again Seth laughed. "Doesn't sound like much the way you say it, but I like living with danger, knowing I have an edge over any man in front of me." He leaned closer and half-whispered, "I even liked shooting Bart Keats the other night. It came down clean and it felt good proving I can still cut it." He leaned back with a grin. "I liked feeling that again."

Softly Joaquín said, "Perhaps it will pass."

Seth looked at him sharply, then snorted in self-deprecation. They rode in silence through the outlying adobe homes of the pobres as they entered town on the main road. A few other riders passed, barely camouflaging their curious scrutinies, and with an oath of impatience at his notoriety Seth turned abruptly into an alley then asked his friend, "Don't you ever get restless?"

"Sí," Joaquín answered. "I think of Lobo when I do. He is only seven and needs us a few more years at least."

"We could take him with us," Seth pointed out.

Joaquín nodded. "Teach him to live with his life on the line at every step, to enjoy shooting men and carousing with drunken women? That sounds like a much better childhood than going to school and church on Sundays."

Seth swung down behind Blue's saloon and tied his reins to a pillar. "I like Holcroft," he said.

"So do I," Joaquín said, following him through the back door.

Their footsteps echoed in the empty saloon as they climbed the stairs. The door to Blue's office was open, and Seth stopped on the threshold.

Blue laughed, standing up from behind his desk. "Hey, come on in." When they had, he shook hands with each of them, then asked Seth, "You come to town for the inquest?"

"No," he said. "Was hoping you'd have breakfast with us."

Blue stared at him a minute, then laughed again. To Blue's knowledge this was the first time Seth had come to town in daylight, and now he was proposing eating in a public cafe. "Let's go," Blue said. "I know the best breakfast in town."

They walked out the front door of the saloon and down the street to the corner, turning heads as they went. Another block east was a small restaurant called Amy's. The windows were curtained with red-checked gingham tied open with bright red sashes, and there was a sprig of purple primrose on each table. Blue led them to the corner and let Seth and Joaquín sit with their backs to the wall. A young woman came from the kitchen. Buxom and pink-cheeked with blond braids wound around her head, she grinned at him, then came over.

Blue stood up. "Amy, want you to meet some friends of mine. Seth Strummar and Joaquín Ascarate."

They both stood up and nodded at her.

"How do you do," she said softly, giving a tiny curtsey. "Please sit down, gentlemen. Coffee, all around?"

"Yeah," Blue said, "and three of your breakfast specials with lots of biscuits."

She laughed. "Got a fresh batch just coming out." She returned to the kitchen, calling back, "Only be a minute."

As the men resumed their seats, Blue saw that both Seth and Joaquín were watching behind him. He turned around to see the windows lined with the dirty faces of street urchins.

"Why ain't they in school?" Seth asked.

"They know too much," Blue answered with a snicker.

Amy came back carrying a tray loaded with plates of ham and eggs, a platter of biscuits, and three cups of coffee. After distributing the food among the men, she carried the empty tray over to the windows and closed the curtains, then returned to the kitchen.

"I like Amy," Joaquín said, digging into his food comfortably.

"She reminds me of some barkeeps I've known," Seth said. "The kind who stay in business by accommodating discretion."

"That's a nice quality," Blue said around a mouthful of eggs. "I wish Lila had a little more of it."

Seth lifted his cup and sipped at his coffee as he watched Blue over the rim.

"I've always been careful about the girls I hire," Blue said, buttering a biscuit. "Last night I went out and saw Melinda on the floor." He looked at Joaquín, who had stopped eating and was also watching him now. "I don't care for surprises like that," Blue said before taking a bite of the biscuit.

Seth set his cup down, flicked a glance at Joaquín, then asked, "What'd you do about it?"

"I fired her," Blue said, unable to read anything in Joaquín's dark eyes. "Meant to call Lila to task for it too, but we were busy last night so I let it slide. I'll talk to her today, though, and make sure she understands that I'm to clear everybody she hires."

"I'll talk to her," Seth said, picking up his knife.

They ate in silence a few minutes, then Blue asked, "When?"

"This morning. Where does she live?"

"La Casa Amarilla on the east edge of town."

"That's where I put Melinda," Joaquín said.

Seth laughed. "Least we know how she got the job."

"The inquest is at ten," Blue said. "She'll probably be there."

"I'm likely to catch her awake then," Seth said. "You going?"

Blue nodded. "Sheriff Slater asked me to since it happened in my place."

"You wearing a gun?"

"They won't let any in. Nib'll be right outside the door."

"What do you think of Slater?"

"He's crafty," Blue said. "I suspect he ran on the wrong side of the law at one time." He shrugged. "Tejoe doesn't need a top sheriff and he's up to the job."

"Think he's content with it?"

Blue shrugged again. "I haven't met many men his age who're happy with where they ended up. He seems more content than most. Anyway, he's got an easy job and doesn't have to put himself out."

"Doesn't sound like much of a threat," Seth said.

"He ain't," Blue agreed. "But like I said, Tejoe doesn't need a tough sheriff. Last Saturday was the town's first killing."

Seth winced. "Don't guess they're real happy with me."

"You threw 'em a wild card going to church on Sunday. Nobody expected that."

"What do you think they'll do with it?"

Blue smiled. "I'll let you know after the inquest. You gonna be around?"

Seth shook his head. "Why don't you come out to the house for supper?"

"All right. I'll pick up Lobo at school on my way."

Seth stood up and dug into his pocket but Blue stopped him. "My treat," he said. "I'll let you get it next time."

"Fair enough. You want to keep Lila?"

Blue met his eyes a moment, then said, "Only long enough to find out why she came."

"We're in agreement, then," Seth said, extending his hand.

"Not unusual." Blue smiled, shaking with him. "She's in room fourteen upstairs." When he shook hands with Joaquín, Blue joked, "Don't let him get too rough with her," but Joaquín didn't smile.

Blue watched them leave, wishing he'd gone with them. At the door he saw the gaggle of urchins following them back to their horses, and it made him laugh. Ten years ago he'd been one of those street brats, and if Seth Strummar had ambled through his neighborhood, he would have followed him too.

Seth was uncomfortable with the parade of urchins behind him. When he and Joaquín reached their horses, he swung on then looked at the boys bunched at the end of the alley. "Ain't you got nothing better to do?" he asked them.

·They shook their heads in silence.

He nodded, then reined his horse to approach them, Joaquín following along. As the boys parted to let him pass, Seth studied their faces, dirty and hungry, their eyes alive for any advantage they could find in the situation. He kicked in his spurs and loped away fast, thinking one of them might grow up to kill him.

La Casa Amarilla was a better-class lodging house on the edge of town. Seth thought Joaquín had done too well by Melinda in putting her there, but he kept his mouth shut as he always did about Joaquín's private business. They tied their horses in back and walked up the rear stairs to knock on the door of number fourteen. Joaquín looked at Melinda's door just down the hall and hoped she was asleep. If she was, they had a good chance to come and go in peace because it took a lot to rouse her. That intimate knowledge suddenly made him feel lonesome.

Lila opened her door, looked at Seth, then glanced at Joaquín. "Good morning, gentlemen," she said with a professional smile.

"Mind if we come in?" Seth asked.

The pretense of welcome fell from her face but she took a step back and opened the door wider. "Please," she murmured as they walked past her. She closed the door and moved to stand in the middle of the room. "I'm afraid I can't offer any refreshment."

Seth was looking out the window at their horses below, a corral beyond with only a burro in it, the desert past that, empty all the way to the mountains. In the room behind him was a deadly enemy, he felt sure of it. He turned around and met Joaquín's eyes, knowing his partner would stop him from going as far as he wished in questioning her. He looked at her, then at her bed, still unmade. "Sit down, Lila," he said, nodding at the bed.

She was wearing a dark blue dress that closed down the front with tiny black buttons, the skirt tight in the new fashion but without a bustle beneath the flounce of bows on her behind. Settling herself with difficulty on the soft mattress, she smoothed her skirt across her hips and thighs. From the window, Seth said, "Let's start at the beginning. What are you doing in Tejoe?"

She studied him a moment, looked at Joaquín leaning against the closed door, then back at Seth. "I'm working for Blue," she said softly.

"What brought you here?"

"I came to escape my husband."

"The same one I killed?"

"Do you think I had more than one?" she asked archly. He shrugged. "Why'd you choose Tejoe?"

"I saw it on a map, bought passage on the train to Benson, then hired a rig to bring me here, having no idea what to expect other than a hole-in-the-wall where Bart wouldn't find me."

"Didn't take him long, though, did it? He walked into Blue's saloon less than twelve hours after you did."

"I didn't know he was following me."

Seth came closer until he towered over her. "Why do you think he would?"

"He loved me," she whispered.

"Uh-huh. Was hoping to get you back, I reckon."

"Maybe," she said. "I didn't get a chance to talk to him."

"Mind if I sit down?" He nodded at the rumpled sheets beside her.

A shutter fell across her eyes, making them colder. "Please," she murmured.

He took off his hat and sailed it across the room to land

on a table by the window, then sat down and pulled her back to lie beside him, holding her waist. "You're a beautiful woman, Lila," he said softly. "I can see why a man would take a risk to make you his. But once that happened, I can't see him doing much to keep you around."

Her eyes flashed angrily as her belly quivered beneath his hand. "Apparently he felt differently," she retorted.

"You want me to believe Bart tracked you all the way from Austin, hot enough to be less than a day behind, walked into Blue's saloon expecting to hold you in his arms, then saw me and decided to change course?"

"I guess that's what happened. Like I said, I didn't get a chance to talk to him before he died."

"Did you want to?"

"No!"

Seth smiled. "That's the second time you've said you didn't get a chance. Seems to me you'd be saying you were spared having to talk to him." He began opening her dress.

She watched his fingers freeing her buttons, then met his eyes again, obviously frightened though trying hard to hide it. "What do you want?" she whispered.

"The truth." He untied the bow of her camisole and loosened its laces until he could slide his hand under the garment and caress her skin. "Do you know what the truth is, Lila?"

"In this case I don't," she said. "I hadn't seen Bart since I was in Austin six weeks ago."

Seth pulled his hand out and tugged the laces free, opened her camisole and bared her breasts. He covered one with his hand, feeling her heart pound against his palm.

She looked at Joaquín, watching with his dark, inscrutable eyes.

Seth took hold of one of her nipples and gently rolled it between his fingers, smiling as she bit her lip. "You're right to fear me, Lila. If you cross me, I'll kill you. Do you understand?"

"I have no intention of crossing you," she whispered.

"Then what're you doing in Tejoe?"

"I told you. I came here to escape Bart."

"Now that he's dead, why don't you move on?"

"I like it here," she said.

He raised his hand to her throat and slowly closed his grip. She lurched beneath him, trying to pry his fingers away from her neck.

"Seth," Joaquín said, his voice softly entreating.

Seth let go with a smile. "Maybe you'll change your mind about liking it here."

Her breath ragged, she taunted, "Why don't you just fire me?"

He glanced down at her breasts. "Blue's got the hots for you," he said, standing up and towering over her again. "Might as well let him work it out, though in my opinion he'd be wiser to shoot his cum down a privy." He chuckled and walked over to the window, turning his back.

She sat up swallowing her rage as she closed her dress. "Is that all you came to say, Mr. Strummar?"

Slowly he turned around to face her again, then shook his head. "Contrary to present company, Blue's particular about who works for him. The girls have to be young and pretty, of course, and they have to entertain all comers without prejudice, though who they take upstairs is up to them. He's not running a whorehouse but providing fresh entertainment for his patrons. Melinda's a little too experienced and she doesn't work for him. Next time you want to hire a girl, run her through Blue first."

"All right," she said, shrugging huffily. "You can't blame me. She's unusually pretty and was new to town. I'm sorry she didn't work out."

"You didn't know who she was before you hired her?"

"Who is she?"

Seth studied her. "You're either lying, stupid, or cursed with bad luck," he finally said. "None of 'em sounds good for Blue."

"Apparently he doesn't think so."

"He's been wrong before," Seth said, picking up his hat.

Joaquín opened the door and preceded him out. Seth turned on the threshold and gave her a barefaced smile of contempt. "Enjoy the inquest," he said just before he closed the door.

She stared at it, listening to their boots on the stairs, then their horses trotting away. With trembling fingers she rearranged her clothing and redid her coiffure, then pinned her bonnet on her head and picked up her gloves. She still had an hour before the inquest, so she walked across the hall and knocked on Melinda's door.

After the third knock, Melinda opened the door wearing her wrapper, her dark sun-streaked hair a tangle down her back.

Lila smiled. "May I come in?"

"Sure," Melinda said. Turning away, she opened the drapes. "Where're you goin' all dressed up?"

"The inquest," Lila said, settling herself on the only chair. "Why didn't you tell me you knew Seth when I offered you the job?"

Melinda looked at her sharply, then laughed as she crossed to the washbowl. " 'Cause I knew my only hope was to weasel my way in and then count on Joaquín defendin' my right to be there."

"What does he have to do with it?"

"We'd been livin' together the last two years." She splashed water on her face, then grinned up from the towel. "Sunday mornin' I drank a whole bottle of Seth's whiskey and he had Joaquín run me off."

"Must've been more to it than that," Lila said.

Melinda laughed. "Yeah, we go way back, Seth and me. I made a mistake hookin' up with Joaquín, though, and I'm glad I'm out of it." She sat down on the bed with a sigh, still holding the towel. "Don't know what I'm gonna do without a job."

"Maybe I can convince Blue to reconsider," Lila said thoughtfully.

Melinda studied her. "Why would you?"

Lila shrugged. "You're good at your job, and some men will want you just because you were Joaquín's once."

"Seth'll never go for it."

"Why should he care?"

Melinda smiled. "He keeps a tight rein on his world."

"Why are you a threat to that?"

"I'm not. But I said some things I shouldn't have when I got so drunk, and they made Rico cry."

"Who's Rico?"

"Seth's woman. He calls her his wife but he's got another one back in Austin."

Lila nodded. "I know."

That surprised Melinda, but she said, "I can't understand why he chose Rico over me anyway. Why d'ya think he'd want a woman who holds him back in bed? You'd think he'd want one who enjoys it when he lets loose."

"Perhaps he's afraid of what'll happen if he does," Lila said, remembering his smile when his hand closed on her throat. "I would be."

Melinda studied her with a growing suspicion. "Had you met him before?"

Lila quickly shook her head. "I'm familiar with his reputation, is all."

Melinda nodded. "Well, Seth doesn't really hurt women. He just uses us with relish."

"He hung one," Lila countered, "and knifed another in the heart."

"They crossed him," Melinda said.

Lila looked away, her lips pressed tight.

Melinda whispered, "You're not thinkin' of crossin' him, are you, Lila?"

"I wouldn't be so bold," she said, standing up. "I'll talk to Blue about your job. Would you like to meet me for lunch? Beck's Hotel, about noon?"

Melinda was inclined to refuse. She didn't want to be anywhere near a plot against Seth for fear she'd be caught in the crossfire. On the other hand, if she could unearth what that plot was, she would be in his good graces again. Maybe if she did keep working for Blue, in time Seth might even choose her on one of those nights he played around behind Rico's back. Smiling slyly, she said, "I'd be pleased to have lunch with you, Lila."

7

When Blue Rivers arrived at the inquest investigating the first violent death within the township of Tejoe, he found the courtroom crowded with men. They all watched him walk in, and no one failed to notice Nib Carey standing just outside wearing two gunbelts opposed across his hips. Blue saw a self-righteous anger in the eyes of the gentry. It was evident that they'd been expecting trouble in his establishment, and also that they had no intention of cutting him any slack. He took a seat by the door, wary of being trapped in the domain of the law.

Sheriff Slater came in and nodded at Blue, then looked over the others as he walked to the front. He stopped before the window beside the judicial bench and thrust his hands deep into his pockets. As he stared at the empty, barren courtyard, he wasn't thinking about what he was seeing but about the irony of being the lawman who might have to bring Seth Strummar to justice. Earl Boyd, a slight, dark man, came in a moment later. He and the Sheriff nodded at each other, then the court clerk set his satchel on the table at the front of the room and removed a sheaf of papers, several pens and a bottle of ink. He arranged them all neatly and stood waiting, watching the door.

Judge Hunnicutt came in wearing the black robe of his office. He was a tall man, florid and robust, nearly fifty and a widower who had come to the territory after losing his family and fortune to the Yankees. He had been appointed to the bench by a former comrade-in-arms, and he spent one week of each month in a different town in his jurisdiction. Tejoe was usually the quietest of his communities, its normal court calendar sparse with petty civil suits and misdemeanor criminal cases. This morning, however, the judge wasn't surprised to find the courtroom crowded.

Neither was he surprised to see no women in the audience. The men there were the owners of commerce, and their faces wore the hard expressions of an unmerciful intolerance they no doubt preferred their ladies not see. A killing threatened everyone's illusion of safety, and the men had gathered to mete out punishment, not compassion.

The clerk called the court to order as Judge Hunnicutt sat down behind the bench. He looked up to watch the widow come in. Realizing she was alone in her sex, she hesitated on the threshold until Blue Rivers rose and guided her to the seat next to his.

The clerk announced that the inquiry into the death of Bart Leroy Keats had commenced. First the sheriff took the stand and was sworn in. When Earl Boyd asked him to testify as to what he knew of the case in question, Rafe Slater said, "I was out of town at the time. I got home early Sunday morning and was informed by Doc Rawls that a stranger by the name of Bart Keats had been killed by Seth Strummar in the Blue Rivers Saloon the night before. That would be Saturday, the 13th of October, 1883. I talked to Blue Rivers, the proprietor of the saloon, and he told me that Keats had walked into his place of business about nine o'clock that night and drew down on Strummar, who then shot and killed him, the deceased, I mean. I rode out to the Strummar homestead and questioned him. Strummar freely admitted the killing, but said he'd never met Bart Keats before that night and did not know why Keats had challenged him. I felt satisfied Strummar was telling the truth, and I have no more information to offer the court.''

"Thank you, Sheriff," Earl Boyd said. "The court dismisses the witness and calls Dr. Hubert Rawls to the stand."

Dr. Rawls was a short man whose vest buttons were strained over his potbelly. Wearing a dusty black suit and carrying an equally disreputable hat, he settled himself into the chair after being sworn in, then looked at the judge and said, "I've been awake all night, Your Honor, tending the birth of a child, and have driven five hours to arrive here in time. I hope you'll forgive me if I'm not at my best."

Hunnicutt smiled. "You are forgiven. Proceed with your testimony."

"What is it y'all need to know?"

"Just tell us what you found when called to the Blue Rivers Saloon last Saturday night."

Dr. Rawls shrugged. "I found the deceased on the floor with a bullet in his chest." He reached into his vest pocket, straining the buttons even further, and extracted a slug. "This is it," he said, holding it up. "A .44 in near pristine condition. The heart, you know, is a powerful muscle that'll stop just about anything. Mr. Keats was prob'ly dead when he hit the floor." He grinned at the judge, fingering the bullet. "Figured I'd keep it as a souvenir."

Hunnicutt restrained a smile. "Since there's no doubt that bullet inflicted the fatal wound and came from Mr. Strummar's gun, I see no harm in your retaining possession. You may go home now."

"Thanks." The doctor stood up and scanned the room as he squeezed the bullet back into his pocket. "Important audience you got this morning, Judge," he said. "Think maybe I'll stick around after all.'' He trundled from the stand and found a seat in back.

The clerk called Blue Rivers. Blue stood up slowly, not seeing any friendliness in the eyes watching him. He crossed to the witness stand and was sworn in, then sat down and gave his testimony without any prompting. ''About nine o'clock last Saturday night,'' he began, choosing his words carefully, ''I was in my office when I noticed the saloon had gotten real quiet, so I went out to see why. I saw a stranger facing off in front of Seth Strummar. I asked the stranger what was going on. He said he was gonna kill Strummar. I was looking right at him, and Seth was behind him in my line of vision. I saw the stranger draw first, then Seth draw and fire.'' He stopped, scanning the faces watching in silence, then shrugged. ''It was Seth's luck. That's all there is to it.''

Sheriff Slater stood up. ''I've got seven affidavits from witnesses who say the same thing, Your Honor. They're all here if you want to parade 'em onto the stand and hear it again.''

Hunnicutt looked at the audience. ''Will those men please stand up?'' He watched them: three of the leading merchants, two members of the school board, a deacon in the Protestant church, and the town mayor; all upstanding citizens who patronized the Blue Rivers Saloon even though they knew it was backed by an outlaw. Maybe because it was, the judge mused, thinking sin was more enticing when it carried an edge of danger. In a stern voice he asked, ''Do any of you disagree with Mr. Rivers' statement?''

They all shook their heads.

''Is there anything you wish to add?''

''Not to the facts,'' Maurice Engle said. He owned the county's major mercantile firm, was tall and dark with a craggy face and piercing blue eyes. ''I got a question or two for Mr. Rivers, though, if I could have Your Honor's permission.''

''Proceed,'' Hunnicutt said.

Maurice Engle scowled at the witness, then asked, "What brought Bart Keats to Tejoe?"

"I don't know," Blue answered.

"Had you ever seen him before?"

Blue shook his head. "He was a stranger to me."

"You're employing his widow."

"I hired her that morning. I didn't know her husband."

"Did you know she had a husband?"

"I didn't ask," Blue said.

Hunnicutt interrupted. "That's more than two questions, Mr. Engle, and I don't see how Mr. Rivers' personnel policies are relevant. Get to the point, please."

Maurice Engle shifted his mouth around as he watched the witness. "My second question," Engle said, "is how likely it is this'll happen again?"

"I can't answer that," Blue said.

"Somebody better goddamn well answer it!" Engle bellowed.

Hunnicutt pounded his gavel. "Any more profanity and I'll have you removed, Mr. Engle."

The merchant turned to the judge with entreaty for reason. "Keats was a bounty hunter, Your Honor. I got no quarrel with Strummar killing him. Any man'd do the same in that situation. But I got a quarrel with it happening in my town. This is the first killing we've had in Tejoe. We got a right to ask a few questions." He turned back to Blue. "I want to know why Strummar isn't here!"

The room was silent as Blue scanned their faces again. He looked through the open door at Nib, then softly told the merchant, "He would've had to come unarmed."

"Otherwise you're saying he'd be here?" Engle scoffed.

"I think so," Blue answered. "But he couldn't tell you anything more'n what I'm saying. We aren't any happier with what happened than you are."

Engle sat down with disgust.

Tom Beck, owner of the best hotel and also the town

mayor, stood up and smiled at the judge. "May I speak, Your Honor?"

Hunnicutt nodded, suppressing a sigh. The procedure had strayed far from the business of an inquest but he recognized that it provided a needed forum for these men to air their views.

Beck politely addressed the witness: "Our concern is for the complexion of our community, Mr. Rivers. We've worked hard to build stability and prosperity for our families, and we can see how quickly all those years of work can be undone. Tejoe is not a poor town, we all know that. Our bank is quite plump, our stores stocked with merchandise, our establishments full of clientele. We are a thriving community, but the wrong element moving in now could turn everything sour. It was with trepidation that we heard the news of Seth Strummar's residence outside our town. When he kept to himself and was rarely seen, we all put our worry on a back burner and tried not to think of it, but we all knew he was a powder keg of potential violence. When you opened your saloon and word got out Strummar was your silent partner, we all felt that worry sputter on the stove. As time passed, we were beginning to think it would be all right. Then this happened. Now we're afraid, Mr. Rivers. Afraid of losing what we worked so hard to achieve because of one bad apple in the barrel."

"Seth's not a bad apple," Blue said. "He's put his past behind him and wants only to raise his children in peace."

Alfonso Esquibel, owner of the town's largest livery, stood up. "That is what we all want. But we do not threaten Strummar's peace. He threatens ours."

"He doesn't mean to," Blue said quietly. "You're right in that he backed me in the saloon, but we pay a good chunk of taxes on our business. He pays taxes on his wife's land, and the plumpness of your bank is due in part to the size of his account. I can't see he's hurt Tejoe any. What happened was unfortunate, but hopefully the results will discourage future contenders."

"I wish I could believe you," Esquibel retorted, "but

violence breeds itself. Other bounty hunters will learn he is here, and now they will always come, thinking Strummar is a little older, a little slower, easier to take. It will happen until some kid comes along and beats him. You know it as well as I and every man in this room."

Softly, Blue said, "Seems to me you'd have some compassion for the man who has to face that."

Esquibel sat down as J. J. Clancy, owner of the Bank of Tejoe, stood up. He was dapper in his fancy suit, and he wore an amused smile. "I agree with Mr. Rivers entirely. Mr. Strummar has brought capital to our community, as discreetly as he has distributed it, and we are better off for his residency because there is a silver lining to the cloud of his presence. Reverend Holcroft mentioned it yesterday morning." He paused to nod at the minister across the room. "As everyone here has pointed out, our community is an affluent one. In some circles, gentlemen, we would be considered a plum to be plucked. It can only discourage criminals to know we have a citizen well capable of defending his interests."

Buck Stubbins, owner of the Red Rooster Silver Mine, stood up. "You're playin' with fire, Clancy. I told Rev'rend Holcroft the same thing yestiddy. You're thinkin' to use Strummar for your own purposes, but I'm here to tell ya that's like smokin' a cigarette sittin' on dynamite!"

The room erupted in vociferous agreement. Hunnicutt watched the minister stand up. After pounding his gavel, the judge asked, "Do you wish to say something, Reverend Holcroft?"

The minister walked to the front where he could look into the faces of his parishioners as he spoke. He nodded at Blue Rivers, a man he hadn't met before, then addressed the room.

"It seems to me there's truth in all the words spoken here today. I even agree to some extent with Mr. Stubbins. We are smoking a cigarette on a keg of dynamite, but the explosive isn't Mr. Strummar. It's the violence innate in all of us to some degree, and in the frontier around us to a great degree. Look at our neighboring city of Tombstone if you have any doubt. Killings there are frequent. It's the wealth of the mines that attracts the less desirable elements to our part of the country, a danger much larger than any created by the presence of one man. I met Mr. Strummar for the first time in church on Sunday, and later that day, by a fortuitous circumstance, I dined with his family. I was impressed by the care he is expending to raise his son to fruitful manhood, and by the love evident in his home. We are all children of God, gentlemen, and it seems to me that accepting Seth Strummar into our community can only benefit us. Believing the best of a man tends to bring it out in him, and from what I saw, Mr. Strummar has a lot to offer. Not only his wealth, as has been pointed out, and not only his ability to protect his holdings, which also has been pointed out, but in the example he provides our youngsters of a man who went astray in his youth but is trying hard to make amends and follow the straight and narrow now. I believe that if we give Mr. Strummar the benefit of the doubt, he will prove worthy of our confidence and be a credit to our community.''

''That's easy to say from the pulpit,'' Maurice Engle shouted, ''but on the streets where the rest of us live, Strummar is a scourge on this community that will only attract more of his own kind! I'm saying we oughta make it loud and clear that he's not wanted in our town.''

The anger of his words was met in silence as each man contemplated the difficulties inherent in telling the outlaw to leave.

Sheriff Slater stood up. ''The facts are these, gentlemen: we have no legal right to run Strummar out of town. He hasn't broken any laws in Arizona, and unless one of you wants to try'n collect the bounty from Texas, there ain't a thing we can do about him being here. Ain't that right, Judge?''

''Yes,'' he said. ''Back to the business at hand, gentlemen. I find that Seth Strummar acted in self-defense when he shot and killed Bart Keats in the Blue Rivers Saloon on Saturday last. There are no charges to be filed. The remains are released for burial. Case closed.'' He pounded his gavel. ''We will recess for half an hour before continuing with the calendar,'' he said, then stood up and walked out as the clerk echoed his last words.

Blue smiled at Nib through the door, and the gunman grinned in congratulation of the verdict, then Blue left the witness stand and walked back to where Lila was waiting. He knew it didn't look good to be so close to the widow, it tinged the killing with ulterior motives that weren't true, and he was sorry it had to be muddied because of him. But he also knew if he were to walk out and leave her on her own, the men would think less of him, so he took her elbow and guided her from the room, feeling the eyes watching them leave.

Outside the gate, Nib unbuckled the right-handed gunbelt and gave it to Blue. He strapped it on, then smiled at Lila. ''Can I walk you home?''

''I'm not going home,'' she answered forlornly. ''I'm going to the graveyard.''

''Oh yeah,'' he said. ''You want some company?''

She shook her head. ''Sheriff Slater is escorting me. There won't be a ceremony and it'll be over soon. That's all I want, and to lie down before work.''

Blue nodded. ''See you tonight, then.''

He walked away with Nib, but a block down the street Blue turned back and watched Lila waiting for the sheriff. When Slater came out, they fell in step beside each other without a greeting and walked in the other direction. Blue looked at Nib. ''Do you get the feeling Lila knew Sheriff Slater before she got here?''

Nib's bullet eyes turned slowly away from the retreating couple to meet those of his boss. ''Seems like they would've said hello or something, don't it?''

Blue nodded. ''I'm going out to Seth's for supper tonight. I want you to watch Lila real close. If she does anything that doesn't seem connected to business, I want to know about it.''

"All right," Nib said. "Won't be hard. She's easier to look at than most any woman I've seen."

Blue nodded again. "Makes me wonder what she's doing in Tejoe."

8

When Melinda met Lila for lunch, their presence created a stir. Not only because they were both brightly attired, Melinda in blue and Lila in green, and not only because they chose the table in front of the window, but because they were ladies of the evening and Hotel Beck was the best in town.

If they hadn't both been beautiful, Tom Beck would have thrown them out. He admired them sitting in the window of his dining room, however, and since their frocks were modest, if bright, and they comported themselves respectably, he allowed them to stay. He even went over and extended a welcome. Feeling tempted to invite himself to join them but knowing he'd never hear the end of it from his wife, he contented himself with offering them a bottle of his best burgundy. They accepted as if gifts from gentlemen were to be expected, then turned back to their conversation as if he'd already disappeared, which he quickly did.

As soon as they were alone, Melinda whispered, "So Seth's in the clear?"

Lila studied her across the sunlit table. "Why do you care so much?"

Melinda's laughter was tinged with bitterness. "Guess I shouldn't," she said, looking away.

"I would tend to agree," Lila replied, "unless you think there's a chance he'll leave Rico."

Melinda shook her head.

"Any woman can be pushed out," Lila murmured. "It only requires a carefully played hand."

Slowly Melinda turned her gaze back on the conniving woman.

Lila smiled. "The hard part is making him choose you when it happens. I've seen the plot ricochet so bad the man hates all women and won't have anything to do with any of us." She laughed softly, then asked in a conspiratorial tone, "If Seth left town, wouldn't it pull the rug out from under Blue?"

"I don't think so," Melinda answered warily. "The saloon's in Blue's name. Seth doesn't have any legal connection to it."

"Is that true?" Lila mused. "What about Seth's bank account? Does Blue have access to that?"

"I don't know," Melinda said. "Rico does."

"She can withdraw money without Seth's approval?"

Melinda nodded. "He set it up that way so in case he dies the money'll be hers."

"Avoiding probate." Lila's grin was gleeful. "That's smart, and it proves he trusts her."

Melinda shrugged uncomfortably. "Seth doesn't have any problem trusting Rico."

"Must be hard for him, though, after being a renegade so long."

"You don't understand their situation," Melinda said.

"I'd like to," she murmured, then added quickly, "It would help me do my job better."

"What does Rico have to do with that?"

"Nothing. But Seth's money has a lot to do with it."

The waiter approached with the wine. Melinda kept quiet until he had filled their glasses, taken their orders and left them alone again, then asked, "Did you talk to Blue about my job?"

"I didn't get a chance," Lila answered. "I went right from the inquest to the burial. It was melancholy." She sipped steadily at her wine a moment, then stared out the window with angry eyes. "Bart wasn't always such a fool. When I married him he had a lot of smarts. He's the one found Tejoe on the map when we heard Seth was living here, and it was his . . ." She stopped, then said hurriedly, "I had no idea he'd follow me."

"Seems odd you'd choose a place he knew if you really meant to escape him," Melinda countered, wondering what Lila had stopped herself from saying.

Lila laughed as if it were inconsequential. "He mentioned it once, that's all. I didn't think he even remembered it."

"There must've been other places he never mentioned."

"None where I knew the richest man in town." Lila smiled. "I learned a long time ago how a rich patron can make a real difference in a woman's life."

"So you did know Seth before," Melinda said softly, thinking she'd caught the woman in a contradiction.

Lila shook her head. "I figured once I got here I'd have him eating out of my hand soon enough."

"You intended to seduce him?" Melinda asked, astonished the woman would travel a thousand miles in search of a man she had never seen.

"Not necessarily seduce," Lila scoffed. "Just use him a little. You should do the same. I'm sure he has heart-strings you could pull."

Melinda delicately snorted with disdain. "Esperanza's the one who sealed my fate."

"Who's Esperanza?"

"An old friend of Seth's who lives with 'em."

"How did she seal your fate?"

"She read my cards and told me right in front of Rico. That's what made her cry, then Seth stormed in and blamed it on me."

"Esperanza tells fortunes?" Lila asked eagerly.

Melinda nodded. "Seth says he doesn't believe her cards, but her word carries a lot of weight out there."

"Do *you* believe her cards?"

"They predicted my death," Melinda said dourly. "Who'd want to believe that?"

"Not many. Is that why you left?"

She shook her head. "I made my mistake hookin' up with Joaquín. Once I realized that, I knew I had to leave 'cause I'd done the one thing to guarantee Seth would never touch me."

"Apparently he doesn't feel the same about Blue," Lila murmured.

"What d'ya mean?" Melinda asked sharply.

"I mean Seth came to my room this morning, pulled me into bed and had his way with me. Joaquín stood there and watched. As he was leaving, Seth said the only reason he's letting me stay around is because Blue has the hots for me. So Seth knows how Blue feels yet still took his pleasure."

"Joaquín watched?" Melinda whispered.

"With wide eyes," Lila said, then sipped her wine. "He's a handsome kid, dressed all in black with his black, black eyes. I'm surprised you couldn't get along with him."

"Joaquín gets along with everyone, but only Seth pleases him."

"Do I detect a nasty insinuation there?"

"Just that I didn't want to play second fiddle to God on Earth."

Lila laughed. "You'd rather play goddess, eh?" She softened her tone. "That's what I thought of Seth's wife in Austin: like a princess, so tiny and pretty, and both she and the child so well dressed and protected by an armed guard all the time." A cold glint lit her eyes. "I heard

Seth gave Johanna fifty thousand dollars when they split up.''

Melinda stared at her. ''You think he has that much money?''

Lila nodded. ''And plenty more right here in the Bank of Tejoe.''

''That's why you came,'' Melinda whispered.

''Partly,'' Lila admitted. ''I intend to get my hands on as much of it as I can. I mean, it's just sitting there waiting for someone to spend it. I might as well provide a need to be filled.'' She winked at Melinda, then gave a radiant smile to the waiter bringing their kidney pie. As she cut through the steaming crust with her fork, she asked, ''Does Espèranza ever give readings to strangers?''

Melinda was wondering why she'd ordered kidney pie since she disliked the dish. At the time, she had simply echoed Lila's choice in order to get rid of the waiter, but now she felt ravenous and the aroma rising with the steam was unpleasant. When she watched Lila slide a forkful of meat into her mouth, the redness reminded Melinda of the blood and guts of Esperanza's loyalty to Seth. ''She might,'' Melinda finally answered, ''if you pay her. I don't think Seth ever gives her money.''

Lila licked the bloody juice off her lips. ''All women need a nest egg of their own, don't you think?''

''Something that'll still be there when the man isn't,'' Melinda agreed.

When Blue rode into the schoolyard that afternoon, he saw the three Nickles boys fighting Lobo. Watching the kid take it hard, Blue wasn't sure Seth would want him to interfere. Lobo was getting his licks in, he was just taking a lot more than he was giving. Finally one of the boys tripped him and he fell. They surrounded him with their fists and yelled ''So there!'' a couple of times. When they looked up and saw Blue watching, they turned and ran into the sandy arroyo reaching into the foothills.

Blue sat his horse and waited for Lobo to pull himself

to his feet. The boy walked toward the trough with his head down, washed the dirt off his face and wiped his bloody nose on his sleeve, which made Blue wince anticipating Esperanza's reaction, then climbed the fence into the corral and saddled his horse.

He rode the pinto out and leaned from the saddle to latch the gate, closing two ancient mules inside. Only then did he look at Blue and say, "They belong to those fellows who were punchin' me. Think I should run 'em off?"

Blue shook his head.

"That's what an outlaw would do," Lobo said.

"Yeah," Blue agreed as they ambled toward the road. "But an outlaw would leave with the mules; he wouldn't have a home here and have to face those fellows again tomorrow."

"I'm bringin' a gun tomorrow," Lobo said.

Blue laughed. "You better talk to Seth about that."

"What am I s'posed to do?" the boy cried indignantly. "There's three of 'em and they always stick together."

"Try making friends with 'em," Blue suggested.

"Who wants to be friends with a bunch of pig farmers," Lobo muttered.

"You like bacon and sausage, don't you?"

"Yeah."

"Well, if it weren't for folks like the Nickles, you wouldn't have any. So what's wrong with being a pig farmer?"

"We could raise our own."

"Then *you'd* be a pig farmer."

"I don't like 'em!" Lobo cried with passion. "They ride stupid ol' mules and don't wear any shoes 'til it practically snows and never do wear boots! They're low class and I don't care to associate with 'em."

Blue studied him a moment, then said softly, "Seth paid a hundred dollars for that pony you're riding and another forty for the saddle. Your boots cost fifteen dollars and you outgrow 'em every year. It ain't the fault of the Nickles that they don't have money like that."

"It ain't my fault!"

"Maybe it is, in a roundabout way. You know where Seth got his money?"

Lobo sniffed and looked away. "He stole it," he said softly.

"From people like the Nickles. Only they lived in Texas and put their money in banks in Texas and Seth took it out. You know that, Lobo. So if I was you, I wouldn't go flaunting my daddy's ill-gotten gains in the pobres' noses. It ain't apt to build your popularity."

"I don't flaunt it," he argued. "I just want to have a race but nobody'll do it 'cause they know I'll win. I want to play craps but nobody else has any dimes. I want to sneak into the saloons and watch the poker but none of the other boys have the nerve. They say their ol' man'll beat 'em good if they're caught in a saloon. I hate 'em. They're all a bunch of pansies."

Watching him carefully Blue asked, "So who do you do those things with?"

"The kids in town," Lobo said.

"When?" Blue asked with astonishment, knowing Joaquín usually rode him back and forth to school.

"I wait 'til Seth's in bed with Rico, then I sneak out."

Blue looked at him hard. "You're asking for trouble, Lobo."

"A man's gotta have a life of his own," the child replied.

Blue decided Lobo was boasting of something he wouldn't dare do. "Are you trying to tell me you get a horse out of the stable without Joaquín hearing you?"

Lobo shook his head. "I keep one in the arroyo half a mile toward the road."

"What do you mean you keep a horse?" Blue asked, scarcely able to believe it.

Lobo shrugged. "I bought one and keep him staked in the meadow there. I move him every day, whether I go to town or not, and always make sure he has water."

"And Seth's never seen him?"

"Seth never goes anywhere," Lobo said with scorn, "except to town to visit your saloon."

Blue picked up the bitterness in the boy's voice. "It ain't easy," Blue said softly, "being who he is."

"It ain't easy bein' his son, either," Lobo retorted. "I'm learnin' to use it, though. At first the town kids thought I was a dandy, but I showed 'em otherwise 'fore they suspected who I am 'cause my name's Madera. Then when they found out I'm Seth Strummar's son, I saw it worked for me and I didn't deny it after that."

"Had you denied it before?"

"Yeah. Not 'cause I'm ashamed or nothin' but 'cause I got tired of explainin' why my name's different."

"Have you ever asked Seth about changing it?"

"He doesn't want me to, says I'll take grief all my life if I carry his name."

"Maybe he's right."

Lobo shrugged. "Yesterday he was talkin' about his brother. Did you know he had a brother named Jeremiah who died?"

Blue nodded, keeping quiet because he didn't know how much Seth had told the boy.

"Seth said I've got a brother named Jeremiah now, too. He lives in Texas with a woman named Johanna."

"What do you think about having a brother?"

"I don't think it's fair he gets to be a Strummar when Seth don't even live with him."

"Maybe it's one or the other," Blue suggested. "I bet Jeremiah would rather be called Madera and live with Seth."

"You think so?"

"I'd bet money on it."

Lobo snorted. "Life's fucked, ain't it?"

Blue was startled. "Who taught you to say words like that?"

"Seth!" Lobo chortled with glee.

When they rode into the yard, Seth walked out to meet them. He stood beside Lobo's horse, reached up and took the boy's hat off, then studied his face in silence a minute. "How'd you do?" Seth finally asked.

Lobo shrugged. "There was three of 'em, so I lost."

"To only three?"

Lobo stared at him in silence. Blue said, "One of 'em must've been twelve years old, Seth."

"I did the best I could," Lobo said earnestly. "But then one of 'em tripped me and I was down."

"Who were they?" Seth asked.

"The Nickles boys."

"What were you fighting about?"

Lobo looked away.

Seth watched him a moment, then asked, "You gonna answer me, Lobo?"

"They called you a killer," the boy said softly, hiding his eyes.

With a sigh Seth lifted his son into his arms. "Put his horse up, will you, Blue?" he asked, carrying Lobo toward the house.

"Sure," Blue answered, watching the kid's arms come around his father's back and hold on tight.

Blue edged his horse close to the pinto and picked up the reins, then turned toward the corral and saw Joaquín standing by the gate watching Seth and Lobo disappear inside the house. Blue clucked his horse forward and Joaquín opened the gate, then followed him into the stable and unsaddled the pinto while Blue tended his own horse. They worked in silence, comfortable with each other's company and bonded by their own memories of childhood fights. As they were leaving the corral, they saw Melinda in a hired hack coming into the yard.

9

Blue gave Joaquín a commiserating smile then walked into the house, leaving him alone. Melinda pulled the buggy to a stop in front of him. They looked at each other a moment before he asked, "Have you come to visit Rico?"

"Oh, you're cold, Joaquín," she retorted. "Is that all you have to say after living with me for two years?"

"You stayed in my room," he replied without rancor.

She glanced down at her gloved hands holding the reins, then met his eyes again with determination. "I had lunch with Lila Keats today. I learned some things Seth should know."

"Like what?"

She looked at the familiar collection of buildings she had lost as her home, the house brightly lit in the falling dusk, then back at him. "Aren't I even to be allowed in? I haven't become an enemy, Joaquín."

He shrugged. "It's not up to me whether Rico allows you in her home."

Trying to picture him watching Seth with Lila, Melinda

wanted to ask if it was true but was afraid of his answer. "There was a time," she said softly, "when I thought you were incapable of cruelty."

"Have you changed your mind?" he asked with an amused smile.

She nodded. "You'd do anything for Seth. You've already committed murder for him."

Joaquín shook his head. "To challenge Seth with a gun is like swimming upstream with a pocket full of stones. I only added a little lead to those men's burdens. By being here you are adding weight to Seth's and I doubt if you will help anyone, including yourself." He smiled playfully. "But my opinion is only one of five. Go on in and test the water among the others."

"What did I ever do to make you hate me?" she whispered.

"I don't hate you, Melinda. I like you most of the time." He held his hand to help her down. "Are you going in?"

She took his hand, the familiar strength of which was hers only for polite duty now, then stood before him on the ground, looking up at him from so near. "I wish things had worked out dif'rent, Joaquín."

"I'll tether your horse," he said, backing away.

She sighed and walked alone toward the bright lights shining from the windows of the house. The front door was open to the cooling breeze of evening, and she stopped on the threshold, seeing a sliver of light beneath the closed door of Lobo's room. Then she heard Blue's easy laughter coming from the kitchen. She crossed the dark parlor and stopped again on the threshold.

Blue was at the table and Esperanza at the stove, Elena in her cradle fussing with quiet puckering sounds. Melinda smiled at Esperanza. "I've come in peace," she said hopefully.

Esperanza shrugged. "Sit down, niña, since you're here. You want some coffee?"

"Please," she said gratefully, taking the chair across

from Blue. She pulled her gloves off and smiled at him.

"What're you doing here?" he asked.

She looked up at Esperanza setting a cup of steaming coffee before her, then asked, "If it would help Seth, would you read the cards for Lila Keats?"

Esperanza exchanged wary looks with Blue before answering. "How could that help Seth?"

Melinda suggested with sarcasm, "You could tell her the same thing you told me. That oughta make her clear out."

Esperanza shook her head. "I never lie about the cards."

Melinda felt stung. "Then it was true," she whispered, "what you saw for me?"

Esperanza nodded.

Melinda tossed her head in a gesture of defiance. "Tell Lila the truth then. Her future can't be any better'n mine since nearly every word out of her mouth is a lie. All I want to know is if you'll do it."

"Where?" Esperanza asked. "Not here."

Melinda smiled. "I'll let you know."

"When you do, I'll let you know if I choose to do it," Esperanza said.

Watching her move away to stare out the window, Melinda was unable to tell what Esperanza was thinking any more than what Blue's thoughts were. She sipped her coffee wishing she had some whiskey in it, but knew it would be ungracious to ask since her last escapade in this kitchen. When she thought back on that, she wondered what she'd hoped to accomplish. Cause a falling out between Seth and Joaquín, she supposed, but she couldn't imagine how she'd expected that to benefit her. Had she really thought either one of them would rescue the person who destroyed their peace? Yet that's what she wanted: to be rescued as Rico had been. Silently Melinda mocked herself, thinking maybe she had to prove she'd die for a man before that happened.

Rico came into the kitchen carrying a basin of water and

a bloodied cloth. She stopped and looked at Melinda sitting at the table.

"Is someone hurt?" Melinda asked with sudden fear for Seth.

"Lobo got into a fight at school," Rico answered. She crossed to the door and threw the water out, then left the cloth and basin outside when she came back and washed her hands at the sink. Drying them on a towel, she faced Melinda and asked, "What are you doing here?"

Melinda laughed to cover her hurt. "I thought I was a friend," she said. "Everyone's treatin' me like an enemy all of a sudden."

"Maybe we don't trust you anymore," Esperanza said.

"Why? What'd I do other'n get drunk on Sunday mornin'?"

"You did more than that," Rico said softly. "You accused Seth unfairly."

"Sweetheart," Melinda said with genuine compassion, "if you don't know he's humpin' half the women in Tejoe, you ought to."

"I don't believe you!" Rico cried.

"Ask Lila Keats." Melinda turned her eyes on Blue. "I ate lunch with her today and she said Seth had his way with her this mornin'."

"Is that what you came to tell us?" Blue asked coldly.

She shook her head. "What I got to say is for Seth, and I'll wait."

Joaquín came through the back door but kept his distance, leaning against the wall. They all listened to the door of Lobo's room open, then the footsteps of the child crossing the parlor. When he came in alone, his face bruised and his lip split, he looked at Melinda at the table. "I thought you didn't live here anymore," he said, pulling a chair out beside Blue.

"Who won?" Melinda asked kindly.

Lobo shrugged. "There was three of 'em."

"Those are hard odds," she said, raising her eyes to his father coming through the door.

"Evenin', Melinda," he said with a sardonic smile. "You run out of liquor?"

Again she laughed to cover her hurt. "There's plenty of it in town, Seth. That's one thing I've got lots of these days."

"What're you missing?"

"Friends," she said.

"You think you have some here?"

She looked for a glimmer of regard behind his fun but saw only the cruelty of indifference in his pale eyes. "You're my friend," she said, entreating with her smile. "That's why I came."

He looked at Joaquín behind her, then at his wife. "Do we have any more whiskey, Rico?"

She moved quietly to take it from a cupboard then set the bottle and four glasses on the table. Seth poured a drink into three and held the bottle over the last as he looked at Joaquín. When he shook his head, Seth set the bottle down, nudged glasses toward Melinda and Blue, and picked up his own. "To friendship," Seth said, meeting Melinda's eyes with a bedeviling smile.

"To friendship," she murmured, sipping the whiskey.

"Tried and true," Blue muttered, downing his shot.

The kitchen was silent, everyone watching Melinda except Lobo, who was reading the label on the whiskey bottle.

"I had lunch with Lila Keats today," Melinda said to Seth. "I thought you'd like to know what I learned."

"I'm listening," he said.

She sipped at her drink, basking in his undivided attention. "Lila was askin' about your bank accounts, who had access to them, whether Blue or Rico could withdraw money, things like that." She saw Seth's eyes darken as he frowned. "Don't worry," she assured him. "I didn't tell her anything. She said you gave Johanna fifty thousand when you split, and that you had that much or more in the bank here in Tejoe." His eyes were darker than she'd ever seen them, a deep slate without light. "I asked if that's why she came and she admitted it was, then tried to pretend she meant to get her hands on it legally, through wages and all, but she told me both she and her husband found out you were livin' here when they were still back in Texas.'' Melinda sipped her whiskey again, seeing from Seth's eyes that she'd won a victory.

''I've never had fifty thousand dollars,'' he said.

''Where'd Johanna get it?'' Melinda asked quickly, suspecting she wouldn't find out if she didn't pounce on it now.

''It was hers,'' he said absently, pouring himself another drink. He looked at Joaquín, then at Blue. ''Sonofabitch,'' Seth whispered. ''They're gonna rob the goddamned bank.''

''Who is?'' Blue scoffed. ''Not Lila alone. And if that was their plan, why did Bart call you out? If they were after fifty thousand, why risk his life for the bounty?''

Melinda was still thinking about Johanna having all that money to herself, and she didn't hear what Seth said next.

''It ain't no fifty thousand,'' he said. ''Most of my money's still in Santa Fe. Here in Tejoe I keep five tops, the other investors ten, maybe fifteen all together. You're right about Lila not being alone, though. But who and where are her *compañeros*?''

''Maybe Slater knows,'' Blue said. ''He went with Lila to the burial today. I watched 'em and when they came together they didn't say a word. I figure, when you fall in step with someone without a greeting you're pretty good friends.''

''I never did trust him,'' Seth said, pulling out a chair and straddling it backwards. ''But I don't trust any badge so I didn't hold it against him.'' He sipped his whiskey then looked at Blue. ''Would you figure him to hit his own town?''

''Maybe he's a patsy,'' Melinda said, ''and Lila's gonna try'n frame him for the job.'' She paused, then added softly, ''Or you.''

Seth's eyes bore into her so coldly she had to work at

not breaking her gaze. Finally he asked, "What makes you say that?"

"Just a hunch." She shrugged. "After your visit this mornin' she came to see me, and I got the feelin' then she was hatchin' a plot against you. That's why I agreed to eat with her, just to see what I'd learn."

"What gave you that feeling?"

"She seemed to know a lot about you. Guess it reminded me of how a person'll study his enemies to find their flaws."

"What'd she know?"

"Details about your past," Melinda answered guardedly. "And then there was something she said about your wife, how pretty she was, like a princess, that was it, so well dressed and with a bodyguard all the time, and envy just rippled in her voice." She shrugged again. "It gave me the shivers."

Seth looked at Blue for a long moment, then at Joaquín, then at Lobo who was staring at him. He winked at his son. "Don't worry, Lobo, I ain't been outsmarted by a thief yet." He stood up and looked at Rico. "Think I'll ride into town."

"Now?" she cried.

"Why not?" he asked, already taking his hat from a peg by the door.

"Supper's nearly ready," she said lamely.

He laughed, then came back and gave her a quick kiss on the mouth. "We'll eat in town," he said, turning away.

She caught his arm, stopping him. "What're you going to do?"

Seth smiled. "Pay a call on the sheriff. Rattle his cage and see what falls out. We'll be back before midnight."

Joaquín and Blue followed him through the door, leaving the women alone in the kitchen with Lobo. Turning hard eyes on Melinda, Rico said, "If anything happens to Seth tonight, I'll never forgive you."

"Would you rather he lose all his money?" Melinda retorted. "Bein' as he ain't exactly employable, you'll be the one who goes back to work." She stood up with a sigh. "Honestly, Rico, you oughta come down off your cloud and look at the real world once in a while." She picked up her gloves. "I'll ride in with the men," she said, walking out.

Lobo stood up and started after her.

"Where are you going?" Rico cried. "Lobo, stay here!"

He ran. Making it outside before anyone caught him, he kept running past Melinda and all the way across the yard where he climbed the fence into the corral. Inside the stable the men were saddling their horses. Seth reached for the cinch under his sorrel's belly, then looked at Lobo sideways as he pulled the strap tight and tied it.

"Can I go?" Lobo asked softly.

Seth studied him, then warned, "We'll be late."

"I can stay awake."

"I'm gonna be busy. I won't be there to catch you if you fall asleep in the saddle."

"I'll be there for you, Seth," Lobo said proudly.

Seth chuckled with pleasure. "Don't make us wait for you."

Lobo ran to his pinto and backed it out just as Joaquín finished saddling his black. He stood a moment watching the boy tug the pinto's head down to get the bridle over its ears, then he swung on and ambled toward the door.

Joaquín didn't think the boy should come but wouldn't disappoint him by arguing about it now. Blue, following Joaquín out of the barn and across the corral, felt the same. They looked at each other with a silent acknowledgement of their agreement as they sat just outside the gate waiting.

Seth swung onto his sorrel and sat there a minute, watching his son saddle the pinto. He thought maybe Lobo could pick up a few pointers in how to conduct a fight, though the meeting wasn't apt to involve anything harder than words, and in the best of circumstances their adversary wouldn't be the sheriff. But then he figured Lobo might as well learn young that because a man wore a badge didn't mean he upheld the law. Seth caught himself short, realizing he was thinking like a desperado again: because a man wore a badge didn't necessarily make him an enemy either. Trying to defend himself from this new vantage point of being on the right side of the law made Seth feel old, and watching Lobo jump to catch the stirrup didn't help. The boy wasn't even eight yet and had no business coming along. But like Joaquín, Seth wouldn't disappoint Lobo now.

They turned their horses out of the barn to join their friends just as Melinda climbed into her buggy. None of the men said anything about her accompanying them. Lobo trotted his pinto through the gate, Seth swung it closed and made sure the latch caught, then they all rode out at an easy lope, the buggy tagging along behind.

A huge moon cast long shadows across the pale desert as Seth and Joaquín led the way, followed by Blue and Lobo, the buggy wheels humming from the rear.

A mile up the road they met Abneth Nickles coming out of town. Seth reined to a stop and the others lined up alongside him, Lobo closest to the buggy. Nickles pulled his team of dray horses to a halt and smiled at his neighbor.

"Evenin', Abneth," Seth said. "I understand our boys got into a tussle today."

"I ain't heard about it," Nickles said, looking at Lobo. "Who won?"

"We'll let them tell you about it," Seth said, cutting off Lobo's reply.

"Fair enough," the farmer said. "Was glad to hear you were exonerated at the inquest this morning."

"Thanks," Seth said.

The men sat in a comfortable silence for a few minutes. The harness on the buggy horse rattled as it shook dust out of its ears, then Joaquín's black stomped one hoof with impatience. Seth asked, "You ain't seen any strangers around, have you? Group of men maybe camped out in the country keeping to themselves?"

"Not on my range," Abneth answered thoughtfully.

"Course, I don't ride it much as I should. Noticed you're holding a bay all by itself in the arroyo 'tween your house and the road. Saw it from Juniper Peak t'other day. You got it quarantined or something?"

"There's a horse tethered there?" Seth asked sharply.

"It's mine," Lobo said.

Seth turned and studied his son.

"You know, come to think of it," Abneth said, "I did stumble on a campfire on the west slope of Juniper. Wasn't more'n a day or two old and looked like half a dozen horses stayed overnight. Might they be the men you're interested in?"

"Might," Seth said, dragging his attention away from his son. "If you catch sight of 'em, maybe you could send one of your boys over to let me know where."

"I'll do that," Abneth said. He smiled at the men. "Y'all make a formidable lineup. If I saw the four of you ride into my camp, I wouldn't think you'd come to talk. It's Kid Madera down there that'd shiver my timbers."

Seth laughed. "If you'd come over to the house for a drink sometime, maybe you wouldn't find him so intimidating."

"Thank you, Seth." Abneth smiled. "The hospitality's mutual, a'course." He peered into the darkness of the buggy, then shrugged. "Ma'am," he said, clucking his team forward.

Seth waited a minute before turning his eyes on Lobo. "You come ride with me," he said, nudging his sorrel along the road toward town. Joaquín hung back with Blue as Lobo kicked his pinto to catch up with his father. After a minute Seth asked, "What're you doing with a horse in the arroyo?"

Lobo ran through the lies he could offer but knew when he was found out it would only make everything worse. "I just wanted it," he answered.

"Don't you like the one you're riding?"

"Yeah," he said, suddenly afraid he would lose the pinto.

"Where'd you get a horse anyway?"

"I bought it."

"With what money?"

"Some I saved."

"You only get a nickel a week. Can't be much of a horse."

"It's okay," Lobo said.

"Who sold a horse to a kid like you?"

"Another kid."

"What other kid?"

"His name's Lemonade. He lives in town."

"Friend of yours?"

"Sort of."

"Where'd *he* get the horse?"

"I didn't ask."

"You know if you're caught with a stolen horse, I'm the one who'll get arrested?"

Lobo looked closely at Seth and realized he wasn't teasing. "Maybe it ain't stolen."

"Did you get a bill of sale?"

Lobo shook his head.

"I'll buy you another horse if you want one, Lobo," Seth said, "but I think we better get that one off our property first thing, don't you?"

"Yes, sir," he said contritely.

"Now," Seth said. "Why are you keeping an extra horse in the arroyo?"

"I like to ride him sometimes."

"To meet Lemonade in town, maybe?"

"Maybe."

"What do you do there?"

"Nothin'."

"What kind of nothing?"

"Play craps some."

"You any good?"

"I do all right," he answered cautiously.

"Is that how you bought the horse, with your winnings?"

Lobo nodded.

"How much did you pay for it?"

"Ten dollars," he said proudly.

"If I was my old man, I'd tan your hide right now. You know that?"

"I'm glad you're not," Lobo said.

"Maybe I ought to think of something else," Seth said. "Maybe I ought to give that pinto to some kid who ain't such a good gambler."

"Why would you do that?" Lobo cried.

"It doesn't seem you need much help to get by in the world. Maybe I ought to start concentrating my attentions on Elena and teaching her what I know."

"She's just a baby, and a girl besides," Lobo scoffed.

"Yeah, but I got her from the start. Not like you. And when Elena grows up and I say jump, she's gonna jump. She ain't gonna hide horses in arroyos so she can sneak into town and do things she ain't supposed to in places she's not supposed to be in the company of people she'd be better off not knowing. Anybody who acts like that, I figure trying to teach him anything is a waste of time."

"You did it when you were a kid," Lobo said. "You told me yourself."

"I was fifteen when I started gambling, Lobo. That's more'n twice as old as seven."

"I can't help that," he said stubbornly.

Seth laughed. "You keep pestering me to buy you a pistol. You think sneaking into town is showing me you're responsible enough to handle a sixgun?"

"Does that mean you won't?" Lobo asked, crestfallen.

"Not for a long time," Seth said. "And if I find out you've bought one on your own, I will take a strap to you. Do you understand me?"

"Yes, sir," Lobo said.

Joaquín and Blue kept a good distance behind, so the voices of Seth and Lobo were lost in the noise of hooves on the hard road and the creak and whir of the buggy wheels. After a while, Blue asked Joaquín if he had known about the horse.

Joaquín shook his head. "Did you?"

"He told me on the way from school this afternoon. I guess that fight rattled him and he let out a lot of stuff that surprised me. He rides into town at night after everyone's asleep and hangs out in the saloons."

Joaquín stared at Blue. "Alone?"

"With some street kids. Those we saw at breakfast, most likely."

Melinda laughed from inside the buggy. "Like father, like son," she said.

The men ignored her. Blue lowered his voice and asked, "Will Seth whip Lobo for it?"

"Seth never hits Lobo," Joaquín said with pride. "He vowed not to when he took him from his mother, and he has kept that promise."

Blue grinned. "So far."

"Perhaps," Joaquín conceded with a smile.

In front of La Casa Amarilla, Seth reined up beside the buggy. "We'll return it for you, if you like," he said to Melinda.

"Thank you, Seth," she cooed. "I'm afraid I promised to pay 'em when I got back but I haven't enough in my purse."

"I'll take care of it," he said, swinging off his sorrel. He gave his reins to Lobo, then offered his hand to help her down.

She clung to the first touch he had given her in years. His eyes were kind, and she thought she had a chance to kindle something if she played her cards right. She smiled up at him as she murmured, "Anything else I can do, let me know."

"Thanks," he said, then climbed into the buggy and slapped the reins, making the little horse lurch into motion.

She tried to catch Joaquín's eye to give him a smile, too, but he wouldn't look at her. Neither did Blue, though she got a smile from Lobo as he trotted past leading Seth's sorrel. Melinda stood outside the gate for a long time, savoring the memory of Seth's touch. Then she walked upstairs to her room and sat in the darkness, wondering how she could make him so grateful he would act to keep her in his life.

10

Rafe Slater was sitting in his office staring down the line of empty jail cells, well aware of the edge he walked that kept him on the keeper side of the bars. In his life he had done a few things against the law but nothing for which he felt shame, so he didn't figure he dishonored the badge he wore, though he didn't figure he especially deserved it either.

He was a native of Alabama and had fought for the Confederacy. After the war he felt a hollowness inside that no enterprise could satisfy, so he kept drifting and along the way improved his skill with weapons more in the interest of self-defense than procuring a livelihood. He had been pushing forty when he ambled into Tejoe, a small mining town in need of a sheriff, and he'd taken the job by appointment until the election when he was voted unanimously into office, there being no contender to oppose him. Tejoe's previous sheriff had died in his sleep in one of the cells, and Rafe had thought he had a good chance of achieving the same fate until Lila Keats blew into town.

Rafe knew the killing last Saturday was just the beginning of a chain of violence that could cost his life. He sure didn't want to tackle Strummar, but he found himself caught between a compromise of his duty and the cravings of his lust and didn't figure he had much chance of escaping retribution from both.

The thing of it was, his lust didn't have much power anymore and he'd slept with Lila more for old time's sake than anything else. Years ago, he'd ridden for her husband in Texas, back when Bart Keats had been Clay Barton and Lila had called herself Esmeralda. When Rafe finally cut himself loose from their gang of outlaws, he figured he'd done himself a favor, though the memory of Esmeralda often haunted him at night. She'd kept on haunting him until he walked into Blue's saloon and met her green eyes again. Then her memory didn't haunt him; her reality plagued him.

When she came to his office later that night, he felt an agonizing mix of desire and repulsion as he watched her walk in. Desire kindled by her still-vibrant beauty flaunted in his face, and repulsion born of a sure knowledge that she was trouble. Yet he'd allowed her to seduce him on the bunk of the farthest cell, and when she asked him to accompany her to the burial, he couldn't see how he could refuse since as sheriff he was required to be there anyway. But Lila hadn't paid any attention to the casket being laid in its grave; she'd thrown herself at Rafe right in front of the undertaker's crew until he promised to visit her in her room later.

Unable to fathom what she could be scheming now that she was on her own, he figured the least he had to know was her plan before he could act one way or the other. If he serviced her in bed while finding it out, he guessed that was all right, though making love to a woman who was only using him didn't come anywhere near to fulfilling his fantasies about her over the years. Neither was his pleasure augmented by the suspicion that whatever she had up her sleeve would result in his opposition of Strummar.

Now, staring down the long, dark row of empty cells, Rafe Slater had made himself melancholy with thoughts of his own death. When he heard the horses stop outside, he stood up and looked through the window, then inwardly groaned as he watched the four riders swing down and tie their reins to his hitching rail. Of all the people he didn't want to see right then, Seth Strummar was about the last. But Rafe arranged his face into what he hoped looked like polite welcome as he opened the door.

"Evenin', Rafe," Seth said. "Mind if we come in?"

Slater stood aside and let them all pass. Noting that Lobo had been beat up, Rafe hoped that was why they'd come to see him. Softly he closed the door. "Want some coffee? I could brew a pot."

"No thanks," Seth said, looking at the empty cells with their iron doors open as if in invitation.

Rafe figured he knew some of what the outlaw was feeling as he stared into their darkness. In an instinctive act of separating himself from that fate, the sheriff sat down and put his boots up on the corner of his desk. "Have a seat, why don'cha?" he offered.

Seth moved to the window instead. Joaquín and Blue were standing near the door as if already poised to leave, but Lobo walked over and peered into the closest cell with curiosity. Seth studied the street a moment, then turned around and met Rafe's eyes as he said, "We heard a rumor that someone's after the bank."

"Our bank? Here in Tejoe?" Rafe asked in surprise.

Seth nodded.

"They'd get more money in Tombstone," Rafe argued.

"Have to fight more'n one lawman to take it."

"That's true," he said.

"Nobody here to back you up," Seth said.

"I can deputize men when I need 'em."

"Who'd you have in mind?"

"Haven't thought about it," Rafe said carefully. "Never had the need."

"Maybe you better think about it," Seth said.

"Would you do it?"

"No."

"Joaquín?" Rafe asked, looking at him. The Mexican shook his head. Rafe shifted his eyes to Blue and again received a negative answer. "Why?" he asked. "You're the best guns in the county."

"We ain't lawmen," Seth said.

"You'd be protecting your own interests," Rafe pointed out.

"Don't need a badge to do that."

"No, I guess not," he said. "Who do you think is after the bank?"

"Lila Keats."

Rafe smiled, though he felt his heart go cold. "All by herself?"

"Figure she's got some men lying low."

"What're they waiting for?"

Seth shrugged.

They studied each other in silence. Finally Rafe said, "Don't make sense, Seth. If Bart Keats came here to rob the bank, why would he call you out? Few men could walk away from that, and even if he overestimated his abilities, why risk it if he was after the bank?"

"Lila knows," Seth said.

"I've talked to her more'n once and didn't pick up any hint of a bank job. Has she said something to one of you?"

Seth shook his head.

"Why don't you just fire her?" Rafe asked Blue. "Without a job she'd be forced to move on."

"You could roust her," Blue said.

"I got no cause," Rafe objected.

"I've been rousted by the law plenty without cause," Blue said.

Rafe studied him a moment, then shifted his eyes to Seth. "Are you boys asking me to roust her as a favor to you? Is that the kinda sheriff you want in your town?"

Seth's smile was whimsical. "I'd just as soon do without and let each man fend for himself, but that ain't the way the world's going. I got my money in that bank and I expect my sheriff to protect it."

Rafe couldn't resist a grin. "I'll do my best, and I'm sure it'll be enough since Strummar and Allister are out of business."

Seth laughed. "I ain't the only one with stolen money in that bank."

"I know that," Rafe said.

"Nobody else is gonna be any happier if they lose it."

"I know that, too. But maybe they aren't as adept at preventing it as you might be."

Seth stared at him hard. "We pay three hundred dollars a year in taxes to this county, give money to both churches and contribute to the schoolmarm's salary. I stay home the livelong day, and when I come to town I patronize my friend's establishment so as not to upset anyone. I don't aim to do more'n that along the line of becoming a good citizen."

"I doubt it'll be that easy," Rafe said, striving to keep his voice lightly undemanding. "You can stand 'em off from taking too much but you can't act like you're not connected to everything going on in this town. You're our most famous citizen. It's a little late to try'n pass unnoticed."

"You're not telling me what I want to hear, Rafe."

"You wouldn't like me if I did."

"Okay." Seth nodded. "What're you gonna do about the bank?"

"Come running when I hear shots, I guess. Can't arrest nobody for a crime that ain't happened yet."

"You can't stop one that's already come down either."

"You can keep the culprits from getting away. With any luck that's what we'll do. Then maybe we can send Lila Keats off to prison."

"Jesus," Seth said. "It'd be kinder to kill her."

"Are we talking about kindness?" Rafe smiled. "I lost the topic, if we are."

Seth turned away to look out the window again, and

Rafe studied the men with him. Joaquín was as loyal a follower as a man could have. He'd stand by Seth even when he thought the outlaw was wrong. As for Blue Rivers, Seth had saved him from a hanging back in Texas and there weren't many debts stronger than that. The three of them made an impressive front against the world, each of them owning a top-notch ability with weapons as well as the kind of survival skills that only come from living outside society's protection. Lobo was their Achilles heel, the desire of both of the others as strong as the father's to see that the boy reached manhood without becoming a fugitive. In order to achieve that, Seth had to set an example, and the sheriff well knew it demanded changes that went against the grain.

Rafe studied the boy, his hair blonder than his father's but with the same lanky straightness, his eyes as pale, his mouth set in lines suggestive of a bitter amusement which looked uncanny on the child's face. Even the way he dressed was a copy of his father: quality boots, tailored trousers and vest and linen shirt. The only things missing were the gunbelt and jacket, emblems of authority denied the boy. Smiling at the bruises on Lobo's face, Rafe asked gently, "You get in a fight?"

"Yeah," Lobo said with defiance, making Seth turn around and look at him. "You gonna arrest me for disturbin' the peace?"

Rafe shook his head. "Haven't received a complaint from anybody. Guess you didn't disturb it enough, if getting arrested is what you're after."

"I'll never be arrested," Lobo boasted. "But any time you want to try, go ahead."

Seth took a step across the room and hit Lobo with the back of his hand, sending the boy sprawling into a cell. Except for his initial cry of surprise, Lobo didn't make a sound as he stared incomprehensibly at his father.

"Stand up," Seth said in a low voice.

Slowly Lobo pulled himself to his feet.

"Apologize to the sheriff," Seth said. "Beg his forgiveness for your smart mouth."

"You're shittin' me!" Lobo cried, his eyes indignant with betrayal.

"No, I ain't, Lobo."

He looked at Joaquín, then at Blue, then back at his father. "You never apologized to a lawman in your life!"

"I apologize for my son, Sheriff," Seth said, his eyes on the boy. "He's an ignorant fool who can't control what comes out of his mouth."

"You ain't bein' fair!" Lobo accused. "You're expectin' me to be better'n you."

"Damn straight," Seth said. "We're all waiting for you to act like a man."

Lobo looked at Joaquín again, hoping for help. When Joaquín gave him a small smile of encouragement, Lobo felt like crying. Seth had hit him, and now wanted him to crawl in front of not only Joaquín and Blue but the sheriff. Lobo knew nothing would be the same whether he did it or not. "I don't see I did anything wrong," he said, flat to his father's eyes, "and I refuse to apologize when it'd be a lie."

Seth laughed. "You little shithead," he said with affection. "You're too slick with your words. Go wait outside."

Lobo walked warily across the room, half expecting his father to hit him again, but Seth didn't move except to follow his son with his eyes.

When the boy was out the door, Seth looked at Joaquín, communicating without words how helpless he felt. Lobo was the same rebel he'd been as a child, and Seth well knew the end of that road and was doing his best to spare Lobo the grief. At the moment, though, he felt he'd failed. Joaquín shrugged as if to make light of the incident, but they both knew as well as Lobo that things were different now.

Giving the sheriff an ironic smile, Seth said, "Sorry," then left. Lobo was already on his horse, watching Seth come out, untie the reins to his sorrel and swing on. They looked at each other across the emptiness as Joaquín joined them.

Blue stayed on the boardwalk. "See you around," he said, giving Seth a playful smile. Blue watched the three of them ride away until they were lost in the dark, then he looked at the sheriff. "That's the first time Seth's hit Lobo."

Rafe winced. "Feel like it was my fault."

Blue shook his head. "Seth knew what he was doing bringing Lobo here. He's trying to teach him to get along with the law. Trouble is," he smiled again, "Seth don't really know how to do that himself."

Rafe laughed. "Truth be told, I didn't either 'til I pinned on a badge."

Seth and Joaquín rode abreast as they habitually did, and Lobo followed along a good distance behind. He seethed with anger at Seth, wishing he were big enough to hit him back and do some damage. Someday he would be. Until then he had to build his strength for the challenge he was born to conquer: being better than Seth Strummar.

They rode in silence the whole five miles to the cutoff and halfway home on the trail before Seth turned up the arroyo. Lobo followed with dread to where the horse he'd bought from Lemonade grazed on the stubby grass.

Seth reined up and looked around. "You picked a good spot, Lobo. Course you'd have to move the stake when the forage is this scarce."

"I moved it every day," Lobo said, still wary.

"You want to move it now?" Seth asked.

Lobo slid down and handed Joaquín his reins, feeling Seth's eyes on him as he walked over to the horse and untied the rope from the stake then led the horse back, reclaimed his reins and climbed onto his pinto. Without another word, Seth headed for the road again. Lobo looked at Joaquín, who gave him a gentle smile, then he followed his father, hearing their friend fall in behind.

For hours they rode south across the moonlit desert. In

the distance the San Pedro River was like a satin ribbon reflecting the milky moonlight back at the sky. Twice they approached towns they didn't enter. The lights appeared on the horizon, gradually growing until they filled the desert, then were left behind to be quickly swallowed by the dark. They entered the third town. It was considerably smaller than Tejoe and seemed to consist of little more than the bawdy district. A nearby stamp mill shuddered the ground with its pounding.

Lobo rode between Seth and Joaquín along the street lined with adobe saloons. Their hitching rails were crowded though Lobo figured it must be nearly midnight. Seeing men in front of open doors watch them pass, he realized with a thrill that Seth was known in this town.

They turned off the street and rode through an alley to the back of a saloon where the men dismounted and tied their horses. Lobo still sat his pinto, waiting to learn if he would be allowed inside. Seth studied him a moment then said, "I'd leave you here if I could trust you to stay out of trouble. Since I can't, you're coming in. But you're not to speak unless spoken to. Understand?"

"Yes, sir," Lobo said. He jumped down and tied his horse beside the others, then looked up at his father with a smile.

Seth didn't smile back. He looked at Joaquín, then led them inside.

The room was a swirl of activity. Near the door, a man with his shirtsleeves rolled up was playing a piano, hammering the keys to be heard above the noise that seemed loud enough to lift the roof. Men shouted at the roulette wheel and joked with the painted women, who seemed to squeal at everything they heard. With Joaquín close behind, Lobo followed his father across to the bar, seeing men at the tables quickly look away when Seth turned to face the room. The keep came from the opposite end of the bar and leaned close to hear above the noise.

"Is Ayres around?" Seth asked, barely flicking his gaze

at the keep before returning his attention to the room at large.

The keep nodded, walked from behind the bar and threaded his way through the tables to a door marked private. Lobo watched him knock then disappear inside. In a moment the man came back out and beckoned them over.

Seth walked away as if he'd forgotten Lobo. He tried to stand up proud as he followed his father, feeling so many eyes watching them, but when he looked at Seth's back he felt abandoned and it chiseled away at his courage. As if sensing how he felt, Joaquín laid a hand on his shoulder, and Lobo smiled up at his father's partner with gratitude.

The barkeep passed on his return trip, not looking at them, and Lobo saw that another man was standing in the doorway now. The man smiled and extended his hand. "Seth, good to see you." He turned and shook hands with Joaquín, saying, "Joaquín," then looked at Lobo. "Who's this?"

"Lobo Madera," Seth said. "This is Mr. Ayres."

Lobo felt a rankle of resentment that because his name was Madera this man didn't know he was Seth's son. But all he said was, "Pleased to meet'cha," as he held out his hand.

Ayres laughed and shook with him. "Come on in." He ushered them inside and closed the door, leaving them in quiet. While he was pouring shots of whiskey he asked, "What can I do for you, Seth?"

"Lobo's brought a horse he wants to sell," Seth said.

Ayres handed glasses to the men and raised his own in a toast. "*Salud*," they all said, downing their shots. "What kind of horse?" he asked Lobo.

"A bay gelding," he said.

"Is it a good one?"

"Pretty good," he said.

Ayres laughed. "Why are you selling it then?"

Lobo looked at Seth, who nodded, so Lobo said, "We think it might be stolen."

"Let's take a look," Ayres said. He led them all back outside into the relative quiet of the alley.

Ayres hesitated when he saw the horse. Thoughtfully he approached and examined the animal thoroughly, tracing the overgrown brand on the left hip with his finger, then he leaned on the horse's rump as he looked at Seth across its back. "Where'd you get it?" he asked.

Seth looked at Lobo.

"Bought him off a kid in Tejoe," Lobo said.

"This horse belongs to Fred Dodge," Ayres said. "He lost it chasing train robbers, was left afoot and had to walk back to town."

"What happened to the men he was chasing?" Seth asked.

Ayres smiled. "Two of 'em are sitting inside playing blackjack."

"They from Texas?"

"Matter of fact, they are. Think you might know 'em?"

"I'd like to find out."

"Where do you want it to happen?" Ayres asked amiably.

"Why not right here?"

"Now?"

"Seems easiest," Seth said.

Ayres looked at the horse belonging to Fred Dodge. "All right," he finally said, "but Fred's gonna be disappointed if you kill 'em before he can make an arrest."

"I'm just looking for information," Seth said.

"All right," Ayres said again. He stood up away from the horse and went inside.

Seth nudged the keeper strap off his pistol, then picked up Lobo, set him on the pinto and handed him the reins. "Just sit still and stay quiet," Seth said. He untied his sorrel, draped his reins over its withers and leaned casually with his left elbow on the saddle. Joaquín moved to his own horse and slid his rifle half out of its scabbard. He too draped his reins, ready to leave in a hurry. Lobo patted the warm neck of his pinto as if to calm the horse, but it was his own heart that was pounding.

The door opened and two men stepped out with Ayres. He closed the door and stayed in the shadows, listening.

"Evenin'," Seth said.

The men nodded warily, their hands near their guns.

"Name's Seth Strummar," he said. "This is my partner, Joaquín Ascarate, and the kid's Lobo Madera."

The two men looked at each other, then back at Seth. "Jim Tyler," one of them said, "and my brother Joe."

"I heard Bart Keats used to ride with you boys," Seth said, and Lobo felt a nudge of misgiving that the horse he'd bought from Lemonade might be connected to the killing.

Again the men looked at each other, then Jim said, "We din't have nothin' to do with what happened."

"You weren't there, I know that," Seth said. "What're you doing in Arizona?"

"It's a free country, ain't it?" Joe asked with an edge.

"Long as you follow the law," Seth said with a cool smile. "Selling stolen stock to kids ain't doing that."

Both brothers looked at the bay horse, then at Lobo Madera, then at Seth Strummar taking the part of a street brat. Jim said, "We sold that horse to a kid in Tejoe. What's it to you?"

"That kid's a friend of mine," Seth said. "And I take offense at anyone selling my friends stolen stock."

"Lemonade knew it was stolen," Joe scoffed.

"Lemonade's just a child," Seth said. "He sold that horse to Lobo here, who's a child too. Now all of a sudden Lobo's living with stolen property and that doesn't set well with me."

Joe shrugged. "We'll buy the horse back."

"It belongs to Fred Dodge," Seth said. "Ayres is gonna see it's returned."

"So what're you after?" Jim asked nervously.

"Nothing," Seth said. "I just wanted to get a look at you. If I see you in Tejoe, however, I'll feel different."

"Is that a threat?" Jim snarled.

"Yeah, it is," Seth said. Without taking his eyes from the men, he said under his breath, "Get moving, Lobo."

Lobo reined away, staring back over his shoulder. Joaquín swung onto his black and pulled his rifle from its scabbard. When he was abreast of Lobo, Joaquín raised the gun and rode looking backward. Seth stepped into his stirrup and slowly swung onto his sorrel, watching the men on the ground below, then he yanked his horse around and dug in his spurs. As he caught up with Lobo, he leaned close to slap the pinto's rump. "Move!" he said.

The pinto was already doing that but Lobo kicked in his heels and leaned into the whipping mane. He glanced at Joaquín ahead of him, sliding his rifle back into its scabbard with his horse at a dead run, then at Seth bringing up the rear, and Lobo laughed with excitement. They tore out of the alley onto the main street, turning heads whose faces flashed pale around coldly glinting eyes, then scuttled downhill off the road, galloping into the dark of the desert.

The cadence of running hooves was wild in Lobo's ears. He wished he could fire a gun to express the jubilation he felt, galloping at breakneck speed across the rocky soil. His heart pounded with excitement as he watched Joaquín choose their course with eagle eyes, hearing and feeling Seth's sorrel strain to stay behind his pinto pony. Lobo thought nothing could beat this thrill of being together against the world.

Joaquín was remembering that when he first started riding with Seth they always left town at a dead run, usually with bullets whistling around them. Joaquín didn't like going through it again. Most of all he didn't like the laughter from Lobo, worried that despite Seth's best efforts he was training his son to be a desperado.

A mile out of town they slowed to a walk that soothed them all into a somnolence, and before they were halfway home the young desperado had fallen asleep in his saddle. Seth pulled his son into his lap as Joaquín took the reins and led the pinto along. He smiled at Seth riding ahead with his son nestled against his chest. More than anything, Joaquín wanted to help raise Lobo to an honorable manhood, believing that achievement would balance the crimes of Seth's past and help fulfill his own aim to save Seth's soul.

When they reached the road into Tejoe, Joaquín reined to a stop. "Think I'll ride into town and visit Melinda."

Seth laughed as he took the pinto's reins. "See you in the morning." He waited until Joaquín had disappeared from sight, then he turned his horse and followed his friend toward town.

The hour was so late the saloon was almost empty, and the few men still there didn't seem to notice Seth carrying a child upstairs. He left Lobo asleep on the settee in Blue's office and went back to the balcony to look over the girls still on the floor. There was only one he hadn't had yet. When he smiled his invitation, she came up the stairs swishing her skirts and smiling too.

11

Joaquín jimmied the lock on the back door of La Casa Amarilla and crept silently up the stairs. With the blade of his knife he opened the lock on Melinda's door, latched it behind himself and turned to watch her sleeping.

The moonlight fell across the bed from the open window, and her hair was like a wayward dark stream flowing across the white sheet. When she stirred beneath his gaze, he moved quickly to cover her mouth. Her eyes flared with fear before they softened with recognition. Joaquín smiled and sat up away from her.

"What're you doin' here?" she whispered, sliding deeper under the covers.

"I need to talk with you," he said.

"Couldn't it wait 'til mornin'?"

He shook his head.

She smiled enticingly. "Did'ya come to talk with words or something else, Joaquín?"

He laughed gently. "Now that I'm no longer yours, you want me again?"

"I don't like being alone," she murmured.

He nodded. "What would it take, Melinda, to make you feel that you are not alone?"

"What d'ya mean?" she frowned.

"If you had Seth in your bed, would you feel you had lost your loneliness?"

She smiled again. "A man like him could overpower anything else in a girl's life."

"And to lose such a man? Would that also overpower anything else, even a husband?"

"I don't have a husband," she said.

"Lila Keats did."

Melinda studied him in silence a moment, then threw the covers off and stood up. In her transparent nightgown she walked across to the washstand and slowly poured herself a glass of water. Just as slowly she drank it down. When she turned to face him, she smiled as he raised his gaze from her body to meet her eyes again. "I can see you want me, Joaquín," she whispered in a baffled tone, "yet you stayed away from me all those months. Why?"

"You didn't want me," he said.

"I do now."

"Only because we are alone. If Seth were here you would prefer him. Or if Blue walked through that door, you would also choose him over me. I wonder if you would be content even then, or if you would covet me because I wasn't yours."

She threw her hair back off her face in the gesture of defiance he knew well. "You're sayin' I'll never be happy no matter who's in my bed."

"Not quite." He smiled gently. "It's just that I don't think the man in your bed has much to do with it."

"What does?"

"You tell me. What is it you really want, Melinda?"

She didn't answer but moved to the window and looked out on the moonlit desert. He walked across to stand behind her, lifting the weight of her hair away from her neck and kissing the damp warmth of her skin. "Tell me what you want, Melinda,'' he said softly, ''and I will help you get it.''

''Why?'' she whispered.

''Because we both love Seth. Isn't that enough?''

She snorted with disdain. ''So you admit you love him.''

''I have never denied it,'' he said, turning her to face him. ''But I didn't take your advice.''

''What advice?''

''Don't you remember what you said the last night we slept together?''

She shook her head.

He sighed. ''You said I should let Seth rape me to learn how it was done.'' He brushed her hair back, watching the memory tremble on her face. ''Do you remember now?''

She looked at him, her eyes full of pain.

''Don't worry,'' he said. ''The hurt you gave has been gone a long time. I don't understand why you want to be raped, why you would choose that over love, but I understand that we both want the best for him, and I came tonight seeking your help.''

After a moment she asked, ''What can I do?''

''I suspect Lila has a grudge against him, but he doesn't remember her, so maybe it was a brother or father. Find out if she ever used another name; maybe that would help Seth remember. Can you do that?''

''Yes,'' she said, then studied Joaquín with a mischievous light in her eyes. ''Did you really watch him have his way with her?''

''I watched. I wouldn't say that's what happened.''

''What would you say?''

''He frightened her.''

''Oh yeah, he scared her, all right.'' She moved away to sit on the edge of her bed. ''When she came over here she was shakin' like a leaf. If she's goin' up against Seth, it's takin' all of her courage to do it. What d'ya think could drive her so hard?''

''I don't know,'' he said.

She hesitated as if weighing her odds, then asked, "If I help, will you get Blue to give me her job?"

Joaquín too hesitated before asking, "Do you know he uses the girls who work for him?"

She shrugged. "Most men who own saloons do that."

"Do you know what he likes from his girls?"

"I can guess," she answered softly.

"Would you enjoy that?"

"As long as he didn't get too rough."

"Sometimes Seth watches. Did you know that?"

"No." She smiled impishly. "What about you, Joaquín? Do you watch, too?"

He leaned against the wall with a sigh. "I stay downstairs and watch the goddamned door." He laughed. "Sorry. It's an old joke."

"Between you and Seth?"

He nodded. "Would you like to know what it is?"

"Yes," she answered eagerly.

"It was when he was married. I convinced him it wouldn't be real unless sanctified by the Church, but when we went to the priest he refused to do it. I promised that if he performed the ceremony, I would dedicate my life to bringing Seth to God. Even then, when we were standing before the altar, the padre insisted Seth take off his gun and kneel. Seth didn't want to do it, but finally he looked at me with such humor in his eyes, such mockery and yet love, too, for my soul, and he handed me his gun and said, 'Watch the goddamned door.' " Joaquín laughed. "That's what I've been doing ever since."

She stared with bewilderment a moment then whispered, "Is that enough for you, Joaquín?"

"It is too much." He stood up straight and moved almost silently across the room as he said, "I will visit you again tomorrow night to find out what you learned." He turned back at the door with a smile. "Don't wait up for me."

*   *   *

The next morning Seth woke up in Lobo's room. At first he didn't know where he was, then he saw his son asleep and remembered putting the child to bed and stretching out beside him, telling himself he'd just lie down for a minute. Now he recognized that as self-deception. The question was why he'd chosen not to go to Rico's bed.

From the angle of sunlight, he guessed it was close to seven. He stepped into his trousers and gathered the rest of his clothes, then tiptoed across the room and eased the door open to peer out. Though he could hear the women working in the kitchen, the parlor was empty, the door to Rico's bedroom wide open. He looked back at Lobo, awake now watching him. "You best move or you'll be late for school," Seth said softly.

"Do I have to go?" Lobo asked.

"No. But the next time you ask to tag along on a late night errand, I'll have to say you can't 'cause you'll miss school the next day."

"I'll go," Lobo said.

Seth smiled, then eased the door shut behind himself.

Lobo looked at Seth's gun and hat hanging on the bedpost. Carefully he lifted the hat off, laid it on the pillow, and eased the pistol from the holster. It was a Colt's .44 that Lobo knew Seth had carried way back when he rode with Allister, when he'd been an outlaw and committed the crimes Texas still held against him. Lobo raised the heavy gun with both hands and sighted down the barrel, imagining how a lawman would look facing Seth Strummar's gun. He didn't mean to pull the trigger. He barely touched it. But the gun boomed in the early morning quiet, shattering the window glass and throwing Lobo backwards. He was sprawled on the bed with the barrel between his knees when Seth opened the door.

Lobo grinned. "Guess it's got a hair trigger."

Seth nodded. "I've told you more'n once not to touch it."

"I was just lookin' at it," Lobo said.

"Put it back."

Lobo did, then settled the hat carefully above it again.

"I'll let it slide this time, Lobo," Seth said, " 'cause I don't guess I should've left it there. But if you disobey me again, I'm gonna have to do something about it."

"You gonna hit me?" Lobo taunted, the cockiness in his voice undermined by a quiver of fear.

"If that's what it takes," Seth said. "Now go wash up for school."

Lobo approached cautiously, keeping his distance as he slid past his father in the door. Seth sighed and went into the room, settled his hat on his head and lifted the gunbelt off the bedpost, then walked back out. Rico was standing in the kitchen door watching him.

"Mornin'," he said, returning to her room. Tossing his hat and gunbelt on her bed as he walked to the washstand, he filled the basin from the pitcher. He disliked a cold shave but wouldn't ask for hot water, didn't want to talk to her at all, though he couldn't explain it any more than he could say why he was suddenly calling it her room instead of theirs. He scraped his razor across his whiskers, dunked it in the basin of water, then looked into the mirror to do it again and saw her standing in the door behind him. He kept on shaving until he was done, dried his face with a towel, and walked across to the chiffonnier for a clean shirt. It wasn't until he was buttoning it that he looked at her without having the mirror between them.

"I missed you last night," she said with a hopeful smile.

"We got in late, didn't want to wake you." He knew it was lame; he often came in late and not only slept in her bed but woke her with his attentions.

"What kept you?" she asked carefully.

"Rode down to Charleston on our way home."

"Any special reason?"

He turned his back as he opened his trousers to tuck in his shirttails, then looked out the window as he buckled on his gun and said, "Think I'll ride Lobo to school again today."

She crossed the room to stand beside him. "What happened last night?"

He ran through all the things he could tell her. Settling on the one that mattered most, he said, "I hit Lobo."

"Oh, Seth," she moaned with compassion. "What had he done?"

"It was what he said. Sassing the sheriff like a hundred two-bit punks I've known."

She reached up and tucked a strand of hair behind his ear. "Lobo only wants to be like you, Seth. Imagine how it confuses him when you fight it so hard."

"I'm right, he's wrong."

She smiled sadly. "How many times did your father say that to you?"

"With every lick of the whip," he admitted.

"Nothing's changed, Seth," she argued softly. "Just because it happened once doesn't mean all your efforts have been wasted."

"We'll see," he said.

She waited for him to touch her, but he kept studying the view outside the window as if he'd never seen it before. "What about Lila Keats?" she asked. "Did you learn anything useful?"

He shook his head. "I found out Lobo was keeping a horse in the arroyo between here and the road. That's what we went to Charleston for, to get rid of it."

"Keeping a horse? Why?"

"He's been sneaking into town after we're asleep, hanging out in the saloons and playing craps in the alley."

Rico sighed. "He's only seven."

"That's a helpful observation," Seth said.

She had to admit the justice of his sarcasm. "I guess I haven't been much help lately, have I?"

Finally he looked at her. "No, you haven't. All I've heard from you is one accusation after another."

"I'm sorry," she said. "I've been feeling out of sorts lately."

"Why?"

She hesitated, then plunged ahead, "We're going to have another child."

"Jesus Christ!" he exploded. "Elena's barely a year old!"

"That's a helpful observation." She smiled through her tears.

Seth whirled around, swept his hat off the bed and stalked toward the door. On the threshold he turned back and said, "Get rid of it, Rico."

"You don't mean that," she whispered.

"The hell I don't! I don't want any more responsibility!"

"Neither do I!" she shouted. "But I won't kill our child! I can't believe that's what you really want." She crumpled to the floor, hugging her knees as she cried.

He stared at her, then quietly closed the door and tossed his hat on their bed. Sitting on the floor in front of her, he pulled her into his lap. "Don't cry, Rico. You're right, it's not what I want. I wasn't ready for it, is all. We'll handle it, just like we've handled everything else. I mean, it's only another baby, right? What's so hard about a baby?"

"Nothing for you," she sobbed against his shirt. "You don't have to carry it for nine months and then have your insides torn out bringing it into the world. All you have to do is love us, Seth. Can you do that?"

"Yeah," he said, lifting her face to kiss the tears from her cheeks.

She met his eyes. "Are you sure? I need your love so badly."

He smiled. "Don't worry, Rico. I'll always be here to take care of you."

"Always?"

"As long as I'm alive."

"And you'll stay alive, Seth? For as long as we need you?"

"I'll do my best," he said.

She sighed deeply and leaned against his chest as they sat on the floor. Her hair was the golden color of sunlight, its wispy tendrils smelling of flowers. He closed his eyes and surrendered for a moment to the familiar comfort of holding her body, a feminine enclosure promising succor that thrived in his strength, withered in his weakness, survived only as well as he did.

A low knock came on the door. Sorry to be disturbed so soon, Seth said with a patient sigh, "Come on in, Lobo."

The boy pushed the door open and stood staring at them. "What are you doin' on the floor?" he finally asked.

Seth smiled. "We like it here."

Rico sat up and wiped her nose on her handkerchief, then she, too, gave the child a smile.

"I just came to say goodbye," Lobo said. "I'm leaving for school now."

"I'll ride with you," Seth said. "Wait for me outside."

"Okay," Lobo said, closing the door as he left.

Seth looked at Rico. "I'll get a board to cover the window in his room. It'll take a while to order new glass."

She nodded but didn't say anything.

"Guess we'll need a new bed, too, so we can move Elena out of the cradle when the baby's born."

Again she nodded, this time with a smile.

He laughed. "You're happy about it, ain't you."

"Yes," she answered. "But only if I get to keep you too."

He stood up with a sigh, looking out the window as he adjusted the weight of the gun on his hip. "Well, as long as Lila Keats doesn't get away with whatever she's got up her sleeve, reckon I'll be around." He gave Rico a smile, then walked through the parlor and across the yard to find out if Joaquín had made it home last night.

12

Lobo left them at the turnoff to the school yard. Seth sat watching after his son a moment, then he and Joaquín ambled on toward town. Though the sky was blue and the sun bright, the breeze carried the chill of winter. "Next January I'll be thirty-five," Seth said with a wry smile. "Never thought I'd live this long."

Joaquín smiled back.

"Rico's pregnant again," Seth said glumly. "She told me this morning."

"Congratulations!"

Seth snorted. "That makes four I know about. I think it's enough, don't you?"

"That is never for us to say."

"There's ways to stop it. Working girls know how to get rid of it when they want to."

"Yes," Joaquín snapped, his eyes suddenly angry. "I'm sure Rico knows all about it, and if she wanted such a solution, I am also sure she wouldn't take you into her counsel."

Seth smiled. "Don't get mad at me, Joaquín. I'm just making conversation."

"As lightly as you make love," he muttered. "You said you have four you know about. Were you trying for another at Blue's last night?"

Seth laughed. "It's a natural urge, you know. Not all of us can be monks in control of our baser instincts. Besides, what about your visit to Melinda?"

"I haven't made love to her since I knew we weren't right for each other. It's been well over a year now."

"You slept with her all that time without touching her?" Seth asked, incredulous.

"I slept in the loft," Joaquín said, looking away.

Seth laughed gently. "I only kept her around 'cause I thought you wanted her. Why didn't you speak up?"

"She needed us."

"And now she doesn't?"

"It was because her friendship with Rico went sour that Melinda had to leave."

Seth frowned. "Would you have given up your room forever?"

"It was only a bed." Joaquín shrugged. "The loft was just as warm."

"Not as warm as a bed shared with a woman."

Joaquín met his eyes. "I'm not the sort of man who finds rape a comfortable prelude to sleep."

"Seems to me," Seth drawled, "a woman sleeping in a man's bed can't fairly cry rape if he takes advantage of the situation."

"The world often seems different to you than to me," Joaquín replied.

"Can't argue with that," Seth agreed. "How long you gonna pay her rent?"

"Until I don't feel like paying it."

"Fair enough. If you didn't sleep with her last night, why'd you go see her?"

"To ask her help against Lila Keats."

"Is she gonna help us?"

"Yes. She asked a favor in return."

"Not surprising. What does she want?"

"For Blue to give her a job."

"I don't mind if Blue doesn't," Seth said, "but wouldn't you rather she go back to Tombstone?"

"And whore for a living again?"

He shrugged. "It ain't your fault you couldn't change her."

"We did change her, Seth. We showed her another kind of life, made her think it was hers, then dumped her back where we found her. I don't think it was right."

"What do you suggest we do about it?" he asked, straining for patience.

"Give her Lila's job."

"That's up to Blue," Seth hedged. "He doesn't like Melinda much, you know."

"That should make it easy to keep his hands off her."

"You laying that down as a condition of the arrangement?"

Joaquín nodded.

"I'll run it by him, Joaquín. But I ain't gonna push him to agree to it."

"If he knows it's what you want, he will agree."

"Can't see how he could since I don't. You're the one who wants it."

"Doesn't that affect your opinion at all?"

Seth sighed. "Looks like Melinda's got a job."

They found Blue in his office, and they all walked over to Amy's Cafe for breakfast again. By the time they were seated at the same corner table, the dirty faces of the street boys were pressed against the windows. Amy closed the curtains before coming over to greet them.

"Good to see you, Seth, Joaquín," she said, then with a warmer smile, "Mornin', Blue."

He smiled back. "Mornin', Amy. You got biscuits in the oven?"

"Just about to pop out," she said. "Specials all around?"

Blue nodded and watched her until she was gone, then grinned at his friends. "Never hurts to have a good cook on your side."

The men sat in a comfortable silence until Amy came back with their breakfast. She gave Blue a mischievous smile, then returned to the kitchen. He cut open a biscuit and spread butter to melt in the steam. "Look at that biscuit," he said. "Ain't it perfect?"

Seth laughed. "Sounds like you're in love, Blue."

"I'm in love with these biscuits, I'll admit that," he said.

"How about Lila?" Seth asked, cutting a wedge of ham. "Think you could part with her?"

Blue poured cream in his coffee and stirred it a while, then laid the spoon quietly in the saucer and met Seth's eyes when he said, "Anytime."

"What's the hesitation?"

He leaned back with a sigh. "We have a lot of wicked fun. You know what I mean, Seth. The kind I haven't had since I became a respectable property owner."

Seth sipped his coffee to camouflage his smile. "Joaquín suggested you give Melinda the job."

Blue glanced at Joaquín then looked at Seth. "I don't like her much."

"I think she'll do well by you," Seth countered.

Blue studied Seth, then Joaquín. Finally he gave Seth a sardonic grin and said, "Maybe the fun'll be more wicked with a woman I don't like anyway."

"That isn't what I had in mind," Joaquín objected.

"You staking a claim on her again?" Blue asked.

Joaquín shook his head.

"Then once she's in my employ," Blue said softly, "what happens between us is nobody else's business."

Knowing this wouldn't be the last time he'd have to intercede, Seth said, "Joaquín thinks Melinda needs us, and there's enough of a priest left in him to want to help her out.''

''Help her do what?'' Blue asked testily.

''Have a nice life,'' Joaquín answered.

''Managing my saloon?''

''So you will be free to indulge your wickedness until perhaps you become weary of it.''

Seth laughed. ''He'll save your soul, Blue, if you keep company with us much longer.''

''Sounds like a fate worse'n death,'' Blue muttered, reaching for another biscuit. He carefully split it with his knife and spread the two halves with butter, thinking of the pink skin of the woman who'd made the biscuits. He had vowed to stay away from her because she deserved better than the likes of him. But as he met Joaquín's dark eyes across the table, Blue decided maybe his wicked days were over. ''Okay. I'll hire Melinda as my manager and I give my word not to touch her. Does that please you, *padre*?''

Joaquín smiled. ''Yes,'' he said.

When they walked outside, the urchins were still on the boardwalk. Seth looked them over then asked, ''Is one of you named Lemonade?''

''He is!'' several boys chirped, pointing their fingers.

The kid was a scrawny twelve, thirteen at the outside. His clothes were close to rags and he was barefoot, his face angular with a cupid's bow mouth and watery blue eyes under a shock of dirty brown hair. ''Are you Lemonade?'' Seth asked him.

The kid nodded.

''I heard you'd do a favor with discretion.''

''Might,'' he said.

''Need you to take a ride with us. Are you free?''

''Where to?''

''Out in the country.''

''What for?''

''Looking for something.''

''What?''

"I'll tell you on the way."

"What's in it for me?"

"Five bucks and supper."

"Five bucks?" the boy asked with suspicion. "Jus' to help ya find something?"

Seth tossed him a gold piece, halfway expecting him to run with it. Lemonade pocketed the coin, however, and stepped forward. "I ain't got a horse," he said.

"We'll get you one," Seth said. He turned to Blue. "Can you handle your personnel problems?"

"Yeah," he answered unhappily.

Seth laughed. "Don't blame me. It was Joaquín's idea." He smiled at his partner, then the street urchin he had just taken on. "Come on," Seth said. "Let's get you a horse."

Blue watched them walk away, puzzled as to what Seth wanted with Lemonade. The kid was as dishonest as he was dirty, a punk about to cross the line into true criminality, and Blue wouldn't have conducted any business with him no matter how petty. He expected the kid to get away with the horse, if not a lot more, and he wondered if maybe he should have warned Seth. But apparently Seth had heard otherwise about Lemonade. That made Blue doubt himself, something he didn't do often. He had to concede he'd made a mistake hiring Lila, though, and couldn't help wonder if he hadn't made another by agreeing to replace her with Melinda, a woman he didn't even like. Now he was watching Seth walk away with the worst punk in town, and Blue could only think either he was losing his edge or Seth was, or maybe the world was changing around them so fast nothing fit right anymore.

Blue turned and saw the boys watching after one of their own walking away with a top gun. An honor like that could change a kid's life, set it straight again just because a man of Seth's stature had picked him out of the gutter. Seth had done that for Blue, saved him from being hanged and taken him out of the outlaw life. By setting him up in business, Seth had also given him a semblance of respectability, and Blue guessed there was a chance Seth could do the same for Lemonade. He turned away from the boys who hadn't been chosen and walked toward La Casa Amarilla, where two women lived across the hall of opportunity from each other.

Seth looked down at the filthy kid walking beside him. "Lobo tells me you sold him a horse," he said with a friendly smile.

Lemonade didn't believe the smile. "Ya mad about it?" he asked cautiously.

"No," Seth said. "Curious where you got it, is all."

"Bought it off some men," the kid said.

"Where?"

"Out in the country."

"Could you find the place again?"

"Sure."

"That's what I want you to do," Seth said.

Lemonade thought a minute, then asked, "What's gonna happen if they're still there? Ya gonna kill 'em?"

"Would that bother you?"

"No," he said.

"Then don't worry about it," Seth said.

They reached their horses at the back of Blue's saloon. Seth swung on and held a hand down for Lemonade. When he took it and leapt up behind, Seth had to suppress a cough at the kid's stench. He kicked his horse into a canter to create a breeze, then reined up in front of the general store. "Get down," he said gruffly.

Lemonade slid over the horse's rump.

Seth swung off and tied his reins. "We'll just be a minute," he told Joaquín, then jerked his head for Lemonade to follow him.

Inside, everyone stopped what they were doing and stared at the outlaw coming in. Lemonade stayed behind as Seth walked across to the counter, the metallic ring of his spurs accompanying the echo of his footsteps in the sudden silence.

Seth turned around at the counter and looked at the kid, then at Maurice Engle behind the register. Rumor said the merchant had once robbed a bank in Arkansas, and it seemed to Seth their common history should create a bond of camaraderie between them. But from the sour expression on Engle's face it was evident he didn't share that expectation.

"Can I help you, Mr. Strummar?" he asked with stiff politeness.

"Need some clothes for the boy," Seth said. "Something sturdy and not too expensive."

"Certainly," the merchant said, going to the shelves and taking a pair of dungarees down. "What color shirt?" he called. "Blue, brown or green?"

Seth looked at Lemonade.

"Green," the kid said.

Engle came back and laid the garments on the counter, pushing them gingerly toward Seth. "Anything else?"

"Socks and drawers and some boots, I reckon," Seth said. "And you might as well throw in a handkerchief. Maybe he'll learn how to use it."

Engle's smile was cool. He added the items to the pile and asked, "A belt?"

"All right," Seth said, knowing the milking was about to commence.

"How about a hat?" Engle asked.

Seth smiled at Lemonade. "You want a hat?"

"Sure!"

"Go pick one out." Watching him move eagerly to the display, Seth called, "Don't touch any of 'em."

When Lemonade chose a slouch in fine, black beaver, Engle gloated as he found the right size in the row of boxes on a high shelf. He set the box on the counter and asked, "Will he be wearing them home, Mr. Strummar?"

"No, he needs a bath first. And you best throw in some kinda medicine for lice. What do I owe you?"

"Thirty-seven-fifty," the merchant said, wrapping the bundle with paper that crackled in his hands.

Seth took the bills from his wallet, then fished into his pocket for the fifty cents. He slid the money toward the merchant, but Engle wouldn't meet his eyes. Seth looked at Lemonade and said, "You can carry it."

At Esquibel's livery, Seth bought the cheapest horse and the sorriest saddle the hostler had. Esquibel was so cowed he didn't even bother to haggle but agreed to Seth's first offer. Again, when the money was exchanged, the businessman wouldn't meet Seth's eyes.

Waiting for Lemonade to saddle and mount his new horse, Seth looked at Joaquín, whose dark eyes were warm with affection. Seth smiled, thinking it would be a cold world without his partner.

When the three of them had ambled a short distance out of town, Seth reined up and looked across at the kid. "The clothes are yours, the horse and saddle are mine. You run off with 'em and I'll hang you as a horse thief. Do you understand me?"

"Yes, sir," Lemonade answered.

"All right," Seth said. "Now I'm taking you home. My wife and daughter and another lady live there. I expect you to act like a gentleman. You think you can do that?"

"Yes, sir," he said again.

"Tonight after supper," Seth said, "we'll go looking for your friends, so don't get too comfy in my home. If you do a good job, I'll give you the horse on the condition you skedaddle and I never see you again. Agreed?"

"Yes, sir," the kid said with a smile this time.

"All right," Seth said. "Let's go."

When Lobo came home from school that afternoon, he saw a strange horse in the corral. The horse was too scrawny to be one Seth would buy, and Lobo approached slowly, wondering who was visiting. Then he saw Lemonade hunkered in the shadow of the stable. He was wearing new clothes, even boots, and a hat better than Lobo's. Lobo reined up and stayed on his pinto. "What're you doin' here?"

"Seth brung me," Lemonade answered, squinting into the sun.

"What for?"

"Says he needs my help to find some men."

Lobo thought about that a minute, then said, "The ones who sold you the horse?"

"Yeah," Lemonade said. "Is Seth gonna kill 'em?"

"I'll kill *you* if you say that again," Lobo snarled.

"Take it easy," Lemonade wheedled. "Bein' as I'm gonna be along, I think it's a fair question."

"Why don't you ask *him,* then?" Lobo snapped. He jerked his horse around and trotted to the gate, opened it and rode through, then latched it behind himself.

Lemonade climbed the fence and followed him into the stable. "Nice place ya got," he said.

Lobo swung down and lifted the stirrup to untie the cinch. Being only seven, he had to reach the full stretch of his arms to pull the saddle off, then heft with all his strength to throw it across the rack. Breathing hard he turned around and looked at Lemonade. "Did Seth buy you those clothes?"

"Yeah," the older boy said proudly.

"That horse too?"

He shook his head. "Only if I do the job good."

Lobo went back to his pinto, tugged its head down so he could pull the bridle over its ears, then slapped it out into the corral with the other horses. Looking at his friend again, he asked, "Do I get to go along?"

Lemonade shrugged.

"Sonofabitch," Lobo said. He started out then turned back to look at Lemonade still standing there. "Why don't you come up to the house?" he asked. "What're you doin' down here in the barn anyway?"

"Waitin' for ya," Lemonade said.

"Well, come on," Lobo said, letting him catch up so they walked abreast out of the stable.

They climbed the fence and crossed the yard toward the house. Lobo felt strange walking in with a friend at his side. That the friend was working for Seth made it feel even stranger. He wondered why nothing was ever normal

in his family. As they walked through the parlor he tried
to imagine how Lemonade was seeing it.

They had hardly any furniture, just the settee covered
with an old Indian blanket in front of the hearth. There
were no portraits on the wall or flowers on the mantle,
none of the stuff typical in other peoples' parlors. Then
Lobo remembered that Lemonade usually slept in Engle's
warehouse, and if he didn't sneak in before the last door
was locked he slept outside. If it was cold, Alfonso Esquibel let the boys sleep in the loft of his livery, but when
it was warm he said they carried bugs and ran them off
with a pitchfork if he caught them in his hay.

Hearing quiet laughter from the kitchen, Lobo caught a
fleeting look of envy on his friend's face.

"Sounds like a party," Lemonade said, "but I don't
guess they'll let us drink."

Lobo didn't bother to answer. When he entered the
kitchen, the men were at the table, the whiskey in plain
view, while the women worked at the stove. Lobo sat
down in his usual place as if nothing were different.

"Sit over here, Lemonade," Joaquín said, pulling a
chair out beside him.

"Thanks," the kid mumbled, sitting down and not looking at anyone.

"How was school?" Seth asked.

Lobo shrugged. "All right."

"You talk to the Nickles boys?"

"Yeah."

"What'd you say?"

"I'll give 'em more any time they want it!"

"What'd they say?"

"That their father whipped 'em for it."

Seth sipped his whiskey. "How'd that make you feel?"

"He shouldn't't've done it!" Lobo cried indignantly. "It
was between them and me."

"Guess Abneth didn't see it that way," Seth said. "It's
a funny thing about being a father. You feel responsible

for what your children do, but I don't expect you to understand that for another ten years or so.''

"At least," Rico said, giving Seth a teasing smile.

Lobo hated seeing it, the way Rico could make his father's eyes light up just by smiling in a certain way. He couldn't figure what was so great about her. Esperanza did the laundry and kept the house clean while Rico spent a lot of time alone with Seth in their bedroom. Lobo knew what they were doing in there and that his father liked it. He just couldn't figure why Seth liked Rico. All she did was parade around with Elena as if the baby was a badge of honor.

Lobo didn't even especially like his sister. She was cute when she laughed, but most of the time she was just a bundle of crying and diapering as far as he could see. Sometimes, though, Seth sounded as if he liked her better than Lobo. There were too many women on the homestead, in Lobo's opinion. He wished Rico and the baby weren't there and it was just the men and Esperanza. She did the work and was a constant source of comfort, never a problem. Lobo thought she was pretty near perfect, whereas Rico was always coming between him and Seth.

Like right now. Seth was watching her at the stove rather than paying attention to his son. Lobo felt angry that Seth was playing with him by not saying straight out whether he could go along to find the outlaws. Losing patience, he jeered, "Why don't you just tell me?"

Still, it took Seth a minute to drag his eyes off Rico. Then he gave Lobo an amused smile. "You want to go?"

Lobo was tempted to deny it just to spite him, but Esperanza was faster.

"No, Seth!" she protested. "He is too young."

Seth looked at Rico. "What do you think?"

"I agree with Esperanza."

"Joaquín?" Seth asked.

"I, also," he said softly.

Seth smiled. "Lemonade?"

Lobo held his breath.

"We might need someone to hold the horses," Lemonade suggested.

"Yeah, we might," Seth agreed, smiling at Lobo. "What do you think, Joaquín? If we leave him back with the horses, he should be up to the job, don't you think?"

"*Sí,*" Joaquín said in a flat tone. "He is up to the job but defenseless if shot at."

"What have you got to say, Lobo?" Seth asked.

"I want to go," he said.

"Why?"

Lobo ignored everyone else as he met his father's eyes. "I want to be a man."

Seth smiled. "Okay, you're in." He looked sharply at the women. "That's it," he said.

Esperanza turned her back and Rico shook her head.

"If supper ain't on this table in five minutes," he said, "we're going without."

"At least you can feed your son," Esperanza huffed, "before you keep him up 'til dawn for the second time in a row."

"We were home by midnight," Seth said.

"It was four-thirty," she answered, lifting the whiskey from the table. "I looked at my clock."

"Next time I'll come bang on your door so you be sure· and not miss our return."

She smiled. "That would be thoughtful. Then I could sleep peacefully, knowing my family is safe at home."

Seth laughed and slapped her bottom as she moved away, then met Rico's eyes. "Well, hurry up," he said. "I don't think I can stand all this feminine censure much longer."

13

Esperanza eased the corral gate open as quietly as she could, then opened the stable door, too, with care for her silence. She moved through the familiar darkness to saddle Rico's palomino, knowing it was the only horse on the place she had any hope of controlling.

Carefully she led the palomino through the barn door and corral gate, leaving both open so she wouldn't risk waking Rico when she returned. Esperanza stepped into the stirrup and pulled her bulk into the saddle, sat gathering the reins a moment as she stared at the dark house, then slowly eased the mare out of the yard. Only when she was beyond the mountain did she urge the horse into a lope that cut distance fast.

She had never been to the tenderloin, but she followed the music of the tinny pianos through the quiet of the sleeping town. The street was illuminated with light spilling from the saloons, and Blue's was easy to spot. Its sign was the most brightly lit, its hitching rail crowded with the best quality horses, and the din escaping from inside car-

ried the loudest laughter with its ribald music. Esperanza
tied the palomino in a shadow and pulled her shawl close
over her breasts as she stepped onto the boardwalk. Years
had passed since she'd approached a saloon, and even back
then she hadn't been alone. She stopped warily at the edge
of the batwing doors and peered in.

The front room was the least congested. Only a few men
were drinking sociably at the tables, a few more bellying
up to the bar. The sweeping staircase separated them from
the gaming room in back. The tables there were crowded,
and beyond them, on a small stage against the far wall, an
old man played a piano. A singer sat on top of it with her
skirts drawn up above her knees. Remembering the lustful
stares of men in saloons, Esperanza almost turned around
and went home.

It had been easier when she was young and could laugh
at the greedy hunger in men's eyes. She and all her sisters
in the profession had known how men's insatiable need
could provide a living, and they'd used that knowledge
with a frivolous disregard for anyone's opinion of women
who satisfied men for money. Now that she was older she
couldn't ignore how the men's eyes demeaned those very
women, naming them receptacles of pain.

Esperanza, however, was no longer one of those women.
It was true Seth often came to her bed in the middle of
the night, but her staying at the homestead wasn't dependent on servicing him. Sometimes she even felt he made
love to her more because she wanted it than because he
did. She was forty-four, after all, and Seth certainly had
his choice if variety was his only motive. But Esperanza
suspected he had taken on the duty of her satisfaction because he felt responsible for Ramon kicking her out. Seth
would never tell her that, of course, just as she would never
tell him she felt responsible for his having hanged Oriana.

In Esperanza's mind, people were responsible for what
they didn't prevent as much as for what they caused to
happen. And though she'd loved Seth from the beginning,
she hadn't warned him of Oriana's existence or the poison

Allister's letters had planted. When Oriana used that weapon to destroy what was left of the men's friendship, she was able to do it because of Esperanza's silence.

Determined not to fail again, Esperanza resolutely entered the saloon. A few men glanced at her and looked away without even curiosity, though the barkeep studied her with suspicion. She smiled as she approached, then stood on tiptoe to lean across the bar and ask for Blue. The keep raised his eyes to the second floor. Esperanza followed his gaze and saw a burly, bearded man watching from the top of the stairs. The man nodded and walked deeper into the shadows of the balcony. He came back with Blue, who stood at the railing a moment before coming down and crossing the room toward her. He nodded at the keep, then took her elbow as he steered her toward the door.

"What are you doing here, Esperanza?" he asked softly.

"I came to see Lila Keats."

Blue stopped and studied her a moment. "Where's Seth?"

"Hunting," she answered with a smile.

"Is Joaquín with him?"

"Lobo, too. I don't like leaving Rico home alone, so I must hurry." She let her gaze drift across the women in the gaming room. "Is Lila Keats here?"

"Upstairs," Blue said.

Esperanza looked at him sharply. "Is hard for a manager to watch the floor from behind a closed door, no? Or perhaps you wish more that she watch the ceiling?"

Blue chuckled deep in his throat. "You know Seth wouldn't like you being here."

"If I wish to earn a few dollars telling fortunes, are you gonna make me take my business down the street?"

"No," he said reluctantly. "But I'll give you money if that's what you're after."

"It is more'n that," she admitted.

He nodded. "You best watch your step. It's hard to

predict what Lila's gonna do. If you give her dire news, she may not jump the way you expect."

"I will only say what the cards reveal," Esperanza answered.

Still he hesitated. "Okay," he finally said. "I'll send her down, but as soon as you've read her fortune, Nib'll take you home."

"I got here on my own, and I can get home that way, too."

"I don't doubt it, but I'm still gonna send Nib with you."

She shrugged. "Suit yourself."

"I intend to. You stay down in this end of the room."

"How can I get business from here?"

He looked around at the solitary drinkers and the few clusters of men engrossed in conversation. "I'll send some of the girls over. How much you gonna charge?"

"One dollar." She smiled. "Is a fair price to know the future, don't you think?"

He studied her morosely. "I'll tell Gus to keep an eye on you. If you need help, he's there at the bar."

"Thanks," she said.

He nodded and walked away. She watched him take a girl aside and give her a silver dollar from his pocket. The girl stared apprehensively at Esperanza a moment, then warily walked toward her.

Lemonade led the way into the mountains, followed by Seth, Lobo, and Joaquín. They caught an old Indian trail heading southeast, then climbed an arroyo onto a plateau, traveled the ridge south and stopped on the edge of a natural bowl gouged out of the range. From a spot in the far end of the valley, the smoke of a campfire rose gray into the black sky.

"That'll most likely be them," Lemonade said softly.

"How many?" Seth asked.

"Was five last time."

"Was Bart Keats one of 'em?"

Lemonade nodded. "I was there when ya killed him. I saw him come in and was tryin' to vamoose 'fore he seen me, then when he called ya out I stopped and watched, knowin' it wasn't me he was after."

"Why'd you think it might be?"

Lemonade squirmed in his saddle, looked back at Lobo, then squinted unhappily at Seth. "Do I have to tell?"

"You're working for me now, Lemonade, and I need to know everything I can."

Again the kid twisted in his saddle to look at Lobo. "I din't do it to hurt ya, Lobo."

"What'd you do?" he cried, already angry that Lemonade had been there to see Seth shoot Bart Keats.

Lemonade looked at Seth again. "It was Bart told me to sell Lobo that horse."

"Why?"

"He promised he wouldn't harm Lobo none, but that he wanted ya caught with stolen prop'ty."

"Didn't you think hurting me would hurt Lobo?"

Lemonade's eyes flashed with fun. "I figgered ya was up to it, Mr. Strummar. 'Sides, I went into the Blue Rivers that night to tell ya 'bout these men."

"What were you gonna say?"

" 'Bout the horse and all, and how they was up to no good agin ya. I figgered maybe I could get a job from it."

"Why didn't you tell me before you sold Lobo the horse?"

"I din't have no proof! The horse was the ev'dence."

"Okay," Seth said. "You and me are going down to that camp and you're going in alone. I'll be close enough to hear everything said, so watch your mouth. I want to know when they're gonna move on the bank. Understand?"

Lemonade nodded.

"Mention of the bank doesn't surprise you, does it?"

"Nope. I heard 'em talkin' 'bout it."

Seth looked at Lobo. Disappointed in his son's gullibility, he blamed himself for not teaching the boy to be more suspicious of people's motives. But Seth also felt a begrudging admiration for Lobo's spunk, so he let that emotion shine through his smile. Giving Joaquín a playful wink, he said, "You men wait here. The fewer we are, the less noise we'll make." He turned back to Lemonade. "Let's go."

Lobo watched his father and Lemonade disappear in the forest, then listened until he couldn't hear their horses anymore. Joaquín swung off and sat on a boulder, his silhouette dark in the moonlight. Finally Lobo dropped down from his pinto, tied it near Joaquín's black, and found himself a boulder with some loose sand in front of it that he could kick at. The horses shuffled their bits and shifted their weight with a dull clump of hooves. Varmints scurried beneath the underbrush. An owl hooted from across the valley. Otherwise it was quiet.

Lobo felt hollow, knowing he'd let himself be used against Seth. Remembering how proud he'd felt while doing it, often wishing his father could see him win at craps or sneak in the back doors of saloons, only proved his total idiocy. He looked across at Joaquín and said, "I fucked up bad, didn't I?"

Joaquín smiled forgiveness. "It was a mistake," he admitted.

"Seth won't ever buy me a sixgun," Lobo said, kicking at the sand. "When he found out I'd been goin' into town, he said it proved I wasn't responsible enough for one. What's he gonna say now? That I proved I'll never be responsible?"

"Never is a long time," Joaquín said.

"Why do people hate him so much?"

Joaquín shrugged. "Usually they do not even know him, but hope to use his fame for their purpose."

"I wish he wasn't famous then," Lobo said, digging his heel into the soft sand.

"The past will fade and people won't remember so often," Joaquín said gently. "Even terrible mistakes can be forgiven in time."

"I wish Seth's brother hadn't died," Lobo muttered.

As always, Joaquín felt stabbed with sorrow at the thought of Jeremiah. "Why do you say that?"

"I'd like to ask him what Seth was like as a kid, maybe then I could see if I'm doin' all right."

"You're doing fine," Joaquín reassured him.

"How did Jeremiah die?"

"What did Seth tell you?"

"Not much," Lobo said, leaning forward with his elbows on his knees, as Seth often did. Lobo looked at Joaquín with eyes the same smoky gray as Seth's, except unlike the man's, the child's eyes were full of need. "Tell me, Joaquín."

Regretfully he said, "Jeremiah was lynched."

"By who?" Lobo gasped.

"Townspeople."

"Why?"

Joaquín looked into the dark valley. "Why some things happen is a mystery, Lobo. I have thought of it many times but never found an answer. I will tell you what I know. Jeremiah was eighteen. Seth was only three years older, but he had been riding with Allister a few years by then. They had stopped in Austin and were spotted by some Texas Rangers who tried to arrest them. In making their escape, a Ranger was killed and another man, too. The people of the city were angry that such a thing could happen on their streets. They went to the home of your grandfather looking for Seth. He wasn't there, but they were so caught in their rage, they hung Jeremiah instead."

"Had he done anything wrong?" Lobo whispered.

Joaquín shook his head.

"What did Seth do?"

Joaquín sighed. "He took his vengeance against the leader of the mob."

"Did he hang him?"

Joaquín nodded.

Lobo's eyes were fierce. "He deserved it."

"Perhaps."

"What would you have done?"

"I would have left him to God."

Lobo stomped away to peer over the edge of the precipice. He knew how badly Seth must have felt about Jeremiah's death because he knew how he'd feel if Seth died because of his mistake. Suddenly the world seemed a vicious place to Lobo, the games of self-defense his family played no longer fun but precautions of deadly earnest. He had been told that when a stranger rode into the yard he was to make for the nearest door, and once inside to stay away from the windows. Yet as dangerous as Arizona was, Texas was worse.

Texas wanted to hang Seth. The state still offered a thousand dollars to any bounty hunter who killed him. Lobo wasn't sure why. He knew his father had been an outlaw with Ben Allister, that they had robbed banks and Seth had saved enough of the loot that he didn't have to work. Lobo also knew Allister had been a rough desperado, and that he and Seth had killed men in the years they rode together. But all that had been before Lobo was born.

He tried to imagine what Jeremiah had looked like, then remembered he had a brother named Jeremiah, too. Lobo felt confused by his kin, they were so disconnected and spread out. He had lived his first years on a ranch in Colorado with his mother, Esther, and her husband, a man named Angel Madera who had given Lobo his name. Lobo had been happy there, but it had nagged at him that he was missing out on knowing his father. Then one night Seth walked into the house. As soon as their eyes met, Lobo knew they were together and nothing would ever change that again. He hadn't realized, however, what it would mean to leave Esther.

He still missed her, and even Angel. Once in a while he thought of their other son, who was his brother in the same way Elena was his sister. Now Seth had told him he had yet another brother living with kinfolk in Texas. Lobo had never met any of them: Seth's father, a man named Abraham Strummar who lived at 600 Grackle Street in Austin, and Seth's wife and son, Johanna and Jeremiah Strummar, a whole other family who got to carry Seth's name.

Lobo turned back around to Joaquín. "Did all that happen in the same house Seth's father lives in now?"

"I think so," Joaquín said.

"Wasn't Abraham home?"

"Yes, he was."

"Why didn't he stop 'em?"

Joaquín smiled at the four-foot tall Strummar demanding an answer to that question. "A mob is a frightening foe," he said. "It is the ugliest of human faces."

"So he was afraid!"

"Yes," Joaquín said sadly, "he was afraid."

"And let 'em do it!"

"He watched helplessly."

"Seth wouldn't have."

"No. He would have died saving Jeremiah."

Lobo walked back over and sat on his boulder, digging the heel of his boot into the sand until he hit rock. "If Seth had died savin' his brother, I wouldn't be here. Neither would my brother Jeremiah."

"That's true." Joaquín smiled. "And we wouldn't be sitting here talking."

Lobo laughed. "Where would you be?"

"México, probably."

"But you're an American now."

"The older I get, the less American I feel."

"Why?"

"Their hunger is insatiable."

"What's that mean?"

"You, for instance," Joaquín teased. "You have a horse as good as mine and dress as well as Seth, two women fussing over you like mother hens, a beautiful baby sister and a ranch of a thousand acres to roam freely, yet you sneak into town and gamble for more."

"I don't do it to get stuff but to have fun," Lobo argued.

"When I was young, getting stuff was all we did because we never had enough, and having fun was an acci-

dent that happened when we felt so bad we didn't care
anymore. Many of the boys you think you are playing with
are working, as I was at your age.''

"Hangin' out in alleys ain't the same as a job,'' Lobo
protested.

"It is if you're there to earn your supper,'' Joaquín said.

Lobo looked into the darkness where his father and
friend had disappeared. "Lemonade's like that. Some days
he doesn't eat at all.''

"You should try it some time,'' Joaquín suggested.
"Then you would understand what drives half the world.''

"Do you think Lemonade was tellin' the truth when he
said he didn't think I'd be hurt?''

"Yes,'' Joaquín answered without hesitation.

"What makes you think so?''

"He wouldn't lie to Seth.''

Lobo laughed. "I can't. Can you?''

"No,'' Joaquín said with a smile.

Esperanza watched Lila Keats walk down the stairs stick-
ing pins back into her coiffure. Even from that distance,
Esperanza could see how perfectly the green of her dress
matched the hue of her eyes, a color Esperanza distrusted.
When Lila came close and stood above the table, her smile
seemed as hypocritical as the cool aspect of her gaze. "Are
you Esperanza?'' she asked.

Esperanza nodded.

"Have you come to tell my fortune?''

"If you wish it, señora.''

"And if I don't, you would leave feeling content with
your night's work?''

"A few moments ago, I would have said yes,'' she replied, suppressing a shiver at the chill in the woman's eyes.

"But no longer?''

Esperanza shook her head. Gathering her shawl, she rose
to her feet and started for the door.

"Wait!'' Lila commanded. When Esperanza reluctantly

turned back to face her, Lila mocked, "Don't you wish to tell my fortune?"

Again, Esperanza shook her head.

"Come, come," Lila scolded. "Isn't that why you're here?"

"I came in the hope of making money," Esperanza answered, "but some visions are not worth the price."

"Not worth five dollars in gold?"

"I charge only one."

"I will pay you five."

"You will not influence the cards with generosity." Lila shrugged.

"Are you certain," Esperanza asked, "that you wish to see the future?"

"Do you think my fortune so unsavory?"

Esperanza nodded.

The green eyes darkened. "Come, vieja. Stop trying to frighten me and show me the truth if you can."

"The cards will reveal it."

"Well, let's have it then," she said, yanking a chair away from the table and sitting down.

Slowly Esperanza returned to sit in the facing chair. She pulled the deck of cards from her pocket, unwrapped them from their silk scarf and laid them on the table. "Shuffle them with a pure heart, señora, and divide the deck in two."

Lila expertly shuffled and cut the deck. Esperanza rejoined it with the top on the bottom, closed her eyes a moment, then dealt four cards face up in the form of a cross. She studied the message a long moment before raising her gaze to meet the green eyes watching so intently.

"Well?" Lila demanded.

Esperanza touched the king of swords. "This man behind you is cruel and capable of great malice. You should not oppose him."

Lila laughed. "His name isn't Seth Strummar, by any chance?"

"The cards do not share names," Esperanza answered, "but I feel this man is dead."

Lila paled, then laughed again. "What harm can he do me then?"

"Sometimes behind you does not mean his influence is past, but that he is riding hard to overtake you."

"How can he do that if he's dead?"

Esperanza shrugged, then touched the five of cups. "This card covering you signifies loss. And because this card," she touched the nine of wands, "is before you, the loss will be great. I feel the chill of the grave, so death is close. Perhaps it is not yours but the king's. For you I see defeat through deception."

Lila hugged herself as if she, too, felt the chill. "And the last card?"

"Reveals the aspect of what is coming," Esperanza said. "The Tower signifies misery, and again, deception. You would be wise to watch your tongue in the days ahead. All of these influences come from inside you and can still be avoided."

Lila stared at her for a long moment then asked coldly, "Did Seth tell you what to say?"

Esperanza shook her head. "I never lie about the cards, *señora*. Your best hope is to carry the weight of what is yours. Only then can you reclaim justice."

Lila smiled. "Justice can still be mine?"

"If you resist treachery."

"If I do, then how would you read these cards?"

Esperanza studied the message again. "If you conduct yourself with honor, the king will not overtake you but will be left behind where he belongs. Your joy will be clouded but only for a time, then the loss will be of your sorrow."

"And all I have to do is conduct myself with honor?"

Esperanza nodded.

"Since vengeance is an honorable endeavor," Lila said smugly, "it seems my future is rather bright after all."

"The indications are grim, *señora,*" Esperanza warned. "Be cautious."

"Thank you," Lila said. She stood up and smacked a five-dollar coin on the table. "Tell Seth his trick didn't work."

Esperanza watched her in silence.

"You can tell him something else, too," Lila gloated. "Tell him I came to return the favor he did me years ago. I'm sure he'll understand what I'm talking about."

"He does not remember you," Esperanza said.

"You expect me to believe that?" she jeered, then whirled and walked away.

After watching her climb the stairs without looking back, Esperanza reached to the top of the deck and turned up the next card, the signifier if the seeker asked further questions. It was the Beast, predicting that Lila Keats would not outwit death. Esperanza sighed deeply, then left the gold coin glimmering on the table and walked into the darkness where Rico's horse stood tied to the rail. She had barely pulled her weight into the saddle when Nib came through the door and caught hold of her reins.

"I've been told to see you home safe, Señora Ochoa," the gunman said. "You wouldn't want me to fail my boss, would you?"

She shook her head with a smile, thinking only the grace of Seth's protection allowed an old whore to be treated with such respect.

Seth tied his sorrel a safe distance away from the glow of the campfire and left his spurs in his saddlebags, then rode behind Lemonade the rest of the way. When they could see the men in the circle of light, Seth slid down quietly and laid his hand on Lemonade's leg, meeting the kid's eyes with warning that it was a rough game they were commencing. Lemonade smiled with childish confidence, then walked his horse slowly forward, calling out, "Howdy, Mr. Norris!"

"Lemonade, is it?" a gruff voice asked as a short, husky man stood up.

Seth could see his face plain but didn't recognize him.

"What'cha doin' here?" Norris asked.

"Jus' got lonely," the kid answered. "Mightn't I have some coffee?"

"Reckon." Norris studied the kid as he tied his horse to a tree and approached. "Got yourself new duds."

Lemonade grinned, hunkering down by the fire. "Decided I was comin' up in the world so I best look like it."

"You still ain't got a gun," Joe Tyler snickered from where he lay in his blankets.

"I'm workin' on it," Lemonade said, filling a cup with coffee.

Seth could smell it from where he was standing behind a tree. He studied the men in the erratic light from the fire: the Tyler brothers he'd met in Charleston, Norris, and another man half-shadowed in his blankets. Seth didn't recognize any of them from his past but knew their breed.

"How much longer ya gonna be around?" Lemonade asked.

"What's it to you?" Norris answered. He still hadn't sat down, was still watching the kid warily.

Lemonade shrugged. "Thought I might ride along when ya go."

Norris snorted. "Come back in ten years and maybe I'll consider it, if you're still alive."

"If *you're* still alive," the man in the shadows said.

Norris glared at him. "You're goin' the way of Bart, you know that?"

"Uh-uh," he answered. "I ain't so stupid as to go against Strummar. Seems to me you're the one doing that." He stood up and came forward to squat by the fire and pour himself a cup of coffee, then sipped at it without looking up, his face hidden by his hat.

"I ain't even gonna see him," Norris said.

"You got that right," the man said, blowing noisily on his coffee, " 'cause you'll be dead 'fore it happens." He looked up with a grin, revealing a long, narrow face beneath the brim of his hat. He was a stranger to Seth.

"When you agreed to come on this job," Norris said, "you didn't ask for a list of depositors."

The man smiled coldly. "Guess I'll have to in the future."

"Does that mean you want out?" Norris asked.

"Guess it does," the man answered. "I'll mosey now, if it's all the same to you."

"It ain't," Norris said. "We already lost one man. We can't pull it off bein' two short."

The man shrugged. "I'm cutting out."

"The hell you are!" Norris bellowed. "You make a move, Webster, and I'll blow you to kingdom come."

Webster stared at him a long moment, then chuckled. "Seems to me Bart already did that to our chances. Or maybe I should say Strummar blew 'em to hell with Bart."

"I saw it," Lemonade said proudly.

"You did?" Jim Tyler asked with interest. "How'd Bart look?"

"At first he jus' looked mad," Lemonade said, staring into the fire as he remembered. "Then he looked kinda sick."

Tyler snickered. "Lead in your heart's apt to make anybody sick."

"How'd Strummar look?" Norris asked.

"Bored," Lemonade said.

Webster and Norris laughed, but Joe Tyler growled, "That's how he looked in Charleston, like he was tired of us even though he'd never seen us before."

Lemonade studied Joe thoughtfully, then said, "Maybe he is."

Seth smiled, thinking Lemonade was a smart kid.

"You know," Webster said in a conversational tone, "I heard J. B. Ayres is an undercover agent for Wells Fargo."

The fire crackled in the silence.

"Where'd you hear that?" Jim Tyler finally asked.

"Around." Webster shrugged. "You ever hear anything like that, Lemonade?"

He shook his head. "I don't believe it, neither."

"Why not?"

" 'Cause when they dragged that man Lafferty outta his place and lynched him, Ayres stood there with a shotgun and watched it happen. Any kinda lawman would've stopped it."

"No man can stop a mob," Norris scoffed.

"I'd try," Lemonade said. "If it was mine to do, I would."

"You ain't even got a gun!" Joe hooted. "How you gonna help us in Tejoe?"

"When're ya goin'?" Lemonade asked.

"We don't know," Webster said with a mocking glance at Norris. "We're waiting to hear from the boss lady."

"But we gotta be ready," Joe taunted. "And you ain't, are you?"

Lemonade shook his head, then stood up as he looked at Norris. "If I get me a gun, can I ride with ya?"

"Come back when you got one and ask again," Norris said.

All the men watched Lemonade mount his horse and ride into the dark. Seth moved quietly to intercept the kid. They smiled at each other when they came together again, but didn't speak until after Seth had retrieved his sorrel and they were back with Joaquín and Lobo, who had heard them coming and were already mounted.

"What happened?" Lobo asked.

"Not much," Seth said. He met Joaquín's eyes and communicated without words that they'd discuss it later, then reached across and slapped Lemonade on the back. "You handled 'em real smooth, kid."

"Thanks," he said, smiling proudly at Lobo, who didn't smile back.

"Let's go home," Seth said. Turning his horse, he kicked it into a fast trot down the mountain.

14

When the men returned, all the horses were in their stalls and the homestead slumbered peacefully. Seth told Lemonade he could sleep in the loft, then asked Joaquín to come to the house. Lobo went to bed, and while Seth checked on Rico, Joaquín heated the coffee left from supper.

Coming back into the kitchen just after Joaquín had filled the cups, Seth took a bottle of whiskey from the hutch and joined him at the table. "They're waiting for word from Lila," Seth said, adding whiskey to his coffee. He offered the bottle to Joaquín, who shook his head.

"Fellow named Webster," Seth continued, "tried to get out of it but Norris backed him down. Apparently he's the ramrod. The other two are the Tyler brothers we met in Charleston." He stopped and drank half his coffee, refilled the cup with whiskey, and took another sip.

"What will you do now?" Joaquín asked.

Seth smiled. "I'd like to run Lila out of town but it doesn't seem neighborly to push her off on someone else."

"What other choice do we have?"

"Slater can arrest her and send her to prison." He drained his cup, then asked with sarcasm, "Ain't that the civilized thing to do?"

"But she hasn't acted yet, so he must wait for her to rob the bank and catch her while she's doing it."

"She won't likely be there," Seth said, refilling his cup from the bottle. "Those clowns up on the mountain are gonna be the ones who're caught."

"If they are taken alive, they will testify against her."

"We'll still have to nab her before it comes down to make sure she doesn't get away."

"A few minutes, perhaps," Joaquín agreed.

Seth smiled playfully. "Let's take it a step closer and make it happen."

"What do you mean?"

"Let's visit Lila and convince her to give the word. When they walk in the door, the sheriff'll be there to welcome 'em." He chuckled at his cleverness. "It's perfect."

"Maybe too perfect," Joaquín said. "There is more to her plot than robbing the bank. You're forgetting they put Lobo on a stolen horse. When he wasn't riding it to town, it was a trap waiting to be sprung on your land. And don't forget Melinda's suspicion of a frame-up. If you are with Lila when she gives the word, it will be difficult to prove you weren't in on it. She is after more than money, Seth."

"Smells like vengeance, doesn't it?"

Joaquín nodded.

"It would explain why Bart challenged me. Maybe he didn't intend to but just went to see Lila, then saw me and couldn't stop himself."

Softly Joaquín said, "It seems you would remember people you had touched so deeply."

Seth chuckled with affection. "If you were a priest, Joaquín, I'd turn Catholic just to receive your absolutions. Anybody who can call the things I did 'touching people deeply' has a silver tongue, that's for damn sure."

"Maybe if we knew Lila's maiden name," Joaquín said, watching Seth sip more whiskey.

"A woman like her uses a dozen names."

"I asked Melinda to find out."

"I doubt if Lila let anything slip." Seth thoughtfully sipped at the whiskey until his cup was empty again. "I'm gonna keep Lobo home tomorrow. Think I'll keep Lemonade here, too. I may need him again."

"I don't think he's a good influence on Lobo."

Seth laughed bitterly. "Neither am I."

He reached for the bottle, but Joaquín took hold of it first. "It is never wise to get drunk," he said gently. "You told me that in El Paso."

Anger flared in Seth's eyes, then was quickly replaced with the familiar glint of self-mockery that made Joaquín ache for his friend. Seth smiled and stood up. "You're right. See you in the morning." He touched Joaquín's shoulder on his way out of the room.

Joaquín smiled as he listened to Seth open and close the bedroom door, then he blew out the lamp and walked across the yard to the stable. He intended to saddle Rico's palomino and let his black rest, but when he went to smooth the blanket on, he discovered the mare's back was wet with sweat. He puzzled over that a moment, then saddled his black after all.

In the dark bedroom, Seth sensed Rico was asleep and moved quietly to undress. As he slid under the covers, she turned unconsciously to take him in her arms, and the warmth of her body aroused him. He slid his hand beneath her nightgown, across the rise of her hip to nestle in the crook of her waist, then felt her kiss on his cheek. Smiling that she never refused him, he kissed her with gratitude, and also with guilt that he didn't do right by her love. He used the girls in Blue's saloon at will, and when his hunger wasn't strong enough that he felt inclined to participate, he sometimes watched another man use the girl. In Seth's mind all that was disconnected from Rico, but he knew she didn't see it that way. Breaking their embrace, he lay back alone.

"What is it, Seth?" she whispered.

He sorted through his mind for an approach to what he wanted to say. Finally he asked, "Why is it important to you that I be faithful?"

She took a long moment to answer. "I don't like to think of you with other women," she said softly.

"What difference does it make? It's got nothing to do with us."

"Unless you find one you prefer over me."

"That ain't gonna happen."

"It happened to Johanna."

"Johanna was a child I had no right to marry," he retorted with impatience. "What she and I shared wasn't like what you and I have."

"What *do* we have, Seth?" she asked carefully.

"If you don't know, my saying it won't make much difference."

"It will to me."

He rolled onto his belly and hid his face in his folded arms as he thought back over his life, remembering the loneliness he'd felt when whores were his only feminine companions. He turned his head to look at Rico. "A man ain't complete without the love of a woman, and you love me for what I am, not my reputation or even my money. You have your own money, and you're not half-bad with a gun either." He chuckled. "Despite all your carrying on, you don't need me. I guess that's why your wanting me around means so much."

Knowing what she was risking, she said, "That's not true, Seth. I do need you."

"You say that," he scoffed, "and you may even believe it, but it ain't true."

She hesitated, then asked, "You know what I did when you left me before?"

"No," he said, feeling bad that he'd never thought about it.

"I tried to kill myself," she said.

"Say that again," he said, sure he'd misheard her.

"I lied about the scars on my wrists. I did it to myself, because I couldn't face life without you."

He jerked out of bed and backed away until he hit the door. "I can't carry that, Rico."

She sat up, knowing they had to have it clear between them or everything that followed would be a lie. "I'm not saying I'd do it again," she explained. "I have Elena now, and soon another child who'll need me. I'm just saying that without you there would be an emptiness in my life no one else could fill."

"Why did you lie to me?"

"Because when you first asked about the scars, you would've left if I'd told you the truth."

"I've never lied to *you.*"

"Not even about Lila Keats?"

"Jesus Christ!" he exploded. "What's she got to do with anything?"

"Melinda told me you had your way with her."

"I unbuttoned her dress and played with her body to scare her. If that's having my way, I guess I did, but there wasn't any pleasure in it."

"That's not a pretty picture, Seth," she whispered.

"That's why I didn't take you along. All of life ain't pretty."

"No. Some of it's sordid."

"Like what I did with Lila Keats?"

"I don't care about that."

"What then?"

"Melinda implied things," Rico said gently, "about you and Allister. She said they were the same with you and Joaquín."

"What kinda things?"

She struggled to find the words. "Even saying it sounds ugly."

"What are you trying to say, Rico?"

"I did it with Melinda," she said, hoping to help him.

He was silent as her meaning came clear, then he said, "I never fucked Allister and I've never fucked Joaquín. Is that what you want to know?"

"Don't be angry, Seth. It hadn't occurred to me until Melinda brought it up."

"Was kind of her," he muttered. "And I'm glad to learn you have so much faith in me."

"Please, Seth. It's just that I felt like a fool when she told me about Esperanza. I thought maybe I was blind about this too."

"Don't you trust your own judgment more'n that?"

"It gets confusing when half the time I have to deny what my senses tell me."

"Like what?"

"Smelling perfume on your clothes when you come home from Blue's."

He shrugged. "A lot of women work there."

"You must get pretty close to pick up their perfume."

"They're just whores, Rico. There's no goodness in what I do with them."

"Why do you want it then?"

If he had been dressed he would have left rather than answer that question. But he was naked standing against the door, and it made him hesitate long enough to appreciate her courage. Finally he said, "Old habits, I guess."

"Habits you learned from Allister?"

"Everybody gives him a lot of credit for who I am."

"Don't you?"

"Allister's dead."

"Then let him go," she pleaded. "Don't pass onto your son the lessons he gave you." When Seth was silent, she asked, "Don't you think Lobo knows what happens in Blue's saloon?"

"How could he?"

"He spends a lot of time trying to figure out why you're different from other fathers. It was Allister who made you different."

"Bullshit!"

"Is it? If you'd never met him, your first killing would've been forgiven. You would never have robbed those banks or killed all those men. And something else: your brother would still be alive."

"You think that was Allister's fault?"

"Yes," she said. "Whose fault do you think it was?"

"Mine. I should've stopped that mob."

"No one can stop a mob, Seth."

"I could've. Well, maybe not then. I wasn't smart enough then, but I could stop 'em now."

"It isn't happening now," she said sadly.

"No," he admitted. "Nothing's happening anymore. I'm just an old man who only fights with his wife."

"You're considerably more than that." She smiled, then sighed. "You've often said you'd marry me if you could. Is that the truth?"

"Yeah."

"Marriage is being true to each other. Can you give me that?"

"What, exactly?"

"I want you to stop hurting yourself by abusing the women at Blue's."

He frowned. "Abusing them? Well, maybe," he conceded. "But if I stay away from 'em, what am I gonna do with my grief, Rico?"

"Give it to me," she answered. "I can handle the part that's truly yours. Why don't we let the rest die of neglect?"

"You think it will?"

"Yes," she said.

Hungrily he approached the bed, then stood looking down at her. "All right. I give my word not to touch another woman for carnal pleasure. Will that satisfy you?"

"If you also give your word not to watch other men do it."

He was surprised he had assumed her ignorance of that, given their history. He chuckled, sliding under the covers to hold her again. "You continue to amaze me," he murmured into her hair.

"And please you?" she whispered.

He answered her with a kiss, hoping she wouldn't notice he hadn't given his word on the second part of her request. Rico did notice, but for the time being she felt content with her partial victory.

La Casa Amarilla was dark as Joaquín tied his horse in the shadow of a cottonwood a short distance away. He walked slowly toward the rooming house, suspecting he was there as much to fulfill a need of his own as to help Seth. When he had jimmied the locks between them, Melinda greeted him with a smile that said she'd been waiting, and he felt pleased with the thought.

He crossed the room lit only by starlight and sat on the edge of her bed. "*Buenas noches,*" he said, amused with himself for falling back on his native tongue.

"*Buenas noches,*" she repeated, then laughed softly. "You're quiet as a cat, Joaquín. I didn't hear you until you were outside my door."

"To move in silence is a useful skill," he answered modestly. "And not so difficult if I remember to take off my spurs."

She laughed again. "Blue came to see me today. He offered me a job."

"Did you accept it?"

"Yes," she whispered, sitting up and leaning close to kiss his cheek. "Thank you, Joaquín. He told me it was your idea."

He shrugged. "We discussed it together, the three of us."

"Ummm," she said, knowing the truth. "When I said I hadn't enough frocks, he gave me an advance on my salary so I could order some from the dressmaker. Wasn't that generous?"

"Yes," he said. "Have you placed your order?

"I gave the woman a small amount to begin. Tomorrow

I'll put the rest in the bank.'' She giggled. ''I'll have a bank account, Joaquín, for the first time in my life.'' She slid closer and put her arms around him. ''I'd like to thank you for what you've done.''

He shrugged out of her embrace and moved a scant distance away. ''Did you find out any more about Lila Keats?''

''Blue told me she was dangerous and he thought it best I stay away from her.''

''So you haven't seen her since we talked last?''

Melinda shook her head. ''I spent most of today at the dressmaker's choosin' patterns and material. I had a lot of fun, Joaquín,'' she cooed, sidling up close again. ''Wait 'til you see my gowns, I'm gonna be so beautiful.''

''You don't need fancy dresses for that.'' He gave her a smile, then said, ''I should go now.''

''Don't hurry away,'' she said, sliding onto the floor in front of him and reaching to unbuckle his gunbelt. ''Let me thank you first.''

''No,'' he said, catching her hands.

''Why?''

''I don't use women that way.''

''Not even the girls in Blue's saloon?''

He shook his head.

''Why not?'' she asked, astonished.

''I feel sorry for them.''

She climbed onto his lap, pushing him back to lie beneath her. ''Do you feel sorry for me?''

''No,'' he said, ''but I don't want to love you either.''

She pulled her nightgown off over her head so she was naked on top of him. ''You just now said I don't need fancy dresses to be pretty,'' she teased.

Her breasts were lovely in the starlight, but he said, ''For over a year we slept a short distance apart and you never wanted me.''

She sighed, resting her weight on his hips as she unbuttoned his shirt then ran her cool palms over his chest. ''I do now, Joaquín.''

He knew he should resist but the perfume of her hair overpowered his resolve. When she unbuckled his gunbelt, he let her pull it out from under him, then listened to its quiet thud on the floor. Taking hold of her waist, he lifted her off and nestled her in the blankets, kissing her mouth as he dipped his fingers inside to discover she was wet.

She laughed deep in her throat and whispered, "Now that's something Seth would do."

Joaquín retreated to the far side of the bed.

"Jesus, I'm sorry," she moaned. "I said the wrong thing again. Forgive me, Joaquín."

"Why did you say it?" he asked, his desire gone.

She shrugged. "It just slipped out."

"It wasn't an accident," he said. "It has already happened twice. The last time I left, and this time I will, too. But first I want to know what you expect when you say something like that."

"I want to make you mad."

"Why?"

"It's how you get started in this game. You know, things get a little rough, then the sweetness comes." She stared at him a moment. "You've never hit a woman, have you?"

"Not for fun," he said.

She laughed. "Well, that's why I have to say it, Joaquín. When I mention Seth, I'm tryin' to make you mad enough to hit me. But you always get up and leave instead, just like you're doin' now."

He stood by the bed buttoning his shirt.

"Don't leave," she pleaded. "I don't want to be alone."

"I have to go home."

"Because Seth needs you?" she asked with sarcasm.

"Yes," he said.

"Will you always choose him over a woman?" she taunted.

Joaquín walked around the bed, buckled on his gunbelt, then raised his eyes to hers. "Seth and I shared a woman once. Her name was Rosalinda. She was like you in more than her name, though, because she also wanted men to hurt her, and she was good at making it happen. I do not think you want to be like her, Melinda. Or perhaps it's that you are not yet like her, but you are on the same road. Do you know what happened to Rosalinda?''

She shook her head.

''She asked to be hurt one time too many and Seth killed her.'' Joaquín settled his hat low above his eyes. ''You should learn to seek love from men, and to accept it when you find it.'' Quietly he walked to the door, slipped out and was gone.

Melinda stared bleakly at the emptiness he'd left behind. But as she listened to the hoofbeats of his horse diminish in the distance, she thought he'd be back another night. If not, the next time he came into Blue's she would tease him until he laughed in the old way again. She knew how to please men, and he was just one more.

Across the hall, Lila Keats heard a creak on the stairs and then a few moments later a horse loping away. She rolled over and shook Rafe's shoulders. ''Wake up,'' she hissed. ''You idiot, someone's been here.''

Sheriff Slater stood up and pulled on his pants, then walked over to the window as he buttoned them. Studying the dark desert, he said, ''I don't see anybody.''

''He's gone now.'' She started picking his clothes off the floor and throwing them at him. ''You should be, too.''

He turned around in time to catch the crumpled wad of his shirt and vest. ''I'm going,'' he said. ''You can stop throwing my stuff.''

She sat down on the bed and glared at him.

When he looked down to button his vest, he saw the silver star of his badge. ''Seth's onto you, Lila,'' Rafe said, ''so if your boys try for the bank, you best be gone.''

''What do you mean 'try for'? Who's gonna stop us?''

''I am.''

''Since when?''

"I'm telling you, Lila. Bart spoiled the pudding when he called Seth out."

"Good old Bart," she muttered. "It was an appropriate legacy, don't you think?"

"Maybe it was," he said, sitting on her bed while he pulled on his boots. "Maybe he was telling you to walk the straight and narrow for a change."

"That's something he never tried," she retorted.

"Maybe he regretted it. And think about this, Lila." He turned to face her across the rumpled sheets. "Bart didn't have a chance in hell against Seth and knew it. That means he chose to die right in front of you. Don't you think there was a message in that?"

She shrugged. "I didn't even know it was him 'til it was over."

"Yeah, well, that was sort of Bart's luck all the way through, wasn't it." He stood up and lifted his gunbelt off the floor then buckled it on, watching her.

"Seth made him crawl," she spit out. "That's what ruined Bart."

"Seth says he never met the man."

"He's lying!" she shouted.

"Take it easy," Rafe said. "You want to wake the whole house?"

"He remembers me," she whispered hoarsely. "And he remembered Bart, too. He couldn't forget us after what he'd done."

"What'd he do?" Rafe asked, looking around for his hat. He found it but didn't put it on.

She glared as if she hated him as much as the man she was thinking about. Finally she said, "Made him eat shit. The human kind."

Rafe swallowed hard.

"Ben Allister is the one who crammed it down his throat," she said, "but Seth Strummar told Allister to do it."

"What'd Bart do to Seth?"

"Nothing! He talked to a *federale*, just passing the time

of day, that's all. Seth said it looked like Bart didn't know the difference between a desperado and a dog so he made him eat shit, saying that's how dogs learn to recognize their own kind.''

Rafe sniffed loudly as if a sudden stench pinched his nose. ''Allister's been dead almost ten years, Lila. When did all this happen?''

''What difference does that make? You know what Seth did afterwards? He took me to his room and played with me all night. Now he says he can't remember us!''

''Who'd want to remember something like that?'' Rafe muttered. ''You'd be better off forgetting it, too. Anyway, Seth ain't the man he was, and Bart ended his part Saturday night. I can't see what's it got to do with you.''

''He raped me!'' she hissed. ''The other morning he lay with me on this very bed and I thought he was going to do it again. I think he would have if Joaquín hadn't been with him.''

''He didn't though, that's what counts. Anyway, I can't see that a woman living with outlaws has much claim to virtue. I seem to remember you sashaying between beds freely enough.''

''I took my pleasure,'' she said. ''Bart wasn't any good after what happened. If I hadn't been there, he might've gotten over it. But I begged Seth to stop and all that did was increase Bart's humiliation. As if that wasn't enough, Allister made Bart watch Seth drag me into his room. They destroyed my husband as surely as if they'd killed him. Seth did kill him! Bart was a fool to challenge Seth, though, I admit that. We came here for the money and Bart thought he could let the other slide, but I guess when he saw Seth again he couldn't. I don't care about that. I haven't cared for Bart in years, but I'll never stop hating Seth Strummar. I'm going through with our plan and I'm gonna live soft the rest of my life on his money.''

''Aren't you forgetting your partners? There ain't enough in that bank to set you all up.''

"They're just making wages, whatever they think is going on."

"You're in over your head, Lila. Soon as you make your move, I'll arrest you." He smiled. "But I promise to visit you at night long as you're in my custody."

"You'll be in jail too," she threatened.

He shook his head. "A man can't be arrested for loose talk, only for what he does." He put his hat on. "That's why you're still free: it goes for women, too." He opened the door, looking back over his shoulder. "My advice is to get out of Tejoe while you still can."

By the time he reached his office, Rafe Slater was feeling melancholy. He lit the lantern at its lowest wick and poured himself a drink, then put his feet on his desk and stared down the dark corridor of empty cells. He knew it was a fine line which side of those bars he was on, as well as for Seth, Blue Rivers, and even Joaquín. Rafe had inherited wanted posters on all three of them when he took the job. The posters were old and the money probably wasn't there anymore, except for the thousand-dollar bounty against Seth. That was for killing a Ranger and Texas wasn't likely to drop it soon, but Texas Rangers weren't real popular in Arizona.

Rafe remembered the scene when he'd told J. J. Clancy that Seth Strummar expected the bank to be robbed. "What's he doing about it?" the banker had demanded angrily.

"He told his sheriff," Rafe answered. "And I'm passing it along so maybe you can take precautions."

"He stands to lose as much as the rest of us, more than most," Clancy bristled indignantly. "Why doesn't he take precautions?"

"I don't guess he figures it's his job," Rafe said.

"But he has the experience," Clancy argued.

"What d'ya expect him to do? Stand around the lobby with a rifle?"

"It would certainly discourage thieves."

"I don't think that's what Seth wants to do with his life. He could keep his money at home if he did."

"So what are you doing about it?" Clancy barked.

"Not much I can 'til something happens. Being as I don't have the budget for a deputy, I thought you might want to put on a private guard."

The banker frowned. "For how long?"

"Hard to tell." Rafe shrugged. "I'd be careful picking him, though. Don't hire a stranger."

"Do you think I'm an imbecile?" Clancy shouted.

"No, sir," Rafe said, swallowing his bile at the man's tone. "Just trying to help out."

"Trying and doing aren't the same, though, are they?" Clancy asked with a sneer.

Rafe had pounded his boot heels in anger all the way back to the tenderloin. Blue bought him a drink and let him run on about the arrogance of the rich longer than he deserved, then Lila came down and he watched her falling all over Blue until he couldn't stand it anymore. He'd returned to his office and gotten drunk alone, staring at the empty cells as he was doing now.

Tonight the prospect was too melancholy, and finally he walked outside and began his midnight rounds. As he passed the Protestant rectory, he saw a light in the parlor. On impulse, Rafe stopped and knocked on the door.

Homer Holcroft opened it fully dressed. "What a pleasant surprise, Rafe." Homer smiled, opening the door wider. "Won't you come in for a nightcap?"

"Thanks," Rafe said, then followed the pastor into his study, accepted a drink, and carried it over to the window.

He stared out in silence so long that Homer finally said from behind him, "You're pensive tonight. Is something bothering you, Rafe?"

He turned around and studied the minister. Deciding to take a cautious tack, Rafe said, "I was surprised to see you at Seth Strummar's the other day."

Homer chuckled. "I was returning from visiting the elder Mrs. Nickles when I encountered Joaquín on the road. He invited me home for supper.''

''Didn't know you knew him.''

''It was the first occasion I'd had to talk with him. I liked him, though. As I did Mr. Strummar.''

Rafe nodded. ''I like 'em too. You know who Lila Keats is?''

''The widow of the man killed in the Blue Rivers Saloon?''

''Yeah. She came here to take vengeance on Seth.''

''For what?'' Homer asked softly.

''Something that happened a long time ago, when he was still riding on the wrong side of the law. Bart Keats was, too, and according to Lila, they had a falling out which was bad enough that it's festered all this time. At least for them. Seth claims he can't remember either one of 'em.''

''What was it he did?''

''That don't matter. Thing of it is, I know something's gonna happen but legally I can't act 'til it does. Makes me feel helpless just waiting for it to come around.''

''Have you warned Seth?''

''He warned me.''

Homer frowned thoughtfully then asked, ''Is it going to be bad for the town?''

''Yeah, if Lila's friends succeed.''

''Is there anything I can do?''

''Can't think of it if there is,'' Rafe answered with a smile, then turned around and stared into the darkness again. After a long moment he said softly, almost as if he wished the minister wouldn't hear, ''It's my fault it's happening.''

Homer waited a moment before asking, ''How is it your fault?''

Rafe sighed and turned to face him again. ''Remember six months ago when I took a holiday?''

''You visited your family,'' Homer said.

''My family's dead. I just used that as an excuse to get

away for a bit. Rode halfway across New Mexico to El Paso, ran into Lila there, Lila and Bart.''

''You knew them before?'' he asked cautiously.

Rafe nodded. ''You see, Homer, there was a time when I was an outlaw too. Oh, I never had Seth Strummar's class but I broke the law more'n once. Back in those days I was in love with Lila, only she called herself Esmeralda then. When I saw her in El Paso I had a lot of those old feelings, and I figured she'd be tickled to learn I was wearing a badge now, so I told her that, her and Bart. She was tickled all right, especially when I told 'em Seth Strummar was living right outside our town. 'Cause Bart, see, he had this notion Seth had saved all the loot he stole with Allister, and Lila came up with the idea that Seth had it on deposit here in Tejoe.'' He shrugged. ''I didn't persuade 'em otherwise. I let 'em think what they wanted, and even that I'd help 'em if I could. I was just talking through the wine, you know how it is. I never expected 'em to show up.'' He laughed grimly. ''But they did.''

''It seems to me,'' Homer said slowly, ''if you know for a fact they're about to rob the bank, you could arrest them.''

''Who? Lila? You think anyone would believe it? And I haven't seen hide nor hair of her partners. I told Clancy my suspicions and he hired Bob Tice to stand around the lobby with a rifle, but Bob's about the worst shot in town.'' He sighed deeply. ''Tell you the truth, I feel like taking another holiday, this one permanent, head west to California and forget I ever took an oath to uphold the law. I asked Seth and Joaquín and Blue Rivers if they'd let me deputize 'em but they all refused, said they weren't lawmen. Well, I don't feel like one either. I feel like a damn fool waiting to get caught in his own trap, and it ain't a good feeling.''

''No,'' Homer agreed. ''When do you think Mrs. Keats is going to act?''

Rafe shrugged. ''It's bound to be soon. Blue fired her today so she hasn't any excuse to stick around. Not that she needs one. Like I said at the inquest, until a person breaks the law they're free to live where they please.'' He looked into his empty glass, then smiled wryly at his friend. ''Well, I'll go finish my rounds. Thanks for listening, Homer. I feel a mite better, and maybe something'll open up so I can see what I should do.''

Homer smiled. ''Solutions often present themselves at the oddest moments. I'm sure when the time comes, you'll do what's right.''

Holcroft walked the sheriff to the door and tried to send him on his way with an encouraging smile. But Homer's smile disappeared as soon as he was alone. As he poured himself another drink, he admitted ruefully that he wasn't much different from Lila Keats since he, too, wanted to get his hands on Seth Strummar's money. That he intended to use it for the good of others was in his favor but didn't change the fact that he was in competition with thieves to obtain the use of funds already stolen. He remembered Joaquín saying his purpose in life was to protect Seth from himself. Assuming that included plots of revenge stemming from the outlaw's past, Homer decided to seek the Mexican's advice.

Early the next morning, Holcroft drove his buggy to the turnoff from the east road toward the schoolyard. He knew Joaquín usually rode Lobo to school, but the time came and passed without their arrival. When Holcroft heard the school bell ring, he drove into the yard and watched the children file into the building. Seeing neither Lobo among them nor his pinto in the corral, Holcroft turned his buggy east toward the Strummar homestead.

The corral there was empty. When the door of the house opened and Esperanza walked from under the shadowed portal, Holcroft clucked his horse forward to meet her in the center of the yard.

He smiled. ''Good morning, Esperanza. I've come to see Joaquín.''

She shook her head. ''The men left before dawn to hunt deer in the mountains.''

"Lobo, too, I suppose?"

She nodded.

"I went by the school hoping to catch Joaquín." He sighed. "Well, there's nothing to be done. Even if I could track them, my buggy couldn't follow where they go."

She smiled. "You couldn't track them."

"No, I suppose not," he conceded.

"Would you like to come in for coffee?"

"Very much. Thank you."

She trundled ahead while he tied his horse to the corral then followed across the yard. At the door he turned back and watched a white dove cooing from the highest branch of a saguaro. The homestead seemed so peaceful, the dove an emblem of love, it was difficult to remember that it was owned by a man reputed to be the worst killer in the Southwest.

Holcroft crossed the parlor and entered the kitchen just as Esperanza was taking an apple pie from the oven. Near the back door was a cradle with the sleeping infant. Esperanza smiled, sliding the pie onto the counter. "Sit down, Señor Holcroft. In a few minutes this will set and I can cut you a slice."

"Thank you, it smells delicious." He sat down and watched her fill a cup with coffee. "Did Mrs. Strummar accompany the men?"

Esperanza shook her head. "Rico goes riding alone every morning."

"An unusual woman," he murmured.

"Yes," she said, setting the strong coffee before him. "She is carrying a child and I argued against it, but she said she needs time to herself."

Holcroft puzzled over that a moment, then latched onto the familiar sentiment. "A child! How wonderful for them. Their third?"

"Only second," she said, sitting down across from him. "Lobo is not hers."

He nodded. "Usually when a child has a different name,

it's because of the father. But Lobo is obviously Seth's son."

"He is a little Seth, no doubt of that," Esperanza said with a twinkle in her eyes.

"Have you been with the family long?" Holcroft asked.

"Two years," she said. "But I have known Seth much longer."

Holcroft blew on his coffee to cool it. Trying to stifle his curiosity, he said obliquely, "You're obviously fond of him."

"My life is his."

The commitment stated so simply gave the minister pause. He smiled. "Joaquín said the same. Mr. Strummar must be an extraordinary man to inspire such loyalty."

"He is," she said.

Holcroft sipped his coffee, then carefully set the cup in its saucer. "The sheriff came to see me last night. It was because of what he told me that I was looking for Joaquín. I was hoping we could help each other."

"Do what?"

"I'm not sure." He smiled. "Do you know Lila Keats?"

"I have met her."

"Sheriff Slater said Seth claims he doesn't remember her. Is that true?"

"If Seth says so."

Again he was impressed with her loyalty. "The sheriff said she used to go by the name of Esmeralda." He watched Esperanza's eyes darken with recognition. "Does that ring a bell?"

"I heard Allister speak of her once."

"What did he say?"

She shrugged, veiling her eyes. "It was a long time ago."

"The sheriff is worried, Esperanza, that Mrs. Keats has brought trouble to our town. Do you think there is anything I can do to avert what he sees coming?"

She shook her head. "Lila Keats will die. How many people die with her is in God's hands."

"Surely there's something we can do?"

"Forgive me, Señor Holcroft," she said with an edge of anger, "but a minister is like a woman in this world. Our power lies in the men we can petition. For us on this homestead, that man is Seth. If he weren't trying to live under the law, Lila Keats would be no problem. It seems the law gelds men by placing their power in the hands of a sheriff who cannot act without legal cause, so people like Lila Keats are free to spread their poison until they break the law. Isn't that what the sheriff told you?"

Holcroft nodded.

"So there is nothing to be done," she said.

He studied her uncomfortably, then asked, "Are you saying we are all impotent before the virility of evil?"

"That is what the law has made us."

"But surely, Esperanza, you see rule by law as a good thing?"

She shook her head. "I believe in the rule of a strong man. Seth is such a man. Your lawmen are weak, your judges without honor, your laws written by the rich to protect themselves. I believe in the power of the gun. It requires skill and courage to be its master, and in my heart I do not believe a man without skill and courage deserves to survive. By submitting to the rule of law Seth has crippled himself, and all of us who love him are helpless when he is threatened. Do you know what Seth does?"

Holcroft shook his head.

"He drinks. That is what the law has done to him. He numbs his mind so he can keep himself harmless, so his son can survive into the next century by learning to live under the rule of lesser men." She shrugged. "They call it progress. Myself, I would rather go backward. But I will go where the people I love go. That is the only choice we have."

Homer was disturbed by her vision. "That's a grim view of the world, Esperanza."

"It is how I see things."

"Would Seth agree with you?"

"If he did, he would take his family far into the wilderness where the law hasn't yet found its way."

Feeling a glimmer of hope, Holcroft asked, "What does he expect to find in civilization?"

"Redemption for his crimes," she answered.

"Don't you consider that a worthy goal?"

"Ah *sí*, but his method is mistaken. By raising his son to be a good citizen, Seth is hoping to redeem himself. But Lobo cannot redeem Seth. Only he can do that. Yet the only remedy the world will accept is for Seth to surrender his freedom. That he won't do, so he offers his son instead." She smiled sadly. "But Lobo doesn't want to be Seth's peace offering. He wants to be a man who moves with power. In the wilderness that is possible. In the civilized world such a man is sacrificed for the rule of law. So while Seth is striving to offer his son for his sins, Lobo is striving to become an equal of his father. Both will fail."

"You're making me melancholy, Esperanza," Holcroft said.

"You asked for my thoughts." She smiled. "You and I are the same, are we not? My name means hope, and isn't that what religion offers: the hope that God will set everything right after death? But in this life we can only comfort those close to us. Is that not true?"

"Yes," he said.

"*Bueno*." She laughed. "How about a piece of pie to nourish you for your journey home?"

Rico rode her palomino high into the hills, feeling better than she had in weeks because she now knew it was her pregnancy that upset her equilibrium. She hoped for a second daughter. Seth's love for Elena was a joy to share, and Rico looked forward to watching the girl grow to be a woman beneath Seth's appreciative eye. Lobo, however, was worrisome. As he approached manhood, his challenge of Seth would grow stronger, and Rico was afraid another son might break Seth's resolve to raise his children without violence.

He had a deep well of it which she knew he controlled with severe discipline. She supposed it had been born under the whip wielded too vigorously and too often by his own father. Yet Rico didn't blame Seth's father; she blamed Allister, the seasoned outlaw who had taken Seth on at eighteen and taught him, not only to pillage and rape, but to expend any regret he felt by inflicting more hurt. After watching Allister's solution suck him into an early grave, Seth was trying to change, at least to the degree that he didn't inflict his hurt on his family.

Rico believed if she could help him understand that what he did at Blue's was the last vestige of all he'd learned from Allister, Seth could finally leave those lessons behind and be the man he would've been without Allister's influence. Already his love for Elena was teaching him that the girls working for Blue were other men's daughters who didn't deserve what he gave them. Blue, of course, saw it the same way Seth always had, but Joaquín was Rico's ally.

She spurred her mare to gain the final ascent onto a cliff overlooking the railroad to Benson. Stretching to the distant mountains, the desert was empty except for the two lines of iron slicing the wilderness. A boy carrying a bouquet of roses walked on the wooden cross ties. He was about ten years old and dressed in city clothes, the roses deep red in the bright light of noon. As she watched, he looked up and saw her. He stared a moment, then gave her a shy smile. Wondering who he was, she turned her horse and caught the trail leading down an ancient path left by Apaches who had once claimed this desert as home.

Now she owned the land bounded by the railroad, and she curiously approached the boy who was crossing the edge of what was hers. He stood watching her come, his face freckled, his smile tentative. When she reined to a stop beneath the embankment of the tracks, she was looking up at him as if he were already a man. He offered her a rose from his bouquet, and she stretched from the saddle to accept it, held it to her nose in gratitude a moment, then smiled at him.

"You're Lobo's stepmother, aren't you?" he said.

She nodded. "Who are you?"

"Rick Clancy," he answered.

"Your father owns the bank in Tejoe," she said.

"Yeah. I'm taking these flowers to my mother. They come from Mrs. Nickles' garden."

Rico laughed to think of roses growing on a hogranch. She thought she and Mrs. Nickles might be friends if things were different, if she weren't the supposed wife of an outlaw whom people shunned.

"I've seen you in town," the boy said, "when you come to Engle's Mercantile to buy supplies."

"And you know Lobo from school," she said.

"Yeah," he said. "But we're not friends."

"Why not?"

He looked down the long line of rails shining in the sun. "My father told me to stay away from him. All the kids were told the same."

"Did he tell you why?" she asked, feeling sad for Lobo.

The boy's dark eyes met hers. "He said Lobo's a bad seed, but it doesn't make much sense to me." He looked at the roses withering in the heat. "My mother said different, though."

"What did your mother say?" Rico asked with a smile.

"That it's not Lobo's fault what his father did, and he won't have a chance to be good if nobody'll be his friend. That a person needs friends to get along in the world, and maybe if the outlaw had better friends when he was young, he wouldn't have done the things he did."

Rico smiled again. "I think I'd like your mother."

"She said the same of you. After you came to church, she told my father at supper that you looked like a lady coming in on your husband's arm, and that maybe everybody should forget the past and bring you all into the fold.'' He smiled awkwardly. ''She talks like the Bible sometimes.''

Rico smiled back. ''What did your father say?''

''He doesn't think the same. I can't make much sense of the world, they see it so different.'' Again he looked down the iron rails toward town. ''My father'll whip me when I get home because I ditched school.'' He looked at the roses, then back at Rico. ''Lobo told me his father never whips him. Is that true?''

She nodded.

''I wish he was my father then. I don't like my father much, and it's plain Lobo likes his a lot.''

''You'll like him better when you're a little older,'' she said. ''Things will make more sense then.''

He shook his head. ''I don't see how a man can love his son and take a whip to him too.''

''He's only doing what he believes is right,'' she said gently. ''Just because a person's grown doesn't mean they never make mistakes.''

The boy watched her a moment, then said, ''Sometimes I think about how to hurt him back. You know what's the worst thing I could do?''

She shook her head.

''Grow up like the outlaw. Then no one could whip me.''

''Seth regrets the things he did,'' she said quickly. ''In his mind he whips himself, and that's worse.''

The boy frowned in puzzlement. ''Can't see how it could be.'' He looked at the flowers again, then gave her a smile. ''I have to get home now. Tell Lobo hello for me, will you?''

She nodded and watched him trudge off between the rails. When he was just a speck in the distance, she saw him leave the tracks and cut across the desert toward town and the whipping he knew was waiting. Sadly Rico turned her horse and headed home, lifting the rose to smell its fragrance.

15

It was late afternoon when Seth and Joaquín came down from the mountains with the two boys and the carcass of a deer. The yearling buck had been draped across Lemonade's horse, and he rode behind Lobo.

At the homestead, the men left the carcass with the women and rode into town. The boys, too, were supposed to stay with the women and help if they could, but as soon as the men were gone, Lobo and Lemonade followed them. From a safe distance they watched Seth and Joaquín leave their horses in the high-plank corral behind Blue's saloon.

"What about supper?" Lemonade asked, feeling the pangs of hunger.

Lobo shrugged. "I'm thinkin' more of where we can leave our horses and get to 'em in a hurry if need be."

"There's the corral behind the courthouse," Lemonade suggested. "If we tie 'em to the fence, they can reach the water trough easy."

"Okay," Lobo said, reining around toward the right alley.

The courthouse corral was empty except for the sheriff's horse, a huge bay that snorted warily as the boys tied their reins to a rail. When Lobo pumped the handle to fill the trough, the sheriff's horse came over with its head down, blowing great sighs that raised dust from the hard-packed dirt of the corral. Lobo stopped pumping and leaned on the fence as he watched the horse drink.

"You can tell the caliber of a man by the horse he rides," he told Lemonade, who looked sheepishly at his own rather sorry mount. "You should've kept that bay you sold me," Lobo went on. "Did you know it belonged to a lawman in Tombstone?"

Lemonade shook his head. "Just as glad I din't keep it, if that's the truth."

"You callin' me a liar?" Lobo asked, standing up straight to face him.

Lemonade laughed. "For such a little tyke, ya sure are ready to fight at the drop of a hat."

"I ain't little," Lobo argued.

"How old are ya?"

"Almost eight."

"Well, I'm fourteen. Reckon I could beat ya pretty easy."

"You want to try?"

"No," Lemonade said with disgust. "Ain't we gonna get any supper?"

Lobo looked at the back of the courthouse. "When I was in the sheriff's office the other night, I saw a basket of apples in the corner. Reckon we could snitch some if he ain't around."

Lemonade groaned. "I'd rather snitch from 'most anybody but the sheriff. If he catches us, it ain't far to jail, is it?"

"He won't put us in jail for stealin' apples," Lobo scoffed.

"How d'ya know?"

" 'Cause he and Seth are friends, for one reason."

"Yeah? Give me another."

"He's afraid of Seth."

"Who isn't?" Lemonade agreed.

"I ain't," Lobo said.

"How 'bout when he hits ya. Ain't ya afraid then?"

"He never hits me," Lobo said, unable to look at his friend.

Lemonade knew he was lying but let it pass. "Let's go get some of them apples. If'n we're caught, reckon I'll find out, huh?"

"We won't get caught," Lobo said.

They climbed the fence into the corral and ran across to the stables. The door leading to the long aisle in front of the cells wasn't locked. Neither were the cells; all their doors stood wide open. As the boys moved through the dark shadows toward the office in front of them, Lobo walked nonchalantly, figuring if anybody was there he'd just say they'd stopped by to say hello. He knew he could ask for an apple and be pretty sure of getting one, but stealing it seemed a lot more fun. The office was empty, however, and the bushel basket still in the corner as he remembered.

Lemonade picked out the apple he wanted, then bit into it as he watched out the window for the sheriff. Lobo turned around and looked at the cell Seth's blow had sent him sprawling into. He even walked inside and stuck his wrists through the bars as if he had been in there so long he was bored. "Please, Sheriff Slater," he joked, "don't hang me. I promise I won't ever steal apples again."

Lemonade laughed and walked over to the case of Winchesters against the wall. "Now here's something worth stealin'," he said, then took another noisy bite of his apple.

Lobo went over and stood beside him, both of them appraising the chain that ran through the trigger guard of each rifle. It was closed with a padlock. "You any good at pickin' locks?" Lobo whispered.

Lemonade snorted. "If Seth caught ya with one of them

rifles, I know for a fact he'd hit ya so don't try'n tell me dif'rent.''

"I wouldn't let him see me," Lobo argued.

"Like ya weren't gonna let him catch ya with that horse?"

"Abneth Nickles told on me is the only reason I got caught."

"Well, a seven-year-old kid totin' a 'spensive rifle's gonna get told on too," Lemonade said.

"I'm almost eight," Lobo reminded him, looking around the office. He walked behind the sheriff's desk, sat down and put his feet up. "Wonder what it'd feel like to be a lawman."

Lemonade laughed with ridicule. "Seth Strummar's son wearin' a badge. That'd be somethin'!"

"Yeah," Lobo said. He lowered his feet and opened a drawer. Seeing a stack of wanted posters, he lifted them out and flipped through them. "Look at all this money just for catchin' somebody."

"Ain't that easy," Lemonade said. "Those men are killers, like as not." He walked across to look over Lobo's shoulder at the posters the kid was rifling through.

Lobo stopped and pulled one out. SETH STRUMMAR, it said across the top. ONE THOUSAND DOLLARS, DEAD OR ALIVE, FOR THE MURDER OF A TEXAS RANGER. POSITIVE IDENTIFICATION REQUIRED. "There it is," he whispered.

"A lotta money," Lemonade said.

"I'd kill the man who tried to collect it."

"Uh-huh. You and who else?"

"Joaquín."

Lemonade pulled the next flier out of the pile and held it up, grinning at his friend. JOAQUÍN ASCARATE, ALIAS SAMANIEGO. WANTED BY THE TERRITORY OF NEW MEXICO FOR ATTEMPTED MURDER AND LARCENY OF A HORSE.

"Gosh," Lobo whispered. "I didn't know he had one, too."

"Here's another," Lemonade crowed, pulling one out with BLUE RIVERS, DEAD OR ALIVE printed across the top.

"Jesus," Lemonade said. "Blue killed a judge. Did ya know that?"

"Sure. It was a fair fight but they was gonna hang him anyway, so Seth rescued him from the Rangers in Isleta. Didn't you ever hear that?"

Lemonade shook his head.

"That's what I mean," Lobo boasted. "There's no way Seth would let me be arrested for nothin'."

"Huh," Lemonade said, knowing he wasn't included in that protection. "Maybe we best get outta here, Lobo."

"We only came 'cause you was hungry." He smiled. "If you've had enough to eat, we can go anytime."

"I'll just get one more apple," Lemonade said.

Lobo folded the three posters together and stuffed them into his back pocket, then replaced the others in the drawer and slid it closed.

"Don'cha think he'll miss 'em?" Lemonade asked.

Lobo shrugged. "Won't know where to look if he does."

Lemonade turned around and peered through the window again. "Here he comes!"

"Shit," Lobo said. Spinning on his heel, he ran into the corridor.

Lemonade was right behind, but they'd only made it into the deeper shadows when the front door opened. Lemonade pulled Lobo into the darkness of a cell where they huddled in a corner, trapped until the sheriff went out again.

Melinda left the dressmaker's and walked down the street toward the bank. After giving the seamstress half the cost of the dresses, she still had a hundred dollars in her purse. Since Joaquín had paid the rent on her room for the rest of the month, she planned on putting the full amount in her account and eating off Blue until payday. That hadn't been part of their arrangement but she figured she could milk him good as long as Joaquín was taking her part.

She smiled fondly, remembering Joaquín's sweetness.

How he ever hooked up with the likes of Seth Strummar was a mystery she didn't have to understand to use to her advantage. By plying Joaquín's leverage, she might end up half owner of the Blue Rivers Saloon and eventually have enough money to buy Blue out. Then she'd be the one welcoming Seth into her domain. For that to happen, though, her nest egg had to accumulate interest from the beginning, and she meant to add to her account every payday.

Seeing Lila Keats go into the bank, Melinda quickened her pace, wanting to crow about the coup she'd pulled. She smiled as she walked through the door and saw Lila standing at a counter filling out a transaction slip. Melinda walked over and stood close enough to see that Lila was only doodling, making Melinda wonder who she was trying to impress with her presence in the bank. When Lila looked up, Melinda smiled and said, "Afternoon, Lila."

She laughed. "Heard you got yourself a job."

Melinda nodded. "Figure I'll last longer'n you."

Lila shrugged. "My working days are over."

"You find yourself a sugar daddy?"

"Yeah, I did. His name is Seth Strummar." Lila looked at the clock on the wall. "Excuse me," she said with sarcasm. "I have someplace else to be."

"Ain't that just too bad," Melinda said, blocking her path. "Are you tryin' to tell me Seth's keepin' you now?"

Lila laughed, looking past her as the door opened.

Melinda glanced over her shoulder and saw three men come in with their guns drawn. "Holy shit," she whispered. "I walked right into it."

"Don't stick your neck out and you won't get hurt," Lila warned.

Bob Tice had been watching the two woman talk, distracted by their beauty. He flicked his gaze at the men who had just come in, not expecting them to be of any interest, but their guns told him otherwise.

"Hands up!" Norris barked, pointing his pistol at the guard.

Tice raised his hands, wishing he had the rifle he'd left leaning in a corner.

Webster came close and took the sixgun out of Tice's holster, then said with a grin, "Go stand with the ladies."

Tice moved over against the wall with the women, the only other people in the bank besides the teller, who was staring with an open mouth.

Joe Tyler stayed by the door, nervously glancing outside at his brother holding the horses, as Norris went behind the counter and stuck his gun in the teller's face. "Open the vault," Norris said in a pleasant tone.

"I can't," the teller said.

"Open it or die," Norris said calmly.

The teller looked at the guard.

"You best do it," Bob Tice advised.

The door to the office opened and J. J. Clancy stood framed on the threshold. "What's going on?" he demanded.

Norris laughed. "Came to make a withdrawal, Mr. Banker. Why don't you open the safe?"

Clancy hesitated, loath to give in so easily.

"You best do it," Tice said again.

"All the money in the world ain't worth your life," Norris agreed.

Still Clancy hesitated. "You won't get away with this," he warned.

"Who's gonna stop us?" Norris mocked. "You do it now and both you and your teller'll still be alive. One more minute and one of you's gonna be dead."

Clancy looked at Bartles and saw sweat beading on the teller's upper lip. "He can't," Clancy told Norris. "No sense in hurting him."

"No sense a'tall if you move." Norris grinned. "If you don't, a little blood's a prime spur to action, don'cha think?"

"He has a family," Clancy argued.

"Don't you?" Norris asked.

Slowly Clancy moved toward the vault, trying to think

of a solution. Only last month a drummer had come through and tried to sell him a time lock, but he'd scoffed at the notion that Tejoe needed such protection. Realizing the robbers couldn't know he hadn't bought one, he toyed with the idea of trying to convince them he had. His mind was a blank, though. He couldn't remember one thing the drummer had said that might sound convincing. "You're stealing the money of Seth Strummar," was all he could think to say. "You sure you want him for an enemy?"

Norris guffawed as if at a joke. "Ain't a more famous thief in the West, Mr. Banker. I figure he'll admire our pluck. 'Sides, everybody knows his money was stolen once, so it don't make no nevermind we're stealing it again."

"It's not just his money," Clancy pointed out.

"All money's the same to us," Norris said. "Get busy."

Clancy looked at the two women, recognizing one of them. "You're Lila Keats," he said.

She smiled. "I came to make a withdrawal."

"I didn't," Melinda said.

"You come to make a deposit?" Webster asked, eyeing her purse.

"I came to stop you," she said.

Lila thought that was funny. She laughed when Webster tore Melinda's purse off her arm. He rummaged inside, found the hundred dollars, and held it high as he grinned at her.

"You sonofabitch," Melinda yelled, grabbing for it.

Webster hit her with his gun. She fell with a cry as blood poured from a cut in her forehead.

Norris frowned. "That enough blood for you, Mr. Banker, or you want some more?"

"I'll see you hang," Clancy threatened.

"If you don't open that safe right quick," Norris answered, "you ain't gonna live to see nothin'."

Believing him, Clancy knelt on the floor and spun the dial. His hands were shaking so badly, however, that when he'd turned the combination and yanked the lever, the lock held. "Just a minute," he wheedled.

"You got one more chance," Norris said.

Clancy looked over his shoulder at Lila Keats. "The sheriff told me you were planning this," he told her.

She smiled. "I guess he was hoping to ride clear after it was over."

"You saying he's in on it?" Clancy asked, astonished.

"He's not here stopping it, is he?"

"Hurry up," Norris said, jabbing his pistol into the banker's neck.

Clancy told himself to concentrate as he spun the dial again. He didn't like the dark bore of the gun leveled at his jugular any more than he liked the chill of Mrs. Keats' smile. He had one more number to find when he heard the other woman moan. Looking over his shoulder to see the blood oozing from her forehead as she sat up, Clancy felt ill. He couldn't breathe well, and it amazed him that the men holding guns were smiling as if they were having a good time. He wanted to strike out at the ugliness of their arrogance. It wasn't that he'd worked so hard to accumulate the money they wanted, but his depositors had. Not Strummar, of course, though he wasn't the only man in town whose livelihood had come from a shady source. Clancy heaved the lever down and opened the door, revealing the town's lifeblood neatly stacked and bundled.

"Goddamn," Webster whispered, moving closer to his newfound wealth.

Melinda touched her wound, then looked at the blood on her fingertips as she struggled to think. She knew her money was in the hands of the thieves and she'd never see it again. That didn't bother her so much as the thought that Lila Keats would get it after all. Melinda looked up at the woman standing just above her, but Lila was watching the safe and smiling at the sight of all that money.

Webster was smiling at it too, though he was supposed to be watching the guard. Bob Tice began inching toward the rifle he'd left leaning in the corner.

Joe Tyler was watching the street. Nobody was coming so he gave his brother a wink to say everything was going according to plan. Thinking of the good times ahead, Webster laughed as he watched Norris rake the bundles of bills and sacks of coins into his saddlebags.

Lila looked down at Melinda and gloated, "You be sure and tell Seth I got what's mine. Tell him my name was Esmeralda when he knew me before, and the man he killed wasn't Bart Keats but Clay Barton. I think he'll remember us now."

Melinda grabbed hold of Lila's skirts. "Why don't you tell him yourself?"

Lila tugged at her dress. "Let go," she snapped.

Melinda held on. The waistband tore, then caught again, and Melinda laughed because the seamstress had done a good job and doublestitched the skirt to the bodice.

Norris turned with the bags heavy in his hands. "Let's go."

"What about them?" Webster asked, nodding at the banker and teller watching with ashen faces.

Joe Tyler was already outside, taking his reins from his brother.

Bob Tice reached his rifle just as the banker's son came in from the alley. Rick Clancy stopped, bewildered by the chaos in front of him: one woman bleeding on the floor and holding onto the skirts of another who was kicking her, two men with guns on his father and Mr. Bartles. Mr. Tice was raising his rifle, the front door wide open and empty. In panic, the boy ran toward the sunlight.

Tice fired at Norris but missed. Webster whirled and pulled the trigger, not taking time to aim, hitting the kid instead of the guard. Rick Clancy sprawled and slid face down toward the ribbon of sunlight just inside the door. Norris shot the guard, who fell over backwards as the banker bellowed in anguish.

"Help me!" Lila screamed, kicking at Melinda.

Norris ran. Webster did too, spraying bullets at Clancy and Bartles who ducked behind the counter. Knowing she

could betray them, Webster saved his last shot for Lila
Keats. She grunted as the bullet pierced her side, then she
swung her fist at Melinda. "You goddamned bitch! Let me
go!"

Melinda hung on. "Not 'til Seth sees what I've done
for him."

Bob Tice knew he had failed. Only the woman was left,
struggling to escape. In a last ditch effort to redeem his
honor, he took aim at the purple bodice of her dress, but
he slumped into death as he pulled the trigger, so his bullet
went low and hit Melinda's heart.

Bartles huddled behind the counter, hugging himself
with fright as he listened to the horses gallop away. When
he heard footsteps, he raised himself to a crouch and
peered over the counter in time to see Clancy fall to his
knees beside the body of his son, lifeless in a pool of
blood. "Lord have mercy," Bartles whispered.

When Lila whimpered as she tried to pry open Melinda's hands, Clancy rose and hurtled himself across the
room. "You'll hang!" he sobbed, wrenching Lila free of
the dead woman's grasp. "Let's get the goddamned sheriff!" he yelled to Bartles.

The teller followed as his boss dragged the bleeding
woman through the door, then Bartles stood stunned on
the boardwalk as Clancy half-carried the woman down the
street. Men were coming out now, their faces stern with
expectation of danger. They looked at the banker hauling
the shrieking woman toward the sheriff's office, then at
Bartles standing alone.

"What happened?" Maurice Engle yelled from in front
of his store.

"Robbed the bank!" Bartles shouted.

"Them just now?"

"Killed Rick Clancy, too!" he yelled. "*She* was in on
it." He nodded toward the woman leaving a trail of blood
behind as she was dragged up the street.

Tom Beck opened the door of his hotel and stood a

moment watching Clancy and the woman, then looked at Engle. "What happened?" Beck asked.

"Robbed the bank!" Engle shouted angrily.

"Who?" Beck asked, stunned.

"Her," Bartles said, thrusting his chin after Clancy. "The others got away."

"Killed Rick Clancy!" Bartles repeated, then added, "And Bob Tice and a woman, too!"

Men jostled him out of the doorway as they pushed into the bank to see for themselves.

"Sonofabitch," one man whispered.

"Lord Almighty!" another said.

"Where's the sheriff?" Engle demanded of Bartles.

"That's where Clancy's gone," he answered.

Engle bolted back across the street and inside his store, then came out carrying a shotgun. "We'll need a posse," he yelled, running toward the sheriff's office. "Get your guns, men!"

Bartles followed, his feet like wood. He could see the entire length of the block ahead of him: ladies staring from the boardwalks at Clancy and the woman, men ducking through doors and coming back out with guns, accumulating in number until they were a wave of rage rolling toward the sheriff's office. When someone took hold of Bartles' arm, he turned around to see Blue Rivers beside him.

"What happened?" Blue asked in a low voice, as if soliciting his confidence.

Bartles had often admired Blue, his easy nonchalance as he rode rein over his saloon, his wholesome good looks and confident walk. Feeling flattered that Blue had singled him out, Bartles told what he knew.

Sheriff Slater had heard the shots and hesitated a moment too long. Standing in front of the rack of Winchesters, he'd barely managed to unlock the chain on the rifles when Clancy burst in dragging Lila Keats, followed by twenty men rabid with outrage. "The bank's been robbed," they all yelled at once, "an innocent child killed!"

The woman was hideous, a painted face screeching betrayal as the men shoved her into the front cell and slammed the door. Holding her bloody side, she snarled, "Rafe Slater knew all along! He told me and Bart how rich the bank was! We came here to rob it under his protection!"

The eyes of the men turned on their sheriff.

Rafe shook his head. "She's lying," he said weakly.

"We need a posse!" Tom Beck said.

"Gotta have the law for that," Engle said.

"The law was in on it!" Clancy shouted. "Slater told me it would happen." His face crumpled as he bit back tears. "They killed my boy, you bastard!" He lunged for Slater.

Beck caught and held the banker. "That doesn't make sense, Clancy. He wouldn't have told you if he was in on it!"

"He's in on it!" Lila confirmed. "He was just trying to cover himself when it came down. It's his fault the boy's dead."

"We elected you to protect us!" Clancy yelled, struggling within Beck's grip.

"Let's hang him!" Engle uttered. "Then catch the others."

"Put him in jail," Beck argued. "Isn't that easier?"

"He knows this jail inside out," Engle answered. He reached across and disarmed Slater, then tore the badge off his vest. "I say hang him!"

"Deserves it sure as hell!" someone shouted from the back.

"Wait a minute," Rafe pleaded. "Think about what you're saying, Maurice."

"Nothin' worse than a sheriff who hits his own town," Engle retorted. "What do you say, Clancy?"

"Hang him!" he sobbed.

"The sooner we're done," Engle growled, "the sooner we go after our money!"

"Hang him!" Lila echoed. "Robbing the bank was his idea!" Weakening from loss of blood, she sat down hard on the bunk and laughed, a curdled sound.

"You gonna take her word over mine?" Rafe asked incredulously.

The men all looked at her collapsed on the bed, then at the blood dripping into a pool on the floor beneath her.

"The woman is dying," Esquibel said. "No one lies facing Judgment."

Men grabbed the sheriff and jostled him onto the street.

"You're making a mistake," Rafe argued.

"Our mistake was trusting you," Engle said. "But we're gonna rectify that damn quick."

Rafe tried to meet the eyes of the men crowding him along, but no one would look at him. Men he had eaten lunch with in Amy's Cafe, drank with in the Blue Rivers Saloon, men he had sat with in the courtroom to mete out justice, in the council chambers to decide town policy. Their faces were closed against him now, their eyes blind to what they were doing, shuttered to the agony of remorse he knew would be theirs with dawn, a regret so powerful they couldn't allow themselves to contemplate it in the heat of action.

Like a stampede to disaster, the mob surged down the street toward Esquibel's livery. Women in shadowed doorways watched with pale faces. A child stood on the boardwalk with his hands stuck straight down at his sides and his mouth open in silent terror as the men swept past. Flinging open the corral gate and swarming inside, they frightened the horses so the herd escaped into freedom. Rafe Slater watched after the animals with envy as he was pushed under the crossbeam outside the loft and a dozen men shouted for a rope.

Esquibel brought a horse from inside, and Rafe was lifted onto its back by men he had thought were friends. Feeling the animal's warmth between his thighs, he thought it was the last thing he'd remember, then someone put the noose around his neck and he felt the rough rope prick his skin with the promise that soon he wouldn't remember anything.

Across the heads of the noisy mob, he saw Blue Rivers standing in the empty street. Rafe smiled to let Blue know he understood there was nothing one man could do, it was just his luck this time. Blue lifted his hands in a gesture of helplessness, then turned and hurried away. Rafe stared at Blue's retreating back, not wanting to miss his last glimpse of a friend across the bestiality boiling around him.

Esquibel yelled from the loft that the knot wasn't right, and Engle shouted for him to hurry up because the horse was scared. The horse, Rafe thought, they're worried about the horse.

Lobo and Lemonade had huddled in the back cell as the mob stormed into the sheriff's office and took him away. Slowly Lobo crept into the silence left by their departure and looked at Lila Keats dying in the first cell, then he ran for the tenderloin hoping Seth hadn't gone home.

Inside Blue's saloon, the tinny piano blocked all sounds from the street. Lobo saw Joaquín at the bar. Joaquín saw him, too, and Lobo was dimly aware of the anger on Joaquín's face, then that the anger was replaced by alarm.

"Where's Seth?" Lobo shouted.

"Upstairs," Joaquín said softly. "What is it, Lobo?"

Lobo ran up the stairs. The music quit and his footsteps sounded frantic in the sudden quiet. At the top he stopped, confused by all the closed doors along the hall, then he heard Joaquín behind him. "Where?" Lobo cried.

Joaquín grabbed him. "Tell *me*, Lobo!" he commanded.

But Lobo wouldn't. "Where is he?"

Joaquín looked at a door and it was enough. Lobo twisted free, lunged for the door, and flung it open to see his father drinking at a table with Nib Carey. There was a woman on Nib's lap. Her dress was open, her breasts bare between the dark wings of cloth. She lurched to her feet, backing away as she covered herself. Slowly Seth stood up, his eyes colder than Lobo had ever seen them.

"This ain't no place for a child," Seth said.

"A mob's got the sheriff!" Lobo shouted. "Someone robbed the bank and they think he was in on it. They're gonna lynch him, Seth!"

Silence in the room. Seth's eyes a cold slate gray. The woman looking sick, Nib Carey astonished, Seth standing there wearing a gun but not moving.

"They'll lynch him!" Lobo wailed. "They'll hang him, Seth, and he didn't do nothin'! Ya gotta stop 'em!"

The woman murmured, "Honey, no man can stop a mob."

"You would've done it for Jeremiah," Lobo told his father. "It's the same, ain't it? Ain't it?" He felt Joaquín's hand on his shoulder but shook it off. "Ain't you gonna do nothin', Seth?"

Seth's gray eyes softened with hurt. "You shouldn't be here, Lobo."

"So what?" he screamed. "Ya gotta stop 'em!"

Into the silence footsteps rang out ascending the stairs, then Blue ran into the room. He opened his mouth to speak but didn't, seeing Seth and Lobo staring at each other.

Seth asked his son, "You expect me to defend the law?"

"Who else can do it?" Lobo answered.

Reverend Holcroft sprinted up the street toward the livery. Minutes earlier, Tulia had told him what happened, chattering in Spanish at first then finally using English to say the town had gone mad over the death of the Clancy boy.

"I told you!" she crowed. "The outlaw has doomed us all."

Holcroft didn't contradict her. He ran outside, following the hideous siren of the mob to disaster. "Wait!" he wanted to yell as he ran, but he couldn't find the breath.

Tom Beck caught hold of him at the corral gate and

pulled him aside. "You can't stop them," he said sadly. "They're bent on doing it, Reverend."

Holcroft took one more faltering step, then stopped, appalled at what he was seeing. He looked around for help and saw Lemonade behind Beck.

"Ya best pray," the boy said cheerfully.

Holcroft stood on the other side of the fence from the frenzied agitation of the mob, feeling sick. Never had he seen humanity so ugly. He wanted to do as the boy said, drop to his knees and beg God to stop what he was seeing, but his knees wouldn't bend.

Esquibel called from the loft that the knot was ready now, and Rafe Slater almost laughed that all his striving to go straight had ended with a noose. A hush fell over the men as Engle told Clancy to let go of the horse's head and get out of the way, but Clancy was staring up the street and didn't move. Twisting around to follow the banker's gaze, Rafe felt the rope prick his neck with tiny feelers of warning that soon his life would be over. He heard gunfire, then saw Seth galloping his sorrel toward the corral, Joaquín on his black like a shadow, both of them firing rifles over the heads of the mob.

Homer Holcroft fell to his knees with a prayer for mercy.

"Back off or die!" Seth shouted, aiming his rifle at Engle about to slap the condemned man's horse.

Engle met the cold gray eyes behind the gun and took a step away, his hand frozen in the air. "This is right what we're doing!" he yelled. "Don't interfere where you don't belong!"

"I ain't," Seth said. "I don't like lynching in my town."

"They killed my son!" Clancy shouted.

"Robbed the bank, too!" Engle added. "Cleaned it out and got clear away!"

"Seems to me you oughta be chasing them," Seth drawled with disgust, " 'stead of committing a crime yourself."

"They're gone!" Engle retorted. "Slater's caught and we're gonna teach him an irrevocable lesson."

"He'll be dead," Seth said. "You're the ones facing a hard lesson."

"You say that to us!" Esquibel shouted from the loft. "You who has hung not only the man who killed your brother but the woman who killed your partner!"

"I know all about lynchings," Seth agreed. "I'm sparing you some of the knowing I carry."

"Don't listen to him!" Engle bellowed.

Seth fired a shot over the roof of the barn. "I got eight bullets left and Joaquín's got twelve. We'll kill at least half of you before you stop us. Is that what you want?"

"What will you gain?" Engle sneered. "You'll be dead, too." When Strummar met his gaze, Engle took another step away. He saw that the outlaw knew about the bank in Arkansas and thought him a hypocrite.

Seth shifted his gaze, lowered the sight on his rifle, and pulled the trigger. The sheriff's horse jerked as the severed rope fell free, and the men gasped at the accuracy of the shot. As the irony of who they were opposing came clear to them, the mob was restored to a collection of individuals.

Seth laid his rifle across his lap and waited for the next move.

Alfonso Esquibel challenged him. "Let me ask you this, Señor Strummar. We had no trouble before you arrived. Now we try to rid ourselves of trouble and you interfere. Why should we listen to a man who has lived outside the law all his life?"

Seth studied the faces waiting for his answer, then spoke directly to Esquibel. "If you think I give your town a bad name, what do you reckon this'd do to it? That ain't the worst, though. A man can learn to live with the ill feelings of his neighbors, but all the times you wake at night in a cold sweat 'cause of what you've done, the times you look in a mirror and 'stead of your own reflection see your victim's face blacken above the noose, see his boots kicking for ground that ain't there, what his feet'll find is your soul, and I guarantee you won't like the kick of his death.'' Seth stopped and scanned the faces again. ''I made a lot of mistakes in my life. This ain't one of 'em.''

''What'll happen to Slater?'' Engle jeered.

''We'll put him in jail and you can hold him for trial.''

They all stared in silence at the outlaw enforcing the law. Rafe Slater sat with his hands tied behind him, bareback on a horse whose bridle was held by the banker.

Clancy's face crumpled with grief. He leaned heavily on the head of the horse, clutching a cheekstrap in each hand as he sobbed on the animal's nose.

Joaquín lowered his rifle and slid it into the scabbard. He edged his horse into the crowd, then leaned to touch the banker's shoulder. Clancy looked up and met the gentle eyes of the man who had once wanted to be a priest.

''Go comfort your wife,'' Joaquín said with sorrow.

In silent acquiescence, Clancy turned and stumbled away.

''All of you go home,'' Seth said to the rest of them. ''Give it to your wives. They'd rather have it than a husband with blood on his hands.''

In humbled silence, the men dispersed. Joaquín pulled his knife and cut the rope holding the sheriff's hands, then smiled across the now empty corral at Seth.

Homer Holcroft stood up, seeing Lobo standing in the open gate. He embraced the boy, whose body trembled as much as the minister's knees. With pride shining in his eyes, Lobo whispered, ''Seth stopped 'em.''

''Yes,'' Holcroft said.

Blue walked into the corral. ''Holy shit!'' He laughed. ''I ain't never seen anything like it.''

Seth slid his rifle into its scabbard, then smiled at the sheriff. ''First time I've defended the law,'' Seth said.

Rafe yanked the noose off and threw it into the stable. ''You've restored my faith in humanity.''

Seth laughed. ''You got any whiskey in your office?''

Rafe nodded.

"Let's go have a drink before we tuck you in," Seth said, turning his horse to amble away. At the gate he stopped and looked down at his son standing with the minister.

"God bless you," Holcroft murmured.

Seth snorted in self-deprecation, then held his hand for his son, who took it and leapt up behind him.

Blue swung on behind Joaquín, and they followed with Rafe and the minister. They tied their horses in front of the office and went in. With shaking hands, Rafe opened a new bottle of whiskey as Seth stood looking into the cell at Lila Keats dead on the bunk. Blue was explaining what had happened as he'd heard it from the teller, but Seth was only half-listening. He tried the cell door and discovered it wasn't locked. After hesitating a moment, he walked in to look at Lila more closely.

He could see she had bled to death from a wound just below her ribs that wouldn't have been fatal if she'd been tended by a doctor. Seeing her face of despair on the bed beneath him, a memory flashed in Seth's mind, bringing back his recollection of Lila and Bart Keats, though that hadn't been their names and they'd all been a century younger.

Joaquín came in and stood beside him. Nodding down at the woman with a baffled frown, Joaquín said, "She would have escaped if not for Melinda."

Seth thought about Melinda having the will to hold on to Lila's skirts even as she died.

"If I hadn't tried to help her," Joaquín said, "Melinda wouldn't have been in the bank."

"Maybe," Seth said, wanting to squelch his partner's guilt. "Then again, she might've ended up like Lila, living for vengeance 'stead of giving her life to fight it."

"She gave her life fighting for us," Joaquín said.

Seth gave him a playful smile. "Which proves you have good taste in women."

Joaquín was affronted by the joke. He stared at Seth with new eyes across the dead women between them.

"Seth," the sheriff said, offering the bottle of whiskey from the other side of the bars. "Don't have enough glasses." He shrugged in apology.

Seth walked out of the cage and accepted the bottle. As he drank, he saw the chain reaching through the trigger guards of a dozen rifles in their rack. The lock had been opened and the end of the chain dangled free, catching light on the last link as it twisted in the sun like an empty noose. Seth shuddered. Something had been finished in the cell behind him, and he shivered with dread of what would replace it.

He knew only that he had a job in front of him, and the fact that he would rather be home with his family was as peripheral to his purpose as the suspicion that Joaquín had just broken free from whatever power held them together.

When Seth passed the bottle to Blue, he took a sip, then asked, "What'll you do now?"

"Reckon I'm going after my money," Seth said.

"You want me to ride along?"

He shook his head. "I'll take Nib, if you can spare him."

"Sure," Blue answered hesitantly. "But don't you want me to go?"

Seth looked at Joaquín still standing in the open door of the cell, his dark eyes fierce with vengeance, a drive Seth knew well. He looked back at Blue. "Figure Joaquín's got more of a claim. I need someone to stay with the women."

"All right," Blue said.

"What about me?" Lobo asked hopefully.

Seth shook his head. "Tell Rico I'll be back soon as I can." He looked at Reverend Holcroft. "Can you take charge of the sheriff?" When he nodded, Seth said, "Let's move."

16

Outside the sheriff's office, Seth saw Maurice Engle, Tom Beck, J. J. Clancy, Alfonso Esquibel, Buck Stubbins, and Abneth Nickles walking toward him. He and Joaquín swung onto their horses, then sat looking down at the townsmen bunched a few yards away.

"Ya goin' after the robbers?" Stubbins asked gruffly.

Seth nodded.

"Any objection to our riding along?" Engle asked with sarcasm.

Except for Abneth Nickles, Seth hadn't received an overture of friendship from any of them. "I suggest you go home and stay out of it," he said, reining his horse around.

"Wait!" Clancy yelled.

Seth turned back.

"We got a right to ride along," Stubbins said.

"It was our money, too, señor," Esquibel argued.

His voice shrill with emotion, Clancy yelled, "Five hundred dollars to whoever gets the man who killed my son."

"Hold it!" Seth shouted. "Since none of us has a badge, I think you should let me handle it."

"It's our money you'll be handling," Engle growled.

Seth shrugged with contempt. "Suit yourself," he said, then turned his horse and trotted out of town with Joaquín. After a moment, Nib Carey loped down the road after them.

The six men stood their ground watching the dust settle.

"I'm going," Engle finally said.

"Me, too," Stubbins grunted.

Esquibel appraised them quickly, then said, "I, also."

Beck, Clancy, and Nickles gave their assent by following the others back to the stable where Esquibel supplied them mounts from the ones remaining in the stalls.

The hostler looked regretfully into the distance where his corraled horses had escaped, thinking he should be chasing them, not bandits. He was also risking the mounts he put under the posse, and abandoning his business to scavengers and vandals while he was gone. He would have stayed home and placed his bet on the outlaw retrieving the money except that he didn't want it falling into the hands of Engle or Stubbins. Esquibel had picked up enough gossip to know they were riding the edge of bankruptcy, and he felt certain one or both of them would skim off the top and lie about how much they'd recovered. So he went along hoping to make sure that didn't happen.

Beyond the edge of town, Seth saw Lemonade waiting beside the road, his clothes so new they were still stiff. Seth reined up and smiled at him.

"Can I go, Mr. Strummar?" the kid asked hopefully.

Seth evaluated the horse he'd bought the kid and didn't think much of it. Then, too, Lemonade didn't own a gun. Stacked up against those flaws was the kid's ability to be cheerful in dire straits, a quality shining with charm next to the gloom coming from Joaquín. Seth asked the kid, "You know where the dunes are?"

"Yes, sir," Lemonade said.

"Go to the homestead and trade horses. Tell Rico I said

you could take one of the chestnuts. Take the one with the blaze rather than the star; it's better trained to the saddle. Tell Esperanza I need food for four men for three days, fill all the canteens on the place and bring 'em. And tell Rico I said to lend you the Winchester I keep in the well-house. You got all that?"

"Yes, sir!"

"Don't forget bullets for the rifle. Meet us at the north-east edge of the dunes quick as you can."

Lemonade yanked his horse around, kicked in his heels and galloped back toward town.

Seth looked at Joaquín and Nib. "Let's try'n stay ahead of the good citizens. Agreed?"

Joaquín nodded, his face hard.

"You bet'cha!" Nib said.

They all touched their spurs to their horses' flanks and headed south toward the dunes.

Through the open door of Esquibel's livery, Buck Stubbins watched Lemonade ride past. He'd heard about the outlaw buying new duds for the kid, and Stubbins guessed Lemonade was going to the Strummar homestead for supplies. As he pulled his cinch tight, Stubbins muttered to Engle, "What d'ya reckon, Maurice? Think Strummar's on the level 'bout helpin' us?"

Engle swung onto his horse and smiled grimly. "If he turns outlaw again we can shoot him down easy enough, him and his Mexican shadow."

Abneth Nickles jerked around. "I ain't gonna let that happen! Strummar's taking a risk helping us, and you know it. He's got my support clean down the line."

Engle scanned the faces of the five men watching him. "I'm just saying that if Strummar reverts back to old habits, we got him outnumbered."

"I'm not making a move against Strummar," Tom Beck said. "He could kill us with his eyes closed."

"I've always maintained," Clancy said, struggling for dignity while he felt devastated with grief, "that Strummar is the man with the most experience in this sort of thing."

"Don't forget," Esquibel warned, "he has not only Ascarate behind him, but also Nib Carey. Those men are professionals."

Engle sneered. "Maybe you oughta stay home, Alfonso."

Esquibel shook his head. "I am interested in my money, the same as you. I also think the outlaw has the best chance of success, so I will follow, not oppose him."

"Seems to me," Stubbins said, swinging onto his horse, "that'll depend where he leads us." Not waiting for a reply, he reined down the road, intending to get his money back any way he could. The rest of the men followed with sour faces.

Maurice Engle rankled with resentment that he'd been outmaneuvered. Though he was beginning to feel a smidgeon of gratitude that the lynching had been stopped, he had no intention of letting Strummar lead the posse.

Alfonso Esquibel and J. J. Clancy had been humbled by the outlaw's act and felt profound gratitude for what he'd done. Their only intention was to take custody of the money once it was retrieved.

Abneth Nickles had arrived in town after everything was over. Impressed with Strummar, and wary of Engle and Stubbins, Nickles disapproved of the banker offering a reward, doubting that blood money to promote civic action would foster the reign of reason. He suspected, too, that contemplating the reward might tempt someone to try for the thousand dollars Texas still offered for Strummar, dead or alive. So Nickles rode along to help the outlaw if he could. Otherwise his first loyalty was to his family, and he intended to stay out of the fray.

Tom Beck went along because he had a vague notion that it was incumbent on his duties as mayor. The posse had scant claim to legitimacy without a sheriff, and the fact that it was led by an outlaw made it even shadier. Beck wasn't any kind of warrior, however, but a hotelier. He, too, felt grateful that Strummar had stopped the lynching. Such a sordid event could discredit a town and poison its future overnight, so in Beck's estimate, Strummar had already saved Tejoe. The loss of the money was survivable.

The six men traveled at a tense trot, covering the miles quickly. Except for Nickles, they were businessmen accustomed to walking on floors and sitting in chairs, winning their living with words and signatures on paper. Now they were embarking with various degrees of determination on a cross-country chase, carrying only weapons and water. Before them a dust storm obliterated the horizon. They rode blindly into the abyss, pursuing a man who knew the way.

At the dunes, the road forked east and west, and the strong wind showered the posse with tiny, cutting crystals of sand as it erased even their own tracks. In the distance, Nickles spotted Strummar and his men riding huddled into the storm. He pointed them out to Beck, who nudged Engle. Stubbins caught them all staring in the same direction and saw the riders just before they disappeared in the blowing sand. He led the posse in a gallop after them, but Engle wanted to be first. He spurred his horse into a dead run, passed Stubbins, and had to rein up hard to keep from crowding Nib Carey off the road. Nib swore under his breath and jerked his horse out of the way, glowering at the merchant.

Strummar turned to look at the posse bunching up behind him. He squinted against the sand, his hat pulled low above his eyes and a bandanna across his face.

Engle kicked his horse past the Mexican to ride abreast with Strummar, then leaned close to shout above the wind, "Where're they headed?"

Strummar pointed with his chin. "Chiricahuas."

"Think they're still together?"

"Were before the wind came up."

Engle looked back and saw that all the posse had covered their faces with handkerchiefs now, so he did the same, then looked at Strummar again. The outlaw's eyes were the cold gray of knife blades, making Engle feel unwelcome. Keenly aware of the Mexican riding right behind him, Engle felt it imperative to establish some degree of authority. To his way of thinking, merely riding alongside the jefe achieved that.

Seth knew why Engle was there, and he was willing to humor the merchant until he got in the way. Joaquín also knew, but in his experience claiming a place you couldn't hold only made a fool of a man.

For an hour, they rode through the swirling dust peppered by sharp crystals of sand. The horses walked into the wind with their heads down, their manes and tails buffeted by the wind. At the edge of the dunes, Lemonade waited on a palomino. With his face covered with his new, white handkerchief and his crisp clothes and shiny boots, he looked the image of a storybook highwayman. As the posse approached, Lemonade fell in on the other side of Seth.

Seth nodded a welcome but said nothing. Gunnysacks of food and canteens of water were tied to the kid's saddle, and the Winchester was snug in the scabbard. As for the horse, Rico had loaned him her mare rather than one of the chestnuts, animals trained more to harness than riders. That meant she supported Seth's endeavor and had made her contribution, slight as it was, to his success. Letting his mind drift along the pleasant currents of Rico's pleasing ways, Seth jerked back with the realization that he'd been woolgathering the comforts of his woman instead of concentrating on the task at hand long enough that the terrain had changed around him.

The wind carried only dust now, dry and stifling. An improvement over the stinging sand, it was still debilitating. The posse was soon winding between red rocks carved into eerie visages by the constant wind as the horses ascended the Chiricahuas through the thickening light of dusk. Halfway up, piñons crowded the trail. The men pocketed their bandannas and slapped the dust from their clothes with their hats as the horses snorted and shook their ears, clanking their bridles. Accustomed to the solitude of a renegade, Seth thought the posse sounded like an army moving into the mountains. In the cold dark of a moonless midnight, they entered the yard of an isolated homestead.

Seth swung down and handed his reins to Lemonade, then approached the cabin, stopped and hollered, "Hey, Dan! It's Seth Strummar. You home?"

His voice rose up against the mountains, echoed faintly in the distance, then was lost to the cold wind sighing in the trees. The door opened a crack, and a grizzled codger peered out at the men in his yard. "Hey, Seth," he said in a voice hoarse from disuse. "What'cha doin' ridin' with so many?"

"Tracking four men," Seth said. "They robbed the bank in Tejoe."

Dan studied him morosely. "Ya mean this is a posse?"

Seth nodded.

"Ya can come in," Dan said, "but I don't want the whole herd."

"You mind if they rest in your barn? Get out of the wind for a spell?"

Dan looked across at his barn and studied it for a long while, as if he didn't know every sliver and notch in it. Then he looked at the men sitting their horses, their faces chapped and wind-burnt. "Reckon," he finally said. "But no fires!"

Seth looked at Nib Carey, who nodded and led the posse toward the barn. Joaquín swung down and gave his reins to Lemonade. Maurice Engle dismounted and did the same, then arrogantly met Seth's eyes. Disliking the merchant, Seth merely turned and walked into the dim, smoky cabin of Hermit Dan.

The old man knelt before the hearth, building the fire up strong as the men filed in, first Seth, then Engle, then Joaquín closing the door. Dan carried a grinder over to a hundred-pound sack in a corner, dumped in several handfuls of coffee beans, closed the lid on the grinder and worked the crank as he looked at Seth. "I know Joaquín," Dan said. "Who's the other'n?"

"Maurice Engle," Seth said.

Dan snuck quick glances at Engle. "Sit yourselves," he finally said.

Engle sat at the table in the middle of the room. Seth pulled a chair into an empty space between the far wall and the table, straddling the chair backwards to face Joaquín, who remained standing by the door. Lemonade came in and looked at everyone as Hermit Dan looked at him.

"Name's Lemonade," Seth said with a smile.

Dan nodded, then snickered. "S'prised to see ya ridin' with a posse, Seth."

"Life's full of surprises, ain't it?"

"Allister'd be tickled," the hermit said.

"Reckon he would," Seth agreed.

" 'Member the time he Pecos'd that fella in Seven Rivers?"

Seth nodded.

"Why'd he come at ya shootin' like that?"

"Never found out," Seth said.

Dan looked at Joaquín. "Allister killed 'im fair. Then they was left with the corpse, though. Corpses ain't good things to have to account for. So Allister lassoed the feet and drug it away. Few minutes later he come back and says he Pecos'd 'im." Dan giggled through his broken teeth. "Threw 'im in the river, is what he done."

Joaquín smiled politely, feeling too hurt to laugh. But he thought if a river happened to be nearby when he caught up with Melinda's killers, he might Pecos them, too.

Seth asked, "You ain't seen the men we're after, have you, Dan?"

He shook his head. "Ya'll never catch 'em with so many. These mountains're riddled with overlooks, they'll see ya comin' and skedaddle. Ya oughta move like the Apaches, quiet and few."

"I'd prefer it," Seth said. "But those men feel they have an interest in the money."

For the first time, Hermit Dan looked straight at Engle. "Ya oughta trust Seth. He'll not double-cross ya."

"Never said he would," Engle muttered, throwing Seth a surly frown.

Seth shrugged. "I don't care if you come along, Engle. But what do we need the others for? I'd bet money most of 'em can't shoot well enough to win third prize at a county fair."

"All right," Engle said. "Let's each keep a backup, one man. That suit you?"

"Who do you want?"

"Stubbins."

Seth nodded, already having assessed the miner as the most aggressive of the bunch. "I'll keep Joaquín," he said, then called to Lemonade, "Go ask Stubbins to come in, and tell Nib to take the rest of the men home."

"What about me, Mr. Strummar? Can I stay?"

"I don't care," Seth said, looking at Engle. "You got any objections?"

When Engle shook his head, Lemonade grinned and ran out to deliver the message.

Hermit Dan dropped the ground beans into a huge blackened pot he filled with water from a bucket. Kneeling before the hearth, he hung the pot on the trivet and swung it over the flames, then stayed there, tending his fire.

Seth smiled at Joaquín, trying to soften the grief obviously consuming his thoughts. "We'll sleep here tonight," Seth said. "Get an early start in the morning."

Joaquín nodded.

"Is it all right with you, Dan," Seth asked, "if we bed down in your barn?"

The old man stood up and squinted across at him. "No lanterns. No smokin'."

"Agreed," Seth said.

A few minutes later, Buck Stubbins came in alone, though Nib Carey stood outside the door holding the reins of his horse. Seth walked out to talk in the shadows of the hermit's porch.

"Ya sure this is what ya want?" Nib asked. "Neither one of those men is your friend."

Seth smiled. "I ain't their friend either."

The posse was already shuffling tiredly across the yard to the trail down the mountain. Abneth Nickles waved at Seth. He waved back, wishing the farmer was staying instead of Engle.

"I'm worried about Joaquín," Nib whispered, blunt because they didn't have much time.

Seth evaluated the apprehension in the depth of Nib's bullet-hole eyes. "Appreciate it," he said.

"Any message for home?"

"Tell Blue thanks." He smiled. "And give Rico my love."

Nib nodded and turned away to mount his horse.

Seth took a step closer and spoke softly. "Tell Lobo I'm proud of him. Will you do that, Nib?"

"Sure," he said, gathering his reins. "Good luck."

Seth watched Nib ride away at the tail end of the posse, then went back inside and stopped by the door to lean against the wall near Joaquín. Stubbins and Engle were whispering between themselves at the table. Hermit Dan was crouched before the hearth, pulling the coffeepot out of the flames. Meeting Joaquín's eyes, Seth winced and said, "It wasn't your fault."

"What wasn't?"

"Melinda's death."

"Nothing I did helped her."

"You did your best. Can't expect more from a man."

"God expects the impossible," Joaquín retorted bitterly. "Yet even when I achieve it, He destroys my accomplishment before I have time to catch my breath. I'm beginning to suspect I missed my calling."

Seth studied him carefully. "You wish you'd become a priest?"

Joaquín shook his head. "If we had followed your plan, the men we are now tracking would have been arrested when they walked into the bank. No one would have died. Whose plan was better? Mine that sought to save lives and avoid complicity? It cost the lives of four people and prevented nothing.''

"It wasn't our job to stop those men."

"It is now," he said, his dark eyes angrier than Seth had ever seen them.

"We took it on," he admitted.

"Whatever happens next," Joaquín bit off, "four people are dead because I held you back."

"You didn't kill them," Seth said, straining to keep his voice low. "Seems to me you're shouldering more than your share of blame."

"We have already agreed," Joaquín muttered, "that the world often seems different to you than me."

"This ain't the time to fight about it."

"I will not fight your instincts again. I hope to develop more of my own."

"This ain't the time for practice either," Seth argued. "You go off half-cocked, you could get yourself in as much trouble as the desperados we're chasing."

"Are we not already outlaws?"

"Yeah, in some circles. Most, I reckon."

"Then whatever we do will be outside the law. I see no need to draw the line finely."

"I see the need. Will you grant me that?"

"Yes," Joaquín said. "But if a chance comes that even hints at a cause to kill those men, I will not hesitate."

"Neither will I," Seth agreed.

Lemonade came through the door, carrying bags of food. He looked at the two men huddled over the table, then at Seth and Joaquín watching him. "You want I should make supper, Mr. Strummar?" he asked.

"You know how to cook?"

"Enough for what we got."

Seth smiled. "Be sure you make plenty to share with our host."

Hermit Dan brought them cups of coffee, then leaned against the wall nearby, all of them watching the kid hunkered in front of the fire laying slabs of jerky in a skillet.

Dan said, "My eyes are goin', did'ya know that, Seth?"

He shook his head with sympathy.

"Usually, this time of year, there's deer in the oak thickets down b'low. Think maybe ya could kill me one 'fore ya ride out? Would get me clear through winter, almost."

"I'll go down at first light," Seth said.

Hermit Dan smiled. "I'm glad ya come visitin', Seth. Though you're movin' in strange comp'ny. Those two at the table look shady to me."

Seth chuckled. "One of em's the owner of the biggest mercantile firm in the county, and the other owns the Red Rooster Silver Mine. Those are high-class gentlemen, Dan."

"You talking about us, Strummar?" Engle asked huffily.

"Just telling Dan what upstanding citizens he's got at his table tonight." Seth finished his coffee and moved away from the wall. "Hey, Lemonade, did the women pack me any whiskey?"

"Yeah, they did," he said, bringing it over to the table.

Seth broke the seal and pulled the cork. "To successful partnerships," he said, lifting the bottle then taking a swig.

He offered the whiskey to Engle, who stood up and raised the bottle, took a sip and passed the bottle to Stubbins. He did likewise, then extended it toward Joaquín. As Seth watched to see if he would come out of his self-imposed exile, Joaquín pulled himself away from the wall, advanced into the half-moon of light thrown by the fire, and accepted the whiskey. Holding Seth's eyes with his own, Joaquín took a sip and offered the bottle to Lemonade.

He looked at Seth, who nodded, so the kid took the bottle, raised it in agreement to the toast and sipped, then gave the whiskey back to Seth. He recorked it and set it on the mantle, smiling at Dan, who wet his lips in anticipation of the gift. Then everyone but the hermit sat down and watched Lemonade finish cooking supper. Dan stayed by the wall, nervous at having so much company. After the meal, the visitors walked out to bed down in the barn, and only then did Dan come out of his corner to eat.

Dawn was still a rosy smudge above the ridge when Seth and Joaquín carried rifles down the slope behind the hermit's cabin. From the distant pines an owl hooted its melancholy murmur of vigilance, but the men hadn't yet spoken. Walking quietly through the dense underbrush, Seth glanced at Joaquín and asked, "How'd you sleep?"

Joaquín looked over with surprise. "I didn't."

"You gonna sleep on the trail?"

"Don't worry about me. I am not your concern."

"The hell you ain't! I need you, Joaquín. Don't get independent on me in the middle of this."

"Don't you trust my judgment?" he retorted sarcastically.

Hearing the barn door creak open, they both turned and watched back through the sparse forest of juniper among the tangle of rabbitbrush. After a moment, Lemonade appeared and stared down at them. Seth beckoned the kid closer, then smiled at Joaquín. "This is the grand adventure of Lemonade's life, and neither one of *us* wants to be here."

"I do," Joaquín said. "Men who commit such acts must be brought to justice, and I intend to see that they are."

Seth studied him, then pointed out warily, "I used to commit such acts on a regular basis. I had more finesse and didn't leave so many bodies behind, but I hurt plenty of people. Those men are no different from me and I feel damn uncomfortable tracking 'em. I don't need God's avenger for my partner right now."

"Now or ever?"

"Ever, if it comes to that." They could hear Lemonade crashing through the brush, and Seth lowered his voice. "I know you're hurting, Joaquín, and I understand how you feel, but let's keep it simple: we're after vengeance and restitution. Any notion that we're delivering justice is suicide."

"Do you not feel justice has its own power?" Joaquín asked archly. "Isn't that what you felt when you hung the man who lynched your brother? Can you honestly tell me you didn't see yourself as the hand of justice at that moment?"

"That was different," Seth muttered.

"Why?"

" 'Cause what Pilger did was a deliberate act. What happened to Melinda was bad luck. She got in the way, is all."

"That makes it worse," Joaquín said with disdain. "To kill randomly, with no regard for whoever has the misfortune to be in your way, is barbaric."

"No more'n what you'll be doing."

"My aim is not random."

Lemonade came up beside them and asked with a grin, "Where we goin'?"

Looking away from the dour face of his friend to the beaming enthusiasm of the kid's, Seth smiled. "We're gonna bag Hermit Dan a deer," he said, leading them downhill.

"Will you let me shoot it, Mr. Strummar?"

"Can you do it?"

"Sure!"

"I don't see why you shouldn't then." He caught Joaquín's eye but couldn't get a smile out of him.

The sky was a luminous dark blue, the morning star glimmering alone with the crescent moon, the horizon now a wedge of crimson thickening fast. Within the oak grove were two does and a yearling buck, glossy and plump as they grazed on the fallen acorns scattered among the crisp, yellow leaves. Seth handed his rifle to Lemonade and whispered, "Get the buck."

Lemonade raised the gun and took his time aiming. One of the does lifted her head and looked straight at the men. Nobody moved. She stared, chewing a minute, then the buck raised his head and stared at them, too. When Lemonade pulled the trigger, the three deer turned on their toes and bounded in the other direction. Lemonade pulled the trigger again and again, but missed. Joaquín raised his rifle and dropped the buck with one shot.

Amazed, Seth asked Lemonade, "Who taught you to shoot?"

"Nobody," he admitted.

"I believe that. We just used six bullets to bag one deer and prob'ly woke up every man within a hundred miles. Next time I ask if you can do something, don't lie to me."

"No, sir, I won't," Lemonade promised, undaunted.

Seth smiled at Joaquín. "Good shot."

"Thanks," he said.

"Lemonade, get us a pole," Seth said, starting toward the carcass.

"What're we gonna do with it?" the kid asked.

Seth stopped and looked at him with fresh amazement. "We're gonna tie the buck to it and tote him back to Dan."

"A big stick, then," he said.

"Yeah," Seth said. He watched the kid go into the forest, then said to Joaquín, "I was never that ignorant. Or that bad a shot, either."

Joaquín shrugged. "There's not much chance to shoot deer while living in town, or need to carry a carcass, either."

They walked through the carpet of golden leaves to the fallen deer. The bullet had gone into the back of its head. Seth gave his friend a teasing smile. "I call that a righteous killing, Joaquín."

"A lucky shot of desperation," he admitted wryly.

Seth laughed, pulled his knife and slit the deer's belly open, stepping back as he cut the innards loose with his blade and they swamped steaming onto the ground. By the time Lemonade came with the pole, the carcass was ready to be loaded. They tied the feet over the bar, and each man toted an end. Lemonade carried the rifles.

"If I hadn't come along," he said, "ya would've had to tote your guns and the deer, too."

"We've done it before," Seth said, still disgruntled at being lied to. "What's your real name, anyway?"

Lemonade was quiet.

"You don't have to tell me if you don't want," Seth said.

"Warren Walker," the kid said.

"How'd you get the handle 'Lemonade'?"

"It started out as a joke," he said, glancing at Joaquín.

"They usually do," Seth said. "You want to share it? I could use one right now."

"It sounds silly," Lemonade hedged. " 'Specially considerin' who ya are."

They walked in silence a few minutes, climbing the slope back toward the cabin, then Lemonade said, "It was at a orphanage in Topeka. I liked lemonade a lot so this lady who worked there started callin' me the Lemonade Kid." He laughed awkwardly. "It jus' stuck, is all."

Seth chuckled.

"I told ya it was silly," Lemonade said defensively.

Seth shrugged. "If I'd known I was riding with the Lemonade Kid, I would've minded my p's and q's a little sharper."

"Aw, Mr. Strummar, ya don't mean that. Ya wouldn't change your ways for nobody, would ya?"

"Nobody but women and children and a partner who's always giving me trouble," he muttered.

Lemonade glanced over his shoulder at Joaquín, who didn't appear to be listening. It seemed a troublesome partner might be replaced, and Lemonade's failure to make the kill didn't diminish his opinion of himself as a likely contender.

17

As they were hanging the deer from a tree in the yard, Hermit Dan came out of the cabin and stood nearby. Seth nodded for Joaquín to take Lemonade inside.

"I need you in the cabin, Lemonade," Joaquín said, walking away.

Lemonade looked at Seth securing the deer, then followed Joaquín.

Dan came closer. "Fat buck," he said with approval.

"Joaquín shot it," Seth said. He walked over to the water trough by the corral and cleaned his knife, dried the blade on his pantleg and slid the knife back in its sheath on his belt, then returned to the old man admiring the deer. Seth waited, not looking at him.

"I know those men," Dan whispered.

"Do you know where they are?" Seth asked softly.

The old man shook his head. "One of 'em, Dirk Webster, is keepin' comp'ny with Micah Wells' wife." He snickered naughtily.

Seth smiled. "You don't miss much for being a hermit."

"These mountains are infested with men! Must be a dozen of 'em livin' in this range. Can't be no decent hermit."

Seth laughed. "I know what you mean."

"I bet ya do," the old man said, his eyes bright with scorn. "Ridin' with a posse chasin' robbers!"

"It was my money they took. Can't let 'em get away with it."

"Pshaw!" he scoffed. "If ya collected all the blood's been spilt over money, ya'd have to be Noah to survive the flood." The glare of his eyes softened. "Did Joaquín lose someone?"

Seth nodded.

"I knew it! He's got vengeance in his eyes. Ya watch 'im, Seth. He ain't under your wing no more."

Seth sighed, turning around to watch Stubbins and Engle come out of the barn. "Where is the Wells ranch?"

"Toward the ass end of the Pedregosas. On a mesquite flat bordered by a ridge blockin' the view of Mexico."

"How far south?"

"Hundred miles." Dan smiled. "As the crow flies."

"Guess we better move," Seth said, sighing again.

An hour later, they rode out with Seth in the lead on his sorrel, followed by Engle and Stubbins, both on dark bays, then Joaquín on his black and Lemonade on Rico's palomino at drag. The trail wound down the west side of the mountains toward the valley floor fifty miles south of the dunes. An expanse of ancient lake bed, the valley below was immense and flat, the only trees stubby mesquite. All morning the men rode down the shady side of the mountain. At noon they stopped to let the horses graze on the last of the grass, then continued their descent with the afternoon sun in their eyes.

At dusk, they camped in an arroyo that opened on the valley. Towering into the darkening sky, red rocks stood like sentinels carved by sand and wind into visages of reptilian monsters with human faces. Joaquín settled his horse off by itself and left his gear in camp before walking back up the arroyo toward the mountains. Seth watched him go, then looked at Lemonade waiting for instructions.

"You ever hobble a horse?" he asked the kid.

Lemonade shook his head.

"Ain't too many lessons more important," Seth said. He swung down and pulled his hobbles from his saddlebags, dumped his saddle and blanket in the sand, then knelt by the sorrel's forefeet. Nudging them together, he whipped the leather straps into position and tied them fast. "Let's see you do it," he told the kid.

Lemonade swung off the palomino and found the hobbles in the saddlebags, pulled the saddle and blanket off, then crouched near the hooves. The palomino backed away and stopped with its forelegs spread wide.

"Pick 'em up," Seth said. "A good horse'll let you handle its feet."

Lemonade grabbed a fetlock and pulled the hooves together, wound the strap around and tied it. Seth came over and looked down at his work. "It's too loose," Seth said. "This mare could be halfway to Mexico by morning." He knelt in the sand beside the kid, untied the hobbles and started over. "Quick loop, see, another one, yank it tight and catch the hold. You can undo it just as quick, which sometimes is important."

"Yes, sir," Lemonade murmured.

Seth looked at him. "I'd hate to lose this mare."

"I'll take good care of her," the kid promised.

"All right," Seth said, standing up.

They took the bridles off, slung their saddles and blankets on their backs and returned to camp. Joaquín's gear was in a small cove of rocks affording a good view. Seth dropped his gear there, too, but when Lemonade started to put his down, Seth stopped him.

"You sleep over there," he told the kid, nodding at the far side of the camp. "Joaquín'll be here with me, so watch our backs. And keep your gun where you can reach it at all times. Understand?"

The kid nodded.

"Do it, then," Seth said. He turned and walked up the arroyo, seeking solitude. From a distance, he watched Stubbins and Engle collecting enough wood for a bonfire. Seth shook his head at the company he was forced to keep, then sat down in a deep shadow beneath the wall of the arroyo.

His eyes never stopped moving, scanning his surroundings for any hint of danger. It was a habit established so long ago that he was rarely conscious of performing it, yet tonight Seth felt keenly aware of himself as a pinnacle of defense isolated against the proverbial wall.

With each year, the restrictions on his life grew more severe. He guessed it was the natural result of having spent his youth raising hell, though that hadn't been his aim. It had been to live as he damn well pleased, and he'd done that. It was only now when the repercussions of his past threatened to destroy his carefully constructed sanctuary that he realized to what degree he'd turned the world against him: even acting in defense of the law didn't mitigate the fact that he was a fugitive from both sides of it. His best hope for survival was to stay low and out of sight. Leading posses wasn't doing that.

If not for Joaquín, Seth would have gone home and abandoned the chase to the good citizens. Despite his training and ability, however, Joaquín was a novice at vengeance. To achieve it without provoking the law's retribution would be tricky, and Seth figured the cut would be so close they'd need a sharp edge which he meant to provide if Joaquín didn't.

Within the shadow of the wall, Seth watched the townsmen build the fire so high it could be seen for miles, then stand around it, perfect targets from any angle. When Joaquín finally came back down the arroyo, Seth stood up, and they watched each other as Joaquín came closer.

"How you doing?" Seth asked softly, falling in step beside him.

"Fine," Joaquín answered, though the torment in his eyes denied it.

As they walked back toward camp, Seth shared the tip Hermit Dan had given him.

Joaquín listened in silence then asked, "If you were running from such a crime, would you visit a woman?"

Seth smiled. "There were times I did. Guess I figured if I was about to die, I'd just as soon have my ashes raked."

"Is that all a woman is to you?" Joaquín mocked.

"It's all they were then," Seth answered, uneasy with his friend's new quickness to anger.

Stubbins and Engle were sitting on their saddle blankets on the north side of camp, Lemonade alone with the now-dark valley yawning behind him. Seth sat down next to Joaquín, both of them lounging against their saddles from the comfort of bedrolls. As he studied the townsmen across the fire, Seth wondered what would happen if they got lucky and actually caught the men they were tracking.

He would get his money back, he knew that. Given free rein, he'd probably kill the thieves doing it. In this instance, however, Joaquín's claim had precedence. On the other hand, if Seth let Joaquín kill them, he risked losing his best friend to the same swamp of death Joaquín had pulled him out of. The best solution he could come up with was to deliver the thieves to the law, but sending men to jail went against the grain with Seth.

Neither did he like riding with Engle and Stubbins, both of them as shifty-eyed as any men he'd ever met. They expected the worst, kept themselves on guard against it, and barely managed to be civil. Seth had spent a good chunk of his past in the company of men he wouldn't turn his back on, but he'd enjoyed himself. It surprised him that the businessmen were inept at establishing common ground. Even when he looked straight at them, they were so buffaloed it took several minutes for them to garner the courage to look back. When he finally had their attention, he said, "I think we oughta agree on what we hope to accomplish."

"Get our money!" Stubbins barked.

Seth mentally winced. That Stubbins would answer before considering all the angles didn't bode well for his performance in a showdown. Seth looked at Engle.

"The same," Engle said, his eyes narrow and crafty. "Isn't that your intent?"

Seth nodded. "But these men won't give it up without a fight. Are you willing to kill 'em?"

In the silence broken only by the fire, Engle and Stubbins looked at each other. Stubbins nodded. Engle looked back at Seth and said, "They killed four people. We'll be delivering justice."

"I don't attach that word to my thinking," Seth said. "What we gotta consider is that none of us has a badge or any legal sanction to interfere with those men."

Again, Engle and Stubbins looked at each other, then Engle asked, "Are you saying if we kill them we could be charged with murder?"

Seth nodded.

Lemonade stood up and crossed to kneel before the fire, then slowly added more branches to the pyramid of wood. Engle and Stubbins stared into the flames. Seth and Joaquín kept their eyes on the forest so as not to blind their vision. The pyramid fell and Lemonade quickly leaned logs to catch the heat.

Stubbins cleared his throat. "If we take 'em alive, what'll we do with 'em?"

"You can escort 'em to Tombstone and hand 'em over to the U. S. marshal," Seth said.

"Not a ride *you* care to take, is it?" Engle taunted.

"You knew that before you came along."

"That's precisely why we're here."

"You're here," Seth said, " 'cause you don't have a prayer in hell of finding 'em on your own."

"Let's just say we think your odds are better," Engle

drawled, "being as experienced as you are."

"Let's just say that," Seth agreed, striving to keep the conversation pleasant.

"Who gets Clancy's reward?" Engle asked.

Seth looked away to disguise his contempt. "If you collect it," he said, meeting Engle's eyes again, "that makes you a bounty hunter. That's nothing I want." He paused a moment, then said, "If you try to collect the reward after you've killed 'em, though, you'll be confessing to murder." He looked at Joaquín. "We'd be better off taking 'em alive."

From the shadows where he lay listening, Joaquín shrugged.

Lemonade sat back on his heels, proudly watching the fire blaze into the black sky.

Finally Stubbins said, "I'll go along with that. Except ya forgot to mention what happens to the money."

"I'll take it back to Tejoe," Seth said.

"You expect us to let you ride off with it?" Engle asked incredulously.

Seth smiled across the flames. "Look at it this way: if I held a gun to your head and told you to hand it over, you'd do it. So let's just agree now and save ourselves the trouble."

"We'll think on it," Stubbins muttered.

Seth laughed. "What's for supper, Lemonade?"

"Jerky and biscuits, same as last night."

"Only one thing's missing," Seth said.

"What's that?" the kid asked warily.

"Coffee's always first."

"Yes, sir," Lemonade said, digging into the supplies.

"Don't reckon you oughta call me sir," Seth said, smiling again at Engle and Stubbins. "Name's Seth Strummar, reviled far and wide for doing the same thing these gentlemen did once upon a time. Only I flaunted my crimes before the world. Good citizens hide theirs in shame."

"I ain't ashamed of nothin'," Stubbins said. "I was

wearin' a Confederate uniform when I stole that Yankee gold.''

Seth didn't bother to question if the gold ever made it into the Confederate treasury. "How about you, Engle?" he asked. "You ashamed of robbing that bank in Arkansas?"

"No," he said, meeting Seth's eyes. "I deserved a fair shake and I took it."

"That's the same as me," Seth said.

"Nowhere near the same," Engle scoffed. "I did it once and didn't hurt anybody. You made a career not only of robbing banks but of killing men who got in your way."

Seth smiled. "It's what I'm good at."

"Nobody'd argue with that," Stubbins muttered.

"Had a lot of fun, too." Seth laughed, rubbing it in.

There was a silence broken only by the crackling of the fire, then Engle asked in a confidential tone, "You ever think about doing it again?"

"No," Seth said.

"I've heard it's easy to hold up trains," Stubbins said. "Stop 'em in the middle of nowhere and get away on your horse. They can't chase ya 'cause they're stuck on them steel rails!" He laughed. "Sounds like easy pickin's to me."

"I've heard some of the takes are real plump, too," Engle said.

"Hell, even just a coupla thousand would make a dif'rence to me," Stubbins said. " 'Specially if we don't recover what was in the bank."

"How much you figure it was?" Seth asked.

"Twenty," Engle answered. "That's what Clancy told me. How much was yours?"

"Five," Seth said.

"I'm out four," he said.

"Six for me," Stubbins growled. "I'd jus' moved money down from Santa Fe to pay for openin' a new shaft. Minin's gettin' so goldarned mechanized it costs a fortune to turn a profit. Makes me wonder if workin' for a livin's worth it.'' He squinted across the fire at Seth. "Ya don't have to worry about that, do ya, Strummar?"

"I was born with a six-shooter in my hand," he said.

Stubbins laughed. Engle chuckled nervously. The coffee boiled over. Lemonade pulled the pot out of the flames, filled a cup and handed it to Seth, then poured another and carried it to Joaquín. Hearing him say "*Gracias*" in his soft voice, Seth yearned to have his partner back.

Lemonade gave full cups to Engle and Stubbins, then they all sat sipping their coffee while the kid divided the supper and passed it, too, around.

As they were eating, Stubbins said, "Don't see how they could catch a man robbin' a train like that. If he only did it once. Made sure the take was worthwhile, then sat back fat and sassy while they combed the hills for desperados."

After a minute, Engle said, "It could be done."

"Ain't it gonna hurt ya, Strummar?" Stubbins asked in a sympathetic tone, "if we don't recover the money?"

"It'll set me back," Seth admitted, knowing where the conversation was headed.

"Well, sayin' we have bad luck and lose it," Stubbins said. "Would ya consider pullin' a train job, just once, to recover our loss?"

Seth smiled. "I might."

Engle laughed nervously. "We could pull it off, the four of us. Even use the kid to hold the horses. And we have the perfect alibi: we're hunting bank robbers. Nobody'd suspect us."

"I know which runs are worth it," Lemonade said. After glancing shyly at Seth, the kid told the townsmen, "A while back in Tombstone I heard the freight agent say ev'ry third Wednesday the payrolls for the big mines come in from El Paso."

"That's tomorrow!" Engle whispered exultantly. "I'd say it's fate that we do it."

"What d'ya say, Strummar?" Stubbins asked.

Seth leaned forward and poured himself more coffee,

then sipped at the boiled tar, watching the townsmen over the rim of his cup. "If I did it," Seth said, swishing the coffee to settle the grounds, "I'd kill my partners afterwards so they couldn't give evidence against me." He smiled at Engle and Stubbins, then grinned at Joaquín. "Ain't that what you'd do?"

"It would be the wisest choice," Joaquín answered.

Seeing that Lemonade felt chagrined for having gone along with the plan, Seth winked at him, then stood up and tossed him the empty cup. "Think I'll check on the horses," Seth said, walking into the shadowed arroyo.

Engle muttered, "He'd do it, too."

Stubbins looked at Joaquín. "Would he kill his partners in a job?"

Joaquín shrugged.

In the morning, the men rode out in a tense silence. Only Lemonade felt pleased at the prospects of the day. After running errands for the likes of Bart Keats, being Seth Strummar's backup was an immense promotion for the orphaned street urchin. But he figured he'd already made enough mistakes that Seth wouldn't hesitate to count him out. Missing the deer had been Lemonade's first mistake; agreeing to rob the train was a far more serious miscalculation. Lemonade hadn't caught on that Seth was joshing the townsmen, and he knew that to replace Joaquín as Seth's partner required anticipating the jefe and making himself indispensable.

That he was scheming to usurp Joaquín's place wasn't the only reason Lemonade felt wary of the Mexican. Joaquín had changed from a source of kind encouragement to a cold front of anger that challenged anyone within range, including Seth. Having managed to overhear pieces of their conversations, Lemonade understood Joaquín was grieving for the woman killed in the bank, but that had little meaning in Lemonade's life. Never having loved anyone, he couldn't imagine the loss. Neither had he ever owned anything it would grieve him to part with, until now. Seth had not only bought Lemonade his first new clothes and put him on a horse, the jefe had also loaned him a Winchester, and Lemonade meant to earn it before the game was up.

Riding directly in front of him, Joaquín had a low opinion of Lemonade. The kid was poised on the threshold of true criminality, lied about his abilities and exhibited a sham of arrogance that begged to be redressed. Though missing the deer should have taken the wind out of his sails, Lemonade prattled on undaunted, even including himself in the train robbery talk as if he were an equal. Joaquín couldn't figure why Seth kept the kid around. Lemonade was handy for grunt work, but Joaquín wouldn't bet a brass peso on his loyalty.

Yet Seth seemed to be pulling the kid close, as if he thought there was a man worth saving inside the cocky punk. Seth didn't often single people out for his largess. When he did, Joaquín had to concede that it paid off handsomely. After knowing Blue Rivers a matter of weeks, Seth had risked his life to save Blue from hanging. Joaquín had argued against it and refused to help, so Seth had done it alone. Now Blue was their strongest ally and closest friend in Tejoe. Remembering all that made Joaquín doubt himself more severely than ever.

For years he had been content to be Seth's shadow. Believing the depth of their friendship justified being partner to a man the world considered a vicious killer, Joaquín had become the staunchest advocate of Seth's proclaimed desire to live within the law. It had been an interesting role, full of complexities and an ironic humor, but it was gone now, lost to the profound betrayal Joaquín felt at Melinda's death.

He suspected the fault was his for trying to change others when he was the one who needed to change. Rather than strive to share the blessings of Christ's benevolence, Joaquín intended to strike with the wrath of Jehovah. The thieves had wronged him. Not only by killing a woman he cared for, but by killing an innocent child they had outraged his tolerance of brutality. He thought he would never breathe freely again until they bore the full brunt of what they had done. Which meant justice in Joaquín's mind: suffering and loss equivalent to what had been inflicted. Beyond that, he couldn't contemplate what his life would become, who he would be or where he would go. He only knew he was no longer a shadow to be relied upon no matter what.

Seth was well aware of the change in Joaquín's loyalty. He wanted to approve but wished it hadn't come when he himself felt so vulnerable. Suddenly Joaquín was a wild card in the deal. Having learned the finer points of lethal maneuvers from Seth, he was more than ten years younger and had the edge all along the blade, and Seth sure didn't want his former partner as an opponent. He knew this shift was tricky. He'd been through it with Allister and didn't guess the usual result was a deepening of friendship. Yet that's what Seth wanted: to take Joaquín home better friends than when they'd left.

Buck Stubbins didn't feel friendly toward either Seth or Joaquín. Still smarting from the outlaw's joke the night before, Stubbins might have shot Strummar in the back if not for his *compañero* riding behind. Ascarate's dark eyes seemed to miss nothing. They were mean, too, hard and cruel, as if he would just as soon shoot as look at a man. Stubbins didn't like Mexicans much anyway, and this one struck him like a viper coiled for attack.

No happier than Stubbins, Engle also felt humiliated by the joke. It burned like acid in his throat that Strummar was always playing the high and mighty. If he wasn't so damn good, he wouldn't have a chance in hell of getting away with it, but that was the catch: Strummar was more than a thief, he was a legend. Songs about him were sung in cantinas across the Southwest. Having heard some of the songs, Engle had admired the outlaw before meeting him.

After Strummar moved to Tejoe, however, Engle's romantic illusions of an outlaw's charm died fast. From their first encounter, he'd hated Strummar's arrogance: the cold way his eyes bore into a man, allowing no respite of courtesy; how his hand lingered loose by his .44, the polished bone of its grip a testament that he used it daily; the aggressive way he occupied space, defining limitations and enforcing them, making men back off just by looking at them hard. The outlaw rankled with a balls-to-the-wall approach to life, and any sane man recognized the danger in his company.

Yet Engle was following him into the wilderness. Everyone had long ago given up the pretense that Strummar was tracking sign. He'd heard a tip from the hermit and wasn't sharing it, but the outlaw obviously had a destination in mind. Engle thought it would be smart for bandits to have an accomplice lead the posse on a wild goose chase. Even if Strummar wasn't connected to the robbers, he'd lost five thousand but stood to gain twenty, and there was nothing to prevent him from killing his partners, as he'd threatened the night before. Engle couldn't help wonder if that had been a joke or a warning, and it bothered him that he couldn't read Strummar's intentions.

In late afternoon, they approached a homestead in the middle of a clearing cut from the mesquite forest. The house was a low adobe with a covered well, a water trough and a hitching rail in the hard-packed dust of the yard, with a corral and stable about a hundred yards off. The corral was unshaded and empty, the white dust bright in the sun.

Seth looked across at Engle. "If I got my directions right, Micah Wells lives here. I'd rather you do the talking. I'll just listen and watch." He let that settle in a moment, then asked, "Can you handle it?"

Engle nodded, staring at the house. "Shall I tell them the truth?"

"About everything," Seth said, "except why we're here. Just say we lost the robbers' trail heading south, so we stopped to ask if anyone's seen 'em. Then say our horses are tired and ask to stay the night. They should be amenable. If not, we'll know they're hiding something."

Engle asked with sarcasm, "So I'm to pretend I'm the leader of this posse?"

Seth smiled. "Let's see how you do." He reined his horse back to ride alongside Joaquín as they ambled into the yard behind Engle and Stubbins, Lemonade tagging along at the rear. Seth leaned close to his friend and whispered, "Remember: watch the wife."

Joaquín nodded.

They all sat their horses in the middle of the yard while Engle hollered, "Anybody home?"

18

The door opened and a skinny woman came out. Her dress had once been blue but was now a faded gray from having been washed and dried in the sun too many times. Her dark brown hair was wound into a thick bun on top of her head, and strands had escaped to frame her face with wispy curls. Her eyes were sharp with suspicion, her mouth closed in a hard line beneath jutting cheekbones. She carried a rifle.

The merchant tipped his hat. "Afternoon, ma'am. I'm Maurice Engle, and these men are citizens of Tejoe. We're a posse chasing bank robbers. Do you think we might come in for supper? The Township of Tejoe will reimburse you for the expense."

Seth muttered to Joaquín, "That's a line I'd never think to use." When Joaquín laughed softly, Seth thought maybe his friend's hurt was easing and reason reasserting its welcome claim.

The woman said, "The sheriff of Tejoe is Rafe Slater."

"Yes, ma'am, that's true," Engle said. "He wasn't able to come along."

"Why not?"

"The unpleasant fact," Engle intoned, "is Rafe Slater is now in jail for having aided the thieves."

"That ain't been proved," Seth shouted from the back.

The woman looked at him, at Joaquín, Lemonade and Stubbins, then back to Engle. "I'll ask," she said, returning inside and closing the door behind her.

Engle twisted in his saddle and glared at Seth. "You gonna contradict everything I say?"

"Slater ain't been proved guilty," Seth said.

"If we don't catch these men," Engle retorted, "there won't be anyone to testify against him. Since he's a friend of yours, maybe it would behoove you to let them go."

"Maybe it would behoove you to take 'em alive," Seth answered.

The door opened and the woman reappeared, still clutching her rifle. "Put your horses in the barn," she said. "My husband broke his leg, so you'll have to tend them yourself. You can wash up at the trough." She went back inside, closing the door again.

Jessica Wells was thirty-two years old, had been married ten years, and was childless. Although she had once been pretty, her good looks were fast being lost to the ever-present wind blowing through her home, a house of mud on a parched plot of land in the middle of nowhere. The closest town was Tombstone, a wild and sinful city where prices were outrageously high. Usually when Micah rode into town he went alone, coming home a day later smelling of whiskey and cheap perfume. Jessica wasn't angry when that happened, only envious.

She had been easy pickings for a man who liked his woman safely married to someone else, and Dirk Webster had met with no resistance when he wandered onto the Wells' ranch and sought a warmer welcome than his host offered. Keenly aware of the transitory nature of her romance, Jessica cherished Webster's visits, which were

erratic and announced by his artful imitation of a meadowlark. She thought it a beautiful summons, and always
smiled when she heard it.

A discreet affair of the heart seemed a harmless diversion in the labors of her life—a life she had no intention
of leaving, a husband she valued though their passion had
long ago died. She thought, too, that the problem was not
with her but Micah, and if she could give him a child after
all this time, maybe some essence of love could be restored
to their marriage. Of course, her husband must never know
the child wasn't his, and Jessica did her utmost to ensure
he didn't learn of her lover. They had devised a message
with candles: a taper in the east window was a request that
he wait, a promise she would come; in the west window,
a flame was a forlorn expression of regret. It broke her
heart to place the candle in the west window but she had
done it, then lain awake beside her husband yearning for
the pleasure she was missing.

Since Micah's leg had been broken, he spent his days
on the settee with the cast propped on a chair, querulously
recounting everything wrong with his life. Twice Jessica
had been forced to light the candle in the west window
because Micah was drinking and would neither go to sleep
nor let her escape. He needed an audience for his tirades;
as his wife, it was her duty to listen.

For hours she had endured his whining complaints while
part of her mind never stopped craving her lover's caresses.
She had sat demurely in the parlor, fetching another bottle
from the kitchen when her husband asked, saying little and
agreeing with everything because he wanted to argue and
she didn't. She wanted to be lying on a blanket beneath the
stars, feeling her lover's hands on her naked skin.

She worked now to prepare supper for the strangers.
First she tied an apron over the front of her dress, filled
her big kettle with water from the bucket and set the kettle
on the stove, then stoked up the fire to burn hot. She took
the axe from the woodbox and walked out to the chickens,
caught and beheaded a rooster. Returning to the kitchen,

she poured the now hot water back into the bucket and carried it out to a stump. The rooster still ran headless around the yard, so she looked at the strangers unsaddling in the corral.

The tall one seemed familiar but she couldn't place him. Memory nudged with the Mexican, too, but it was faint and she couldn't catch the connection. The man who had talked to her—Maurice Engle, he'd said his name was—struck her as shady. Bad-mouthing the sheriff of Tejoe didn't sit right with her. She had liked Rafe Slater and would have entertained him as her lover if given the chance. But Tejoe was too far away. Its sheriff didn't often ride across two counties to the southern edge of the territory.

She didn't see how these men could be a posse if none of them had a badge. Neither would she hold her breath waiting to get paid by the Township of Tejoe. She caught the rooster now flopping on the ground and carried him to her bucket of hot water. After immersing his body, she bent to the task of plucking the chicken, inhaling the sour smell of wet feathers and feeling certain the strangers brought trouble.

Pal came over and lay down to watch her, knowing he'd get the innards when she was done. He was a gentle mutt with a fluffy yellow coat and soft brown eyes. "What do you think, Pal?" she asked the dog. "These fellows are up to no good, wouldn't you say?" The dog whined. "Yeah," she said, looking up from her task of yanking feathers that came out with a wet slide then a jerk, a steady rhythm from her fingers denuding the bird.

The men were washing at the trough now with their sleeves rolled up; splashing their faces, slicking their hair back, beating the dust out of their hats against their legs. She noted the kid kept his rifle nearby. The others didn't, but then they all wore sixguns on their hips. When they started toward the house, she looked down at her work, listening to them cross the yard, only the tall one and the Mexican wearing spurs, until the door closed behind them.

When she carried the chicken into the kitchen, she could see them through the open parlor door. The Mexican was leaning against the far wall, watching her. She turned to her workboard and attacked the chicken with her butcher knife, Pal at her feet waiting for the innards. A clink of glass from the parlor told her the men were drinking, and she snorted with disdain. These strangers were as dangerous as rattlesnakes yet the first thing Micah did was get drunk with them. Looking at her rifle leaning by the back door, she wondered if the gun was close enough. She didn't stop cutting up the chicken, though. She finished and fed Pal outside, then washed her hands. Wishing she could ask someone to fetch a pail of water, she remembered the kid and decided he was still young enough to be commandeered. She walked to the door of the parlor, stopped on the threshold and waited to be recognized.

Micah looked up, his face flushed with the pleasure of company. "What is it, Mrs. Wells?" he boomed.

"I was wondering," she said softly, lowering her gaze to the floor, "if the boy could fetch some water and wood for the kitchen."

A silence followed her words. If any communication passed between anyone, it was inaudible. When she heard the boy walk toward her, she looked up and fixed a polite smile on her mouth as she scanned the faces of the men. They were all watching her, except the Mexican, who was watching them.

The kid stopped and said, "I'd be glad to help any way I can, ma'am."

"Thank you," she said to the room at large, then turned and led the boy into the kitchen. She handed him the bucket. "You can fill this first. And be quick about it."

He laughed going out the door. She stood looking after him, wondering how long it had been since anyone had laughed in her kitchen. Shaking off her reverie, she set to work. By the time the boy came back, she was paring potatoes.

"What else?" he asked as he set the bucket on the floor.

"What's your name?" she replied, studying him. He was well dressed, so obviously not alone in the world.

"Lemonade," he said.

"Is one of those men your father?" she asked cautiously.

"Nope. I'm workin' for Mr. Strummar."

"Seth Strummar?" she whispered, putting it together, the memory that had nudged when she first saw them ride up: the tall man with gray eyes on a red horse, his Mexican partner on a black, both of them with the blood of murder on their hands.

Lemonade grinned, tickled by her reaction. "Is there somethin' else I can do for ya, Mrs. Wells?"

"Yes," she said, dragging her mind back to the task at hand. "There's a stack of split by the woodpile. Would you bring it in, please?"

Again she watched him leave, this time feeling a strong foreboding of dread. She couldn't think of any reason an outlaw would ride with a posse. So that was no posse in her parlor. At least that much was clear. Hearing the men laugh over their whiskey, she smothered her anger at her husband beneath the concentration of labor. She poured water into a pot, dropped in the quartered potatoes, and set the pot on a back burner to boil, started the chicken frying in her large skillet, then mixed a double recipe of biscuits. She was rolling them out when the boy came back, his arms laden with wood. She jumped when he dropped it into the box. "Goodness," she said.

"Sorry." He laughed. "I thought ya'd be expectin' it."

"I'm accustomed to being alone," she said.

He nodded, then asked willingly, "What else can I do for ya?"

"You could set the table," she suggested.

"Where's the stuff?"

She crossed to the hutch, took out a clean tablecloth, and handed it to him. Then she went back to the stove and turned the chicken. She added more wood, heating the oven for biscuits, and poked at the chicken again with her tongs. When she looked at the boy, he was fussing with the tablecloth, trying to center it perfectly. It was touching to see him struggle with a task she performed without thinking. Finally satisfied with the way it fell, he looked up and saw her watching. They smiled awkwardly at each other.

"The silverware's in that drawer behind you," she said.

He turned around and opened the drawer, then stood staring at the neat array of utensils arranged in their slots.

"We'll need six of each," she said. "And six plates from the shelf above."

"All right," he said, but there was hesitation in his voice.

She concentrated on moving the chicken around in the skillet. When she looked up again, he was putting the silverware on the table, the three pieces bunched together to the right of each place. She set her tongs down and went to help, lining up the knife and spoon on the right and placing the forks the correct distance to the left.

Watching her mend his ignorance, he liked that she didn't accompany her lesson with a lecture. When she finished the last setting, she met his eyes and asked softly, "What are those men doing here?"

"We're chasin' bank robbers!" Lemonade boasted.

"Do you know their names?"

"Sure. Hal Norris, Dirk Webster, and Joe and Jim Tyler. I know what they look like, too. That's part of why I'm along."

She studied his face, thinking it wasn't fair a child had the power to ruin a person's life. "Will your testimony be the only evidence against them?" she asked, trying to sound merely curious.

He shook his head. "There were plenty of witnesses. Mr. Clancy and the clerk were in the bank when it happened. They both lived through it. Four people died, though. The Clancy boy, the guard, and two women. One of the ladies was in on it."

"God in heaven," Jessica whispered, sinking into a chair. "When did this happen?"

"Day before yesterday. Some say the sheriff was in on it, too. The townsmen was gonna lynch him but Mr. Strummar stopped 'em. Jus' rode into the corral and told 'em all to go home. Can ya beat that?"

"No," she murmured, thinking of Dirk.

"The Clancy kid was only ten," Lemonade said, adding spice to the gossip, death meaning no more to him than that. "And the woman what was innocent, she held onto the other one so she couldn't get away. Died holdin' onto her skirts so they had to pry her hands loose."

"Lord have mercy," Jessica moaned.

"Ya all right?" he asked worriedly. "Ya ain't gonna faint or nothin', are ya?"

She shook her head. "A terrible thing," she managed to say.

"The robbers got away with the money. That's what we're after. We're aimin' to take the men alive if we can."

"Is that true?" she whispered.

"I wouldn't lie to ya."

"No, of course not," she said with an apologetic smile.

Pulling herself to her feet, she returned to the stove, slid the biscuits into the oven, then stared at the chicken sizzling and snapping in the grease. The boy watched her as if still worried she might faint. "You can put the plates on the table," she said, remembering almost too late to start a pot of coffee.

When she looked up again, he was setting cups beside each plate. She drained the potatoes, slid them into two bowls and set one at each end of the table, took the salt and pepper and crocks of butter and marmalade from the pantry and set them on the table, then arranged the chicken on a platter and set it before her husband's place. She surveyed her work, returned to the oven for the biscuits, piled them onto a platter and set it, too, on the table, then looked at the boy. "Tell the men supper's ready," she said.

He left eagerly. She took a deep breath, entered the parlor, walked across to the settee, and offered her shoulder to help Micah up. He leaned on her heavily before he caught his balance between the cast and the cane, then he jerked away as if he didn't need her. She followed him meekly into the kitchen. After repeating the procedure to lower him into his chair at the table, she slipped out the back door.

Seth and Joaquín watched her go, both of them already seated. They glanced at each other, then Joaquín stood up. "I wish to check on my horse," he said, leaving through the parlor.

Seth smiled at their host and said, "He's fussy about his mount."

Once outside, Joaquín skirted the house until he came into view of the back. Mrs. Wells was there, leaning against the wall and hugging herself as if she were cold. A yellow dog, tethered to a stake, lay nearby. Joaquín hunkered down in the dark shadow thrown by a cluster of mesquite. Their lacy leaves bobbing in the wind whispered as softly as a harlot's negligee as he watched the woman, knowing she was yearning for her lover. Joaquín remembered the sweetness of that hunger, a satisfaction he had once found with Melinda. Remembered, too, her fear of being alone, and he shuddered to think of her in a grave. With a start he realized she would be buried long before he returned.

A meadowlark sang from beyond the clearing. He didn't really hear it until the woman took notice. She raised her head at the sound and walked away from the house, threw a worried look back at its lights shining through the dusk, then disappeared in the mesquite thicket east of the yard. Quietly Joaquín followed her. The path wound through the low trees with needle-sharp thorns. He kept himself crouched in the shadows, pausing every few moments to listen. A quarter mile into the thicket, he heard voices and stopped, waited, then crept closer.

An arroyo suddenly opened, a giant gouge dropping into

the lower plains. In its mouth, the woman stood talking with a man whose horse grazed in the shadowed canyon. Mrs. Wells was pleading. Her tone reached Joaquín before he caught her words: "The boy told me they want to take you alive, Dirk. Maybe that's your best chance."

"The hell it is," Webster growled. "Forget it, Jessica. I ain't surrendering."

"But all those people died!" she cried softly. "The law won't forget something so bad. They'll catch you, Dirk, and then there'll be no mercy."

"We only killed half those people. Their goddamned guard killed the other two."

"Two or four, what difference does it make?" she asked frantically. "One is a hanging offense, Dirk."

"We didn't kill no women," he muttered.

"That means you killed the child," she moaned. "For God's sake, surrender and beg the mercy of the law."

"It ain't got none, Jessica. If I'm not lynched, I'll hang. Even if by some miracle I escape that, they'll lock me in prison. Is that what you want?"

"No," she whimpered.

"I'm near starved. Can you bring me some food without attracting attention?"

"It'll be a while," she said. "They're all in the kitchen eating."

"Where do they think you are?"

She shrugged. "I'll bring whatever I can soon as they're done." Suddenly she clung to him, their words too muffled for Joaquín to hear. He watched, aching with his own loss, as they kissed hungrily in the darkening arroyo. When she finally tore herself free, Joaquín stepped back into the mesquite and watched her pass within a yard of him. He waited until he heard the kitchen door open and close, then he followed the path toward the arroyo, walking with the nonchalance of assumed possession.

The moment he cleared the trees, Webster saw him and froze. Keeping his hand close to his gun, Joaquín laughed lightly. *"Buenas tardes, señor.* Are you with the men visiting at the house?"

"Yeah," Webster said.

"I work for Señor Wells. It is unusual to have so many guests at one time. You are keeping guard, eh?"

"That's right," Webster said.

"You wouldn't have any tobacco, would you?" Joaquín asked with a friendly smile.

Webster reached into his vest pocket, pulled a pouch of makings out and tossed it over. Joaquín shook the tobacco into a paper, rolled it tight and licked the seal. Privately swaggering for taking the risk of occupying both hands while facing his foe, he struck a match on the sole of his boot and took a long time holding the glare to his face as he lit the cigarette. Exhaling a billow of smoke, he tossed the makings back. *"Gracias,"* he said.

"So what d'ya do for Wells?" Webster asked.

"Vaquero," Joaquín said with a dismissive shrug.

"You must know this country pretty good then."

"Sí," he said as if bored.

"Ride the range near everyday, don'cha?"

"Sí," he said again, puffing on the cigarette, which was making him dizzy. "Are you looking for something, *señor?"*

"Friend of mine was s'posed to meet me nearby. You ain't seen a man traveling alone, have you?"

Joaquín shook his head. "I have seen no one I didn't know for days now, except you."

Webster began rolling himself a smoke. When he had the bag of tobacco in one hand and the paper in the other, Joaquín lazily dropped his own cigarette and ground it out with the heel of his boot, then drew his gun.

Webster's hands stopped.

"You are under arrest," Joaquín said, "for robbing the bank and killing four people in Tejoe."

"You got a badge?" Webster growled.

Joaquín smiled. "I have a gun, *señor,* and it would give

me great pleasure to kill you, so I suggest you not hesitate when I ask that you raise your hands.''

Webster dropped his makings, the paper fluttering away on the wind as he complied.

''Now with your left—very slowly, *señor*—take out your gun and toss it gently toward me.''

Webster hefted his pistol to land with a thud in the sand, then asked, ''Who the hell are you?''

''Joaquín Ascarate, *a su servicio*.''

Webster thought a minute. ''You ride with Strummar?''

''We ride together.''

''Is he in the house?''

''*Sí*.''

''Who else?''

''Other men. Some of us wish to kill you. Some wish to deliver you alive to the law in Tombstone. It is up to you what happens.''

Webster assessed him. ''What if I cut you into the take?''

''What would I get?'' Joaquín asked.

''The Tylers already took their share back to Texas. Norris and I got fourteen left. We'll give you four and split the ten.''

''Only four?'' Joaquín asked playfully.

''All right!'' Webster barked. ''I'll give you my five.''

''That is not all I would be taking. The blood of murder is on your money. Do you think that is something I wish to own?''

Webster stared at him a long moment. ''If you kill me, you will own it. If you really don't want it, what's to prevent me from riding away?''

''I will not shoot unless you provoke me,'' Joaquín said. ''Melinda provoked no one, yet she is dead by your gun, so I would not consider killing you murder.''

''Melinda? The other woman in the bank?''

Joaquín nodded.

''The guard killed her. I swear it.''

''Do you think that lessens your guilt?''

"Yes! I'd never shoot a woman."

"But a child?"

"Norris hit the kid. It was chaos in there all of a sudden. You've been in tight situations, you know how everything can turn wrong in the blink of an eye."

"You will die in less than that," Joaquín said, "unless you walk now ahead of me to the house."

"All right," Webster said.

Joaquín knelt to pick up the pistol, keeping Webster covered as he groped on the ground. But he couldn't find the gun and glanced down. Webster kicked sand and Joaquín lurched back, raising his arms to shield his eyes. He heard a rifle fire, then a grunt, shook his head and refocused in a matter of seconds. Webster lay on the sand, thrown backward by the force of a bullet, blood spreading across his chest. In his hand was the pistol Joaquín had lost. He stood up and reholstered his gun as Seth dragged a silently resistent Mrs. Wells toward him. In Seth's right hand was a Winchester, still smoking.

The woman moaned when she saw Webster, then she fell against Seth's chest and sobbed in helpless abandon. Seth tossed the rifle to Joaquín, meeting his eyes with an honest assessment that judged him short. They could hear the dog barking and the men shouting guesses of where the shot had come from.

Seth took hold of the woman's shoulders. "Snap out of it, lady," he said, shaking her roughly. "You got one minute to tell us everything you know or you won't be Mrs. anybody for long."

She leaned away as far as his grasp allowed, her pale face streaked with tears.

"Where're his partners?" Seth asked.

She shook her head.

He slapped her, then raised his hand to do it again, expecting Joaquín to object. Joaquín said nothing and Seth's palm came down hard against the woman's cheek. She cried out and fell to her knees. When Joaquín stood immobile, apparently indifferent, Seth felt a cold chill of loss.

They could hear the other men crashing through the brush, searching for them. Seth lifted the woman to her feet. "You best say it before they get here," he warned, "or you'll be telling it to your husband."

Fear filled her eyes. "Dirk was to meet Norris at somebody's cabin," she whimpered. "He just came back to say goodbye." She stopped and looked at her dead lover, grief hollow in her face.

As the others came running into the mouth of the arroyo, Micah Wells bellowed from the porch, "What the devil's going on?" His wife jerked free of Seth's grasp and turned away to hide her tears.

Stubbins stomped over to the corpse and stared down at it a moment, then asked, "Who was he?"

"Dirk Webster," Lemonade piped up.

"Who killed him?" Engle asked.

"I did," Seth said. "He was getting away."

"That right?" Engle asked Joaquín.

He looked at Seth a long moment before he said, "*Sí.* I was careless and Webster gained the advantage. He would have escaped if Seth hadn't shot him."

Engle looked back and forth between them a moment, then at the woman. "What do you know about it?"

"Nothing," she said, shaking her head as if in a daze. "I was out walking and just happened to be near. Everything was over by the time I arrived."

"Ya best go to the house, little lady," Buck Stubbins said kindly. "This ain't no place for ya."

She walked away without looking back.

After a moment, they could hear Micah Wells angrily demanding that his wife tell him what happened. Their voices moved into the house and the door closed, then the four men and a boy stood in the silence of the arroyo lit only by brittle starlight.

"What'll we do now?" Stubbins asked.

"You could try searching his horse for the money," Seth wryly suggested.

As Engle and Stubbins moved eagerly to do it, Seth

stepped closer to Joaquín. "Did you learn anything?"

"He asked if I had seen a man traveling alone," Joaquín answered, staring into Seth's eyes as if he could find a key to survival in their depths.

Seth frowned. "One man?"

Joaquín nodded. "The Tyler brothers have gone back to Texas. Webster offered me a cut, saying he and Norris had fourteen left."

Seth studied Joaquín's face. "You think he'd trust Norris with the money?"

Flicking his gaze at the townsmen searching the horse, Joaquín asked, "You don't think they'll find it?"

Seth shook his head. "Webster would've hidden it under a rock before bringing it here."

"When he made his offer," Joaquín said softly, "it didn't sound as if they had split it yet." He shifted his gaze to the corpse. "I should thank you for saving my life."

"Only if you mean it."

Joaquín met his eyes again. "I was lucky you happened along just then."

"I followed the woman back out," Seth said.

Stubbins left the horse and searched the clothes on the corpse, but both he and Engle came up empty-handed.

"Sonofabitch," Stubbins complained. "Ya sure ya didn't kill an innocent man, Strummar?"

"Yeah, I'm sure," he retorted, losing patience. "Ain't he one of 'em, Lemonade?"

"Yes, sir. That's Dirk Webster."

"Well, he didn't have any money," Engle said.

"So Norris has it," Seth said. "Webster told Joaquín the Tyler brothers are already gone, but he and Norris were supposed to meet up someplace."

Stubbins and Engle looked at each other, then Engle asked with sarcasm, "You didn't find out where?"

"Webster was not stupid, *señor*," Joaquín replied with equal sarcasm.

"What'll we do now?" Stubbins asked Seth.

"Nobody travels cross-country unseen. We'll hit the cantinas and scavenge another lead. Are you up for that?"

Again the townsmen looked at each other, this time longer. Stubbins looked back at Seth. "If that's what it takes."

Seth looked at Engle.

"I'll go," he said.

"All right," Seth said. "I suggest we finish our supper and move out. That agreeable?"

"Will you tell us where?" Engle asked, bristling with resentment.

"Sulphur Springs seems a good bet," Seth said, ignoring the hostility. He looked at Lemonade. "Go ask Wells for use of a shovel and where he wants the grave, then dig it. When it's ready, come get us and we'll help tote the body."

"Yes, sir," Lemonade said, trotting toward the house.

Seth watched the townsmen until they, too, moved across the yard and went inside. He looked at Joaquín and said, "That was an old trick to fall for. You should've left the gun and come back for it later."

"Thanks for pointing out my error," Joaquín snapped.

"Might keep you alive next time," Seth said. He walked over and looked down at the corpse, feeling somewhat better to see he'd hit the heart despite the haste of his aim. After a moment, Joaquín came over and they both stood staring down at Webster. In the distance, they could hear the shovel working. Seth asked, "Would you feel better if you'd killed him?"

"No," Joaquín admitted.

"I don't feel a thing," Seth said, meeting his friend's eyes. "Maybe it's better this way."

"Which way?"

"Letting me spill the blood."

"Do you think I would gain anything by that?"

"I already got a death warrant on my head, but you don't. Seems to me that's worth preserving."

"You think I should live my life in the safety of your protection?"

"Maybe I want to live mine in the safety of yours. Maybe if you become known as a killer, we'll have to split company for the sake of finding a moment's peace."

"Is peace what you're after?" Joaquín mocked.

"Yeah, but I'm having a hard time pinning down what you're after."

"I already told you: I am serving justice."

Seth nudged the corpse with his boot. "Is this a piece of it?"

Joaquín looked down at the dead man between them. "It would have been better to take him alive."

Seth shrugged. "I'd rather die from a bullet than a noose."

"There is a difference, though," Joaquín said. "His death is the result of my careless mistake and his desperate move against the deadly Seth Strummar. It was a game of skill and error. Justice had no time to be heard."

"If I hadn't come along, would you have heard it?" Seth asked, straining to keep sarcasm from his voice.

"I would be dead," Joaquín conceded. "To be both just and dead carries little weight."

Seth laughed. "I'll agree with that."

They both looked down at the corpse again. "One thing we know," Joaquín said, "is that Webster believed Norris is waiting for him somewhere nearby."

"If he was right, that means we have to scour this corner of the territory hoping we're close enough to do something about it when Norris makes a mistake."

"And if Webster was wrong?"

"Then Norris is already across at least one border, maybe two, and we're setting off on a trek admirable only for its ambition."

Joaquín nodded. "I will do what it takes. Will you?"

Seth hesitated, then smiled. "I'll back up whatever you want."

"You have a family," Joaquín pointed out. "Perhaps you should think of them."

Seth looked north, thinking of the warm comforts of Rico's bed, the commodious friendship of Esperanza, the baby Elena with her flashing blue eyes, and Lobo, who had been angry at being left behind. Meeting the dark eyes of his friend, Seth said, "None of 'em are more kin to me than you are."

Joaquín gave him an awkward smile. "This is something I must do. It is not yours."

"We're partners, ain't we?" Seth asked painfully.

"I am releasing you," Joaquín said with soft determination.

Seth looked away. After a moment he gave his friend a playful smile. "We can be partners on this job, can't we?"

"Perhaps," Joaquín answered solemnly. "We'll see."

Lemonade's voice cut between them. "The grave's ready," he shouted, ebullient with happiness at his achievement.

19

Lobo was unhappy at being left behind. The first moment he could slip away, he took his pinto from the stable and rode hard for the dunes. He also took a Winchester carbine from Joaquín's room and two boxes of .44 cartridges, a full canteen of water, and a fistful of jerked venison wrapped in a bandanna along with a dozen oatmeal cookies.

By the time he got there, the wind had swept the dunes clean of tracks. He sat his pinto feeling his hopes dwindle until he spotted fresh dung half-buried in the sand. He chose his direction on the chance the horse had been pointed the way it eventually walked. A mile further on, he came across more dung dropped on the move. He knew that meant the odds were good he was on the right trail.

The women didn't realize Lobo was gone until Nib Carey arrived at the homestead for breakfast. Though both he and his horse were tired from just having returned from the mountains, Nib pursued the boy, expecting to catch him within hours. At the dunes he, too, saw the dung and a few traces left by the pinto's hooves, so Nib spurred his horse into a lope across the ancient lake bed of Sulphur Valley, heading east toward the Chiricahuas.

At noon, Lobo was outside the cabin of Hermit Dan. He sat his horse and hollered, as Seth had told him to do. Lobo's shout echoed against the far ridge and bounced back; otherwise only the wind moving in the trees made any noise. His eyes searched the shadows around the cabin until he spotted the carcass of a deer hanging under a tree. Behind him the corral was empty, the looming barn silent. "Dan!" he called again. "It's Lobo Madera."

The door cracked open and the hermit peered out, then stepped into the sunlight and smiled up at the boy. "Trackin' your daddy, ain't ya?"

"Yes, sir," Lobo said.

"Left early this mornin'. Kilt me a deer 'fore he went."

"Where was he goin'?" Lobo asked, trying not to sound impatient.

The old man shifted his mouth around as he considered the situation. He knew Seth wouldn't want Lobo crossing the country alone, but the boy riding so hard to catch his daddy made Dan feel sad. Finally he said, "It's a long ride after 'im, Lobo. Ya best get down and let your horse breathe a spell."

"Will you tell me where Seth went?"

Hermit Dan nodded. "Give ya vittles for your inner man, too."

Neither of them moved for several long moments. Dan chuckled. "Ya got your daddy's eyes, damn if ya ain't, Lobo. He went to the Wells ranch in the southern valley, thinkin' one of 'em he's chasin' might be visitin'. So don't go in flappin' your lips, if you're a-goin'. Make better time on a rested mount, though."

"How far is it?" he asked.

"Hundred miles, down the mountain into the inferno."

"Thank you kindly for the invitation." Lobo swung his leg over and jumped from the stirrup. "I sure am hungry."

"Put your horse up," Dan said. Camouflaging his relief, he quickly went back inside the cabin.

Lobo led his pinto into the barn, unsaddled and tossed an armful of hay into the manger, then stood a moment listening to the creak and moan of the roof in the wind. Empty except for him and his pinto, the barn was a cavernous structure built to hide stolen stock. Seth had told him that, saying once upon a time Hermit Dan had taken a bite of nearly every steer rustled between the two territories.

It seemed to Lobo that during that mythical "once upon a time" only outlaws, Indians, and a few settlers to provide sport had lived on the frontier. As a baby, he'd heard stories of how exciting an outlaw's life was, but now that he was older he understood there was no future in being an outlaw. Most of them died young to begin with, and those who stayed alive were hermits to one extent or another. Even Seth, though he had a family and rode into town, acted as if the world were an ever-shrinking corral of threat. That's why he never went anywhere but Blue's saloon, and why he stayed in the shadows when someone rode into the yard until he knew who they were.

Now he was crossing the country, wide open for any number of catastrophes to fall on his head. As much as Lobo accepted that Seth's survival was a gambling proposition, he meant to defend his father against the enemies he could fight. If that made him an outlaw, too, then Lobo guessed he was born to it because he was Seth Strummar's son.

Lobo and Hermit Dan sat at the table over bowls of chile beans and a skillet of cornbread, eating with a purpose that excluded conversation. The shuttered cabin was dark, the only light coming from the fire blazing intermittently above a somnolent glow of flickering coals in the hearth. When Lobo looked up, he saw a bottle of whiskey on the mantle. It was the same brand Seth bought, and seeing it made Lobo yearn for his father with a painful ache of anger aimed at himself. He thought if he hadn't been so stupid about sneaking into town on the sly, Seth might have taken him along. Lobo knew he was just a kid, but he meant to prove his worth so Seth wouldn't leave him behind again.

Hermit Dan gathered the dirty dishes and carried them to the corner kitchen, then stayed in the shadows, having exhausted his tolerance of intimacy by sharing a table with the boy. He liked Lobo, though, and thought he should do his best to send the boy home.

"Ya know," Dan said in his husky voice, "Seth won't like ya disobeyin' 'im. If he wanted ya along, he would've took ya."

"Reckon," Lobo mumbled.

"But you're a-goin' anyway?"

"Looks like it," he said, peering into the shadows to meet the old man's eyes.

"What d'ya aim to do when ya catch up?"

"I'm gonna help him."

"He may need ya," Dan admitted with regret. "He's alone with them men."

Lobo preened under the implied praise, then caught the flaw in the hermit's words. "Ain't Joaquín with him?"

Dan shook his head. "There's a bone 'tween 'em. I don't know how it happened, but they ain't together no more."

"What do you mean?" Lobo cried, stunned at the thought of Joaquín not being their friend.

Dan shrugged. "Ya'll see for yourself. If ya go, I mean."

"I'm goin'," Lobo said.

Hermit Dan studied the boy in the flickering light of the fire, his blond hair so angelic, his pale eyes so fierce. Dan had traded Seth a deer for a lead on one of the men being tracked. It was an equitable exchange, worthy of their mutual respect, but Dan never gave anybody something for nothing. Yet he decided to give the other man to Lobo as a buffer against Seth's anger. "I gave your daddy one man for the deer,'' Dan muttered. ''I hear tell the other un's hidin' at Deadman's Cabin.'' He let that sink in a moment, then said, ''Ya might mention it when ya see 'im.''

''Where is it?'' Lobo asked eagerly.

''South side of Guadalupe Pass,'' Dan whispered, ''clear t'other side of the Pedregosas in New Mex Terr'tory.'' He paused, then said, ''Nobody knows what happened to him what built the cabin, not even his name. He's nothin' more'n a dead man now.''

Lobo stood up. ''The trail southeast?''

''After ya get outa the Chiricahuas. Ain't ya gonna sleep none?''

''No,'' Lobo said. ''Thanks for dinner.''

Dan chuckled. ''There be no doubt you're a Strummar. Ya got that drive.''

''It's nothin' to do with the name,'' Lobo said defensively.

''No, it ain't,'' Dan agreed.

''Thanks for everything,'' Lobo said.

He walked into the sunlit yard and across to the barn where his pinto sighed when he threw the saddle on its back. ''Yeah, I know, Bandit,'' Lobo said as he tightened the cinch, ''but it can't be helped.''

He swung on and trotted down the trail, keeping up a good clip as he shortened the distance between himself and his father.

Nib Carey arrived at Hermit Dan's at sunset. While he sat his lathered horse in the yard and hollered three times, Nib could have sworn someone was watching him from somewhere, but no one answered his summons. He stepped down, loosened his cinch and watered his horse, even gave it some feed, and still no one appeared. The silence was broken only by ravens squabbling over a deer carcass hanging from a tree.

Nib cautiously pushed the cabin door ajar. The room was tidy, the dishes washed and put away, the floor freshly swept, the blankets on the bed tucked tight. He went back outside and stared into the forest all around. Seeing the carcass again, he knew the hermit would be wanting to butcher the deer and salt it down, so wouldn't have gone far. Nib hollered once more, trying to keep the anger from his voice. Not wanting to shout Seth's name into unknown ears, he yelled, "I'm lookin' for Lobo!"

The echo of his voice was answered only by the raucous complaints of ravens quarreling in the trees. After unsuccessfully searching the yard for tracks he could identify as Lobo's, Nib stood up straight and scanned the fringe of forest again. Nothing moved except the pines bouncing in the wind and an occasional flash of shiny black as ravens glided between perches.

Nib trounced himself thoroughly as he rode back down the mountain, letting his tired horse pick its own pace. He should have taken a fresh horse and ridden hell out of it to catch the kid. Now Blue would be mad, and Nib might even lose his job. Seth would be mad when he got home, and mad, too, if the kid caught up with him. If Lobo didn't catch up, if he got lost or died somehow, Nib would be the point of failure in Seth's carefully constructed defense of his family. But Lobo could have gone any direction from the cabin, if he had ever been there. Nib had lost him. It was as simple and humiliating as that.

A hundred miles south of where Nib was riding, the border route between Tucson and El Paso met the road to Nogales. The crossing was graced with a scattering of adobe hovels and blessed with a spring. Its water was life-sustaining but unpalatable, giving the town, if such it could be called, the name of Sulphur Springs. It was owned by Raul Ortega. He offered for sale food, lodging, dry goods, whiskey, weapons, ammunition, horses, and the company of women.

Seth figured Raul's Cantina was as good a place as any to pick up gossip of the nature he was seeking. He led the posse to stable their horses in Raul's Livery and walk the block of town to the cantina. Stubbins and Engle bellied up to the bar, sharing a bottle of whiskey, while Seth and Joaquín took beers to a corner table. Lemonade stood awkwardly just inside the door. Flipping him a nickel, Seth said, "Buy yourself a beer."

"He is only fourteen," Joaquín objected.

Seth smiled, pleased to hear Joaquín correcting him again. "It's only beer."

"I don't trust him sober," Joaquín argued. "Will you give me a reason why you want him along?"

Seth sipped his beer and watched Lemonade talking to the barkeep. "Because he tells anyone who'll listen what we're doing, so every man through here tonight will know who I am and why I'm here without my having to say a word. If any of 'em have something to share, they'll let me know." Seth smiled at Joaquín, trying to break through his hostility. "It's a trick I learned from Allister: you let the green kid blow your horn, and all you have to do is watch and see who's interested."

"The green kid," Joaquín replied sharply, "is risking his life every time your name comes out of his mouth."

Seth grinned. "Nobody's twisting his arm."

"You are using his ignorance, leaving him open to danger when he is incapable of protecting himself."

"He dealt himself in. If he's gonna play, he may as well learn how."

"Does that mean you would defend him?"

"If he's acting in my interest."

"And if he isn't, you will let him die because he failed to understand a situation you put him into?"

"I didn't put him anywhere," Seth snapped. "He came along."

"You allowed it. I'm surprised you didn't bring Lobo."

"Why don't you buy yourself a woman, Joaquín?" Seth suggested. "It would do you good."

"It won't be difficult to find more pleasant company," Joaquín retorted. He took his beer over to the far end of the bar and leaned with his back to the wall.

Left alone, Seth felt weary at being jefe again. He was

too old to be riding the trail, definitely too old to change colors and uphold the law. Too slow to face professionals in their prime, that was the truth of it. If he had a predictable backup, or a troop with any degree of loyalty, he might feel more optimistic. But fighting the men he needed to lead, he had no control over what lay ahead and he knew it. Knew, too, that he was vulnerable because he felt divided.

Half of him wanted to go home to his women, lovely Rico and cantankerous Esperanza and the bundle of sweetness called Elena, while half of him wanted to indulge in the rambunctious bedding of a whore to ease his tension. Half of him wanted to camp in the wilderness with Lobo and watch the stars fall; half of him wanted to grind Norris' face in the dirt to prove no man got away with stealing money from Seth Strummar. There were two many halves pulling him in too many directions, and he felt disgruntled.

A bevy of whores came in to milk the new arrivals. The women were colorful and gay, laughing as they dispersed among the men. Seth saw Raul Ortega lead a young beauty through the door. They stopped on the threshold as Ortega pointed Seth out to the girl. She smiled shyly. Nodding his thanks at Ortega as she walked toward him, Seth stood up and held a chair for her, then sat back down and admired her, thinking not all the repercussions of being jefe were unpleasant.

She raised her head under his scrutiny, her exotic features framed by curly black hair falling loose to her shoulders. She was Creole, a breed Seth hadn't seen since the last time he'd been in east Texas. Her skin was cocoa-colored, her cheeks flat and her nose delicate over her sensuously full mouth, her eyes black fire glistening from beneath long lashes she used in the way Spanish girls flirted with fans. He guessed her age at sixteen, and that she was either new to the profession or extremely well trained. "What're you drinking?" he asked.

She turned to the barkeep, expectant of his attention, and signaled with three fingers together. Then she turned back and demurely looked at her lap. Seth nodded with a smile, knowing now that she was a spy. There had been a time when he liked nothing better than spending a few hours with a woman who wanted something from him, a time he would have enjoyed pushing the limits of her desire to please him. Now he thought she would at least provide some diversion while he waited, since he wasn't keeping any secrets.

Two vaqueros came in and stood at the bar between where Engle was with Stubbins and where Lemonade stood alone. Seth watched Stubbins assess the newcomers so aggressively they shied away, which was no way to gather information. Engle was more interested in the woman on his arm. Seth appraised her, trying to plumb the man by his taste in whores. It was a hard call. She was pretty and obviously dumb, if not deliberately stupid, but there were times when Seth had chosen a dim-witted woman because she wouldn't interfere with his thinking. Which wasn't what he wanted now. He watched the barkeep deliver two beers and a shot of tequila, setting them quietly on the table without meeting his eyes. Seth looked at the woman assigned to him. "What's your name?" he asked.

"Heaven," she said in a whispery voice.

He smiled and lifted the tequila. "Is this for me?"

"If you wish."

He drank half of it down, then slid the glass toward her. "We'll share."

"*Gracias*," she said, downing the raw tequila as easily as he had.

He watched Maurice Engle walk out the door with the woman. Stubbins had managed to overcome his clumsy approach and was talking with the vaqueros now. Lemonade listened, sitting cross-legged on the bar and watching the door, his Winchester at his knee, his beer mug empty. Joaquín still had his back to the wall, his hat shadowing his face. The woman with him—small, dark, and plump— laughed often. For a moment, Seth envied Joaquín's youth and bachelorhood and clean slate, then he smiled at the ancient child sharing his table. She smiled back as if guessing his thoughts, but he knew whores were adept at performance.

Seth caught Lemonade's eye. The kid jerked his chin at the vaqueros and shook his head. Stubbins broke away from them, came over and sat down without an invitation. He looked at Heaven a long moment, then shifted his eyes to Seth. "How long we gonna be here?"

"Where do you think we should go?" Seth asked.

"After Norris!"

"Which way?" Seth replied, answering the man's hostility with calm for the sake of peace. Stubbins was so brash he constantly rode the edge of being provoked, and Seth didn't want him to fall over that edge and force a confrontation the miner would lose.

"Ain't ya got any idea?" Stubbins asked impatiently.

"I'm thinking on it."

"That means ya don't," he muttered.

"It's too bad Webster didn't leave us a map."

Stubbins glared at him. "Ya think that makes me afraid of ya?"

"Don't see how it should change your opinion one way or the other."

"Would've been better to take him alive," Stubbins said, as if the idea were his own.

"Would've been worse to let him get away," Seth answered.

Stubbins sniffed loudly, scanning the cantina as he frowned. "Reckon," he said.

Seth winked at the ancient child, and she gave him another wise smile that was almost convincing. He figured if he got drunk enough she would become one hungry ear dripping with desire. Not intending to get that drunk, he made a mental note to congratulate Ortega on his acquisition.

Stubbins asked, "What would ya do in Norris' boots?"

Seth pretended to mull the question over, as if he hadn't

been pondering exactly that for the last two days. As he sipped his warm beer, he saw Joaquín lift a lock of the woman's hair to fall behind her shoulder. Seth smiled, thinking what the kid needed was a good lay to take the edge off his grief, then he looked back at the owner of the Red Rooster Mine. "I'd go to Mexico," Seth said.

"He could be there now," Stubbins complained.

"Yeah, he could," Seth agreed.

"Why ain't we? If he crosses the border he'll disappear."

"We got information he ain't left yet."

"From Webster?"

Seth nodded.

"So we're sittin' here tryin' to catch his wind?"

Seth laughed. "That's about it."

Stubbins laughed, too. "Don't seem a respectable occupation for a man."

"I prefer the running, myself," Seth said.

"What's the dif'rence?" Stubbins asked, suddenly friendly.

"The man out front is making the decisions. All we can do is ride the repercussions."

"We got choices," Stubbins argued.

"Can't see too many right now."

He sniffed his agreement, then asked, "Ya think Norris has all the money?"

"The Tyler brothers took six."

"So there's fourteen left?"

"That's what Webster said."

"There's the reward Clancy put up. That's another five hundred."

Seth shrugged. "Webster said Norris killed the boy. Norris'll say Webster did it. Hard to prove either way."

"We can say anything we want, then," Stubbins muttered.

"That's always true," Seth said. He watched Joaquín walk out with the woman, not even glancing in his direction. Seth's only consolation was knowing Blue and Nib were home with the women and children. Stubbins left the table and went outside alone. Seth looked at Heaven. She flashed her crescent eyes and asked, "Would you like more tequila?"

"Why not?" he said, watching her signal the keep again.

By midnight, the cantina was rowdy with vaqueros and drifters. The whores were busy, and more than one resentful glance was thrown at Seth for having a woman to himself. The resentment was contained only because everyone knew who he was. They also knew the Mexican leaning against the far wall was his *compañero*, that the two surly men and the boy at the bar were with them, and why they were there. The law in Arizona, however, was scattered and scant, and most men approved of vigilantes. Provided, of course, their actions didn't result in a miscarriage of justice.

Ortega's regular patrons had heard rumors that Seth Strummar was living in their part of the country. Now they were seeing him for the first time. They noted Ortega had given Strummar his personal concubine, and they all noticed that the outlaw hadn't touched the girl, though he seemed to be enjoying her company. The Mexican was like a lizard, standing immobile for hours, his eyes missing nothing.

No one missed seeing the vaquero stop beside Strummar's table. Holding his mug of beer, he petitioned shyly in Spanish for permission to sit down.

Seth smiled into the broad mestizo face of a man so recently removed from peonage that his every gesture was imbued with humility. *"Siéntese,"* Seth said in his clumsy Spanish, then caught his partner's eye with a glance that yesterday would have summoned Joaquín, but Seth didn't watch to see if it still worked. He smiled at the vaquero and waited with hope.

Joaquín came over and sat down. Seth watched their faces, hearing the murmur of Joaquín's Spanish as he leaned with his arm on the back of the vaquero's chair and spoke softly.

"*Sí,*" the vaquero said.

Joaquín kept speaking, his Spanish too quick for Seth's ears. The vaquero nodded several times, glanced once at Seth, studied Heaven as if he weren't seeing her, then met Joaquín's eyes and spoke in a fluid whisper.

"*¿Está seguro?*" Joaquín asked.

"*¡Sí!*" the vaquero affirmed.

"*Gracias,*" Joaquín said solemnly, touching the vaquero's shoulder like a priest delivering a benediction.

Seth restrained a smile, then glanced at Heaven. Her face had come alive with yearning aimed at Joaquín, which made Seth smile after all.

Joaquín reported, "There is an abandoned cabin on the land where this man works. He says yesterday it was no longer abandoned."

"Did you find out where?"

Joaquín nodded.

Seth smiled at the vaquero. "*Gracias, señor. Le diga no otra persona, ¿entiende?*"

"*Sí,*" the vaquero said. "*Nadie.*"

Seth smiled again. "*Si necesita ayuda de yo, soy a su servicio.*"

"*Gracias, señor,*" the vaquero said, standing up and bowing. He kept his knees rigid but couldn't help himself from backing the first steps away. Then he went to the bar to glory in his notoriety for having spoken with the outlaw.

"I'm going outside," Seth said to Joaquín. "Can you keep the lady company for a while?"

Joaquín shrugged, not looking at her.

"Thanks," Seth said. "She's a speciality of the house so we can't let her loose with the rabble." He smiled sardonically. "Help yourself if you feel inclined. I'm passing, myself."

"*Sí, ya lo creo,*" Joaquín muttered with sarcasm.

"It's true," Seth said. "I promised Rico—swore fidelity to the marriage bed."

Joaquín laughed with disbelief. "I would like to see you keep that promise."

Seth stood up. "Stick around and you will."

Finally Joaquín looked at the woman. "Take your time," he said to Seth.

Seth laughed and walked out. Every eye in the room followed him, and he stepped into the darkness relieved to be away from the constant scrutiny. Heading north along the edge of the road, he deeply inhaled the cool, night air after so many hours of breathing tobacco smoke and kerosene fumes inside the cantina.

He knew he needed sleep more than anything, which meant the best plan would be to stay at the crossroads and ride out in the morning. If Norris was in the cabin yesterday, odds were good he would give Webster one more day and be there tomorrow. But he would be rested and wary. Best to face him sharp with fresh horses, ready for anything. The plan made sense, and Seth realized that if he could get Stubbins and Engle to fall for it, he could give them the slip. By tomorrow he and Joaquín would have the money and be on their way home. Whatever happened in between would be nobody else's business.

He started back toward the cantina, then remembered Joaquín was with the ancient child and decided to give them more time. Lemonade came outside and stood a moment, letting his eyes adjust to the dark. When they had, the kid saw Seth and joined him. They ambled down the road together, the boy carrying his borrowed rifle proudly, the man feeling the weight of his sixgun heavier than he used to.

Thinking he'd leave the kid behind with the others, Seth asked, "What'll you do when this is over, Lemonade?"

"I hadn't thought on it," he answered with a grin.

"You remember the deal we made?"

"Yeah," he said, looking worried now.

"I want to keep it," Seth said.

"Ya mean ya want me to skedaddle?" Lemonade asked, crestfallen.

"That pretty well fits it. Reason I brought it up now, I don't want you doing something thinking there's a job for you out of it. There ain't."

"No chance?" the kid asked.

Seth shrugged. "Not that I know of."

After a moment, Lemonade asked with chagrin, "I fucked up with the deer, din't I?"

"You missed the deer, there's no arguing that. But you did the part I hired you for fine. We're playing a different hand now, is all."

"I wish you'd let me stay, Mr. Strummar," he said, trying not to plead.

"You can stay for this job. I ain't saying you can't. But there's no payoff for you at the end of it."

Lemonade turned around and stared back at Sulphur Springs, a squat huddle of lights across the distance. "If I left on my own," he asked, "would ya let me take the mare?"

"No," Seth said. "But I'll buy you a horse from Ortega as good as the one you left at my place."

A man inside the cantina laughed. Distorted on the breeze, the guffaw sounded like a plaintive cry of loneliness from where Seth stood in the dark. Feeling isolated on the edge of society was a familiar sensation for Seth, as well as for Lemonade. On the strength of that unspoken bond, the kid pushed for an opening. "Will ya tell me, Mr. Strummar," he asked, "why it is ya don't want me around?"

Seth considered his answer carefully. "You lied to me for one thing. Hard to trust a man who lies."

"That wasn't really a lie," Lemonade argued. "It was more like a brag."

"If that deer had been a sheriff," Seth retorted, "we'd be dead."

"Ya ain't ridin' against sheriffs no more," Lemonade pointed out.

"Outlaws shoot back, too," Seth said, surprised at having made that slip. "What I'm saying," he said gruffly, "is we're playing a dangerous game and you don't stand to gain anything by surviving it. No one would hold it against you if you went your own way."

"I stand to gain a lot, Mr. Strummar," he pleaded. "I'm riding with ya and learnin' from that. For the rest of my life, I'll be proud to say I knew ya. It's all I got goin' for me, that and the clothes ya bought. I'd sure like to stick it."

Seth despised the pitiful tone of Lemonade's appeal, but if his plan worked the kid would be left behind with the others. There was no sense kicking him out when he could spoil the play. "Well, as long as you're here," Seth said, "run back inside and tell the men we're staying the night, to get themselves rooms and be ready to ride at dawn. Can you do that?"

"Yes, sir!" the kid said with vigor.

"Don't shout it from the door. Tell each man quietly. Learn to control your mouth."

"Yes, sir," he said meekly.

Seth took a coin from his pocket. "Get yourself a room, too."

Lemonade laughed. "Thanks, Mr. Strummar!"

Watching Lemonade run back to the cantina, Seth remembered the gaggle of street urchins he'd plucked the kid out of. When he'd first seen those vultures, Seth had wondered if one wouldn't grow up to kill him. Now he couldn't help wonder if he wasn't training Lemonade to do it.

A few minutes later, Seth saw Engle and Stubbins come out and walk to the hotel across the road. Seth stood in the dark for an hour, enjoying the quiet, the stars, and the rising new moon. The land was a humid presence around him, a desert oasis with the faint scent of sulphur evaporating off the spring, and he felt a moment's compassion for Heaven. Such an accomplished beauty deserved a better place to call home, and a better man than one who shared her at whim. Carried on a sudden breeze, the sulphur smell was strongly unpleasant as he watched Lemonade cross the road to the hotel. Seth waited until the cantina's hitching rail was empty, then walked back through the dark to the lighted door.

Only the keep behind the bar, and Joaquín and the ancient child engrossed in conversation, were still there. Seth walked across to their table and sat down. They watched him, their faces as smooth as river stones. Regretfully he said, "I think we should move out while the good citizens are asleep."

After a moment, Joaquín said, "I will go." He didn't move.

"I'll be in the stable," Seth said, then left them alone to make their private adieus.

He chuckled as he saddled his sorrel, thinking if there were ever two people meant for each other, it was Heaven and Joaquín. Their educations meshed, allowing for the difference in sex, of course. Seth thought they would be a dynamite team in any scam a couple could pull, then had to admit they weren't thinking of schemes these days. They were playing it straight, catching thieves and going home when it was over. At least he was.

Finished with his own, Seth saddled Joaquín's horse, too. When he was done, Joaquín still hadn't shown up. Seth swung onto his sorrel and led the black down the road to the cantina. He stopped outside and whistled softly. Nothing happened for so long he was about to dismount and go in when Joaquín sauntered out the door. He took his reins with a smile and slapped his horse so it leapt to a gallop while he swung on with the agility of youth, forcing Seth to dig in his spurs to catch up.

They galloped along the road heading east, then slowed to a trot when they cut south toward the mountains. Seth looked at the newly blossomed Don Juan riding beside him where a monk had been. "It's a good thing you raked your ashes before meeting Heaven," he teased, "or you'd still be back in Sulphur Springs."

Joaquín looked across as if he hadn't really seen Seth before. "The girl and I went for a walk," he said.

"You didn't fuck her?" Seth asked with surprise.

Joaquín shook his head.

"How'd you resist Heaven, then?"

"Ortega gave her to you, not me."

"I gave her to you."

Again Joaquín looked at him with a baffled curiosity. "How can you love Rico and see every woman as a piece of meat?"

Seth laughed. "We're all just people who go bump in the night."

"And sometimes," Joaquín said, leaning close to point his finger like a gun at Seth's chest, "we go bang in the night, too."

Seth laughed again, ignoring the gesture he would not have tolerated from any other man. "Love and death," he quipped. "They're the only things that matter."

"Are they?" Joaquín asked. "What about honor and dignity? Do they not matter?"

"Most people seem to get along without 'em."

"Melinda got along without them," Joaquín replied angrily. "So does Heaven. But it is not their choice."

"Ain't mine," Seth said.

"Wasn't it yours with Lila Keats?"

"Lila brought herself down," he retorted. "Which is what I see you doing."

Joaquín was quiet for a long stretch, then said, "The abuse of women is the worst sin. It amazes me I have ridden so long with a man who enjoys it so much."

Seth reined up sharp and turned his horse head-on to face his former partner. "That's right. I've done things to women that would make you puke. I've killed more men than you've got fingers and toes, and I robbed nearly every bank in Texas. You knew that the moment we met. It's a little late to be getting so goddamned self-righteous. You've used whores and killed men. Now 'cause you're chasing thieves for a crime you never lowered yourself to commit, you think you're the scythe of God out to right wrongs. Well, I'm wrong, Joaquín. Why don't you start with me?"

They stared at each other across their horses' ears. Joaquín said, "I have no wish to kill you."

"You think you could?" Seth scoffed.

"I have no wish to find out."

"Maybe I do."

"Would it make you feel better?"

Seth remembered Allister asking how it would feel when one of them looked down on the other's corpse. Remembered, too, that he had challenged Allister to that final confrontation by stealing his women. Now Joaquín was challenging Seth, again over women, but with a whole new twist. He smiled painfully. "Don't try to kill me 'cause I'm a whoremonger, Joaquín. I gave it up."

"I have no desire to kill you," he answered.

"What are we doing then?"

"Wasting time," Joaquín said, reining his horse around and kicking it into a trot again.

Seth caught up. "Where we going?"

"Deadman's Cabin."

"That sounds promising. Where is it?"

"On the south side of Guadalupe Pass. Have you been there?"

"Yeah, it's rough country."

"Sí," Joaquín agreed. "It's all badlands, though, isn't it?"

Seth smiled. "No rest for the wicked."

Joaquín shook his head. "I want to catch Norris and give back what he gave Melinda. After that, I will be satisfied."

"You'll let the Tyler brothers go?" Seth asked hopefully.

"They are not worth a trip to Texas."

"I agree," Seth said. He turned in his saddle and looked back, nudged by a suspicion of being followed:

"What is it?" Joaquín whispered.

"Don't know," Seth said, facing forward again with a puzzled frown. "Let's quit talking and move."

20

Lobo rode into Sulphur Springs an hour after dawn. He saw Rico's palomino in the corral and felt a moment's jubilation before he noticed neither Seth's sorrel nor Joaquín's black were there. He sat puzzling over that a minute, tired and hungry from having ridden all night. The town was a cluster of low adobes permeated by the sour smell of rotten eggs. As he watched, a door opened and Lemonade stopped abruptly on the threshold and stared at him.

"Well, lookee here!" Lemonade called back over his shoulder. Then to Lobo, "Howdy, Lobo. Ya lookin' for Seth?"

Engle and Stubbins came to the door. The merchant smiled but the miner didn't. "What in tarnation ya doin' here, Lobo?" Stubbins demanded sternly. "If your daddy wanted ya along, he would've brung ya."

"Hold on," Engle said. "Took a lot of courage for the boy to ride this far. We shouldn't chew him out for having gumption. You hungry, Lobo?"

He nodded.

"Well, step down and come on in. Your daddy'll be surprised to see you, no doubt about that."

"Is he here?" Lobo asked.

Engle smiled. "He's not up from bed yet. Had company last night; I'm sure you know what I mean."

Lobo nodded again, swung his leg over and jumped to the ground.

"Why don't you put his horse up, Lemonade?" Engle suggested kindly. "He looks plumb tuckered."

"Thanks," Lobo said, handing his reins to Lemonade. He followed Engle into the house, Stubbins coming along behind.

There was no one else in the dining room, only three plates set at the table, but the food looked good. Hotcakes with honey and fatback and coffee. Lobo sat down and dug in without waiting for a second invitation. Engle and Stubbins sat down and watched him. After a few minutes, Lemonade came in and sat down, too, all of them watching Lobo.

Engle asked, "What brought you here?"

"Lookin' for Seth," Lobo answered, his wariness returning with the coffee and food in his stomach.

"What made you think to look here?" Engle asked.

Lobo looked at Stubbins, who seemed grim, then at Lemonade, who seemed amused. "Seth ain't here, is he?" Lobo asked the kid who had once been his friend.

Lemonade shook his head. "Him and Joaquín left last night after we was all asleep."

Lobo laughed at the townsmen. "So he shook you off, like a dog shakes fleas."

Engle reached across and slapped him.

Stubbins was on his feet. "I'll have none of that!"

"He's a smart-mouthed son of a killer!" Engle shouted.

"He's still a kid," Stubbins retorted with disgust. "I don't go for roughin' up chil'ren."

Engle didn't seem to care what Stubbins went for. The merchant was glaring at Lobo as if ready to hit him again when Lemonade said with disdain, "Ya oughta jus' ask 'fore ya rough him up."

"You ask," Engle sneered.

Lemonade looked at Lobo. "D'ya know where Seth is?"

Lobo looked at the two men watching so intently. "Maybe."

"Don't play games," Lemonade warned. "These gen'lemen are in earnest."

"Believe that, kid," Stubbins growled.

"If Seth wanted you with him," Lobo sassed, "he would've taken you."

"Ya little snot!" the miner yelled.

Engle laughed. "Why don't you hit him, Buck? You'll feel better."

Lobo looked at the door.

"There's no chance we'll let you go," Engle said. "Make up your mind to that."

"What do you want with me?" Lobo asked.

"We want the money your father's after," Engle said in a reasonable tone.

"If he said he'd bring it back, he will."

"He lived his life provin' otherwise," Stubbins grumbled.

"But he always keeps his word," Lobo boasted.

"Then why doesn't he want us there?" Engle argued. "Why did he leave us behind, if not to get away with the money?"

Lobo shrugged. "Maybe you slowed him down. He's accustomed to crossin' the country pretty fast."

The two men stared at him for a long moment of silence, then Stubbins asked in a patient tone, "Where's he goin', Lobo?"

"If I tell, will you take me along?"

"Hell, no! A manhunt's no place for a child."

"Then I won't tell," Lobo said, looking at Engle, "but I'll lead you there."

"It's a deal," Engle said.

"Wait a minute," Stubbins protested.

Engle snickered. "Strummar'll trade the money for his kid in the blink of an eye. What're you complaining about, Buck?"

"I don't like usin' a kid."

"No one's gonna hurt him." Engle looked at Lemonade. "Go saddle the horses and fill the canteens."

Lemonade glanced at Lobo, then left to do it.

Lobo asked Engle, "Can I help him?"

"No," Stubbins said. "Stretch out on that settee there and close your eyes. I'll wake ya when it's time."

Lobo looked at Engle, who nodded, so he laid down and closed his eyes. The next thing he knew Lemonade was shaking him awake.

"Ya been sleepin' for hours," the kid said with scorn. "Mr. Engle told me to wake ya now."

Lobo looked around the room, remembering where he was. Then he studied Lemonade's face, trying to figure if he was still a friend.

"Ya best move," Lemonade said.

Lobo slowly stood up and stretched, trying to collect his thoughts. He knew only that he wanted to be with Seth, so he picked up his hat and followed Lemonade into the bright light of noon.

Engle and Stubbins sat their horses in the road, Rico's palomino standing beside Lobo's pinto. Sight of the golden horse made Lobo feel protective of his stepmother in a way he hadn't before. Knowing she would cry over the loss of the mare but be undone by the loss of the man, Lobo swung onto his pinto and looked at the carbine in his scabbard.

"Take his rifle, Lemonade," Engle said with strained patience. "He's a Strummar, after all."

Lobo watched to see if Lemonade would do it. The kid grinned sheepishly as he came forward and slid the carbine free. He shrugged as if had no choice, but Lobo didn't see it that way. He glared icily at Lemonade until the kid took a step back, his smile wavering.

Lobo reined his pinto around and trotted east toward the badlands, hearing the three horses fall in behind. Hermit Dan had described their destination as a cabin on the south flank of a pass. Studying the mountains looming in the distance, Lobo realized his odds of finding that cabin were slim.

Thirty miles southeast, Seth and Joaquín were bellied down on a rock overlooking Deadman's Cabin. A bay gelding stood in the unshaded corral with one rear hoof crooked, his head lowered as he slept in the sun. Occasionally a sparrow chittered from the scrub brush or a fly droned close, attracted to the moisture of the men's sweat, but otherwise everything was silent. Not a breath of wind moved off the mountains towering starkly red all around, and the thin column of smoke from the cabin's chimney rose straight into the blue sky.

Joaquín searched the scene in front of him for a clue to success. "Any ideas?" he asked.

"I was cornered in a cabin by five Rangers once upon a time," Seth said.

"How did you get out?" Joaquín asked, watching him now though Seth still studied the terrain.

"Set fire to the cabin, crawled underneath and made it to my horse. About the same distance as here."

"You set fire to your sanctuary?" Joaquín asked in amazement.

"I destroyed my cover as a way out. My sanctuary was a horse moving fast between my legs."

"Why were the Rangers chasing you?"

"I held up a high-class poker game in Austin." He smiled. "Pissed off a few legislators, I reckon."

Joaquín looked away. "What did you do with the money?"

"Spent most of it on women without honor or dignity." He met his partner's dark eyes with a playful smile. "Let's see how close we can get, then take it from there."

"All right," Joaquín said.

They approached the cabin from opposite sides, walking silently with their rifles cocked in their hands. As they peered in opposing windows and met each other's eyes across the lethal terrain of enemy turf, Joaquín was struck by Seth's profound alienation. He was a pariah to outlaws as well as the law, and the brutal fact was that his life had been lived and there remained only the repercussions to ride until a young man keen on a reputation killed him. Joaquín shuddered with lucidity: he saw Seth reduced to bones, a skeleton mouldering in the privacy of a grave, if lucky.

In that moment, the existence of the human soul seemed a mirage, a dream born of a yearning so powerful that Joaquín had hung his life on the scaffold of its need. For years he had sustained himself by striving to bring Seth to God, yet the road of that journey led instead to a vision through a window of absolute mortality. Joaquín was now in a territory which wanted him for crimes different only in degree from those committed by the man he sought to kill. That man had as much right to kill him, and Joaquín knew the outcome of what lay ahead would turn on luck and skill, not virtue.

Seth nodded at their prey with a smile acknowledging the honest moment just passed, and he was again the outlaw Joaquín had chosen to follow away from the priesthood: irreverent and in control. Joaquín looked at the man in the cabin—intent on preparing his midday meal—and remembered Webster saying the guard had shot Melinda, which meant she'd been caught in the crossfire as Seth said, only not of the bandits but of the law trying to stop them.

Though Joaquín tried to tell himself it didn't matter, that the bandits were still responsible, it was uncomfortably easy to put himself in their place. At any time in the last few years, if Seth had asked him to help rob a bank, Joaquín might have done it. If in the course of such a robbery, the guard had been so inept as to shoot an innocent bystander, Joaquín wouldn't accept the blame. It was the guard's mistake, which was the banker's mistake for hiring an incompetent. But the banker had paid with the life of his son, so maybe there lay the justice. It put enough doubt in Joaquín's mind that he decided he'd do what he could to deliver Norris to the law.

All Seth wanted was the money. Alive, Norris could produce it. Dead, he was the doom of success. Under normal circumstances, Seth could count on his partner to follow his lead. Now he was worried Joaquín would jump the gun, knowing the money had never once entered his thinking. Catching Joaquín's eye, Seth jerked his head at the door.

They approached from different sides, shifted their rifles to their left hands, drew their pistols and cocked them with their thumbs, then met each other's eyes across the empty space they intended to fill with undefeatable threat. A cognizance of the years they had ridden together flashed between them, a memory of meeting in a sunlit yard, of Joaquín taking Seth's weight when he was wounded and couldn't stand alone, an afternoon spent sharing whiskey and arguing over vengeance, their reunion and midnight talk of what it meant to be a man, another time when Seth came seeking the same courage Joaquín had sought from him. Now they stood opposed across a door to chaos, knowing everything about each other except the future of their friendship.

"Ready?" Seth whispered.

Joaquín nodded.

Seth kicked the door open and jumped in to land solid on both feet with his guns on Norris. "Don't move," Seth said.

Joaquín came in just as Norris jerked around in front of the stove.

"Don't try it," Seth warned.

Norris looked back and forth between them. "Who're you?"

"Seth Strummar," he said.

"Joaquín Ascarate," he said.

"Goddamn," Norris muttered. "It ain't right," he complained, his voice gaining volume. "Thieves catchin' thieves ain't right, not where I come from."

Seth smiled. "Maybe you should've stayed there."

Norris looked at him hard. "So you're Strummar, huh?"

"That's right."

"And you've come after your money."

"That's right, too."

"How 'bout I split with you, bein' as I think I earned it, seein' how things turned out?"

"I agree you paid heavy," Seth said.

"Damn straight," Norris said. "The guard was the one started shootin'. We had it smooth 'fore he opened up."

Seth shrugged. "That doesn't change the fact that I'm taking the money back to Tejoe. All of it."

Norris glanced between them again. "What'll you do with me?" he asked nervously.

"Kill you if you don't drop your gunbelt," Seth said.

"If I do?" Norris asked warily. "How long will I be alive?"

"How long will he be alive, Joaquín?" Seth asked, not taking his eyes off Norris, who was sweating as he waited for the answer.

Finally, Joaquín said, "At least as far as the law in Tombstone."

"There you are," Seth said to Norris. "What're you gonna do?"

"Do I have your word?" he asked in a quavering voice.

Seth laughed. "I wouldn't take your word, Norris. Why would you take ours?"

Norris looked frantically at Joaquín. "Do I have your word you'll deliver me safely to Tombstone?"

"I will do my best," Joaquín said.

Seth laughed again. "That's as good as you're gonna get, Norris. Make up your mind."

"All right," he said, reaching with his left hand to unbuckle his gunbelt. He let it dangle a moment, then gently fall.

"Move away from it," Seth said.

Norris did.

Joaquín picked it up and tossed it onto the bed under the far window.

"Now," Seth said, holstering his sixgun then sitting down at the table and laying his rifle in front of him, "what's for supper? I'm starved."

Norris looked at a kettle on the stove. "Shot a rabbit," he said nervously.

Seth grinned. "Ain't that the way? You pull off a big heist and still have to eat lean 'til you feel safe enough to spend it."

"Yeah," Norris mumbled.

"Where *is* the money?" Seth asked casually.

Norris looked at Joaquín, then back at him. "Webster has it."

"Webster's dead," Seth said. "I killed him yesterday. He didn't have any money on him."

"He was supposed to," Norris wheedled. "Maybe the Tyler brothers have it."

Seth shook his head. "They've already gone back to Texas, taking six thousand with 'em. Webster told us you had the rest."

Norris looked at Joaquín.

"Those were his dying words," Seth said. "I wonder what yours'll be."

"Wait a minute," Norris protested, his eyes on Joaquín. "You gave your word."

"I also gave my word to help Melinda," he replied testily. "If not for that, she wouldn't have been in the bank and would not have died. If I were you, *señor*, I would not put much faith in my word: it tends to ricochet out of control."

"The guard killed the woman!" Norris cried. "I've never shot a woman!"

"Nor a child?" Joaquín scoffed.

"Webster shot the kid! He overreacted, pulled the trigger too quick, aimin' at the guard. The kid was in between, is all.''

"Webster told us it was you," Seth said.

"You've done the same, if not worse!" Norris accused. "How can you turn me over to the law?"

"That ain't my part of it," Seth said. "All I want is the money."

Norris looked back and forth between them. "You mean, if I give you the money, you'll let me go?"

"I won't," Joaquín said.

Seth smiled. "Sorry, Norris."

"Sonofabitch," he muttered.

"Seems to me," Seth said, "giving us the money is your best bet."

"Don't seem that way to me!" Norris retorted. "Soon as you have it, you got no reason to keep me alive."

"My inclination," Seth said, "is to kill you right now and count the money a loss, knowing anyone else who thought to rob me would think twice. But Joaquín's thinking is all tangled up with justice." Seth grinned at Norris. "Doesn't that word send chills down your spine?"

Norris nodded.

"So you see," Seth said, "Joaquín and I ain't partners in this deal. But we're going along unless one of us gets in the other's way. You turn the trick, Norris. You don't give me a reason to kill you, Joaquín wins. You give me a reason, I win. But there ain't no way you're gonna win. Unless you think if you stick it through a trial you might find mercy. In which case you best side with Joaquín and not give me a reason to kill you."

Norris just stared at him.

"Where's the money?" Seth asked.

"Outside."

"Let's get it," he said, standing up.

Norris looked at Joaquín. "All of us?"

Seth laughed. "Don't you trust me, Norris?"

He shook his head.

"But you trust Joaquín. Why is that?"

Norris studied him, then said, "He has the eyes of a priest."

"And what's a priest ever done for you?" Seth teased.

Norris shrugged. "Prayed for me, maybe."

"Think it did any good?"

"Guess we'll find out," Norris said.

21

The rabbit had been eaten and a fresh pot of coffee was simmering on the stove. Norris sat with his hands tied behind him, his legs and body tied to the chair, watching Joaquín, who stood between the door and a window. The Mexican seemed to be drowsing, leaning against the wall with his Winchester beside him, his face hidden by his hat.

Strummar was out there with the money, settling their horses into an arroyo. He thought like an outlaw, all right, Norris told himself. Even while acting for the law, Strummar hid in defense. Didn't let anything rush him, either. Most men, once they had the money, would have ridden hard for home. Strummar was letting their horses rest. He was smart, no doubt about that, and Norris was unhappy with his situation.

He kept chastising himself for being caught by surprise. His only defense was that few men won against Strummar, but that argument did nothing to bolster any hope of escape. Despite Ascarate's promise to deliver him alive to Tombstone, Norris had no doubt the Mexican was lethal.

Even when relaxed, he was like a fist clenched for a blow. Norris suspected he would attack on the least provocation, but provocation was required. He wasn't sure with Strummar.

The outlaw had claimed to be accommodating his partner's notion of justice, but he'd also said they were going along until one of them got in the other's way. That smacked of mutiny to Norris, and he considered it piss poor to be caught in a power play that had nothing to do with him. He was the trick, like Strummar said—a dummy who would turn the game but couldn't win it for himself.

Norris weighed the benefits of throwing what little he had behind the man he chose to win. On one side was Seth Strummar, a renowned bandit and cold-blooded killer. On the other, Joaquín Ascarate, famous for abandoning the priesthood to follow Strummar. With the discipline of a zealot and the training of a desperado, Ascarate tracked men under the banner of justice. He wanted Norris alive, while Strummar was profoundly indifferent.

If he were watching from the sidelines, Norris would root for Strummar because the outlaw had risen above sentiment and lived life honestly. But the honest truth was the world didn't need Norris. He knew that. So did Strummar. Ascarate, however, believed even the worst sinner was a child of God, worthy of salvation. Norris smiled, thinking maybe the Mexican's holy crusade wasn't so bad if he could be moved to mercy. "Hey, Joaquín," he whispered.

The Mexican looked up, his dark eyes inscrutable.

Softly Norris said, "They'll lynch me in Tombstone. You know that, don't you?"

Ascarate shrugged. "That will be the marshal's problem."

"I'm your responsibility. You can't just turn me over to be lynched."

He shrugged again, watching the yard.

"It's the same as murder," Norris wheedled. "You might as well kill me here."

The Mexican turned around with an amused smile. "Do you think that argument is in your favor?"

"If I can get you to see it's the same thing. You don't strike me as a man who wants blood on his hands."

"You have already proved you are such a man."

"Those deaths were a mistake! I didn't go in there intendin' to kill anybody, let alone women and children. It blew up in my face. Webster was too quick and too sloppy. It was out of control 'fore I could catch it."

"Are you saying," Ascarate drawled with disdain, "that you expect me to let you go?"

"Strummar said he would. All *he* wants is the money."

The Mexican looked away, and Norris knew he'd hit a sore spot. Striving to drive a wedge into their already splintered partnership, he said with an insinuating warmth, "It's hard to figure why you're ridin' together. I ain't ever met two men more different in what they value."

"I doubt if you understand what I value, *señor*."

"Oh, I think I got a pretty good picture. Any man who'd ride for justice, after all, must be operatin' from some basic assumptions. Things like love should reign triumphant, kindness and mercy should shower on the heads of sinners, all of Christendom should be a gentle place to live." He paused to smile. "That sound about right?"

"I see nothing wrong with it."

"There ain't nothing wrong," Norris agreed, " 'cept it's not true."

"It could be," Joaquín said, looking out the window at the horizon tinged rose with the beginning of dusk. He hadn't expected independence to be this mournful recognition of solitude. He'd expected strength, not doubt, courage, not fear, and he knew the man whispering behind him was like a viper circling for the exact point to pierce poisoned fangs into his intent.

"If Strummar got what he wanted," Norris said, "it'd be every man for himself and there wouldn't be no law."

"What do *you* want, *señor*?" Joaquín asked sharply.

"To ride away free. Ain't no secret about that."

"And you think the deaths of four people should be forgotten as an unfortunate accident?"

"It's the truth! Strummar killed men the same way. You ride with him. What's the difference?"

"His crimes are in the past."

"Three days ago is in the past."

"Three days ago Melinda was alive."

"So this is a personal vendetta," Norris accused. "That makes you no better'n Strummar. You're both actin' for yourself, and all that talk about justice is nothin' but hot air!"

Joaquín drew his pistol as he walked forward. He pressed the barrel of his gun between the viper's eyes and slowly cocked the hammer with his thumb. "You are right in thinking you will be lynched in Tombstone. If not lynched, you will hang. If I pull this trigger, I can easily call it justice. You will not be alive to call it anything."

"For God's sake!" Norris cried.

Joaquín chuckled, lifted his pistol and eased the hammer back. "I am in no hurry. Perhaps death is a void of nothingness after all, and this time with us will be your only hell."

In a cold sweat, Norris watched the Mexican resume his post by the window and assume the same nonchalant pose—one knee crooked and his boot flat against the wall, his face hidden by his hat except when he scanned the view—giving no indication that anything had happened since he'd been there a few moments before. Norris decided to keep quiet.

Lobo wasn't talking much either. Having told Engle and Stubbins only that he needed to go to Guadalupe Pass, they'd found the way. Now they sat their horses staring at the peaks rising from both sides of the chasm through the mountains, and Lobo had no idea where to go.

Lemonade eased the palomino alongside Lobo's pinto. "What're we lookin' for?" he asked confidentially, as if they were still friends.

Lobo figured he had to tell or they'd never find it. "A cabin," he said.

"Where at?" Stubbins barked.

Lobo shrugged. "On the south side. That's all I know."

"Shit," Engle muttered.

"That ain't no problem," Lemonade piped up. "We'll jus' wait 'til dark and watch for smoke."

"Seth won't build a fire when he's bein' tracked," Lobo said.

"He doesn't know we're here," Engle argued. "He probably thinks he lost us and is feeling real sassy about now. I'll bet he has coffee for supper."

"We should look for a trail leadin' up," Stubbins said. "The only reason anybody'd build a cabin out here is a mine. In this terrain, that means we gotta gain some elevation."

"All right," Engle said. "You lead the way, Lobo. If we stumble across 'em, they won't shoot with you up front."

Lobo kicked his tired pinto along the trail winding through the pass. The mountains were rocky and red in the sunset, treeless even on top, a dry comfortless vision against the fading blue sky. Engle and Stubbins were both in foul moods, Lemonade was treacherous, and Lobo no longer believed he'd done the right thing. Tired and disarmed, he was bringing his father nothing but trouble, not least of which was himself. Now Seth would be forced to make his decisions in the interest of protecting his son.

Even worse was the thought that Seth might not be there. Hermit Dan hadn't told him about the cabin, so maybe Seth didn't know. Maybe he was fifty miles away, looking somewhere else. That meant Lobo was riding unarmed into an outlaw's lair with two businessmen and a former friend who was now a traitor, and Lobo felt stupid for coming.

Seth saw them from the ridge. Studying the pass through his spyglass, he spotted the four horses when they were still distant specks interesting only because of their steady progress closer. After watching them for an hour, standing under a ledge as he studied their pace through the shadowed canyon, he recognized the pinto first, then the palomino. He had seen those two horses together so often he didn't think he was making a mistake, but he studied the pinto's rider a long time before admitting it was Lobo. Seth laughed with pleasure, then frowned and muttered, ''What the hell?''

When the canyon was lost in the shadow of the peaks behind him, he turned to his sorrel and rode back to the cabin. He left his horse with Joaquín's in a box arroyo a couple hundred yards from the corral, an enclosure small enough that he could seal it with piles of dead brush, and carried the saddlebags of money to the water trough filled by a tiny trickle from the windmill. Listening to the blades slowly creak in the breeze of twilight, he washed the dust from his face as he considered the situation.

The game had changed. Any room for play was lost with Lobo's arrival, and Seth wished he'd already killed Norris. Then when Engle and Stubbins got here, the hand would be dealt. Now there was a prisoner to jinx the deal when all anyone cared about was the money. Except Joaquín. Seth wasn't sure what his former partner wanted, but he knew if a play came down and he had to decide which way to jump, Lobo complicated the decision considerably. Scanning the trail his son would ride in a few hours, Seth rolled down his shirtsleeves and buttoned his cuffs, then settled his hat on his head, feeling apprehensive.

The hardest challenge before him was to conduct himself in a manner his son would admire. It was a stipulation Seth had never placed on his behavior before, certainly not in the middle of a skirmish, and to be facing it without Joaquín's loyalty seemed a breach of their contract. Joaquín had promised to help raise Lobo. Now here they were at a crossroads where Seth had to shine as a fatherly example. Without the partner he had come to depend on, he had to perform with grace in a game he'd survived by playing with no rules. Suddenly he had a lot of them, and victory demanded more than survival.

Seth slung the saddlebags over his shoulder and walked across the yard to the cabin. Inside, he moved to the stove and poured himself a cup of coffee. "The good citizens are coming," he told Joaquín, then blew on the coffee to cool it before adding, "Lobo's with 'em."

"How did that happen?" Joaquín asked.

"I don't know," Seth said, "but it'll save me a trip back for the palomino."

Joaquín looked out the window. "How soon will they be here?"

"Little after dark. I figure they'll see our smoke and find us easy."

Norris was nearly beside himself, tied helpless in the chair. "Why do you want 'em to find us?" he cried.

Seth gave the captive a cold smile. "They have my son. What do you think I'd be willing to trade for him?"

"Who are they?" Norris asked querulously.

"Good citizens acting in the interest of their community." Seth finished his coffee and set the cup aside, walked to the window and said softly, "I'll stand guard a while."

After watching Joaquín cross the yard and disappear in the rocks to see for himself, Seth turned around and smiled at Norris. "I'd say your odds just dropped through the floor. Clancy put up a reward for the killer of his son, and these fellows are businessmen. If they kill you, they get paid for their trouble."

"The reward's yours," Norris said with frantic geniality. "Webster shot the kid. Didn't you say you killed Webster?"

Seth shrugged.

"You got the money," Norris argued. "You said that's all you wanted. They'll kill me. If not these men, I'll be lynched in town. None of it was my fault. In the middle of a job, things happen. You got four men who ain't necessarily compatible, the somewhat predictable defense force and totally unpredictable bystanders. Anything can happen. It was bad luck, but none of it was my mistake! I got caught in a disaster. You understand that, I know you do!''

"What makes you think so?'' Seth asked pleasantly.

"I've heard tell of banks you robbed with Allister where people died, innocent people, same as now.''

"If you aim your pleas at someone who cares,'' Seth said, "you might have better luck.''

"No one else is here,'' Norris muttered.

Seth laughed. "Reckon I'd be talking, too,'' he said. "Being as you ain't got nothing but words to fight with.''

"I can't believe Seth Strummar's gonna turn me over to the law!''

"Yeah, I'm having trouble believing it myself,'' he said, watching out the window again.

"Why do it, then?''

"I told you,'' he said impatiently. "This is Joaquín's game. I'll play it unless I see you getting away. Then I'll kill you. Other than that, I ain't taking any action.''

"Will you stand by and let the good citizens kill me?''

"I don't know,'' Seth said. "That depends on how it falls.''

"You sound like it's gonna happen!''

"They were hot to do it when we started out. Can't imagine their mood's improved since.''

"What about your kid? You gonna let him watch 'em kill me?''

"He's here,'' Seth said. "Reckon he's gonna see what happens.''

Norris took no comfort from the conversation. He sat through the lengthening shadows of dusk in the silence of despair. The only conclusion he could draw was that Webster had been right and any man who crossed Seth Strummar was a fool. They all should have vamoosed like the Tyler brothers. But Webster had wanted to see his sweetheart, and Norris to recover from the shock of what he'd helped do. Now Webster was dead, and Norris had dim hopes for a future long enough to see the next sunrise.

It was dark when the good citizens arrived. Strummar and Ascarate had heard them coming and left Norris alone in the cabin, tied to the chair like a stuffed pigeon in the light. Unable to see anything outside, he heard the horses crest the ridge, snorting and sighing with weariness after the climb.

Seth was on a perch overlooking the yard, his Winchester in his lap. Joaquín was behind a boulder on the other side, his rifle in position along the ledge of stone. Lobo came into view first. Seeing that the child was tired and felt ashamed, Seth coaxed silently for Lobo to put some distance between himself and the others.

Lobo nudged his pinto close to the wall of rock directly beneath Seth. Warily, the boy looked around, then up to meet his father's eyes. Seth smiled, though he knew he should be mad. Lobo wanted to laugh but looked away before someone followed his gaze.

Lemonade was watching Engle and Stubbins, who stared at the brightly lit, apparently empty cabin.

"What d'ya think?" Stubbins whispered.

"It's a trick," Engle said. "The question is, what do they want us to do?"

"Go inside," Stubbins said.

"Why?" Engle asked. Looking around nervously, he saw Seth.

"Evenin'," Seth said.

Stubbins and Lemonade jerked around to look at him too. Lobo vainly searched the opposite side of the yard for his father's partner, remembering what the hermit had said about Joaquín being different now. Lobo wanted to know if that meant *he* was different to Joaquín, a man who had been his friend half his life. Feeling the presence of his father on the cliff above him as his only sure connection, Lobo clung to it. Without speaking to or looking at each other, they both breathed acknowledgment of their bond.

"Why'd you go off and leave us?" Engle bellowed.

"Figured we'd be more effective," Seth answered in an easy tone.

"Ya got the money?" Stubbins barked.

"Yeah."

"And Norris?" Engle asked.

"In the cabin."

"Alive?" Stubbins asked.

"Was when I left."

"How about the money?" Engle asked.

"It's with me," Seth said.

Lobo watched Lemonade angling to be in tight with whoever came out on top. Looking at Seth on the ridge, Lemonade's eyes glinted with ambition, and Lobo realized you couldn't be friends with anyone who blew with the wind. He'd heard Seth say that about someone else, but Lobo understood it now: a man could be like a tumbleweed or a tree; it was his gumption that decided whether he had something to offer or was just drifting through. The orphaned street urchin was drifting through with both hands open, and Lobo suddenly remembered he had been the one to bring Lemonade into Seth's circle.

Lobo wanted to look up at his father but didn't because he knew that would be wasting a pair of eyes, so he watched the others for any move toward attack. The only aid he could give would be warning, but it might make the difference.

Stubbins asked, "Ya intend on takin' the money to Tejoe?"

"Yeah," Seth said.

"When?"

"In the mornin'," Seth said. "Our horses are tired."

"Why don't you come down, then?" Engle asked.

"I like it up here," Seth answered. "Why don't you put your horses away and make yourselves at home?"

"Is there grub?" Stubbins asked.

"No more'n you brought."

"Will ya come in and eat with us?"

"Reckon," Seth said. "I'm getting pretty hungry."

"All right," Engle said. "Why don't we all go in together?"

"I want to talk to my son."

"He's coming with us," Engle said.

"The hell he is," Seth said.

A rifle cocked in the opposing shadows, and Lobo finally spotted Joaquín behind the boulder.

"Why don't you gentlemen step down?" Seth suggested.

Engle and Stubbins did, keeping their hands away from their guns.

"Lemonade,": Seth said, "put their horses up."

The kid leaned from his saddle to gather the reins, then led the two horses toward the corral.

"Wait," Lobo said. He kicked his horse alongside Engle's and took his carbine back, then laid it across his lap.

Seth said, "Go on in and start supper, gentlemen. We'll be along."

Engle and Stubbins turned reluctantly and walked into the cabin. Seth watched them a moment, seeing their silhouettes move around the brightly lit room, then he looked at his son. "Come up here," he said.

Lobo dismounted, tied his horse to a creosote bush, and climbed the rock with his carbine in one hand. He settled cross-legged, holding the rifle in his lap as Seth was doing, noting there was a plump set of dusty saddlebags at his father's side. Finally, Lobo met Seth's eyes.

"How'd you find me?" Seth asked, his voice noncommittal.

"Hermit Dan sent me. I was hopin' to catch you in Sulphur Springs but I ran into Lemonade and the others instead."

"Hermit Dan sent you here?"

Lobo nodded. "He said one deer was worth one man, not two."

Seth chuckled. "The old coot."

"How'd you come to be here?" Lobo asked, relieved to hear him laugh.

"Saloon gossip." Seth smiled. "I oughta tan your hide, you know that?"

"Reckon," Lobo admitted.

"If you knew it was wrong, why'd you do it?"

"I wanted to be with you."

"Someday you will be, Lobo," Seth said gently. "But you're still a child. I wish you could understand that."

"Does that mean I should stay home with the women, 'cause I'm a child?"

"Yeah, pretty much."

"How can I learn to be a man if I'm always home with women?"

Seth looked away, into the cabin at Engle and Stubbins cooking supper as comfortably as if they were two prospectors who had lived together for years. What impressed Seth was how easily they dropped their guard. Knowing he wouldn't be that relaxed alone with Joaquín, Seth looked back at his son. "I don't want you to be the kind of man I am, Lobo. I want better for you."

"There ain't none," Lobo said.

Seth studied him a moment, then nodded at the cabin. "See those good citizens down there? They're not thinking of anything but filling their stomachs. Oh, in the back of their minds, they're rolling the problem around, knowing pretty soon they'll have to deal with it again. Right now, though, they're making supper. If I was to move against 'em, now is when I'd do it. They wouldn't think that was fair. They think they should eat first, then resume the skirmish. That's what makes 'em amateurs. You think that makes 'em less than me?"

"Yes, sir," Lobo said quietly.

Seth shook his head. "It means they're doing other things with their lives besides maintaining a constant defense, keeping an offense that changes with every shift of the wind. I live like an animal, Lobo, aware with all my senses all the time. There's a lot to admire in being sharp, but I never had any time for daydreaming. You ever think about that? No time to close my eyes and forget the world.

No chance to love a woman with my full attention. Well, you're too young to know about that. Which is exactly my point. You're a child, Lobo, and you don't belong here.''

"I think I do," he said.

"I don't want you here," Seth retorted.

Lobo glanced down, fighting tears. "You want me to get on my horse and go home?"

"You know I can't let you. If that's what you were gonna do, why didn't you stay there?"

"I want to be with you," he said again.

Seth leaned close with menace. "I want you to stay alive, Lobo. Is that so hard to understand?"

"I want the same for you," he answered bravely. "Why can't we be together?"

Seth sighed. "Com'ere," he said, laying his rifle aside and pulling his son into his lap. The sky was a myriad of stars clustered thick in the west, dimming near the rising moon. The mountains towered overhead, gouged with hidden canyons, while the pass below was lost in oblivion, a whole piece of the world that had disappeared.

Seth asked softly, "Did Nib tell you I was proud of you?"

"No, sir. I didn't see Nib."

"Well, I am. Do you know what for?"

"Helpin' to stop the lynchin'?"

"That's what you did. But what I admire is your drive to act when you see something's wrong. That takes courage and it can't be taught."

Lobo thought a moment, listening to his father's heartbeat. "Are you sayin' I should follow my conscience?"

"It'll hold you in good stead."

"That's what I did by decidin' to find you."

Seth chuckled, the sound rumbling in his chest. "I'm glad you're here. I was feeling lonely."

"Why?"

"I'm too old for this. Reckon I'm ready for a rocking chair on the porch."

Lobo laughed at the notion, and Seth took more pleasure from the sound than he'd felt in days.

After a moment, Lobo asked, "Is Joaquín still our friend?" He felt his father tense behind him.

"Why do you ask that?"

"Hermit Dan said he wasn't."

Seth was quiet, then said, "Joaquín was hit hard by Melinda dying. I don't suppose you can understand that."

"Rico cried," Lobo said.

"Did she?" Seth asked softly.

"And there was gonna be a big funeral for Rick as soon as Mr. Clancy got home."

"Did you know the boy?"

"Jus' from school," Lobo said. "But it felt strange seein' him dead, and Melinda and Mr. Tice, and Mrs. Keats in the jail. I felt like I'd seen dead folks before, though."

"You had," Seth said. "Coming down from Colorado, remember?"

Lobo nodded. "This wasn't like that. Did I ever meet Allister, when I was a baby and don't remember?"

"No," Seth said.

"I feel like I did."

Seth looked down at the top of his son's head. "When Allister died, you were about a month from a seed growing in your mama's belly."

"Did he know I was there?"

Seth shook his head. "Neither did I."

"It might've made a difference."

"How do you figure?"

"Maybe he wouldn't have tried to kill you, if he'd known you had a son who'd get him back for it."

"He didn't try," Seth said. "He wanted me to kill him."

Lobo twisted around to look up at his father. "Why?"

Seth smiled. "Maybe 'cause he didn't have a son to keep him alive."

Lobo laughed with delight.

"Let's go eat," Seth said. Setting his son aside, he retrieved his rifle with his left hand and picked up the saddlebags with his right.

Lobo could tell they were heavy. Carrying his carbine, he jumped off the rock and started toward the cabin.

Seth was thinking about Allister and Joaquín, wondering what they would have thought of each other, opposed as they were across nearly every facet of life. He wondered what it would have been like if they'd met, whether that meeting could have come off without a fight, and where he would have fallen between them, a man caught short by the disparity of his past and his present. Under the false assumption that his enemies were in the cabin, he jumped from the rock into the business end of a Winchester.

Lobo heard Seth jump down behind him, then remembered he had to put his pinto up and turned around to see Lemonade holding a rifle on Seth. Lobo didn't move.

"I'm takin' that money," Lemonade said. "Ya can toss it over real easy, Mr. Strummar, or I can take it off your corpse."

"You're gonna have to kill me to get it," Seth said in a low voice.

"Ya don't mean that," Lemonade answered with cocky assurance. "But I want to thank ya. Your tryin' to send me away, sayin' I wouldn't get no payoff at the end, got me to thinkin'. None of ya gen'lemen need that money. I'm jus' startin' out and I do. So I'm takin' my payoff, along with Lobo's pretty pinto all saddled to go."

"I'll kill you," Seth said.

Lemonade grinned. "I don't believe ya will, not in front of Lobo. Toss that money now, real gentle so I don't have to shoot."

"I already know you can't hit the broad side of a barn," Seth scoffed.

"I'm standin' right nigh close to it, though, ain't I?"

Lobo stood frozen, wondering what he should do.

Seth threw the saddlebags hard.

Lemonade stepped aside and let them pass, not lowering

the aim of his rifle. "I know ya'd track me, Mr. Strummar. So reckon I'll have to kill ya after all." He giggled nervously. "I'm gonna be famous."

Seth reached for his sixgun, sure of his kill even if the kid got lucky. A carbine fired and Lemonade fell. For a long moment of denial, Seth watched a blotch of blood spread over Lemonade's shirt. Moving as if through mud, he holstered his sixgun and retrieved the rifle he'd loaned the kid who tried to kill him. Then he forced himself to turn around and look at his son holding a smoking gun.

A few minutes earlier, Joaquín had gone inside the cabin to check on Norris. Seeing the townsmen eating at the table, Joaquín leaned against the wall and watched.

Norris watched, too, glancing at the Mexican once in a while but finding no encouragement in his stance of waiting. The good citizens seemed indifferent to their captive's fate.

"What do you think?" Engle whispered to Stubbins.

He shrugged, wiping his bowl with a crust of biscuit. "Not much we can do."

"We can take the money away from Strummar," Engle muttered.

"Us and who else?" Stubbins asked with disgust.

"He's got his kid now. He'll give us the money if we raise a stink. Probably be glad to get shut of the whole deal."

"I don't think so," Stubbins said.

"What *do* you think?" Engle asked with strained patience.

Stubbins looked at Norris, then at Joaquín. Raising his voice he asked the Mexican, "What d'ya reckon's gonna happen here?"

"Seth will take the money to Tejoe," Joaquín answered. "One of us will take the prisoner to Tombstone."

"Ya volunteerin'?" Stubbins jeered.

"If no one else will do it," Joaquín said.

Engle snarled, "Do you expect us to let a known bandit

ride off with the entire contents of the Bank of Tejoe?''

''That's right!'' Norris said.

''Shut up,'' Stubbins growled. ''Ya got no say.''

''Seems to me I'm in pretty deep,'' Norris said.

Engle sneered at Stubbins. ''Unless you can think of a way to get the money from Strummar, Norris is all we got to show for our trouble.''

Stubbins kept quiet.

''Both of us together could get it away from him,'' Engle argued. He looked at Joaquín. ''Would you stop us?''

''I will kill no one over money,'' he said.

''Are ya tellin' us to try?'' Stubbins asked, exasperated.

Joaquín shrugged. ''That is your decision, is it not?''

''Will you stand with Strummar?'' Engle demanded. ''That's all we need to know.''

''What if I lied to you?'' Joaquín asked with a playful smile.

''What're we gonna do?'' Engle asked Stubbins. ''Let Strummar ride off with the money?''

They both glowered at the prisoner, who was keenly aware he had caused their problem.

When the gun fired outside, Joaquín raised his rifle and cocked it at the townsmen. They lurched to their feet, half-crouched over their chairs. ''Put your guns on the table,'' Joaquín said.

''Would you shoot us?'' Engle mocked.

Joaquín pulled the trigger and splintered wood at Engle's fingertips, then recocked his rifle.

Engle jerked his hand back with a yell. ''All right!'' he said, not moving.

''I suggest you do it now, *señor*.''

''All right,'' he said again, glancing at Stubbins.

The miner was already unbuckling his gunbelt. ''I surrender,'' he muttered, glaring at the Mexican. ''Wash my hands of the whole deal. If Strummar comes back to Tejoe with the money, I'll celebrate. Until then, I'm goin' home to lick my wounds.''

''Stay where you are,'' Joaquín said.

"Am I a prisoner?" Stubbins demanded gruffly.

"At the moment, yes."

From outside, Seth called, "Joaquín?"

"*Sí*," he shouted. To the townsmen, he said, "Back away from the table."

Engle and Stubbins moved against the far wall, their guns left behind.

Seth appeared on the threshold, took his cut of the room, then called over his shoulder, "Come on in, Lobo."

Watching him leave his rifle and the saddlebags of money on the table, then cross to the stove and pour a cup of coffee, Joaquín saw that Seth was different. "What was that shot outside?" he asked.

Seth stared into his cup for a long moment before answering. "Lemonade pulled a gun on me," he finally said, scanning all the faces watching him. "He died."

"Jesus," Engle whispered.

"He was only a kid," Stubbins muttered.

"His bullet could've killed me just as dead," Seth said. "Any of you would've done the same."

Lobo came through the door and stood in the light. "You want me to get the horses, Seth?"

It took Seth a moment to look at his son. When he did, Joaquín knew from the hurt pride in his eyes what had happened: Lobo had killed Lemonade, in defense of Seth. Joaquín felt stunned at the enormity of his own failure. In the name of justice, he had abandoned his alliance with Seth and left a child to fill the empty place in their broken partnership.

Seth asked, "You still taking Norris to Tombstone?"

Joaquín nodded, knowing the break was irrevocable.

In a voice rough with feigned indifference, Seth asked, "Will you ride as far as the cutoff with us?"

"*Sí*," Joaquín answered gently.

Seth gave him a bittersweet smile, then nodded at Lobo, who spun and disappeared. Everyone in the cabin listened to his footsteps running away. Joaquín crossed the room and cut the ropes holding Norris to the chair. He lumbered stiffly to his feet, his hands still tied behind him.

Seth shouldered the saddlebags, picked up his rifle, and collected the two gunbelts. He smiled with melancholy at Norris bound for justice, then looked at Engle and Stubbins. "I'll leave your weapons a mile down the trail," Seth said. He started for the door, but turned back and studied their faces for another long moment. "It's been interesting, gentlemen." He smiled wryly. "See you in Tejoe."

Historical fiction available from

PEOPLE OF THE LIGHTNING • Kathleen O'Neal Gear and W. Michael Gear

A breathtaking epic of heartbreak and passion, warfare and nature's violence—set 8,000 years ago in the gorgeous land we call Florida.

FIRE ALONG THE SKY • Robert Moss

A sweeping novel of America's first frontier. "There is not a single stuffy moment in this splendidly researched and wildly amusing historical adventure."

—*Kirkus Reviews*

THE EAGLES' DAUGHTER • Judith Tarr

War and romance in the Holy Roman Empire! "Seduction, power and politics are the order of the day."—*Library Journal*

MOHAWK WOMAN • Barbara Riefe

This unforgettable third novel in the compelling Iroquois series tells the poignant tale of a young Iroquois woman who must learn what is means to become a warrior in both heart and soul.

DEATH COMES AS EPIPHANY • Sharan Newman

"A spectacular tale made even more exotic by its rich historical setting. Newman's characters are beautifully drawn."—Faye Kellerman, author of *The Quality of Mercy*

NOT OF WAR ONLY • Norman Zollinger

"A grand epic of passion, political intrigue, and battle. History about as vivid as it gets."

—David Morell